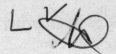

Heart of a Hero

Brave heroes – saving lives and falling in love!

Three passionate novels!

G000128515

By
Request™

In September 2006 Mills & Boon bring
back two of their classic collections,
each featuring three favourite
romances by our bestselling authors...

HEART OF A HERO

The Paramedic's Secret by Lilian Darcy
Police Doctor by Laura MacDonald
Fire Rescue by Abigail Gordon

BILLIONAIRE GROOMS

The Billionaire Bridegroom
by Emma Darcy
In the Billionaire's Bed by Sara Wood
The Billionaire Bid by Leigh Michaels

Heart of a Hero

THE PARAMEDIC'S SECRET
by
Lilian Darcy

POLICE DOCTOR
by
Laura MacDonald

FIRE RESCUE
by
Abigail Gordon

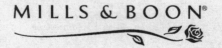
MILLS & BOON®

DID YOU PURCHASE THIS BOOK WITHOUT A COVER?

If you did, you should be aware it is **stolen property** as it was
reported *unsold and destroyed* by a retailer. Neither the author nor
the publisher has received any payment for this book.

*All the characters in this book have no existence outside the
imagination of the author, and have no relation whatsoever to anyone
bearing the same name or names. They are not even distantly inspired
by any individual known or unknown to the author, and all the
incidents are pure invention.*

*All Rights Reserved including the right of reproduction in whole or
in part in any form. This edition is published by arrangement with
Harlequin Enterprises II B.V. The text of this publication or any part
thereof may not be reproduced or transmitted in any form or by any
means, electronic or mechanical, including photocopying, recording,
storage in an information retrieval system, or otherwise, without the
written permission of the publisher.*

*This book is sold subject to the condition that it shall not, by way of
trade or otherwise, be lent, resold, hired out or otherwise circulated
without the prior consent of the publisher in any form of binding or
cover other than that in which it is published and without a similar
condition including this condition being imposed on the subsequent
purchaser.*

*MILLS & BOON and MILLS & BOON with the Rose Device
are registered trademarks of the publisher.
Harlequin Mills & Boon Limited,
Eton House, 18-24 Paradise Road, Richmond, Surrey, TW9 1SR*

HEART OF A HERO © by Harlequin Enterprises II B.V., 2006

The Paramedic's Secret, Police Doctor and *Fire Rescue* were first
published in Great Britain by Harlequin Mills & Boon Limited in
separate, single volumes.

The Paramedic's Secret © Lilian Darcy 2001
Police Doctor © Laura MacDonald 2002
Fire Rescue © Abigail Gordon 2003

IISBN 10: 0 263 84969 4
ISBN 13: 978 0 263 84969 1

05-0906

*Printed and bound in Spain
by Litografia Rosés S.A., Barcelona*

Lilian Darcy currently lives in A̶ustralia̶
with her historian husband and the̶ir̶
They also spend significant amounts o̶f̶
United States. Lilian has written over f̶ive̶
Romances, and also writes for Silhouette. ̶
the Medical Romance™ line for its drama, its
emotion and its heart-warming tone.

Lilian enjoys travel, quilting, gardening and reading,
and is a volunteer with Australia's State Emergency
Service. Readers can write to her at PO Box 381,
Hackensack, NJ 07602, USA or e-mail to
lildarcy@austarmetro.com.au

flight paramedic Anna Brewster, the strongest impression was this one—*she doesn't like me.*

Finn didn't let it bother him. There was too much else to think about and absorb. In any case, he wasn't in the habit of letting emotions cloud his judgement or throw him off balance, especially when he was, essentially, the one on trial, the one they were all curious about and ready to judge.

'Would you like a coffee first, then we'll get started?' Anna Brewster suggested.

It was a wooden invitation, made perhaps because she felt she had to, or perhaps purely because she craved a coffee herself. Vern had left the two of them to their own devices now. Everyone else had melted away, back to their regular duties.

Finn had known Vern for nine years. For the first six of those years they had worked together in the ambulance service in Melbourne. After Vern's move to Teymouth three years ago to head up the northern division of the Tasmanian Ambulance Service, they'd kept in touch. Last year, Vern had actively head-hunted Finn for this position, telling him, 'I want you, as soon as there's a vacancy here for a flight paramedic. Are you interested?'

Finn had been very interested. Now, seven months later, the promised vacancy had opened up, and here he was.

It was just on eight o'clock, a Monday morning in the middle of January, and the weather was foul outside. You wouldn't have known it was summer. The wind blew in strong, erratic gusts, and chilly grey tufts of cloud tore apart and re-formed as they scudded across the sky. Rain fell in uneven gouts, as if tossed by wild eight year old angels from celestial buckets.

The ambulance garage was freezing. Radiant heaters high on the walls had about as much effect on the temperature as candle flames.

'Coffee would be great,' Finn said, in answer to his partner for the day.

'Vern showed you the staffroom before I arrived, didn't he?' she asked.

'Yes,' he said, then tried some humour. 'The new carpet was a design inspiration. Grey. Tones with the clouds. And I particularly liked the smell.'

She didn't laugh. Just stared at him.

OK, right, well, that's cleared that up, then, he thought. She absolutely doesn't like me. I wonder why...

He crafted a series of plausible reasons and mentally inspected them. Doesn't like men. Doesn't like Scotsmen. Last boyfriend was a Scotsman and ditched her in unpleasant circumstances. Current boyfriend—not a Scotsman—applied for this job and didn't get it. Intuition—which he never trusted in the slightest—said no to all of the above, even the last one, which was the most plausible. Certainly he'd had an easier road into this particular job than a lot of people, but after his experience and the extra qualifications he'd worked hard to obtain in Melbourne he deserved it.

'We have an urn down here as well,' she explained. 'Saves time when all you want is a quick cuppa.'

'Saves the body from the stress of too many extreme temperature fluctuations, too, I suppose. If I remember, the staffroom was warm.'

'Mmm,' she said, and this time she allowed one corner of her mouth to quirk upwards. Couldn't call it a smile. 'We can go upstairs if you want to.'

'Whatever you normally do.'

Anna didn't reply at first, just turned and walked towards one of the storage rooms, which apparently doubled as a tea and coffee station. He followed her, idly noting the neat grace of her walk and the way her dark hair bounced in the middle of her back.

Then she flung back at him over her shoulder, 'If you're complaining about the cold, wait till the next heat wave. The garage is like an oven then.'

'In that case, I'll very much look forward to complaining about that, too,' he said politely.

A small bubble of unwilling laughter escaped from her diaphragm, parting her lips briefly before she clamped them shut again.

Gotcha! Finn thought, starting to enjoy himself.

Maybe she'd recently attended a seminar on gender equality in the workplace and was suffering a temporary bout of militancy. She did look like the type who might not be taken seriously by a certain sort of man. Perhaps she'd suffered from it in the past.

She had a trim figure, just on the petite side of average, neat, high breasts, a tiny, unconscious sashay in her walk. It was somewhat disguised—but not much—by the practical, unisex uniform she wore, consisting of dark blue overalls with yellow bands around the arms and legs.

And her face… Big grey eyes, a soft mouth and fair skin, all framed in dark, voluminous hair that glinted with reddish gold. The prevailing impression, therefore, was of a very attractive woman somewhere in her late twenties, thirty at the outside.

Yes, maybe that was it. She felt she had to prove herself to the new bloke. OK, well, she had nothing to fear from him. He came from a background of strong, heroic women, and was the last man in the world who needed to be told that the right woman could handle anything she wanted to, despite deceptively fragile packaging.

'How do you take it?' she asked.

She had grabbed two ugly floral mugs and spooned in some shiny granules of instant coffee. Now she was tilting the lever on the urn, and boiling water was hissing down.

'Black,' he answered. 'Three sugars.'

Got the reaction he expected.

'That's disgusting!'

'Hits the spot, though.'

'Ugh, no!'

He grinned, took the mug from her grasp and raised his eyebrows in a question which she accurately read.

'Be my guest,' Anna said. 'Mix your own poison.'

'The only way to get it how I want,' he agreed.

She looked around for the sugar to hand to him. From experience, he knew that no one completely believed him about the three sugars. No doubt she would have left each spoon half-empty and forgotten to give it a good stir at the end. While she was still looking, he found an empty jar with a hardened scrape of tired-looking white crystals around the bottom of it.

'Uh…?' Finn held it up.

She rolled her eyes, as if the extra work of refilling the jar for him was the last straw. Then she opened one of the cupboards beneath the bench-top, got out a new packet of sugar and ripped it across the top.

'If you want to wash out the jar…' You can do it yourself was her unstated implication.

Finn shook his head.

She poured, didn't spill a grain. She had wonderful hands, with fine, adept fingers. When she slid the jar across to him, he caught it clumsily then scooped out his three sinful helpings and stirred them in vigorously.

'Are you watching in horrified fascination?' he teased.

'I'm horrified. I wouldn't say fascinated.'

'I guess it betrays my working-class background,' he said.

'Does it?' She sounded very offhand. *Too* offhand. *That's feigned.*

It gave him a jolt. He forgot that he didn't trust intuition, and that he never drew conclusions too soon, and let it all happen like a series of dominoes toppling, until he reached the last one.

She thinks she knows me.

Him, personally? Or his type? It had to be the latter, because they'd never met, either in a professional capacity or a personal one. He'd have remembered. A woman like this. And her name wasn't familiar.

So, yes, Anna had to have condemned him on the strength of type. Not hard, probably. He never attempted to conceal his origins, or the sort of man he was—straightforward, someone who'd come a long way and worked hard for what he had—and most of this could be read in a few sentences of his speech.

'Finn, do you know, your accent *literally* makes me dizzy!' an old girlfriend, a serious student of linguistics and speech, had told him once.

Another old girlfriend—at thirty-three, he'd had a few—used to sigh over it, and tell him he sounded just like her favourite rock singer. Like the former lead singer of a legendary Australian band, Finn had exchanged a working class Glasgow childhood for a working class Australian adolescence, and he had the wandering vowels—spoken in a deep voice with a leathery edge—to prove it.

OK, so how do I handle this? he wondered inwardly. Righteous anger and a deliberate, exponential increase in the tension level between them until they could barely tolerate each other's company?

Ah, life's too short for that!

Simmering and glowering weren't his style. Maybe he was wrong and she had other reasons. Give her the benefit of the doubt. He'd win her over. In his own good time, and hers. And he'd make it fun.

Anna added a generous splash of milk to her coffee then picked it up and led the way out into the large, high-roofed vehicle bay.

'We've got a scheduled transport at nine-thirty,' she said, then broke off and dropped the briskly informative tone. 'How did you get rostered onto a flight crew on your first day, anyhow? No ambulance service I've ever heard of has their new recruits jump in at the deep end, even when they've had a lot of experience elsewhere. And your name wasn't the one on my roster. I was supposed to be working with Steve Quick today and tomorrow.'

She looked indignant and angry, as if his sidestepping of normal procedure was a personal affront and a criminal act. He answered her accusations in order.

'I got rostered on a flight crew because I pointed out to Vern that it made sense, despite being a breach of procedure,' Finn explained. 'Since we've known each other for years and he personally recruited me because of my extra experience in a couple of specific areas, it would have been a waste to send me to the bottom rung for three months, the way new staff usually are. Even so, I wouldn't have won the argument if he hadn't had three of his trained flight paramedics out of action for the next couple of days, and a couple more out of town and hard to reach.'

'Who—?'

'Two are off sick, he didn't tell me their names, and Steve Quick's father died in Brisbane last night. He phoned while I was in Vern's office, so it's not general knowledge yet. He'd be on his way to the airport by now.'

'Oh, poor Steve! I knew his dad had been ill, but...' She bit her lip and blinked a few times.

'Yes, it was bad news,' he agreed. 'So I'm with you instead. And I'm new, as you've pointed out, so fill me in,' he invited. 'As much detail as you like.'

Maybe a willingness to listen, on his part, would soften that steely look around her eyes and mouth.

'OK, then, there's a printout in the office—not the main office, but the one the paramedics use, just off the garage—with the scheduled transports listed, for both road and flight crews. Today we're supposed to take off from the airport at nine-thirty and head out to Redfield to pick up a cardiac patient and fly him to Hobart. Twenty-five minutes flight time to Redfield, thirty-five to Hobart, and twenty back here. Including ground time, turn-out and wrapping up at the end, round trip, door-to-door, will take us about four hours, give or take. After that, we're on call.'

'Here until seven tonight, and at home until seven-thirty in the morning, right?'

'That's right. We're together for the next two days, as you know, then I have four days off, while you work another two with someone else. Fairly standard sort of arrangement. I mean, every service does it a bit differently, I guess. I'll then come back on with a fourth person in the middle of your four days off.'

'I looked at my roster for this month but, of course, it may change now.'

'In any case, it's just sets of names till you get used to it, and get to know everyone,' she agreed. 'It's a bit like one of those old-fashioned English country dances, where you keep changing partners all down the line. Eventually, you get to work with everyone. Sometimes you can go for weeks and hardly set eyes on certain people, if your rosters don't coincide.'

Her tone clearly betrayed the devout hope that this would be the case with the two of them after this initial, unexpected and unwelcome forty-eight hours.

Finn hid a grin behind the orange floral mug and gulped some coffee. Felt the sugar and the caffeine fighting the arctic draughts of the garage as one of the non-urgent patient transport vehicles left the building.

'So if we take off at nine-thirty…' he began.

'Yes, we should leave here by eight-thirty or so, especially on your first day,' she agreed. 'Meanwhile, we'll check our vehicle.'

'Cool!'

Again, she stared at him. *'Cool?'*

He grinned unrepentantly. 'I'm enthusiastic.'

'Apparently.' It was scathing.

Come on, he wanted to tell her. You've got a sense of humour. I know you have. I've already seen a couple of little glimmers. Lighten up. Get over your problem…or at least admit to what it is, because I'm still curious.

He almost warned her straight out, 'You know, I like a challenge.' But his intuition—that thing he didn't trust—told him to play this quietly for the moment, pretend he wasn't aware of her hostility, win her over before he challenged her openly on what she felt and why she felt it.

They drank their coffee as they worked, checking inventory and equipment on the vehicle they would use—car number 121—if called out later in the day as a road ambulance crew. Their stock of morphine had to be checked and signed for, too. There were two road crews already on for the day shift. Anna and Finn would only get called out if a third ambulance was needed, and they'd be limited to call-outs within the city of Teymouth itself, making them easily available for a flight emergency.

During this half-hour of routine, Anna gave no ground and Finn accepted the fact. He rarely wasted his energy on minor battles. If she wanted to behave in this clipped, no-nonsense fashion, he could do so, too.

Then, at exactly eight-thirty, she announced with a dismissive glance at his empty cup, 'Time to go. Better wash that out or the sugar sludge will harden like rock in the bottom.'

'I'm aware of the protocol,' he drawled.

'Are you?' Barbed. She was hinting at something else. Again, he let it go.

She suggested that he take the wheel for their trip to the airport. 'You'll learn the route more quickly that way.'

He agreed.

At least she seemed to be genuinely doing her best to be helpful and informative, rather than carrying her feelings into the professional sphere. He had the impression that she would regard pettiness of that sort as beneath her.

It was a fifteen-minute drive. If you had to, you could, no doubt, do it in ten. On a day like today, with the rain still splashing down, pooling in depressions in the pavement and racing along the gutters, the grey view as they emerged from the Tasmanian Ambulance Service's Teymouth headquarters was not inspiring. Normally, however, it was glorious—all the way down the widening triangle of the Tey valley, past Teymouth's higgledy-piggledy houses and modest CBD, almost to the harbour and the ocean at the river's mouth.

The place wasn't huge—Tasmania's second city after Hobart. But as Hobart was situated on the south-east coast of the roughly triangular island, a very scientific logistical study had shown that Teymouth, two hundred kilometres by road to the north, was the best and most central location for the air ambulance section of the service.

The Beechcraft Kingair B200 aircraft could reach Hobart in twenty minutes of flying time, and Melbourne in just over an hour. Given that certain cases were routinely flown to Melbourne for treatment more specialised or sophisticated than that available at the Royal Hobart Hospital, Teymouth's distance from Melbourne was an important consideration.

Finn had been in the city for just one week, but he'd known before he'd made the move that the pace of Teymouth would suit him far better than Melbourne ever had. Tasmania was gorgeous, a study in contrasts and possibilities, and the lifestyle here actually left room for enjoying all that the place had to offer.

Untamed wilderness and welcoming community, beaches which hosted bathers during hot summer afternoons and penguins at dusk, farms which grew and processed the freshest produce, ranging from sweet ripe raspberries to tangy gourmet cheese.

Finn had rented a little farm cottage, within the required distance limit for both the airport and the T.A.S. headquarters. It was surrounded by a sea of carefully fenced and well-guarded blue-green opium poppies, now past their flowering. They were part of Tasmania's extensive cultivation of the plant for the production of licit opiates, the raw material for legal morphine-based drugs, much of it destined for export. The plants would, no doubt, look spectacular when they were in flower.

Meanwhile, his bedroom looked out on a year-round vista of the Great Western Tiers, hinting at the even wilder country beyond.

Lying in bed last night at ten-thirty, with the curtains open to let the moonlight in, and not in any real hurry for sleep to come, Finn had marvelled at the distances—both physical and metaphorical—he'd covered thus far in his life.

From the slums of Glasgow at thirteen, to this place at thirty-three. From the rude, unquestioning health he'd enjoyed at fifteen to the wreck of a youth that he'd been five years later, his body ravaged by leukaemia and almost more ravaged by the treatments that had eventually cured him. Ironically, he had emerged from the near-fatal illness stronger in both mind and body than his twin brother Craig, who had never known more than a day or two of sickness in his life.

During those late teen years, Finn had had just one goal. To live. Once he'd achieved that, he'd set another in its place. To be strong. He'd taken up martial arts and gained a black belt in tae kwon-do, teaching the discipline for several years both full and part time.

But that hadn't been enough. Growing up in a family that had never valued education, he hadn't finished his schooling. Wouldn't have finished it, he knew, even if his illness hadn't intervened. The years of forced physical inactivity during his illness, however, had taught him the value of education and revealed the quality of his mind. He'd wanted to use it. He hadn't wanted to end up on the industrial scrap heap like his father.

So, at the age of twenty-two, he went back to school, taking adult classes at night to gain his university entrance. He had considered medicine, but knew himself too well to suffer the illusion that he would make a good doctor. He needed something more active, but in that same sphere. Something medical. Something with variety. Something where what he did would *matter* on a life-and-death human level.

And eventually he'd arrived at the work he had just been recruited for—fully qualified flight paramedic for the Tasmanian Ambulance Service, trained in rescue and advanced life support, and now with more than nine years of study, on-the-job training and experience under his belt.

He had enjoyed the work in Melbourne, and expected to enjoy it even more here in Tasmania, where he would travel the length and breadth of the island. He'd waited seven months for this opportunity to come up after Vern's initial approach. Hadn't always waited patiently either, since patience wasn't a notable virtue of his.

Poor, spoiled Kendra! She hadn't quite deserved the grilling he'd given her on the subject of life in Teymouth, and what she knew of medical services there.

'Jeez, Finn! I only did nursing training there for a year before I dropped out!'

'And why *did* you drop out? Weren't you satisfied with—?'

'Nothing like that. The place was fine.' A shrug. Kendra Phillips reacted to many things in life with a shrug. 'I decided teaching aerobics and trying some modelling on the mainland would be more fun. And it is. But, of course, I don't want to do it for ever. If I got married...'

For no good reason, Finn had a nagging sense of guilt about Kendra occasionally. He hadn't seen her for five months, and didn't know where she was or what she was doing these days, though his brother Craig probably did...

'Next left, Finn.' Anna's crisp, impersonal voice cut across thoughts that had strayed way too far in the last few minutes. They were almost at the airport.

'Thanks,' he said.

'Here. Just up ahead.' She yawned hugely.

'Tired?'

'Pete and I got a call-out last night,' she explained. 'Road trauma. Spinal case. Had to pick the patient up in Fryerstown and take him to Melbourne. It was four in the morning by the time we got back, and the outlook for the patient wasn't great.'

She meant she'd been dwelling on it and hadn't slept, even after she'd got to bed. He didn't need her to say it straight out.

'Likely paraplegic,' she went on. 'Turned out I'd been at school with the guy, only he was a few years ahead.'

'Coincidence.'

'Not when it's a call-out to Fryerstown. That's where I'm from, and it's not a huge place. Always sets me on edge when I hear that's where we're picking up from.'

'I'll remember that,' he promised.

'I'm only telling you why I'm tired.'

But there was more to it than that, he could tell. It could have piqued his curiosity if he let it. Once again, he chose not to.

At the airport, she directed him away from the com-

mercial terminal and on a little further to the part where
light aircraft were based, and where the aircraft chartered
by the ambulance service were hangared. Finn had flown
in this type—the Kingair B200—before, so it presented
nothing new.

Neither did the pilot. Like Finn, Chris Blackshaw was
in his early thirties, young enough to be active, enthusiastic and just a little bit wild in his private life, but old
enough to have the required experience. No special training was necessary for a pilot to work in the area of
emergency patient transport, just extensive flying hours
in a wide range of conditions. The demarcation was
clear. The pilot flew the plane, the paramedics dealt with
the patients and the medical equipment. Trust in each
other's area of competence was paramount.

Today, for example.

'Nice weather for January,' Chris commented.

'Let's not make weather conversation, Chris,' Anna
teased. 'Keep your thoughts on wind velocity to yourself, please!'

They grinned at each other, and Finn couldn't help
noticing how her voice and manner had lightened. She
was really quite beautiful when she smiled. Those grey
eyes looked bluer. She lifted her chin and showed white
teeth that met in a neat, perfect bite. In the car, she had
pulled her hair up into a high ponytail to get it out of
the way, and now he could see how long and graceful
her neck was, and the clean line of her jaw.

Within half an hour, they were in the air. You couldn't
do this work if you were at all squeamish about flying.
Although the plane was large enough to require a commercial airstrip, it was far less substantial than most passenger aircraft. In bad weather—like today's—you felt
as if you were riding in the stomach of a giant bumble-

bee, and the roaring drone of the engines only added to this impression.

Flying just above the low clouds, Finn could only conjecture about the vistas he was missing below. There would be rolling farmlands first, then the coastline, dotted with houses that overlooked Bass Strait.

Finally, as they dipped below the clouds again, the wild country of this thinly populated corner of the island appeared below them just before they came in to land at the tiny airport. As far as Finn could see, they appeared to be the only aircraft in operation here at the moment, which didn't surprise him.

Feeling the wind broadsiding the aircraft from the west, he was impressed at Chris's skill in bringing the Kingair smoothly to taxiing speed.

Five minutes after their arrival, the ambulance from Redfield Hospital pulled onto the tarmac. It took just under twenty minutes to effect the hand-over. Oxygen and IV lines had to be checked, as did the ECG leads on the cardiac monitor. A patient required more oxygen in flight than on the ground, and additional medication as well. Brian Charlesworth, aged sixty-four, had already been given drugs for motion sickness and pain, as well as a small dose of tranquilliser for nerves. He also had two stick-on foam pads placed on his chest, one just below the right shoulder and the other against his lower ribs directly beneath the armpit.

'For monitoring,' he was truthfully told, but if necessary—no one ever hoped it would be—two defibrillator paddles could be placed against those same pads to administer a lifesaving jolt of electricity.

After a careful exchange of information and a brief exchange of pleasantries between the two ambulance crews, Mr Charlesworth was loaded aboard via the upward swing of the cargo door. Then the door swung down again and Finn and Anna were left with their patient while Chris spoke to the airport controller, based in Melbourne, in preparation for take-off. At a small airport like this one, the onus was very much on the pilot to back up the distant controller's information with visual checks of his own.

Despite the tranquilliser, Mr Charlesworth was nervous. 'Couldn't pick a calm, sunny day, could I?' he joked feebly.

'Actually, you'll be one of the few people in Tassie who does get to see some sunshine today,' Anna told him easily. Her head looked small and nicely shaped within the confining black arc of the headphones. 'Once we get above the clouds, I mean. It's blue and peaceful up there, as if we're skimming over a sea of cotton wool.'

She had painted a vivid, reassuring picture with those few words, and Brian Charlesworth nodded, seeming a little calmer.

But it didn't last. Chris taxied out to the start of the landing strip, received clearance for take-off from the Melbourne controller and revved up the engines. They screamed, and the plane itself began to judder. The wet black tarmac began to race past, faster and faster, and Finn looked up from checking the ECG tracing once more to find that Mr Charlesworth was gripping Anna's hand hard enough to cut off the circulation, though she wasn't complaining. Sweat beaded near his greying hairline and on his top lip.

OK, so we have a nervous and not particularly stable heart patient, and we're flying into worse weather to the south, Finn thought calmly.

His gaze intersected briefly with Anna's and there was

that little quirk at the corner of her mouth again. He gave a slow blink and a tiny nod in reply. They were going to have trouble with this one.

Their shared awareness of the fact vibrated between them and created a connection that felt disturbing. It was as if someone had taken a big spoon and started stirring up Finn's insides, releasing a cloud of butterflies. Sort of ticklish and frightening. He didn't want to admit to himself that he recognised the source of the feeling. Not yet, anyway.

The trouble with Brian Charlesworth started just five minutes into the flight, as the plane battled and bumped its way through the clouds, making the ride jerky and uncomfortable and necessitating the use of headphones for all of them, including the patient.

The tracing on the cardiac monitor suddenly went flat. Fortunately, both Anna and Finn saw it at once. They checked Mr Charlesworth's pulse, checked the ECG monitor then zapped him with the defibrillator within seconds of it happening. The powerful electrical charge generated a substantial amount of heat and would have burned his skin if it hadn't been for the pads. His chest jerked up from the stretcher then thumped back down and a second later he lifted his head a little and said, frowning, through the headphones, 'What happened?'

'You just had a bit of a faint, Mr Charlesworth,' Anna answered casually.

Her hand rested lightly on his shoulder for a moment, and Finn was too conscious of the grace and warmth of the movement. Conscious, too, of the brief clash of her grey-eyed gaze with his own. Those eyes, fringed with dark lashes, were mesmerising…

Flick. Back they went to Mr Charlesworth again, leaving something nameless behind.

'Oh. Right.' The patient nodded. 'I feel a bit woozy, even though they gave me the medicine. It's rough, isn't it?'

'Just bouncing from cloud to cloud today, I think,' Anna agreed. 'Like a baby's pram going over speed bumps, or something.'

She sounded so relaxed about it that once again Finn had to hide an appreciative smile. She certainly had the right attitude, and a handy set of reassuring images.

Smiles aside, he was still watching the monitor, which was bouncing up and down along with the plane, like everything else.

OK, he registered, the patient's heart's going again, but the rhythm is still unstable.

Anna had seen it, too.

'Something to settle it?' she mouthed. Her shoulder brushed against his and then retreated again.

'Definitely,' he mouthed back, leaning closer.

He couldn't help the movement. It fitted their need to be unobtrusive in their communications with each other, but he noted the way her eyes widened for a tiny moment and the way her lips suddenly parted just enough to admit a swift stream of air before she turned to reach behind her for the new medication.

With no fuss, she added the drug to the swaying IV line and Mr Charlesworth's heart rhythm soon stabilised. He was so busy listening to and feeling every judder and lurch of the plane that he didn't even notice their concern, or the fact that Finn barely took his eye off that monitor for the rest of the thirty-five-minute flight. Anna's hand looked white and pinched from the patient's grip, but she said nothing.

All three of them let out a controlled sigh when the plane finally slowed on the tarmac and the onslaught on their ears and bodies ebbed. Anna removed the patient's headset, grinned rather cheekily at him and said, 'There! Roller-coaster ride over. Welcome back to the ground!'

Here in Hobart, hand-over to a road crew from the Hobart ambulance service took place at the airport. This was accomplished with no fuss or drama today.

Brian Charlesworth seemed relieved to be on the ground and thanked Anna and Finn profusely, although he still didn't know quite how much gratitude he truly owed them. By the time the twenty-minute hand-over was completed, Chris had checked his plane and was waiting for them.

As they waited for clearance for take-off, Finn engineered the conversation quite deliberately, making it as neutral and professional as possible, keeping Anna off her guard but learning quite a lot about her all the same. She took her job seriously, but still managed to smile about it. She didn't panic easily, but she occasionally took things too much to heart.

Now came the twenty minutes of air time between Hobart and Teymouth. Anna had retreated behind her shell of hostility again, after her quietly cheerful professionalism during the Redfield to Hobart flight. She spoke a couple of times to Chris through their headsets but said nothing to Finn. She looked very tired.

By a quarter to one they were back at headquarters and Finn told her, 'It's OK by me if you hide out in the stand-down room for a while.'

'I'm going to grab some lunch first,' she answered. 'Then, yes, I'm going to try and sleep. How about you?'

'Might watch some TV.'

'I meant lunch. Did you bring something?'

'A couple of sandwiches.'

'I'm going to heat some soup in the microwave.

You're welcome to have some.' She used that same cool politeness he was starting to recognise.

'Thanks,' he said. 'But my sandwiches will do. I noticed there's a toaster oven, so I'll toast them and they won't taste like they were made last night.'

'Resourceful,' she commented.

Purely making conversation, Finn realised.

They were alone together in the staffroom as they heated their respective lunches, and it was a little awkward. If she hadn't been giving out such clear vibes to leave her alone, he'd have asked some more questions. Casually personal ones, like what part of Teymouth did she live in and what had she done before her paramedic training.

No one came to it at eighteen, straight out of school. It was actively preferred that new recruits had lived a little first, worked in some other area. The profession drew former teachers, nurses, tradesmen, policemen, and the work and training were both demanding enough that anyone who came to it on impulse didn't stay the course—if they were accepted into it in the first place. Selection procedures were also rigorous, and by the end of it all Tasmanian paramedics were amongst the best trained in Australia.

So where had she been before this? When and why had she left Fryerstown?

Clearly he wasn't going to find out today. He blew out a sigh between his lips. The timer on the toaster oven rattled around to zero and the orange of the heating element inside began to fade. Anna was already eating her soup, spooning it neatly in between mouthfuls of buttered toast while she read the newspaper.

I wonder what she'd do if I just leaned on the table,

took her face between my hands and kissed her? Finn thought.

Suddenly, he understood…or admitted to himself…that he wanted to, and he had to fight a series of too vivid mental images of her response. At face value, she wouldn't like it. She'd push back her chair, leap to her feet. Her eyes would be blazing…not just with anger, though…and her cheeks would be flushed. She'd undoubtedly give him quite a dressing-down.

But beyond that, and beyond every chilly degree of her conduct towards him today, there would be an elemental part of her, he somehow knew, that would respond. The certainty of this understanding glowed inside him like the coals of a fire, dangerous and welcome at the same time.

CHAPTER TWO

'RISE up, sunshine.'

Somewhere on the very edge of Anna's consciousness came the sound of a hand thumping against a door. Flattened palm on wood.

The male voice, newly familiar, came again. 'Rise and shine, Anna. Your pager's not working.'

Groggily, she rolled over and began to swim up out of a sleep that hadn't lasted nearly long enough. She peered at her watch through one eye. Only three-thirty. That meant she'd had a bare hour. Could have done with ten.

'OK, I'm coming in,' said the voice.

'No, it's all right, I'm awake,' she called back, sitting up.

Too late. Finn McConnell had appeared, making her instantly self-conscious about her body, although she'd slept on top of the bed covers in her uniform and therefore wasn't remotely indecent. She wasn't happy with this strange response to the man, but seemed helpless to change it.

'Sorry, but we're called out,' he said.

'I assumed so.' She nodded. 'My pager…'

She unclipped it from her belt and discovered that it had accidentally got switched off, something she'd been too tired to check. Not good. She made a huge effort and shook off the last vestiges of sleep, aware of him in the doorway, watching her.

So aware of him, and of her own body's response to

that male bulk. She didn't want to be at all, and perhaps that only made it worse. She knew too much about him, and from the moment when Vern had introduced them this morning, with no explanation about why Steve Quick wasn't working today, she hadn't hidden it well enough. Finn knew something wasn't right.

She was torn between thinking, And so he damn well should, and wishing fervently that she was a whole lot better at hiding her feelings.

Anna wasn't in any hurry for a confrontation. They had to work together for two days, that was all. After this, their rosters might not coincide for weeks, and they'd only connect occasionally.

Her dislike, based purely on what she knew about recent events in Finn's private life, had no bearing on her work or his. Conversely, the fact that her cousin Kendra was, in many ways, a very silly girl had no bearing on the moral issues involved. Finn McConnell had made Kendra pregnant and was so far showing not the remotest sign that he was intending to do the right thing. It wasn't a subject she had time to dwell on just now.

'What are we dealing with?' she asked.

'Priority one. Chest pain.'

'Today's theme.'

'So far. A common one, in our line of work. You drive,' he suggested.

She nodded. 'You can learn the roads when it's not so urgent.'

They reached the vehicle. The keys were dangling in the ignition and she started it smoothly. Seconds later they were out of the garage and on their way, siren singing loudly and lights flashing. A priority one call-out meant they were authorised to use these warning devices, as well as breaking traffic regulations if necessary.

Anna wondered what had taken the first two crews out, so that she and Finn, as back-up, were required. And she wondered what they would find. Chest pain, male patient, age forties, with a question mark. As diagnoses went, it was at the vague end of imprecise. The emergency had been self-reported by the patient, so it could be a case of unwarranted panic. Could even be a hoax. The problem was, you were never sure.

Glancing sideways at Finn for a fraction of a second, meeting only his sober profile, Anna wondered if she could apply those same words to him. Hearsay was inadmissible as evidence in court. With human beings, you could never be sure.

Maybe she was misjudging him. Maybe he was going to take on his share of responsibility for Kendra's unborn child after all. He was here in Teymouth, not on the mainland. Did that mean anything? And Kendra still believed. Or claimed to.

But Kendra was such a bubble-head. She had been spoiled as a child, and hadn't grown up one bit, it often seemed, in the ten years since they'd both left Fryerstown after finishing school. Oh, Lord, it was a mess! And Finn himself had no idea that Anna knew anything about it.

He was an incredibly well put together specimen. Anna didn't have to look at him through Kendra's eyes in order to see the attraction. Tall and solidly built, broad-shouldered, rugged-featured. He wasn't wearing overalls as she was, but had chosen the more formal of the two uniform options today—dark navy blue pants, and a white shirt with navy epaulettes. It suited him.

He wore his dark hair short, as if he didn't care what people thought of the shape of his head, which wasn't perfect and regular and eggy, like a male model, but rather square. His forehead was high and blunt and his jaw stuck out stubbornly, except when he grinned. He had a very wide grin, which crinkled up his dark eyes and made you think of all the wicked but well-intentioned things he must have done as a boy.

He had that weird mish-mash of an accent, which could either be incredibly annoying or incredibly seductive. Probably both.

And Finn was bright. Not the kind of intelligence that had been hot-housed by expensive schooling and conscientious parents, she sensed, but a raw intellect which had flourished like a weed on a garbage heap with no assistance from anyone whatsoever.

He had slipped so smoothly into the job this morning, absorbing each instance of their protocol here being different from that of his former service, and it was impressive enough that he'd talked Vern into letting him do it in the first place. Then he had done everything right with Brian Charlesworth.

Earlier, before they'd set out, he'd even made Anna laugh, although she hadn't wanted to.

Kendra, you picked a good one this time.

They arrived at the address they'd been given, a small, blue, weatherboard cottage with a red-tiled roof, and the sound of the siren died away with a final yelp as Anna switched off the engine.

The place seemed quiet. No one came out to greet them. The front door was closed. Locked, too, they found, after they'd rung the bell and obtained no response.

Finn looked at Anna. 'Force it?'

'Or try round the back. The side gate was open, I noticed. This isn't Melbourne. A lot of people don't lock their back door. Of course it may be a hoax call…'

'Let's do it.'

He led the way, over the roughness of dense, springy couch-grass. Some late sun broke through the thinning clouds, making an untrustworthy promise of fair weather for the morning. They heard a radio playing in the back yard, tuned tinnily to the cricket in some city where it hadn't rained today.

And here was the patient, inert, eyes closed, flung on his back on a low metal and plastic lounging chair, as if in search of the fickle sunshine. He looked to be in his late thirties, rather than the forties this afternoon's ambulance dispatcher had estimated.

'Unconscious...' Anna suggested aloud.

'Asleep,' Finn corrected cheerfully.

And Anna realised immediately that he was right. The man's chest rose and fell, to the accompaniment of a light, fluttering snore. On the cement path beside the lounger stood a small group of beer cans, a mobile phone, the radio, the racing form guide and the remains of some take-away food wrappings. Hamburgers, or fish and chips. The paper was translucent and shiny with grease.

'Eh, mate,' Finn said, reaching down to shake a shoulder. 'Stomach feeling a'right now, then?' His wonky accent sounded stronger and odder. There was something compelling about his voice, which Anna did not want to recognise.

The man opened his eyes blearily. 'Huh?'

'Indigestion gone now?' Finn said.

'Indigestion?'

'You called the ambulance, remember? You were having chest pains.'

'That's right.' Memory returned. 'Hell, they were racking! I'd never had anything like it. *Indigestion?*'

'Can be pretty severe.'

'Never had it in my life.'

'There's a first time for everything. Seriously, though…'

Finn asked some searching questions to confirm what he and Anna were now both pretty sure of. False alarm. As a final check, Anna felt the man's pulse and took an ECG strip. Both were normal, and the man agreed without a blush that he'd overreacted this time.

'Still, you have to take these things seriously,' he said.

And, of course, he was right. It was part of the job. Not nearly as bad as the types who thought the emergency OOO was the appropriate number to phone when they felt like making a prank call or getting a free trip to the hospital for some nice drugs.

Since there was no urgency on the return journey, Finn took the wheel, the siren was silent and Anna gave him a few tips on Teymouth traffic patterns at peak hour—which streets to avoid in which direction, which short cuts worked best. He seemed to absorb it all without fuss as his lean, strong hands manipulated the wheel, and she decided he probably wasn't someone who needed to be told things twice.

Which led to her thinking about a few things she would like to tell him at least twice, which had nothing whatsoever to do with the job. Back at headquarters, she was still thinking about it as she relaxed with a cup of tea in the staffroom. Finn had been sidetracked by today's second ambulance crew, back from the hospital after delivering a woman with acute asthma to the emergency department, and it was a relief to be free of his presence after so many hours together today.

To be honest, she hadn't expected a man like this, despite the over-abundant detail of Kendra's emotional ravings. She had taken most of that with a pinch of salt. As she let the hot, fragrant tea fill her mouth in satisfying gulps, Anna thought back to her last meeting with her cousin.

They had both been in Fryerstown for Christmas. Anna had been rostered on for work the previous Christmas, her first in Teymouth. The Christmas before that she had still been based in Hobart and had made a quick two-day visit home, but Kendra hadn't been there. That meant it had been three years since they had last connected. Still, the old intimacy of their middle teen years had returned straight away, unchanged.

And that was wrong, of course, Anna realised now, pausing with her mug halfway to her lips before she took another thin gulp. Their relationship should have changed in ten years. Why hadn't it?

Her immediate impulse was to blame Kendra herself, but perhaps that was unfair. Yes, it had been Kendra who had grabbed them each a tumbler of down-market, over-sweet cream liqueur on Christmas Eve and pulled Anna into her old bedroom.

Kendra's old bedroom, that was, not Anna's. Anna's room at her parents' house had been converted into 'my craft den' by her mother, and there Mum pottered about making souvenirs for Fryerstown's slowly growing tourist trade. Dabby little paintings on polished cross-cuts of beautiful Tasmanian timber, or picture frames, purchased in bulk and then embellished with pressed flowers, gumnuts, fabric or more painting. To be brutally honest, they weren't all that good. A little twee. But some of them sold and Anna was proud that her mother was resourceful enough to try.

Kendra's mother, Auntie Rona, didn't try anything very much, so she didn't need a 'den' and Kendra's old room was unchanged since she had left it in a blaze of drama and rebellion and wild optimism at eighteen to study nursing in Teymouth.

The room was still painted pink, like a little girl's. It was still crowded with dolls and cuddly toys gathering dust on a set of knick-knack shelves, while the back of the door and most of the wall space was covered in pin-ups of Kendra's teen idols. Jon Bon Jovi, Kevin Costner, several obscure rock stars and some anonymous semi-nude hunks.

But perhaps I'm as guilty as Kendra for going along with it, listening to her, not challenging anything she said, Anna thought now.

Their conversation, as those silly liqueurs had rapidly disappeared, had matched the teenage decor. Only one thing had been different. Kendra had been more than five months pregnant.

But apparently it wasn't a problem.

You see—to tell it in Kendra's way—there were these two brothers she'd met in Melbourne. Twins. Craig and Finn. Both hunks, but Finn was a ten and a half out of ten. They had both worked out at the gym where Kendra taught several aerobics classes each week, despite her lack of formal qualifications in the area.

She had liked Craig at first. Well, he had been the one she'd first met. He was a part-time security guard and bouncer at a nearby nightclub.

But then he'd introduced her to Finn. Sigh. Gorgeous!

Anyway, to cut a long story short—which Kendra *hadn't*—a party, too much to drink. 'Et cetera, et cetera, blah, blah, blah.' Ho hum. In the family way. 'Didn't even think about being careful!' Giggle. These things could happen when you both lost control.

Unfortunate. Kendra had lost her job a short time

later, and she was broke, which was why she was back in Fryerstown, dump though it was, back at her parents', just riding out the pregnancy. Morning sickness, stomach bloating, 'et cetera'. Couldn't teach or model. No choice but Fryerstown. Wasn't going to pressure Finn about a decision on their future.

He was a paramedic, like Anna, 'But at Teymouth.'

'But I'm at Teymouth now!' Anna had exclaimed at that point. 'Didn't Auntie Rona tell you?'

'Oh, probably.' Another wave. 'I guess I didn't take it in.'

'I've been there nearly two years, and there's no one called Finn there.'

'Well, maybe he hasn't started yet. He was waiting for an opening or something. He used to ask me about Teymouth a fair bit at first. I said to him once, "You're only interested in me 'cos of Teymouth, aren't you, Finn?" Then I was talking to Craig and he said he'd got the job. Finn had.'

'What's his name.'

'I told you, Finn.'

'Finn what, Kendra?'

A huge yawn and another giggle. 'Sorry, pregnancy makes you so vague. Finn McConnell. You'd know if you'd met him.'

'Of course I would! There's only thirty of us, covering everything from routine patient transport to emergency rescue. Only eight flight paramedics.'

'I mean, you'd *know*, sweetie.' Suggestive drawl. 'He's…'

There followed a lot of rose-coloured detail, which Anna, to be honest, hadn't listened to with her full attention. Kendra hadn't seemed to notice, or care. 'He's

got a lot more going for him than Craig. A *lot* more!
He's a winner.'

But Anna wasn't interested in that. 'What's he going
to do about the baby?' she asked, when she finally got
an opportunity to break in. As far as she was concerned,
that was always the most important question in a situation like this. Sometimes the only question.

Kendra didn't seem to feel the same way. 'Oh… You
know… I don't want to put pressure on him. I think a
man's always going to be more interested once it's born.
I'm not interested in stuffing up his life, and I'm sure
he knows that. I mean, I understand the male perspective, I really do. I think I'm good that way. I think that's
why men like me.'

A giggle.

'Well, and certain other attributes of mine. When I get
my figure back, and my skin… You see, Anna, I know
why men feel trapped, and I just don't want to do that
to someone I really care about.'

She probed at this subject for quite a while, drawing
on a vocabulary of psycho-babble which Anna privately
thought was nonsense. Given a choice, she always preferred to look at life's big issues in a simple way, and
as far as she was concerned Kendra's situation *was* simple.

She was single, jobless and pregnant, and the man
who was fifty per cent responsible for getting her that
way ought to be somehow involved in helping her make
the best of the situation. Not that he had to slip a ring
on Kendra's finger and declare undying love, if that
wasn't how he felt. A baby made very poor glue for
sticking two ill-suited people together.

But Finn needed to let Kendra know where she stood,
get rid of those rosy fantasies of hers with some plain

talking if necessary, and live up to his biological fatherhood by making a financial and emotional contribution
to the future of his child.

And I'm going to have to bite my tongue to keep from
telling him that, Anna realised. Even though it's none of
my business.

When her pager buzzed against her hip a few minutes
later, she wasn't sorry. Thinking about Kendra, thinking
about her cousin's situation and her own past in
Fryerstown, it was only making the issues twist more
tightly inside her.

As distractions went, however, an urgent call-out to a
three-car pile-up in the CBD was effective but not exactly fun.

This time there was no question that she and Finn
were wasting their time or their role as back-up to the
two main road crews. Wet roads and lapse of driver concentration were the culprits. Two people were seriously
injured, and two more needed hospitalisation in
Teymouth for minor injuries. One patient was taken directly from the accident scene by helicopter to Royal
Hobart with a suspected head injury. Later, once stabilised—if he survived—their own service would probably
have to fly him to Melbourne for ongoing treatment in
a specialised unit there.

By the time Finn and Anna were back at headquarters,
it was time to leave for the day and downgrade to being
on call at home.

'Quiet, from the flight perspective,' Finn commented
to her. 'About a hundred flights a month from here on
average, right?'

'About that,' Anna agreed.

'So we should theoretically run a bit over three a day.'

'"Average" and "theoretically" being the operative words,' she agreed. 'And the day's not over yet.'

Their next call-out came at six-fifteen the next morning, just as Anna had rolled out of bed and was about to lunge for the shower. She shrugged at the disruption to her morning routine. She'd had a shower last night as she always did as soon as she arrived home from work. Sometimes the job wasn't very clean. But the service aimed at a turn-out time of one hour outside normal working hours, and that did not include the luxury of a shower.

And this one was definitely going to be serious. A thirty-eight-year-old female patient, admitted to Fryerstown Hospital in unstoppable and rapidly progressing premature labor with triplets at just twenty-six weeks gestation. Two aircraft would be needed. Anna and Finn would each fly in separate planes to Hobart to pick up a neonatal transfer pack and a NETS team, consisting of a neonatal specialist and a neonatal intensive care nurse.

The teams would be flown to Fryerstown, where they would spend several hours stabilising each baby for transport to Melbourne Children's Hospital and handing over to the neonatal staff there. The two Hobart teams would then be returned to Hobart before the planes could finally head for home base in Teymouth once more. The five legs of the journey and ground time in between would take the whole day and much of the night.

Finn had just arrived at the ambulance service's airport office when Anna pulled into the parking area. She hadn't asked him yesterday where he lived. She'd told herself she hadn't wanted to know that much about his circumstances. Maybe he already had another woman in tow, after leaving Kendra in the lurch.

But today she was more curious, or perhaps simply less stubborn about admitting it. Either he lived closer to the airport than she did, or he was lightning fast at getting out the door, because Anna knew she hadn't wasted any time.

They had swapped uniforms. He was wearing overalls, and she had on the more formal outfit.

'I grabbed it off the hangers automatically. Why?' she muttered to herself.

Because it's Fryerstown, she realised.

It hadn't struck her before, but there were other times when she'd been called out from home for a trip to Fryerstown, and each time she'd chosen the dark pants and crisp white shirt with its natty epaulettes.

To show everyone in my home town how far I've come in life? Or to show myself?

Finn looked as good in the overalls as he had in the shirt and trousers. Looked even better when still rumpled from sleep than he had when fresh and neatly groomed as he had been yesterday. He hadn't had time to shave, and his new growth of beard was pushing through as thick and fast as a tropical forest. One side of the open collar on his overalls was folded in, and Anna had to resist a strong urge to reach up and tidy it for him. Her fingers tingled suddenly, and she closed them into a fist.

She said instead, 'Lucky you got a good workout with the equipment yesterday. You'll be all right on your own?'

'I'll spend the time between here and Hobart running through it to make absolutely sure,' he said, acknowledging her right to ask this question with a brief nod.

'But so far there's been nothing significantly different from what we had and how we used it in Melbourne.'

'You go with Chris, then,' Anna said, and again he nodded, this time so quickly that she knew he'd already planned to suggest this himself. 'I'll go with Rick.'

Both pilots were already there, turning over their engines and running through their pre-flight checks. In the office, the phone rang and it was a message from Fryerstown Hospital. The first baby had already been born, by Caesarean. She was in better shape than she might have been, and she was surviving so far. The hospital had the equipment but not the experienced specialists, so it had to be a matter of prayer and teeth-gritting determination.

The second baby, born just ten minutes ago, hadn't made it, and they hoped he would turn out to be the smallest of the three. His placenta had been smaller than the first little girl's, and all the Fryerstown staff's attempts at resuscitation hadn't enabled him to breathe or keep his little heart going.

Finn's comment was practical, and Anna herself had been around long enough not to find it callous. 'Solves one problem,' he said laconically. 'I wasn't sure we'd get a plane off the ground with two babies, two teams and two neo-transport units.'

The units weighed a good hundred kilograms each, containing a portable incubator, oxygen, compressed air and monitoring equipment.

'This way,' he went on, 'at least each baby gets its own plane.'

The aircraft were both ready. Anna and Finn closed the office again and separated. They'd meet up in transit in Hobart, no doubt in a flurry of early morning activity as the teams and the equipment came aboard.

There would be separate flights, spaced a few minutes apart, to Fryerstown, and then a painful hiatus once each specialist team had been delivered to the hospital. Stabilising a tiny premature baby for transport could take several hours.

By the time they reached Hobart at five to eight, the Hobart teams were waiting at the airport with their transport cots, which needed special brackets to anchor them in the plane. The teams had already received a report on the birth of the third baby—a boy, bigger and stronger than the little one who'd died, not as big as the girl but doing well.

Picturing tiny Fryerstown Hospital with its outdated collection of brick and fibro buildings, Anna knew how tough it must be for all concerned. And she was thankful, at heart, that her role between Fryerstown and Melbourne would be limited to dealing with flight safety issues, assisting the NETS team with the equipment and responding to their needs and instructions. Today, hers wasn't the ultimate life-or-death responsibility.

She gave a standard pre-flight safety briefing to the NETS team, pointing out emergency exits and explaining the use of life jackets in case of a water landing, as much of their flying time today would take place over the waters of Bass Strait. When this was done, she had time to wonder about the parents of the babies. They were a tourist couple. The end of the second trimester seemed like an odd time to chose for a holiday in Tasmania's rugged south-west when you were pregnant with triplets.

Neonatologist Paul Swanson made the same comment during the flight from Hobart, through clear weather and over increasingly rugged and sparsely populated terrain. He had received more detailed information from both

Fryerstown and the patient's own obstetrics specialist in Melbourne by this time, and so far he didn't seem impressed.

'These women!' he complained loudly into his headset. 'They get to thirty-five and suddenly their career isn't enough and they want a new lifestyle accessory. Doesn't happen within a week, so they go and badger a fertility specialist. Treatment is premature and over-enthusiastic, and three embryos implant.

'Well, great. They wanted it all, and now they're getting it all. Only they won't accept that it's going to change their lives in any way whatsoever. This one went against Gordon Leggett's express advice in taking this holiday and, boom, this happens.' He shook his head. 'It's her own fault, and it makes me angry.'

'But, Paul,' the neonatal intensive care nurse said sensibly and carefully, 'wouldn't it be all the worse for the mother now—for both parents—to feel that it's their fault? And couldn't this have happened to her at home? You know it could!'

He snorted, then admitted, 'I'm just mouthing off, Sarah. Want to get my hands on those babies before someone does something ghastly. She was having pains for two hours before she did anything about it, apparently. The safest way to transport premmie babies is *in utero*. This aircraft could probably have got her to Melbourne for delivery if she'd made a move sooner, and none of this would be happening.'

'Only a few more minutes,' Nurse Sarah Comstock said, as sensibly as before.

Anna recognised now, too, that this was Paul Swanson's way of expressing and partially relieving the same tension that they all felt.

The plane touched down in Fryerstown at ten past nine.

CHAPTER THREE

HOME.

It was jarring for Anna, as always, to find herself suddenly here, at a few hours' notice. It felt like Lewis Carroll's looking-glass land, not quite the same Fryerstown that she knew so well—the place where she had been born, at the same hospital as the three premmie babies, and had spent her first eighteen years. This was a sort of parallel universe Fryerstown, which she moved through in a bubble, separate from everyone else.

Normally, whether a flight was a routine patient transport or a medical emergency, she wasn't here for long. It could take less than an hour for patient hand-over and equipment checks. Sometimes she didn't even leave the airport, and only saw the town itself before landing and after take off, passing the windows of the plane at some crazy, tilted angle so that it took her some seconds to recognise landmarks. That's the mine manager's house. Those are the slag heaps and the waste water channels. There's Sulphur Street.

Today was different. Her first task, and Finn's, was to assist with the transfer of the equipment from the two planes to the ambulances, driven today by local volunteer crews. Once this was done, and each ambulance had left for the hospital with the two neonatal teams on board, the urgency ceased.

Anna and Rick made another check of the plane's equipment, Rick from a pilot's perspective and Anna from a medical one. Had anything been damaged or

moved or disconnected during flight? Knowing the repertoire of likely drugs and supplies for the trip to
Melbourne, were they all to hand and in order?

Parked adjacent to them, Chris and Finn were doing
the same thing in the second aircraft. Finn took a little
longer at the task than Anna did, and she knew he was
taking extra care that everything was right. This wasn't
a scenario he'd have wanted to plunge into on his second
day in a job where he'd had to argue to bypass the usual
gradual augmentation of responsibility.

Sorry you were so pushy now? she could have asked.
She thought about it, then rejected the idea. He might
not catch the humour.

In any case, so far there had been no suggestion whatsoever that he wasn't equipped to handle anything that
was thrown at him.

He came over to her when they were both finished,
grinned easily at her and said, 'So, this is your native
soil, right?'

'If you want to put it that way.'

'Is there somewhere in this town where we can get
something to eat?'

At which point it fully hit home.

That's right. I'm here for the next few hours with
nothing to do, and it looks as if Finn McConnell is expecting me to play host.

She glanced around for the pilots, and crossed Rick
off the list at once. He was a quiet man, trying to turn
his thirty years of experience as a pilot into a blockbuster
adventure novel. If ever he had a spare moment, he'd be
holed up in some flimsy shack of an airport office with
his laptop, his Thermos and the packed meals his wife
always prepared for him, rattling away on the keyboard,

slurping coffee and munching. He wouldn't be interested in driving into town.

Chris was making plans of his own. 'It's possible,' he said, 'that I have a girlfriend in this town.'

A quick phone call apparently confirmed that he did, and he wore a wide grin when he informed Anna and Finn, 'She's picking me up in ten minutes. Nice. Haven't seen her in a year.'

'Would she be open to giving us a lift into town?' Finn asked, as if he and Anna were joined at the hip.

She drew in a breath to protest, then thought better of it. Not really fair to abandon the man, and it wasn't as if there was any lure in the prospect of spending what might be some hours in Fryerstown on her own.

Mum and Dad were away on their annual January trip to a caravan at a beach camping ground on the east coast. Her brother Rod lived down in Strahan, operating a tourist boat. She'd lost contact years ago with any friends from school who'd stayed in Fryerstown.

You could see Kendra.

Ugh. They'd had a fight just after Christmas. Was Anna wrong in thinking Kendra had promoted it quite energetically?

'You're *always* critical of my choices!' she had claimed. 'You *always* make it clear that you would have done better in my situation! You have no respect for me! You never have! You look down on me! Well, you can just get down off your high horse, you smug, snooty-nosed…!' As Kendra herself would have said, Et cetera.

Anna was still waiting for an apology. Eventually, she suspected, she would be the one to mend fences without one. Underneath, she was very fond of her spoiled, wayward cousin, and perhaps there was some truth in some of Kendra's accusations, too.

At the moment, however, Kendra's ex-lover seemed like the lesser of two evils.

Unless she took the bull by the horns for the baby's sake and played matchmaker, got Chris's obliging part-time girlfriend to drop both herself and Finn off at Auntie Rona's little green fibro house in Oxide Street for a rapturous reconciliation.

Oh, brilliant idea! She wanted to stay out of the situation, not place herself strategically as a punching bag between the two of them.

Chris's Maddy had a 'the more the merrier' response to the prospect of two more passengers in her ancient and tiny European car, which meant that Finn and Anna were squashed into the back seat.

So squashed, in fact, once Chris had slid the front passenger seat back as far as it would go, that Finn had to turn his legs sideways and stretch his big arm across the back of the rear seat. Anna had the choice of scrunching herself up hard against the window handle and looking like a scared rabbit, or letting her limbs fall more naturally and having them nudge against Finn's thigh and torso. She went with the latter option.

Regretted it.

Fryerstown airport was some minutes from the town itself. With the rugged nature of the surrounding terrain, a closer location had not been possible. The road into town was sealed and smooth, but it wound sickeningly from side to side and up and down. With each change of direction, their bodies lurched together, goading him to mutter at one point, 'I'm not doing this on purpose, you know.'

'I know,' she muttered back fiercely. 'Neither am I.'

'Got that straight, then.' Suddenly he grinned. 'You know what? I'm not going to fight it any more.'

For a few seconds she didn't know what he meant, then his right arm dropped onto her shoulder, he shimmied himself a few inches closer and now, instead of colliding, they moved in unison on the bends and the pressure between them was steady and warm.

Her skin crawled and heat began to pool inside her. Oh, this was just great! Her body responded to his with a life of its own. She felt the softness of her breast nudge against his side, and knew he was aware of it, too. He seemed relaxed, totally confident in the rightness of their contact, not pushing it but not fighting it either.

Something was very wrong with the springs of the seat. This car was beyond old, barely fit to be on the road. Their shared weight was making the seat sink in the middle, pushing them even more heavily against each other. Effectively, she was nestled right into his arm.

Arms.

There was nowhere for that big left limb to go except across the front of his body and onto her thigh or hip. Her choice. The hip felt too intimate, sending a jet of heat straight for the core of her, just inches away, but when she used an elbow to nudge his hand lower, its flattened weight on her trouser-clad thigh felt even worse.

Well, even *better*, actually, but in this case better *was* worse!

Oh, it was crazy!

He gave a lazy growl of laughter at the way she kept trying to wriggle into a safer position. 'Hope you don't get car sick!'

'That's not the problem!'

In front, Chris and Maddy were catching up on their news with a fervency which suggested they'd last seen each other drifting in opposite directions in separate life-boats shortly after a shipwreck. Maddy was gabbling out her life story, Chris kept interjecting 'No! You're joking!' and Maddy wasn't paying the requisite attention to the road.

Screech! She took a bend too fast, and Anna felt Finn's face…his lips and nose…against her hair. It tickled, and was almost like a kiss.

'Mmm! Honey and almond,' he murmured, before another bend changed their weight distribution again.

'Peach and almond,' Anna corrected, as if it mattered. The man was a connoisseur of shampoos? That sounded dangerous.

Speaking of danger…

'Hey,' he said to the front seat, with a mix of cajoling and desperation, 'Maddy, we're ambulance drivers. It really hurts us to have you driving like this. Can you, please, develop a greater interest in the road?'

'I'll tell you later, Chris,' Maddy said obediently, and they reached the approach to town in one piece. 'Where am I taking you?' Maddy wanted to know.

'Drop us opposite Cassidy's—that would be fine,' Anna said.

'They tore down Cassidy's two years ago.'

'OK, opposite the big slab of old concrete floor where Cassidy's used to be.'

Maddy wasn't a Fryerstown native, clearly. If she had been, she would still have said 'Cassidy's', although the old-fashioned department store no longer existed, and 'the mine manager's house', although it was now an expensive bed-and-breakfast, and 'the railhead', although the rails themselves were now rusted to pieces and grass grew up through the metalled bed of the track. Copper was still mined in Fryerstown, on a small scale, but it went out by truck these days.

'Here we are,' Maddy said. 'Do I have to pick you up again?'

'No,' Finn answered. 'We'll be staying in touch with the hospital, and the ambulances will take us back to the airport when they're ready.' Chris would be paged, too, of course.

'Right.' Maddy didn't seem concerned about the emergency which had brought them to Fryerstown, fortunately. Anna didn't feel like talking about it right now. The team would be at the hospital by this time, working over the two tiny babies…if both of them still lived.

Their temperatures and blood gases needed to be stabilised, their respiration and fluids brought up to the right levels. Were they breathing on their own? They'd need IV lines for fluids and nutrients to keep up their strength. More than one IV, probably. One to a vein in the scalp, perhaps. A central line to the chest. Not desirable, but often necessary. They would be stuck with sensors and taped with wires and tubes until there was hardly a square inch of skin left free. Their little nappies would be the size of folded sandwich bags, and almost as thin, and their urinary output would be measured to the millilitre.

Meanwhile…

Chris and Maddy drove off, after Maddy had barely brought the car to a halt for Anna and Finn to get out. It was fairly obvious that the two of them were going to rush off to Maddy's and leap into bed. Whether any form of future commitment was on the agenda, Anna didn't care to speculate.

Meanwhile… Meanwhile…

The sun was shining on the slab of concrete that used

to be Cassidy's. The miners' monument and fountain ran with bubbling water. The surrounding mountains dreamed in the summer air, bare of trees and clad only in stark spills of rock in colours of rust red, yellow ochre, dirty pink, bark brown and leathery white. The streets, with their mean little fibro or weatherboard dwellings and brave shopfronts were quiet.

Lord, but it was an ugly town!

No! No, it wasn't, it was *beautiful*. It *was*! The colours of those mountains were so rich. The skies were so hugely blue when it was fine, and so dramatically clouded or silkily fogged when it wasn't.

The green little gardens that people had made were like oases, not on streets like shadeless Oxide Street, which marched straight up the hill and boasted only tired yellow lawns, but on the two streets that bordered innocent, unpolluted Dangar's Creek, tucked just below the mine manager's house high on a hill.

And, not so far away, there was the lushness of the temperate rainforests on the way down to Strahan and the dark waters of Macquarie Harbour.

How was it possible to hate and love this town the way Anna did? To love all those rich earth colours on the mountains, even though she knew they were the result of stripping the ancient forests until not a tree was left to stem the ravages of erosion, and of poisoning the air with chemicals from the copper smelter. To hate the lack of choices for its young people, even though in so many ways she loved the uncompromising isolation of the place. To hate the poisonous dominance of the mine, even though she loved the stories of the early days, when copper ore had first been found here, and hard lives had been lived by the miners who'd wrested the mineral from the earth.

'Anna...?' Finn was watching her carefully.

Lord, how long had she been standing like that, staring up at the mountains and breathing the morning air?

'I'm sorry,' she said automatically.

'What for?'

'You're probably starving,' she improvised.

'Aren't you?'

'Yes, actually,' she admitted.

'Then let's eat. There must be somewhere.'

'We'll head up the main street. There are a couple of cafés. You choose.'

'If you like.'

The choice came down to the Wild Rivers Café, which doubled as a gallery, selling local paintings and hand-crafted Tasmanian wood products, and the Paradise Take Away, which would serve you a deliciously greasy breakfast until eleven, and then metamorphose into a pizza place, serving deliciously greasy pizzas, until ten at night.

Finn picked the Paradise, and she was a little surprised. The atmosphere at Wild Rivers was far more genteel.

Somehow he didn't need her to ask him about it, and explained when she hadn't even spoken, 'My theory is that the servings will be bigger at this one.'

She laughed. 'They will be.'

Anna was starting to relax a little more, Finn decided. Earlier it hadn't been hard to sense her strong, conflicting moods. In the background, there was the grey wash of tension they all felt about the two fragile lives which were the reason for this whole exercise. Overlying that, for Anna, was a complex pattern of feeling about her memories of this place and her past here.

He could easily see how someone could get attuned

to the raw beauty of the town, how its poisonous chemistry could seep deep into their bones.

Then, in the car...Oh, boy, the car. He hadn't known whether to fight it or go along with it. He certainly hadn't wanted to give her the impression that he was using the car's movement as an excuse for touching her, but in the end there hadn't been a choice. The cramped space, the wrecked seat springs, Maddy's wild driving. He couldn't have kept himself from touching her if he'd tried. And, of course, he hadn't tried, because he hadn't wanted to.

She had felt so good. She had *smelt* so good. He'd almost named the scents in her shampoo correctly. And if his masculine perception was worth anything at all, she had been every bit as aware of him as he had been of her. It hadn't been one-sided.

At the moment, sitting opposite her at a table in the corner and watching her study the menu, he felt as if they were the only people in the whole world who mattered, and as if this interlude in Fryerstown might never come to an end.

They both ordered a big, hot breakfast of eggs, bacon, sausages, grilled tomatoes and toast, washed down with orange juice and coffee. She winced at his dollops of sugar again. There were three other people there, just finishing off their own late breakfasts, but otherwise the place was deserted. Outside, even the main street was quiet.

'Isn't this the tourist season?' Finn asked.

'For what it's worth,' she agreed. 'A lot of people prefer Strahan. It's by the ocean. There's fishing, and the Gordon River cruises. But Fryerstown is starting to invest in tourism now. It's a good jumping-off point for some of the wilderness hiking routes.'

'Would you like to see it develop in that direction?'

'If it keeps the town alive, gives people employment, of course I would.'

'I thought you might be happy to see the place die a natural death once the mine finally closes altogether. I get the impression not all your memories are happy ones.'

'That's not— Well, yes,' she revised. 'It *is* true. It was hard, growing up here at a time when the mine was scaling down its operations year by year. There was a sense that you had to leave or go under, yet most of us knew our parents couldn't afford to finance an education elsewhere.'

'What did you do?'

'I went to Hobart and half killed myself, working my way through art school, then realised at the end of it that, not being as talented as I'd once thought, all I'd qualified myself for was a very minor career as a commercial artist, and it wasn't what I wanted at all.'

'So you became an ambulance officer.'

'So I became an ambulance officer,' she agreed. 'I still draw a fair bit in my spare time, but professionally I realised I wanted to do something that mattered. I did the full paramedic training, moved to Teymouth, did the flight training—and here I am.'

'Here you are.' He decided to take the statement literally, though he knew she hadn't meant it that way. 'No one you want to go and see while we're here?'

'My parents are away.' That was all she said, and he could tell that she was holding something back, and that it was an effort for her.

He thought about pushing, then decided against it. Her body language was pretty explicit. She'd sat up higher in her chair, pushed back a little. The confiding posture, which had suggested she might be willing to reveal more, was gone, and her expression was cool.

'What would you like to do next?' Anna enquired politely. 'We'll probably still have another hour or more after this, even if things are going well.'

'Go for a walk?' he suggested. 'End up at the hospital? I'd like to see the babies, if possible, to see what we're in for while we're still not under any pressure. Get to know everyone a bit. I expect I'll be involved in flying the parents up to Melbourne in a day or two.'

'Yes, I suppose you will,' Anna agreed. 'I'll be off but, yes, the mother ought to be fit enough to travel by tomorrow or Thursday, when you're on with…'

'Simon Petty, I think,' Finn supplied.

'He's good. You'll like him.'

'I like you.'

It just slipped out. What was that old line? 'Caution, do not engage mouth before putting brain into gear.' Well, he'd just done it. It had definitely not been the right time to slip in a line like that, although the more time he spent with her, the more he meant it.

'Fast worker, aren't you?' was her sour comment.

Exactly why he shouldn't have spoken. Despite those fierce moments of awareness in Maddy's car, and the soft shreds of her past self, her inner self, which Anna had begun to reveal to him—like strips of bright, torn silk, he thought fancifully—she hadn't abandoned her hostility. Not one bit. She had only…forgotten about it at times, because of the strength of the elemental connection between them.

Which was interesting. Mysterious. Why should there be that conflict inside her? Almost as if she didn't want to be hostile but for some reason felt she had to.

'Fast worker. That's a loaded term,' he told her.

'You're right.'

'You prefer it the old-fashioned way?'

'I prefer a man to at least try to pretend that there's more than one thing on his mind.'

'Even when it's on your mind just as much?'

Snap! Up went her head. Her jaw dropped half an inch and then froze tight. The muscles around her eyes tightened, and one hand came to clutch at the top of her very professional white shirt, where just one button at the neck was unfastened. Time seemed to slow and he waited, had room to think, during her few crucial seconds of silence, What's she going to say? Is she going to deny it?

No.

'I can't help that,' she blurted.

'But you would if you could?'

'Yes!'

'As a general rule, or purely in relation to me?'

'As a general rule,' she parroted deliberately, 'I don't have this problem with my co-workers.'

'I'm flattered.'

'And I—I guess you should be,' she admitted confusedly.

Anna Brewster, this flushed, was a pretty amazing sight. How could you describe that soft pink blooming on her cheeks? What had happened to her eyes? They had been plain blue-grey. Now they were like rainy pools, reflecting dark storm clouds. Breath was coming in and out over a bottom lip that was suddenly moist because she'd licked it nervously, and she was wiping a hand up through her hair in a vain attempt to mask her face. Finn had a vivid image of those slender fingers raking across the top of his own head.

'And I should…apologise,' she went on. 'I'm sorry, I—'

'Why? Why should you apologise?' Finn demanded. Surely she wasn't scared of her response to him, was she?

No, he realised. No, it wasn't that.

She had gathered her inner resources now. 'Because it's wrong, and it's going to go away as soon as I can make it. Believe that, Finn!'

'Should I?' He spoke his thoughts aloud. 'On the one hand, you're a strong-willed woman. On the other, what we were both feeling in the car was pretty strong, too.'

'It wasn't.' He couldn't believe Anna was denying it like that, and just listen to her reasoning! 'It was purely to do with the steamy atmosphere being generated in the front seat,' she said. 'With those two talking each other's clothes off and Maddy driving as if she'd forget how to do it—and I don't mean how to drive—if she didn't get home in the next three minutes…'

He laughed. Her voice had risen without her being aware of it, and the waitress, who had just arrived to take their plates away and offer more coffee, had pricked up her ears.

'Yes, all right, it's funny,' Anna said.

'And it's not true. What was happening to us had nothing to do with what was happening in the front seat. But if that's your story, if that's the best you can come up with, I'm not going to push it.'

'No. Good.' She gave a short nod, her colour still high.

Aagh! This was maddening! Now she almost looked disappointed, as if a part of her had wanted him to keep at her about it. It was too confusing. The only course of action seemed to be to retire from the fray. Temporarily, of course.

If Anna thought that he was the kind of man to be put off by the wishy-washy protests she'd given him so far, then she was very much mistaken. Sure, if he'd been in any doubt whatsoever about their chemistry, but the fact that she'd admitted it herself, bathed in all that graceful confusion…

Finn's groin tightened, and so did his determination. No, this was very definitely not finished yet.

'I'll pay,' Anna said abruptly.

They had both waved away the waitress's suggestion of more coffee a minute ago. Finn threw a crumpled ten dollar note onto the table and Anna squashed it in her hand and went up to the cash resister at the counter. He watched her, appreciative of the way the dark navy fabric of her uniform trousers spread so smoothly and firmly across her neatly rounded backside.

She was chatting to the waitress and he tuned in to the conversation.

'Yes, I'm in Teymouth now. I'm a flight paramedic. We're on a call-out, just here for an hour or two, waiting for two patients to be stabilised.'

They finished with a couple of pleasantries, then she came back to the table and handed him some loose change. 'Here.'

'Thanks.' A quick tally told him that she had scrupulously split their bill, and it seemed easier just to pocket the money than to argue the point. If it was a point of honour with her, he respected that.

'She was in my brother's year at school. I didn't recognise her until she said something,' Anna was saying. 'She's lost weight.'

'Sorry?'

'The waitress.'

'Oh, right,' he said, then added, 'Still up for that walk?'

She nodded, so he stood up and they left the café together.

It was a form of claustrophobia, Anna decided as they began to walk back down the main street. In an open space, with physical exercise to occupy her body, she wouldn't feel the same awareness of him. The secret link between them in the car had been brought out into the open at the Paradise Café, and it was crazy of her to be disappointed because he hadn't pushed just a little further.

She almost wanted to confront him with it. Yes, I'm attracted to you, but if you think I'm going to fall into bed with the man who made Kendra pregnant...

It would have been so satisfying to say it, to set those tiny dark hairs on the back of his neck standing on end with shock, because clearly he had no idea that she knew anything about it. If he had, he would surely have said something.

She was starting to wonder if he'd even bothered to remember...or find out...that Kendra was here in Fryerstown. He hadn't mentioned her by name, or even hinted that he knew anyone in this town.

I'll tell him...

But Anna didn't want to stoop to that. Create a scene? Sordid, and hitting a little too close to home. Mainlanders sometimes joked about the inbreeding of rural Tasmanians. It wasn't fair or accurate, but there had been a couple of families she knew here and in other nearby towns whose shifting relationships were like something out of a sleazy court case. Her own life could so easily have ended up that way as well.

This was one of the things Anna had wanted to escape when she'd left Fryerstown at eighteen. She'd been dizzily in love with Russell Hoxton that year, and certain that their future would be a shared one. The pregnancy scare had taught her otherwise. Russell had been so horrified when she'd told him of her suspicions. And then, in the end, she hadn't been pregnant at all.

Or so she had assumed ignorantly back then when her period arrived at last, four weeks late and unusually heavy and painful. Now she understood that she'd probably had a miscarriage, and that was an odd, unpleasant feeling. To know belatedly that there had once been a baby, and she should have grieved. Should she grieve now, years later?

Impossible, really. Russell, once full of such grand plans for leaving Fryerstown and conquering the world, still lived here, working at the local petrol station. At twenty, even before Anna had left for Hobart, he'd fathered a daughter with Lisa Berg. Less than a year after that he'd fathered another one with Vanessa Simmonds.

I could be like Lisa and Vanessa, she knew. We'd have gone to play-group together, with our three children, half-siblings and almost the same age. Or we'd have fought like angry cats over Russell, who wouldn't really have cared about any of us.

That's not what I want.

She hadn't wanted such a tangle of tenuous connections and dishonoured commitments then with Russell, and she didn't want one now with Finn. She shuddered.

Finn was oblivious. He took a deep, appreciative breath and grinned at her. 'The air's fresh.'

'It is today,' she answered. 'It isn't always. It never used to be.'

The grin turned crooked, more complicated. 'For the

moment,' he said softly, 'I'm only interested in today. Tell me about that big house on the hill.'

They crossed Malachite Street and took a short cut over the derelict concrete floor of Cassidy's, talking as they went. Just a few hundred metres away was the Lyell River, still hopelessly poisoned from the ore processing, and a thick, bright rust orange in colour. It was like a running wound through the town, and didn't begin to get clearer until miles further downstream, where gradually nature somehow miraculously managed to filter out the worst of it before it tumbled, still undrinkable, into Macquarie Harbour.

'It's terrible,' Finn said, studying the water from the car and pedestrian bridge that crossed over it.

'Like it's running paint, not water,' she agreed. 'When I was a child, I used to think that rivers and creeks had personalities... No, I shouldn't be telling this story yet. Wait and see.'

She led the way across the bridge and up into the half-hidden houses behind the grand eminence dominated by the mine manager's house. It was cooler and shadier here. Some people had restored the cheap old houses prettily, and tall tree ferns grew in many places.

Out of the mountains behind the town and down between the houses came tumbling clear Dangar's Creek, and Anna and Finn stood on a much smaller bridge and watched as it scurried on downstream to its confluence with the Lyell River fifty metres further on.

Anna took up her story again. 'I used to feel so sorry for Dangar's Creek,' she said. 'Once, my brother and I tried to dam it up and divert its course. We got as far as flooding someone's garden, then Dad showed us a map and convinced us that Dangar's immolation in the poisoned Lyell was one of life's more inevitable calamities.

There's simply nowhere else for the poor little creek to go.

'He couldn't understand why we cared. He couldn't see that for us Dangar's was alive, like a happy, misbehaving little hobgoblin, while the Lyell was garishly dead, and the moment where the clear water met and mingled with that orange paint was just *painful* to us.'

Finn was silent for a moment. 'You're amazing, Anna,' he finally said.

'Why? Because it can still make me cry?' She brushed away a tear with her knuckle and forced a little laugh. 'That's not amazing, that's just silly.'

'Because you can still invest a mountain creek with personality,' he said seriously. 'Because of what you feel about this town. It *is* amazing. What's your brother doing these days?'

'Rod? He's living in Strahan, piloting a tour boat up the Gordon River.'

'Where the water is pure?'

'Where the water is pure,' she agreed.

They grinned crookedly at each other, and she was alarmed at how much those grins communicated, back and forth.

'And your mother?' he asked. 'What does she get up to?'

'She makes souvenirs.'

'And your dad?'

'Watches sport, drinks beer and collects his pension. I love him, but we don't have a lot to say to each other. He's from the school of thought that believes parenting is a woman's responsibility so, you know, the connections were just never made.'

'Like my father, too, all of that.'

'Really?' Anna nodded, not entirely surprised.

'Something in common.'

'Maybe they watch different sports.'

'Maybe they do,' he agreed, humouring her. But he was right. It *was* something in common, and not the only thing by any means...

Hell, I want to kiss her! Finn thought. Hold her, touch her. 'Kiss' isn't right. *Drink* her. Take her. Give myself to her. It's... It's...

Something he would have to harbour inside himself until the timing was right, which it most definitely wasn't yet. She had folded her arms across her body. That fluent, betraying body language of hers once again. Don't touch! it said. I might want it, but don't do it, all the same.

A'right, Anna, he thought, I'll respect all that confusing conflict inside you, but I'm not going to let you forget what your body is telling you.

They were still standing on the little bridge, leaning rather uncomfortably on the splintery wooden railing. Deliberately, he eased a little closer in order to get a better view of the steps that zigzagged up towards the big house on the hill. His movement had the side benefit of bringing him almost close enough to brush her arm with his, and he knew she had noticed.

She moved a tiny bit away, but not as far as she could have moved if she'd really wanted to. Not nearly as far. The realisation ignited an incandescent spark of promise in Finn's future, and he smiled down at Dangar's Creek as if the water were an old friend.

CHAPTER FOUR

'THERE'S a stick insect on your shoulder. Stop a minute, Anna.'

'Oh!'

'Scared of them?'

'Not really, but—'

'Hold still. It's quite small.'

Obediently, Anna stood on the path. Finn lifted her collar out of the way with one hand, moving very slowly and carefully. She felt the back of his hand brush her jaw. He stuck out the index finger of his other hand and began to coax the brownish-green creature onto it. It took a few moments.

'Hold *very* still,' he said.

He had his gaze fixed on the insect, and Anna couldn't help watching his eyes. They were as dark as a gypsy's and so full and honestly expressive of everything that he was made of—intelligence, humour, warmth, curiosity…And kindness.

Most men would just have flicked the insect off into the bushes and thought no more about it, but Finn didn't. Instead, he let it stalk awkwardly around his hand as it explored. He hadn't stepped away from Anna, so they were still standing very close, both intent on the creature now.

'Want to hold him?' Finn said.

'Um…'

'Go on.'

He didn't wait for her to agree, just took her hand

gently and positioned it next to his other wrist. The stick insect had begun to march up his arm. The dark hairs that curled there caught at its legs like long grass. Anna could feel the hairs, too.

Finn had gorgeous forearms, below the rolled blue sleeves of his overalls—smooth, hair-ruffled skin covering solid, ropey muscles and square, strong wrists.

'Come on, Fred,' he said, nudging the creature with his finger. It wouldn't go in the right direction. 'Press your arm along mine,' he told Anna, and she did so.

His head was bent in concentration, and she felt his forehead brush her hair. The possibility of a kiss was palpable in the air between them, and she kept expecting him to initiate it—her breathing was getting shallower and shallower—but he didn't, and finally the insect stepped across to her arm and began its confused sentry duty up and down.

She gave a tiny screech. It tickled, and felt dry and clingy. Creepy! The kind of sensation it would take a while to get used to.

'What do you think?' Finn still hadn't moved.

'It does look incredibly like a stick. But the poor thing is going to need trauma counselling soon if we don't put it back where it belongs.'

'Want to do it?'

'OK.'

They found a tree leaning over the low fence at the front of someone's garden, and she rested her arm on a branch and waited for Fred to make a rapid and rapturous return to his habitat, but he didn't.

'Not very bright, is he?' she said.

'Here…' Finn's touch again, this time from just one finger sliding along the skin of her arm till the insect clung and he could put it off onto a branch. She watched every hair on her arm stand up to attention and felt her nerve-endings there buzz with life. 'I guess that's the end of nature study for today.' He looked at his watch. 'We should get to the hospital. It's getting on for twelve. They should be ready soon.'

'I feel out of touch,' she said.

'They'd have paged us if they needed us.'

'I know, but…'

Anna couldn't admit to how distracted she'd been over the past couple of hours. She was wearing the uniform, but that was about it. If he guessed that she kept wondering why it was that he hadn't kissed her…

They walked along Conglomerate Street, crossed the poisoned river by a bridge further down and then headed up Calcite Street to the hospital on the other side of the narrow river valley.

'I love the street names in this place,' Finn commented drily.

'It's a company town,' Anna said. 'Some bright spark in mine management in the 1930s thought it would be cute to name them all after rocks and minerals and refining processes. As if mining wasn't dominant enough here already.'

'I take it you'd rather we were strolling up Primrose Lane, or something.'

'Well, it isn't great fun to grow up in Sulphur Street. But, no, not Primrose. Why not name them after some of the pioneering miners, though? Or the explorers?'

'I take your point. You're proud of this town's human heritage, rather than its past generation of mineral wealth.'

'Something like that. I'm sorry, you don't need to get embroiled in the complexity of my feelings about Fryerstown. Here's the hospital.'

He didn't answer, but she felt the brief brush of his fingers against her palm, once more sending a prickling warmth all the way up her arm. For a moment, she thought he was going to hold her hand, but then he'd stopped to let her pass through the entry door ahead of him.

Another mind-bending and too abrupt journey through the looking-glass. That was how it felt. There were only a few other patients at the hospital at the moment, all minor cases. No one was waiting in Casualty. But the sense of urgency in the air was huge.

'They were about to page you,' said the middle-aged receptionist at the front desk, not someone Anna knew.

'Ready to go?' Finn asked.

'Not yet. Likely to be another half an hour, apparently.'

'Problems?'

'Of course! But go on through and hear it from the experts.'

The atmosphere in the hospital's very basic paediatric unit was hectic and tense. Dr Swanson was keeping no one in any doubt about his feelings. The parents of the babies were in the recovery annexe next to the operating theatre where the babies had been delivered, and were fortunately well out of earshot. The mother was showing no signs of any post-partum complication, which was one blessing.

The boy and girl both had names now, written in black felt-tip on cards at the foot of each transport unit. The boy, who would be going with Anna and her team, was Matthew Thomas, and the girl was Ashley Kate. They didn't seem quite human enough to have names, so red and thin and fragile, with skin that was almost translucent as the fat layer beneath it had not yet formed.

Neither Finn nor Anna distracted anyone with questions, just absorbed what they needed to know by listening and looking. As expected, Matthew seemed to be having a harder time. His oxygen saturation level was lower, and the rate on his respirator was consequently higher. As Anna watched, Dr Swanson was cursing under his breath, trying to put another IV line into veins that would be like fine threads. It was distressing the baby, but it couldn't be helped, and when the specialist achieved success at last his relief was very evident.

Finn's team was almost ready to depart, but when they did so, in a flurry of activity five minutes later, Anna hardly noticed, too absorbed in what was happening to Matthew.

'I still don't like his oxygen sat. We've got to get it up, but those lungs are so fragile,' Dr Swanson was saying. 'I'm going to turn up the rate. Just a fraction. And we're going to wait.'

They did, for another hour, by which time Anna assumed Finn and his plane would be long gone. But when little Matthew's blood oxygen levels, heart rate and temperature were finally satisfactory and they drove back out to the airport, she found the plane still there, and both Rick and Chris going over mechanical checks while the medical team inside balanced on a knife-edge of tension. Should they wait this out? Try and fly in another plane? Take the baby back to the hospital?

'What's the problem?' she asked Finn, who was prowling back and forth between pilots and neonatal team, clearly wishing there was more he could do.

'Some damned warning light keeps going on when it shouldn't be going on. Or at least, if it should be going on, it means there's a problem and we can't take off. But Chris thinks it's the light that's at fault, not the engine thing, only they have to check to make sure, because if it *is* the engine we'll drop out of the sky. And you probably didn't understand half of that but, sorry, I'm not a pilot, I'm a paramedic, and—'

'Feeling totally useless either way.' Anna nodded. 'Finn, we have to head out.' She was getting signals from her team, and Rick had returned to his aircraft to complete his own pre-flight checks.

Fortunately, nothing was amiss, and they achieved a quick, fluid departure. Anna hooked up the transport unit's oxygen equipment to the plane's supply, and plugged in the power as well, to save the battery for use in transit. She discussed cabin pressure and temperature with Dr Swanson, and communicated his requirements to Rick in the pilot's seat.

After take-off, she reported the flight's status back to the service's control centre. During all of this, Matthew's condition remained satisfactory, despite the stress of movement and noise.

Once safely in the air, Rick was able to report, via the headphones, 'OK, Chris has clearance for take-off now, too. It was just the light.'

'Thank heaven for small mercies!' Dr Swanson muttered, then said to Anna impatiently, 'There's a rattle between the unit and the frame-thing. This thing here. Can you fix that? Pad it with something? We just don't need any more noise and vibration, and it's driving me mad.'

Having expected to share Finn's recent sense of helplessness, Anna found herself busy for the rest of the flight. Dr Swanson was demanding. The cabin wasn't warm enough after all. Could she find a better position for the IV fluid bag? How many minutes out of Melbourne were they, and how was the vehicle, which was already waiting for them at the terminal, set up? Those brackets would need changing again, wouldn't they?

She dealt with everything as efficiently and clearly as she could, and was rewarded, on landing at Melbourne's Essendon Airport in the late afternoon, with a brief, 'Good work, everyone. He's hanging in there.'

Then came the bustle of another transfer. Unhooking the oxygen and power, locking the unit into the brackets in the ambulance, reporting to the Victorian service's drivers, who would navigate tangled Melbourne traffic while Anna remained in the back of the vehicle with the NETS team, dealing with the equipment.

Finn's plane was coming in to land just as her own crew left the terminal, but they caught up to each other as the transfer at Melbourne Children's was completed in the early evening. Scribbled case notes had to be handed over, and a vital oral report on each baby's condition given by the NETS staff to the hospital's neonatal specialists.

Finally, both teams could let go of their tension. The babies had survived the transfer without any apparent worsening of their status, and for Finn and Anna this was the best that could be hoped for. Since the babies' parents lived in Melbourne, there would be no return flight to Tasmania, and news of the ultimate outcome for these two tiny infants would probably never reach them.

'Which is a mixed blessing,' Finn commented to Anna, as they stood waiting for the two NETS teams to wind up their hand-over. Both having filled the same role in all of this, they were natural allies, and she didn't question the fact that they were standing together, a little apart from everyone else.

'You think so?' she queried, in answer to his comment.

'Yes, why, do you really *always* want to know?' he returned.

'Sometimes not,' she admitted. 'But I'd like to with these ones. My mind can't make the leap to see them as happy, healthy toddlers, even though so often these days they do reach that point, and you'd never know, by the time they hit two or three, that they were premature.'

'Maybe the parents will send some photos.'

'Have a feeling not, in this case. It might be months before they have their babies home, and this part of the process will seem so long ago, and something they just want to forget. Particularly since what Dr Swanson was grumbling about during the flight was right, in many ways. They probably shouldn't have taken that holiday, and it must be hurting them that they did, and this was the result.'

'Think we're about ready to go,' Finn said. 'Takes a while, doesn't it? It'll be getting on for midnight by the time we touch down in Teymouth.'

'Did you handle everything, by the way?' she had to ask. 'I didn't get a chance to ask before.'

'Forgot to plug in the power straight away,' he admitted. 'So we were running on battery longer than we should have been.'

'Not a crucial mistake.'

'Hate any kind of mistake. I was kicking myself. That mechanical glitch with the plane had us all distracted and doing things in the wrong order.'

'You shouldn't have told me,' she teased. 'You could have kept your slip-up to yourself, and I would never have known.'

'Yeah, but there's something about your eyes, unfortunately, Anna Brewster,' he told her lightly in reply. 'Are you an enchantress, or something? I'm starting to wonder. Because I have a feeling I couldn't lie to you if I tried.'

Anna laughed, then felt herself blushing, which she knew was exactly the reaction he'd intended. He was flirting with her, deliberately reminding her that she felt something when they were together, and that he knew it. She ought to resent it, bristle at it, for Kendra's sake, but for some reason she couldn't.

If she was an enchantress, he was a wizard or a warlock, entrancing her not with mystic spells but with his honesty, and he didn't stop at admitting to medical mistakes either...

She made the fatal error of trying to top his wicked remark. 'Of course you could!' she said. 'Just give it a bit of practice, and I'm sure you'll get it right.'

A gleam lit up his wicked dark eyes. 'Don't want to practise,' he said. 'I'd much rather give it to you straight, Anna. You're doing something to me, you know that? And I like it, an' I don't want it to go away.'

What did a sweet threat like that deserve in the way of a comeback? Something. Definitely. A big, fat, squashy put-down to freeze him off. So why was it that all she could manage was a weak nod of acknowledgement, another even darker blush and no coherent comment at all?

She thought about him all the way back in the plane, skimming over the darkening waves below in Bass Strait, and the rugged centre of Tasmania, where scarcely a light broke the thick black of night-time. And when he said goodbye to her at chilly Teymouth airport at a quarter to twelve, her voice stuck in her throat when she tried to reply.

CHAPTER FIVE

'ANNA. Hello, it's Finn.'

She almost said, I know, since his voice was unique and branded permanently into her mind, but changed it just in time to a half bland, half wary, 'Hello, Finn.'

Then she was tempted to add something even more betraying, but managed not to.

It's taken you long enough, was what she wanted to say, because it felt so inevitable and right that she was hearing his voice, addressed just to her, at last. She had been thinking about him in almost every spare moment for days, no matter how hard she'd tried to fight it.

She'd been thinking about Kendra, too. She'd even phoned her cousin earlier in the week, hoping it would be some kind of antidote to Finn's devastating effect on her, but it was an awkward conversation and hadn't really helped.

Kendra had apologised. 'I'm sorry about what I said at Christmas. I didn't mean it, it was just hormones.'

'That's fine, Kendra, I knew that. But…have you been in touch with Finn?'

A beat of silence, then, 'No, not yet.'

'I think you should,' Anna jumped in, almost before she'd heard the word 'no'.

'I told you, I'm not going to—' Kendra began.

'But don't you want to get the situation resolved?'

Anna herself had. She still did.

If there was even the slightest possibility of Finn and Kendra cementing their relationship, whether misguidedly for the sake of the baby, or because they discovered they really loved each other after whatever had split them up so quickly back in Melbourne, then she wanted to know about it. Soon! And if there wasn't that possibility…

If there wasn't, she tried to remind herself, then that still put Finn McConnell well out of bounds, because there was no way she was going to let herself fall for a womaniser who ducked his responsibilities. Surely there was no way! She definitely did not share Kendra's forgiving, boys-will-be-boys, let-him-have-his-freedom attitude.

'It's complicated, Anna, I've told you that,' Kendra said.

And that, as Anna had known before, was where she and Kendra parted company. It *wasn't* complicated!

'I've met him…worked with him for a couple of days two weeks ago, and we run into each other all the time at the station now,' she told her cousin. She hadn't mentioned the emergency trip to Fryerstown.

'Oh, how is he?'

She refused to be drawn. 'Contact him yourself if you want to know. You have his details, don't you?'

'Of course I do. Craig told me—he phoned me last week—but—'

'Kendra, he seems…'

Really, if she was any judge of character, not the sort of man who *would* duck his responsibilities, and that was what she was starting to feel as if she did not understand. He seemed like such a straightforward person, with pure and refreshingly simple ideas about honour and duty and commitment.

'Have you told him how you feel?' she pressed. 'Does he know you'd like his help, and his involvement?

Maybe he feels as if, by leaving Melbourne, you've shut him out, signalled that you're not interested and don't want to acknowledge that he's the baby's father.'

'You don't understand…'

'No, I don't, although I'm trying to. So hard! Why don't you come to Teymouth for a visit? You could stay with me. See him. Talk. Work something out. Soon, please!'

'I have to handle it in my own way,' Kendra had insisted stubbornly, and Anna had eventually ended the conversation, having felt that the situation had been more frustrating than ever.

I need some way to feel on firm ground about this, she had told herself, thinking about it afterwards. If Kendra and Finn had some big knock-down fight and decided they didn't want any more to do with each other, then that would be one thing…and I could accept that the man I…

She had hesitated, groping around in her mind for a way of putting it that hadn't sounded too frightening to her inner ear.

A man I could feel something for, she'd come up with, had once fathered a baby with my own cousin. On the other hand, if they found that they loved each other, I *know* I would…I'd have to be able to…forget completely about the effect he has on me.

The same effect he was having on her right now, on the phone, despite her repeated resolutions to keep her defences up.

'I wondered if you were busy tomorrow,' he said.

'Sounds like maybe I should arrange to be,' she speculated incautiously.

Damn! Where had that come from? She was never as blunt as that, not even with her brother. But, admit it, she was actually light-headed with relief that Finn had phoned at last, had made a concrete attempt to do something about all the unacknowledged yet unmistakable chemistry that had exploded between them.

She had pretended to herself and to him that she was resistant, but she probably hadn't pretended very well. At work, some of the other paramedics were starting to talk, or to rib the two of them, with varying degrees of crudity, about their relationship. Everyone clearly assumed that they were having an affair, or at least teetering on the brink of one.

There hadn't been any concrete evidence, Anna considered.

She also told herself that she was pleased he wasn't making any moves on her…and some of the time she even meant it…but it was maddening and confusing, too. If he wasn't interested, what was the source of that *atmosphere*? It definitely wasn't coming from her.

Well, not just from her, she amended in her more honest moments.

They hadn't been rostered together since those first two days. Steve Quick had returned from Queensland in time to pick up his place on the roster again, and Finn had been moved into road duties, which was where any new recruit would normally begin. In any case, all the flight paramedics returned to road duty for regular blocks of time every few months in order to keep current with skills that were more frequently called upon on the ground.

Before this, Steve and Finn had made another triangular journey between Teymouth, Fryerstown and Melbourne to transfer Matthew's and Ashley's mother to Melbourne, so that she could be with her babies. In the roomy Beechcraft plane, they had been able to take the babies' father as well.

With the way their rosters had chanced to work out, however, Finn and Anna had still seen each other often.

In a job like this, everyone spent extensive though erratically timed stretches hanging around at headquarters. You could catch up on sleep or reading or television. Sometimes there were students or observers who had questions or needed a tour. There was administrative work to be done, report details to be completed. Some people pored over their pay-slips and suspiciously checked the calculations on their overtime. Often, however, groups of paramedics and junior ambulance officers simply gathered in the staffroom at meal and snack times to eat and talk.

And it had to be those times which had people grinning and speculating about herself and Finn, Anna had decided. She would find him sliding a piping hot mug of tea across to her at the big table in the staffroom when he hadn't even asked her if she wanted one. When he was telling an anecdote to two or three others, she'd look across to find that his dark gaze was on her.

And though, on occasion, she was ostensibly reading a book or the newspaper, or watching something on television, she'd suddenly hear herself adding something to the conversation and would realise, as several pairs of eyes focused in her direction, that she hadn't taken in a word of what she had been reading or watching for the past five minutes.

'If you're listening anyway, come and join us, Anna,' Ron or Matt or Louise would say.

Finn always stayed silent, never added his voice to the invitation. He would be studying his fingers, or staring into space with his coffee-mug to his lips, maybe chewing on some take-away Chinese, as if it didn't matter to him in the slightest whether she joined them or not.

But then, as she moved from the grey lounging chairs to the big white laminate table, she would see a little glow in his eyes. They would remain on her for just a moment, and if the chairs weren't arranged right, or if there wasn't a space, he would be the one to quietly shift so that it seemed natural for her to sit beside him.

Then, oh, then it would start. She would be aware of him every time he moved. She'd hear the soft slip of his shirt fabric against his skin as a shoulder shifted. She'd feel the warmth of his thigh, even though it wasn't in contact with hers at all.

If he had to move, she'd hear an apology. 'Sorry, Anna, shift your chair a bit, could you?' It would sound more like a line of seduction in that dark voice of his, with its twisted vowels and thick letter r. She'd feel the colour and heat flooding into her face for no reason at all, and would have to hide behind another mouthful of her meal.

Sometimes there would be a paging announcement, 'Crew to car 118, please, priority one.' And Finn and Diane or Finn and Mark would grimace briefly and get up from the table, perhaps gulping some last mouthfuls of coffee as they went.

'See you later, guys,' someone would say, and Anna would echo it and hear the way her voice didn't sounded quite natural. Too offhand, or too high-pitched.

After they had gone the convivial gathering somehow wouldn't be the same. The spark would be gone. Over the next ten minutes, she'd have to firmly stop herself from turning her head when she heard footsteps coming along the corridor, in case the call-out had been a false-alarm or in case a crew already on the road had been closer and had taken the job instead.

Sometimes, her head would turn anyway then turn back, and she knew that anyone who was watching her would be able to read the disappointment. She would end up gulping the rest of her tea and slinking back to the television chairs, trying to pretend to herself and to everyone else that Finn's absence wasn't the thing that had sent her away.

But she knew she was often an easy person to read. No wonder people teased them.

Now, at the other end of the phone, he laughed at her blunt words. They didn't seem to have put him off in the slightest. '*Arrange* to be busy? You really know how to flatter a man, don't you?'

'Finn—'

'Listen, Anna,' he said, and the sincerity that enriched his voice intrigued her and kept her silent. She wanted to hear what sort of a construction he was going to put on all this—their attraction, her wariness, his slowness to act over the past two weeks and more. 'Let's cut to the heart of this, shall we?' he went on. 'We're hugely attracted to each other.'

The erratic Scottish accent kicked in and made the word 'hugely' sound like something delicious and very decadent to eat.

'Please, admit it,' he said. 'It's been that way from the beginning. It's not a disease or a sin. I know…' He hesitated. 'That you have…or you think you have…some reason for not trusting me, or something. That's why I haven't jumped into this like the hothead I want to be when it comes to you.'

'I—'

'No, I'm not asking for an explanation, a'right?

Maybe you don't even have one. All I'm asking for is a chance to prove that, whatever it is, it's wrong. I've held off in case it all went away, in case you gave me a reason to stop feeling like this about you, but it hasn't gone away, and—' He broke off. 'Come to the beach with me tomorrow. Could you do that? Bring your open mind with you, leave everything else behind, and let's see where we end up.'

Of course, she said yes, and she honestly didn't know whether it was because of what he'd said, the honest arguments he'd used or the voice he'd said it in. She couldn't really claim he hadn't given her a chance to say no. But from the moment she'd heard his voice, that had never been a genuine option. Oh, she had known she was going to agree to whatever he proposed.

He picked her up the next morning at half past nine, wearing casual black shorts and an open-necked knit shirt with a subtle grey and green pattern. He was driving a lovingly restored and maintained classic yellow F J Holden, which was definitely not the vehicle he'd brought to work each day for the past two and a half weeks.

Anna inspected it in the driveway, and her landlady's young teenage son came down and inspected it, too, goggle-eyed with admiration. Finn had to exercise some tact in order to prise fourteen-year-old Tom away from the car, over whose waxed and polished paintwork he was running loving and reverent hands.

'You're a god, Finn,' Anna teased him as they drove away. She felt much more relaxed than she had expected to be, and the reasons for it were simple.

First, his failure to act on their sizzling attraction over the past two weeks had generated huge tension within her, which was now released. Second, she'd made a decision this morning. At some point today, when the timing felt right, she was going to talk to him about Kendra, tell him that she was Kendra's cousin, find out his perspective on the situation and take it from there.

Until then she was going to do as he had asked and give him the benefit of the doubt, keep an open mind, because there was no sense in spending any time with him at all if she did nothing but bristle with tension.

Setting all this out clearly in her mind felt good, an exertion of mastery and control, at last, over a situation she hadn't been in control of from the beginning.

'I don't use this vehicle for day-to-day commuting,' Finn explained as they turned out of Anna's street.

She rented a one-bedroom granny flat attached to a very pleasant house in West Teymouth. Her landlady was divorced with one child left at home, and the arrangement suited all of them. Judy Lawton could go out at night when Anna wasn't working, without Tom feeling as if he was being subjected to the indignity of a babysitter, and it meant that Anna got to live in a tranquil residential part of Teymouth, close to some wonderful parks, which she couldn't otherwise have afforded.

'Did you have to bring two cars across Bass Strait on the *Spirit of Tasmania*, then?' she asked, in answer to Finn's comment. The large car and passenger ferry plied the strait in each direction several times a week, linking Tasmania with the mainland.

'No, I picked the Toyota up a few weeks ago when I first got here,' he answered. 'Used car prices have dropped over the past couple of years, even though I suppose it's still an extravagance to run two vehicles.'

'This isn't a vehicle,' she told him. 'It's an entire lifestyle.'

He laughed, pleased. 'Someone who understands!'

Oh, she couldn't help it, she just grinned at him, feeling as if they shared some magic knowledge that nobody else had. This was making her dizzy, helpless. She'd never known anything like it, and the speed with which it was happening both frightened and delighted her.

Today, wearing a matching set of shorts and vest top in Wedgwood blue instead of uniform trousers and shirt, far away from the busy ambulance headquarters and from Fryerstown and the sombre, unsettling effect it always had on her mood, Anna had faith—faith that she didn't need to question the radiant connection between herself and Finn. It felt right, and therefore it had to be right, and nothing and no one else mattered.

Wriggling deep into the newly upholstered seat, which felt cool against her bare legs, she asked, 'Where are we going?'

'Putting your destiny in my hands?'

'I'm feeling sufficiently crazy today.'

'I'm glad about that.' He glanced across at her, his hands light on the steering-wheel and his dark eyes glinting with naked fire. Then he returned to her question. 'I thought we'd head for the east coast. Takes an hour and a half, according to my map, which makes it closer to two in this old friend. Is that too far for you?'

'No, I like driving. How does that saying go? It is better to travel than to arrive.'

'I was thinking that—or something very similar—just the other day.'

Another glance, smoky and thoughtful this time, made both her statement and his into something significant.

'I like driving, too,' he went on. 'Frees your thoughts. And this scenery's all new to me.'

'I've only been over to this part of the coast once myself, with some friends, and that time we went by the other route. My parents take their holidays a lot further south.'

'When we get there, I thought we'd just pick a beach, preferably deserted, and swim and walk and eat.'

'Eat what? If the beach is deserted there won't be a kiosk.'

'I packed a picnic,' he said.

'Finn! You should have told me to bring something.'

'As I remember, I specially instructed you to bring absolutely nothing.'

'Except my swimsuit and a towel, I assumed.' She had a small leather backpack at her feet containing these items, as well as hat, sunscreen and sunglasses.

'As to your swimsuit, it depends on how deserted the beach is, doesn't it?' The lazy, suggestive drawl made it quite apparent what he meant.

She almost gasped as an image flooded into her mind of Finn's strong body, naked in the foaming waves, streaming with water and glinting in the sun, while she swam and rolled beside him, the cold caress of the water buffing her skin into tingling life.

Oh, she wouldn't dare, no matter how deserted the beach!

He was laughing again. 'You're not shocked?'

'I'm not a prude. I've done it before.'

'After dark, in a pool, with female friends,' he guessed.

'Yes, exactly. Different if it's an open beach in broad daylight, with—'

'Who says it will still be daylight by then?'

'How long are we staying?'

'However long you like.'

'I'm working tomorrow.'

'I'm not. I'll tuck you up in a couple of nice dry

towels and you can sleep in the car on the way home while I drive. When we get there I'll scoop you up in my arms—you'll have given me your key earlier—carry you inside and nestle you into your soft white bed. And then I'll—'

'My quilt cover is blue and green and gold, with sheets to match,' she came in quickly.

'Don't mess my head up with irrelevant details, woman!'

'I think you're the one who's messing up my head,' she muttered, knowing he would hear.

'Maybe that's the idea,' he suggested softly.

They drove in silence for a while, and Anna pretended to watch the scenery. It wasn't a perfect day. The temperature was mild but the sky was overcast, threatening to drizzle. And that only went to prove how unlikely it was that her image of the two of them swimming naked together would be realised, because that fantasy had contained a perfect arc of blue sky and brilliant, glorious sunshine.

'But, you know, I like it overcast this way,' Finn said two hours later.

They'd had a good talk in the car, and Anna had seen a different Finn from the one who sat at the big table in the staffroom yarning and ribbing the other paramedics. He had talked about his serious battle with leukaemia fifteen years ago, and didn't have to spell out for her the way his illness had moulded him as a man.

Then, when she'd tried to put into words a rather cloudy perception that they'd both come through periods of *poisoning* in their lives—his chemotherapy, her childhood in Fryerstown—he had known what she meant.

'Isn't there some saying about that?' he'd said. 'What

doesn't kill me makes me strong, or something. I've always thought that was true.'

Now they had found a long sweep of beach between St. Mary's and Bicheno, accessible only by a dirt track and then a muscle-knotting trek across the deep, drifted dunes. Some of the threatened rain had fallen, just enough to dapple and dampen the sand. Enough, too, to discourage most summer beach-goers. The stretch of sand was deserted apart from a handful of surfers way up the other end. They must have found a different access point, because there were no cars parked near Finn's.

In a backpack larger than Anna's, he carried the picnic, and he had a towel slung around his neck. They had both put on sunscreen back at the car.

'To ensure that we won't see a single ray of horrible, nasty sunshine all day,' Finn said.

'Oh, absolutely,' Anna agreed. 'Wouldn't want sun.'

'Sun is so *obvious*. I mean, everyone wants sun, and all it does is bring the teeming masses crowding onto the beach.'

And they discovered after a while that it was true. Who did need sun? The misty grey sky was what made it special, painting the landscape of sea and sand and sky with the subtlest and coolest of colours.

They ate straight away, spreading out towels on the sand in a little hollow in the lee of the dunes. The picnic Finn had provided was eccentric and spontaneous. Some tubs of fruit yoghurt. A packet of smoked salmon and one of cream cheese. Cracker biscuits, bread rolls, a whole head of oakleaf lettuce. A cold anchovy pizza, with two slices missing. Two bottles of beer, one bottle of cider and some mineral water mixed with juice. A blob of butter in a plastic container and a jar of straw-berry jam.

'Did you shop for this specially, or was it just what you happened to have in the house?' Anna had to ask.

'Uh…a bit of both,' he confessed. 'Is it revolting?'

'That depends. How old is the pizza?'

'Nine o'clock last night, after I got off work late. Wasn't as hungry as I thought.'

'In the fridge overnight?'

'Promise! Anchovy. Goes with the seafood theme, see.' He pointed at the smoked salmon.

'So which is the main course, then, and which is the hors d'oeuvre?'

'Suit yourself.'

Perhaps it shouldn't have been delicious but it was, eaten, in the end, in no order at all. Each flavour seemed somehow stronger and tangier today, with the sea air sharpening their appetites and their thirst. Then they left their backpacks on the sand and went for a walk the length of the beach, splashing up to their ankles in the cold, salty water, both of them happy to let the thunder and hiss of the waves drown the need for conversation.

A faint mist hung in the air over the water and the cool beige sand, and somehow the dullness of the day made the irregular line of foam, as each wave slid up the sand, glow with a pure, almost iridescent white. The air was cool and fresh and filled with ozone and the clean smell of the sea.

On the way back, Finn took Anna's hand and she let him, and again they didn't speak, which gave her all the time in the world to realise, This is important. Already. It's not just a little twenty-four-hour lust virus that's go-ing to be over when I wake up tomorrow. He makes me laugh. That silly picnic! He makes me think and feel. He makes me… Oh, help!

Suddenly, he had pulled her out of these crucial thoughts.

Run and jump in the sand dunes with him until I'm breathless and happy and my hair and clothes are full of the stuff…! 'Finn!' she shrieked aloud.

It didn't take Anna long to catch the mood, and it was wonderful, ten minutes of pure exhilaration. They chased each other back to the wandering pathway which ran from the rutted parking area to the beach, zigzagging up and down the dunes. Their flying feet sent cold sand bulldozing downwards as it tickled and hugged their legs.

Running just ahead of Finn, as they took a short cut towards the path, Anna was laughing too hard to take any notice of where her feet fell, and didn't realise the significance of the patch of charcoal and ash that fanned out across the sand and darkened it to a bluish grey just at this point. Vaguely, she knew that someone must have had a fire here a few weeks ago.

Then her instep pressed down hard on something sharp and painful, and she limped and staggered for a few more paces through the sand until she half fell to a sitting position.

'What's wrong?' Finn said, slowing to a breathless halt beside her.

'I trod on something…'

'Oh, hell, there's broken glass. Some idiots have had a drinking session here and entertained themselves by smashing the bottles afterwards. Look!' He swore again. 'It's everywhere!'

They both saw it now—chunks and splinters of brown

glass on the surface of the sand and half buried beneath it, mingled with the lumps of charcoal.

Anna bent her knee up, twisted her foot and looked at her instep. It was running with blood, getting mixed with the sand encrusted on her feet and making it red and sticky.

'Is the glass still in there?' Finn stepped carefully towards her and dropped to the sand.

He picked up several more shards of broken beer bottle and put them in a pile where they wouldn't be a danger to their bare limbs.

Anna began to inspect her foot, but the reddening sand made it hard to see. Finn pulled a wad of clean tissues from the back pocket of his black shorts, took her foot in the warm curve of his palm and began to wipe the sand away. Anna was distracted by the sober line of his brows and the silken texture of his eyelids as he looked down. She hardly felt the cut for a long moment, just wanted to reach out and explore his face with her fingers.

But the blood kept coming, and now they could both see the clean, slightly curved edges of the cut.

He pressed gently. It hurt, but not too sharply. 'Doesn't feel to me like there's anything in there,' he said. 'How does it feel from your end?'

Fabulous! Keep stroking my foot like that with the ball of your thumb. I don't think you've even noticed you're doing it...

'Nothing,' she agreed in a thin voice that was almost a gasp. 'I don't think it's too deep.'

Wishful thinking? The last thing she wanted was to be compelled to sidetrack from this heart-stopping day in favour of a trip to Casualty in St Helen's for some stitches.

Fortunately, Finn agreed. He stopped that hypnotic caress, gently and carefully pulled the edges of the cut apart with his thumbs just enough to gauge its depth, then pressed them together again and said, 'I've got a first aid kit in the car. I think that'll cover it.'

'Good.'

'But we can go home, if you like.'

'No!'

He didn't say anything, but she could read the gladness in his body as he slid her foot back onto the sand, keeping the cut clear of the dry grains.

'Don't move!' he told her, and she watched him as he made his way crookedly across the spinifex-covered dunes to the car. His legs were strong and tanned and every bit as hairy as a good man's legs should be.

He was back with the items he needed from the first-aid kit in five minutes, and it was a simple matter to brush the dry sand off and dress the cut with antiseptic ointment and several strips of adhesive bandage.

'But I won't be able to swim,' she realised aloud. 'Or those plasters will come straight off and the sand and water will open up the cut.'

'Don't worry, I'll keep you company on the sand.'

'No, you won't,' she retorted. 'You can swim for me! Hope you brought your togs.'

'Yes, in the end. Fortunately,' he added, watching the parking area. 'It was a tough decision, but looks like I made the right choice.'

Another car had just pulled up next to Finn's—an old green station wagon with a light fibreglass surfboard strapped to the top. A rather scruffy man got out, followed by two children, a boy and a girl, aged about seven and four. The kids were already dressed in swimming gear, and carried balled-up towels, clutching them awkwardly in the crooks of their arms.

The man took no notice of them once they were out of the car. He was unstrapping his surfboard from the roof-rack and inspecting it, running his hands over its surface.

The children asked him something, and he pointed at the track leading to the beach. From where they stood in the lee of the dunes, the children wouldn't have been able to see the water. They set off in the right direction while the man stripped naked beside the car and began to put on a sleek, knee-length black wetsuit then zipped it up to his neck.

'Oops,' Finn said. 'Has he seen us?'

'Maybe he doesn't care.'

'That's a surfer's body, if ever I saw one.'

As the man was quickly decent in his wetsuit, they kept looking at him. His skin, during the brief seconds of nakedness, had come in three distinct shades—dark tan on face and below elbows and knees where the wetsuit stopped, lighter tan on his torso because on hot days he obviously surfed only in board shorts, and pallid white from waist to thighs.

The man fiddled about some more, then checked and locked the car. The children must be out of his sight now, but he hadn't taken any notice. They had become distracted by the inviting shapes of the dunes, and started to do what Anna and Finn had done earlier—lots of running and jumping and shrieking, on the opposite side of the sandy path from where Finn and Anna still sat.

'Is it safe over there, do you think?' Anna asked.

'I'd better warn their dad,' Finn agreed. 'Can't see any glass from here but, then, we didn't notice this lot until we got close to it.'

He set off to intercept the surfer, who was now on his way to the beach, with his board tucked under his arm.

Anna began to follow Finn, carrying an empty plastic container left over from lunch and picking up pieces of glass as she went. Probably silly to bother. It would take hours of systematically combing the sand to find all of it, but every little bit helped.

'Clean Up Australia' day was coming in early March. Perhaps she could phone the nearest Scout troop and suggest they make the glass their project this year.

Finn had reached the children's father, and was talking and gesturing. Anna wasn't yet quite close enough to hear his words, but she heard the surfer yell, 'Kids, watch where you jump, OK? This man says there's broken glass. I'm going to catch some waves. You know where I'll be if you need me.'

He thanked Finn politely, then continued his way towards the beach, raising his head to scrutinise the surf. Anna caught up to Finn, who shrugged at her. They didn't need to voice their scepticism aloud. Was a casual warning like that enough for two rather young children? No, it wasn't.

The surfer hadn't even reached the tide line when Anna and Finn saw that the younger child, the girl, was crying and hobbling. Her brother had his arm around her and they were picking their way across the sand-hills toward the beach.

'Dad? Dad!' the boy yelled. 'Kimberley's cut her foot! *Dad!*' He cupped his hands around his mouth.

Their father heard and turned, began to walk reluctantly back, then quickened his pace as the boy repeated even louder, *'Kimberley's cut her foot!'*

Halfway up the beach he dropped his board and began to run, and Anna and Finn, who were making their way towards the two children as well, heard him start to swear. The three adults reached the two children at the same time.

'Oh, hell, you weren't wrong about the glass, were you?' the surfer groaned.

'I cut my own foot a few minutes earlier,' Anna said.

'It hurts,' Kimberley whimpered.

'Have you got two bandages, then?' her father demanded of Anna.

'In the car,' Finn said. 'I'll be back in a minute, a'right?'

'Thanks, mate. Kimberley, sit down, OK? No! Not there! There's more glass!'

The sudden shout frightened the girl and her sobs freshened, although Anna could tell that her father was more alarmed than angry. Remorseful, too.

'This is a stuff-up,' he muttered, as he cleared a safe patch for the girl to sit down. 'Jamie, check if there's any more glass around and, for heaven's sake, watch your own feet. That'd be the last thing we need! What in hell made me think I'd get any surfing in?'

He was still cursing himself, the drunken bottle-smashers and life in general when Finn got back. Kimberley had stopped crying, and Jamie looked pensive and subdued and not very happy.

During Finn's absence, Anna had cleaned the sand from the cut with the corner of Kimberley's towel and had looked at it carefully. Like hers, it wasn't too deep, but she could see that there was a splinter of glass left in it, and it was in a more awkward position, too, slicing up from the ball of the foot to the space between the first and second toes. Fortunately, Finn had brought the whole kit with him this time.

'In case there's still glass in it,' he said.

'There is,' Anna confirmed.

He handed her the tweezers and said, 'I'll defer to your finer fingers.' The child's father seemed to have no desire to tackle the ugly splinter himself.

Kimberley made a remarkably good patient. Anna soon had the glass fragment out, and Finn was preparing a more elaborate dressing because simple adhesive bandages would never hold in such an awkward spot. It was the children's father who needed their best bedside manner.

'Donna's going to murder me!' he was saying. 'It's hopeless! I have them one weekend a month, and every bloody time I do something wrong. Last time I ironed a dirty great scorch mark on Kimberley's party dress. Now it's this. My ex thinks I'm just an idiot—and I am. Jeez, you'd think I'd know by now that you can't turn your back for a minute! But it's hard when you're not with them all that often. You forget how it is. You're not really part of their lives. You're not in the habit of watching out for their safety and putting them first. You just *forget*!'

The two children were silent and large-eyed through all this, as if the flood of complex and very adult emotions was overwhelming for them.

When the cut was dressed, the dad—he'd told Finn and Anna that his name was Anthony—said to his children, 'Wait here, OK?' Then he loped back to the car, rummaged about on the floor of the front seat for a minute and returned.

'You didn't have to wait,' he told Anna and Finn.

'Well…'

'Thanks a million, by the way. Are you doctors, or something?'

'Paramedics,' Finn answered.

'Right…'

'Ambulance officers,' Anna clarified.

'Oh, OK.' His brow cleared. 'Then I guess you would know a bit about first aid.' He was obviously one of the many people who didn't realise just how highly qualified the paramedics of the Tasmanian Ambulance Service were.

Anthony bent down to his little girl and began to pull something colourful up over her foot. An old plastic bread bag, Anna saw. He secured it in place with a thick rubber band and said cheerfully, 'There! Bet you thought we'd have to go home, didn't you, kids? Well, we don't, see! We're going to dig in the sand instead. Might paddle a bit. Jamie can jump some waves. Then we'll stop off and get ice creams on the way home. We're gong to have a great afternoon!'

It was like the sun coming out, which it was starting to look as if it might actually do. The children dropped their cloaks of timidity and fear, as if suddenly discovering that they hadn't done anything wrong after all, as they'd obviously thought, and Finn and Anna realised that the little part-time family was going to be all right.

A few minutes later, after more thanks from Anthony and echoes from the children, the three of them were down near the tide line digging all sorts of wonderful channels and moats, castles and tunnels. Anthony had his wetsuit pulled down, with the arms tied around his waist, and he was directing Jamie to dig towards the incoming waves. Jamie's shouts of excitement carried all the way up to the dunes.

Anna and Finn were collecting their gear, ready to leave. Despite the happy outcome for Kimberley and her brother, the earlier mood of misty solitude on the beach was spoiled now. Anna's foot throbbed, and she and Finn didn't have a plastic bread bag and a rubber band to waterproof it with. She had to try and keep up on her toes as she walked and Finn had just picked up several more lethal-looking pieces of glass.

'It's after three,' he said. 'Feel like finding a café or something, and then heading back? I'm assuming you're no longer up for that naked moonlight swim we've both been looking forward to all day.'

'That was only ever in your dreams, Finn,' she told him.

He didn't let her get away with it. 'Just in *my* dreams, eh? I don't think so…'

She fought against a blush, and lost. Tossed her head instead, and stalked off so that he wouldn't see. Behind her, she could almost hear his smug satisfaction in the rhythm of his footsteps. He caught up to her a moment later, and she half expected him to push the point…or pull her into his arms. He did neither.

Instead, he said thoughtfully and quite fervently, 'Gee, I hope I'm never in that position!'

'What position?'

'Part-time dad. Two nights out of fourteen, or even twenty-eight, like Anthony. Kid, or kids, plonked in my car at six on a Friday evening, to be returned by dinnertime on Sunday night, preferably still in one piece, thank you very much. I mean, an awful lot of people make it work, and that's great. My hat's off to them. They're heroes, the lot of them, mums, dads and kids. But…'

He shook his head.

'I'm no saint,' he went on. 'I've had my share of relationships. A couple of them serious. Some a big mistake. But I can say one thing. I've always been damned careful not to father a child.'

The words washed over Anna like a bucket of cold water.

He's lying. That was her first outraged thought.

Then she arrived at the truth, and knew she wasn't wrong. Finn had spoken so confidently, his opinion as usual straightforward and his conscience clear and unclouded.

Oh, my Lord! Kendra hasn't told him she's pregnant.

That's what this is all about. That's why he's acting as if he's a free agent in the way he and I respond to each other. That's why, intuitively, I haven't been able to condemn him the way I've tried to. It's why he's never mentioned her, and why Kendra herself has been so evasive and strange, with all that talk about not pressing a man.

He doesn't know.

CHAPTER SIX

ANNA was stunned by the realisation, and she was silent, her thoughts churning, as they bumped carefully along the rutted track and back to the main road in Finn's car.

Kendra hadn't told him.

Their relationship had been short-lived. Anna thought back and tried to pick some simple facts out of Kendra's vague and highly coloured narrative. Perhaps it was only the one time that they'd slept together. Then, as far as Finn was concerned, the relationship had ended, Kendra had left Melbourne... Thinking back, Anna had the impression she had kept up a closer contact with Craig.

Yes, because she doesn't *want* Finn to know. Not until the baby is born. And she's scared she'll betray the truth if she talks to him on the phone. She must think he'll be more interested after the birth, when his child is a reality and when Kendra herself has that gorgeous figure of hers back again. Her skin will probably clear up, too. That's it. That's why she's hiding away in Fryerstown. It's not just because she's broke. She wants to give it her best shot with Finn. She really wants him...

And meanwhile Finn could make innocent, idealistic speeches about not fathering a child in a casual relationship because he hated the idea of part-time fatherhood, unaware that there *was* a child of his loins in the world, now less than three months shy of being born.

I have to think. I have to work out what this means for *me*.

Was that selfish? Perhaps. That was irrelevant. At the

moment, it was a matter of emotional survival. Only now did she realise how deep her feelings went. She was twenty-eight years old. She'd had boyfriends. Two at art school. One of the trainee paramedics in Hobart, and another paramedic, here in Teymouth, early last year.

She and Brenton had only gone out together for a couple of months. Working together, it had been awkward and they'd both soon agreed that the relationship hadn't been going anywhere. It had been best to end it before things had got ugly and it had threatened their professional dealings with each other.

Brenton had left the service a few months later, to follow his second love of fine wood-working full time. She had heard he was about to get married.

But neither Brenton nor the others had touched her heart and soul like Finn did. In his case, she didn't care that they worked together, found herself shrugging at the potential risks. She had been so hostile towards him at first, and it was incredible how quickly that had broken down, how quickly she had come to feel that she knew him, and that he wasn't the kind of man she'd conjured up in her imagination—the uncaring father of Kendra's coming child.

Because he didn't know.

'You're quiet,' he said, after a silence whose length she couldn't measure.

Where were they? Coming into the tiny town of Kerry Creek already, nearly halfway home.

'Feeling sleepy?' he wanted to know.

'No, I'm fine.'

'Foot hurting, then?'

'Nothing like that.'

'Then what?'

'I...have a headache.' Extremely feeble, but the best Anna could come up with.

'We'll have some tea, if there's a café here. That'll help. And you can take some tablets. There are some in the kit.'

'It's earning its keep today,' she joked thinly.

'It is,' he agreed.

He was taking the headache at face value, then.

Well, he would, she quickly decided. As she'd observed before, he was a straightforward man, one who wore his virtues—honesty and kindness, for example— easily and openly and without fuss or self-aggrandisement. Precious virtues, they were, too, and much more rare than they should be. It hadn't taken her long to know all this about him. The only jarring note was struck by what she had thought she knew about his attitude to Kendra, and now this contradiction was cleared away.

Oh, sweet heaven, I'm in love with him! I'm not just teetering on the brink. I dived in days ago.

'Here we go,' Finn said, coming to a halt outside an old stone cottage set a little way back from the main street behind a white picket fence. He got out of the car, strode closer and studied it for half a minute, then came back to her, opened the passenger door for her and took her elbow. 'This place looks a'right, d'you think?'

The cut foot was throbbing, and she wasn't quite as steady as usual as she climbed from the car.

'Lace curtains, and little rosebuds in vases on the tables,' he went on, bending to hold her steady. 'Really cute, it is.'

He had her on her feet now, and was looking into her face, his eyes warm and glinting with mischief and...something else. Something important.

'Finn, you hate places like this!' Anna laughed, almost in tears at the same time. Her heart was turning over

She loved him, and he cared about her, she was almost sure of it. It wasn't just a man's short-lived physical need. He would be handling this very differently if it was just that. He wouldn't have frozen like this, with the two of them sandwiched in the space between the seat and the open car door.

'Eh, yes, I always feel as though I'm going to…knock something over with my elbow,' he was saying, as if it had all been important when he'd started the sentence but was getting less and less so with every word. 'But I can…smell the scones baking…and…'

They stood together, both motionless. His face was inches away. He watched her mouth with his dark eyes and she watched those eyes until she couldn't bear it any longer. She let her lashes and her lids sweep down as a tiny sound vibrated in her throat and caught there, a whimper of need that was almost painful.

He was hesitant. They both were. Almost clumsy about it, too. Which side was he going to angle his head? Where did their noses belong? It all happened very slowly, so that her breath was fluttery and shallow in anticipation, and it felt as if the world had stopped turning.

But finally their mouths met perfectly, soft and clinging and tender and hungry. He had one hand resting loosely on her bare arm. She clutched a handful of his shirt fabric near the waist, scrunching it up so that the heel of her hand nudged against silky, warm skin.

The fingers of their other hands tangled together. He took a small step forward and his thigh touched hers, pushing her legs apart a little and shoring her up at the same time. Another tiny step brought his stomach against her ribs and the soft press of her breasts against his chest.

They tasted each other, lingered a little more, then very slowly let each other go.

Anna felt dizzy, and the whole universe had gone soft at the edges. Neither of them needed to speak. They both knew that ending the kiss now, so soon, meant only that they would take it up again later, when they were alone.

The sense of magic and anticipation was all-consuming. The air itself seemed to glow. Anna's chest was tight and there was a heavy fullness deep inside her. It ached. Not pain, but tingling awareness and need. It made her want to laugh and sing.

Finn was laughing already. His fingers were still knotted with hers as he turned towards the café and nudged the car door shut behind him with his hip. She took three hobbling steps and caught up to him, and his arms dropped around her shoulders and pulled her into the hollow between his chest and upper arm.

'How did I know it would feel this good, eh?' he murmured. 'How did I know?'

She couldn't answer, just had to smile and look at him. Everything she felt reflected back at her from his eyes, too.

They ordered Devonshire teas and he made her take two headache tablets, which she did because she was vaguely aware that she did have a throbbing pain at the back of her head somewhere. It might have hurt if she'd been able to think about it.

But all she could think about was him, and they were openly and rapturously lost in each other as they ate and drank and talked, and then as they drove again.

At Anna's flat, Judy and her son didn't seem to be home. The weather was clearing. It must have rained more here than on the east coast, because the ground was wet and the air had that fresh, tangy smell of eucalyptus and earth, but now the sun had broken through in several places and was bringing out the green of trees and grass so that they glowed richly in the golden evening light. It was almost seven o'clock.

It was so obvious Finn was coming in and they were spending the evening together that she didn't even bother to ask. Inside her flat, he seemed too large at first, as he prowled around looking at some of her drawings, mounted on the wall. She had to stifle the urge to clear a space for him—push the coffee-table back against the wall and take half the cushions off the couch, or something. The need soon passed.

He accepted a beer, she poured herself a glass of white wine and they discussed dinner possibilities lazily as they drank. The matter didn't seem at all important. Anna privately felt that she probably wouldn't even be able to concentrate on a take-away restaurant menu long enough to choose anything.

'I have pasta and some jars of sauce,' she offered vaguely in the end.

'Sounds great,' he said, as if he didn't care in the slightest either.

She filled a saucepan with water to boil, emptied the first jar of sauce she found into a second saucepan and said, 'There! Done!' Then she turned away from the stove, to find him laughing at her as he leaned against the humming fridge.

'What?' she demanded.

'Nothing,' he answered, with the laugh still colouring his voice, and she didn't need him to tell her that he wanted her in his arms.

She went to him, hardly able to believe that something

could feel so right and yet so dangerously sensual at the same time. She'd always somehow assumed that love would feel like slipping into a comfortable pair of old slippers.

Instead, it was… Well, maybe they were slippers, but they were slippers of the hand-made, Italian leather, crystal-beaded moccasin variety, fitting with a soft caress like a second skin but utterly luxurious and perfectly worked at the same time.

In short, it was heaven.

He was still smiling as he gathered her against him. 'Anna…' Her name was like melting chocolate in his mouth.

This time he kissed her properly, his mouth coming down slowly onto hers with a sensual precision that had her heart pounding as she waited for it. She was content to stay quiescent in his arms, to hang back and watch while he did all the work.

She was tired, almost drugged by the hours of fresh sea air and a little fuzzy from the effect of the wine on an empty stomach. Her limbs felt deliciously heavy and the hard warmth of his body supporting hers all along its length made her feel heavier still—a different kind of heaviness this time, a fullness deep inside her.

'Mmm, don't let me go,' she murmured against his mouth. 'Please, Finn!'

'I'm not planning to. Not until you tell me to.'

'Can't imagine…that I'll ever find the words…'

She closed her eyes. Sight was simply a distraction, the easiest and most ordinary of the senses. She wanted to sense him in every other way, without her eyes. He smelled of the sea, and of nutty soap and a tiny bit of sweat. He tasted of beer, too. Pleasantly so. It wasn't a drink she normally enjoyed herself, but on a man's mouth it could taste just right, a complicated blend of very male flavours.

He felt warm, soft in some places, hard in others. There was the resilient give of honed muscle cushioning her and supporting her where his arms wrapped around her body. There was the rigid bump and nudge of hips and aroused manhood against her swelling groin. There was the sheer sense of his solid bulk.

The only way she would ever topple this man would be if she caught him off guard. Something just felt right about that—that he was stronger than she was but would use that strength only to shield and support her, never to overpower or dominate.

Even the sounds they made together inflamed her need for him—those growling purrs of satisfaction in his throat, the gentle rasp of his lightly roughened chin and jaw against her cheek.

The pasta water came to the boil and then boiled half away before they stopped to add the packet of thin linguine, and it would have overcooked if she hadn't dragged her mouth from his kiss once more to say, 'I like it *al dente*.'

'You mean like this?' Deliberately, he caught her lower lip softly between his teeth, then licked away the minute sensation of pain with the tip of his tongue.

'I meant the linguine.'

'That means tongue-shaped, doesn't it?'

'Think so.'

'And *al dente* means "on the teeth". Or "chewy", I suppose. Very sensual, the Italians.'

'In my experience the Scots aren't bad either.'

'And how much experience *is* that, exactly? That you've had of Scotsmen, I mean.'

'Keep doing that…and that…for long enough and I'll be able to fill an encyclopaedia.'

By the time they got to the linguine it wasn't very *al dente*, but neither of them cared.

It was after ten when Finn reluctantly left, and Anna knew he would have stayed all night if she had given him the word. Oh, and that word almost burned her mouth with its eagerness to escape.

Stay. Please, stay, Finn.

She had to bite it back, fight it like a chocolate fiend fighting the sweet lure of Easter displays. The temptation badgered at her repeatedly. When he put down his coffee-cup. When he got to his feet. When he kissed her again. When the music on the CD player died to an expectant silence at just the right moment. When he said something hopeful and hinting about how it had chilled down outside now, although it was so cosy here in her flat.

Oh, she knew what he wanted, and he knew that she knew it.

Might as well just say it.

'I'm not going to, Finn.'

'Ah, well, greater powers of control than I have.' He had known exactly what she meant.

'Not *much* greater.'

'Good…'

'Don't kiss me again, because—'

'It would be the last straw? Even better!' He shaped himself to take her in his arms once more.

'I…mean it, Finn.'

'I know you do, gorgeous, and… Aagh!' He groaned. 'Can't believe I'm saying this! What kind of a man am I? Anna, I—*respect*—*that*! Hell, that was hard! Those

words just didn't want to come out. Would you like me
to take them back?' he offered hopefully.

'No, Finn. Yes…but, no. Not yet.'

They both laughed, and she added carefully, 'Sorry,
mixed signals. Can't think tonight, and I *want* to, you
see. You know, that cold-light-of-day thing? Morning
after the night before?'

'I know,' he said. 'And I know it'll mean more that
way when it does happen. And that's important, Anna.
I want you to know that, a'right?'

'Yes…yes, oh, and I do.' She nodded, having to wrap
her arms around herself in order not to wrap them around
him instead and undo all the hard work of the past few
minutes.

He left finally, and she stood in the doorway and
watched him all the way to the car, then watched the car
as far as she could see it down the street.

It was only once she had cleaned up their few dishes
and made her preparations for bed that she was able to
think, I started today planning to tell him I was Kendra's
cousin, but everything has changed now. He doesn't
know that he has any reason to think of Kendra ever
again. He thinks we're both free and that all our problems are over.

It wasn't true. She knew that, almost as strongly and
intuitively as she knew that she loved him, but tonight…the whole day…had been so perfect she just
couldn't see the dark side at the moment. She had as
much confidence and happiness and faith as Finn, and
when she went to bed and to sleep at last, her dreams
were glorious.

He phoned her the next evening, after she got home from
work. Anna and Matt, driving car 118, had been quite

busy today, with several call-outs, but none of them had been very dramatic.

There had been one unappealing idiot with stale alcohol on his breath and a broken toe. He had already made one ambulance trip to the hospital three days previously, two days after the break had happened, to be given strong painkillers—which he hadn't bothered to take, it turned out—and some instructions about rest and care.

Anna and Matt had had to tell him that there was nothing more to be done. He had been given the appropriate treatment the first time, his pain had not been an emergency and he had just been wasting their time.

There had been a collapse that had turned out to be a mild stroke, there had been an asthma attack and there had been another collapse of an elderly man at his home. They had quickly diagnosed this as being due to low blood sugar, which had been easily remedied. Then there had been a case of chest pain in a middle-aged man, who had been admitted to Teymouth Hospital for tests.

Finally, there was a road traffic accident in which no one was injured. Sometimes you couldn't trust an accident victim's claim that there was 'nothing wrong with me'. If you looked at their car and it was in tatters, you had to take such claims with a large pinch of salt and often exercise some tactful persuasion towards a ride to hospital 'just to check things out'.

People were often in shock, hyped up and distracted, and simply weren't aware of their injuries at first. All they could see was the expensive damage to their car. Internal bleeding was silent, and far less obvious than a crushed and twisted car body. But on today's accident scene Matt and Anna could trace the progression of the two moderately damaged vehicles. No sudden explosive halt over two or three metres, but a drawn out skid over about twenty-five metres, creating a much less jarring impact.

The three people involved claimed no injury. They seemed like sensible people and were relatively calm, and on the evidence Anna and Matt believed them.

On the phone to Finn, Anna vented her feelings a little about the man with the toe and described the new black skid marks now sketched on the concrete sides of the Wetherill Street overpass, but didn't need to go into any more detail about her day.

He didn't suggest getting together, and she appreciated that. He understood her need for breathing space. Perhaps he felt it, too. But it was good that he'd phoned. It gave her a warm feeling of hope and confidence and happiness, and he finished their casual conversation with, 'See you tomorrow. You're on at night, right?'

'Yep. I'm yawning already.'

'See you around seven, then.'

It left her feeling as if the whole world glowed.

Although they were both working the night-time roster, Finn and Anna were on different crews the following night. Anna was paired with Ron, while Finn himself was working with one of the service's most experienced paramedics, Diane McMahon.

Diane was a nice woman, a former nurse, married to an architect. They had two school-age children. She was hard-working and calm in a crisis, a jewel with every patient and a complete, ear-bashing motor-mouth at the wheel. Finn's hair stood on end at some of the curses and commentary she flung at other drivers, each word delivered through clenched teeth as she navigated the streets and the traffic with steely concentration.

He knew why she was like that. In fact, he had realised that she was a far better driver than she would have given herself credit for, but the driving, especially on a P1 call-out with full sirens and lights, wasn't her favourite part of the job. She had to get her mental adrenaline up in order to stay on top of, say, speeding the wrong way up Teymouth's busiest arterial road in peak-hour traffic, when startled motorists didn't always manage to veer out of the way as quickly as they should.

Unfortunately for Finn, understanding Diane's psychology on the issue and actually putting up with her driving style were two very different things. In the three weeks he'd worked in Teymouth, this would be the fourth shift he'd been paired with her.

Everyone had different ways of splitting up the driving and the patient care in the back of the car. Some people preferred to go 'job about'. Others liked it when one crew member drove for the whole of one shift, and did reports and patient care the next. The latter was what Diane preferred, and she seemed in no doubt that it was her turn at the wheel today. Finn didn't argue, but had to steel himself mentally for a long night of commentary.

He hoped the shift would be quiet, and his desire to avoid Diane's tirades wasn't the only reason. If things were quiet, he'd get to see Anna.

Ah, didn't that present some great pictures to his mind's eye! He loved the way she pulled her overalls down to her waist when she was relaxing, and used the sleeves to tie them there. Beneath the overalls, she'd be wearing some neat, close-fitting T-shirt in grey or navy or white. Her bare arms were so smooth and graceful, just like that long neck of hers. As for her breasts, softly moulded by the fabric of the T-shirt...

Tonight, if he did get the chance to see her dressed

like that, he knew he was going to torture himself by remembering how those rounded shapes had pressed against him on Saturday night.

At midnight, crews were permitted to bed down for the night, suggesting more appealing images. Anna in the early hours, for example, woken from sleep, all rumpled and warm. Anna curled up in a lounging chair at dawn, waking herself up with coffee, her fine hands wrapped around the mug to steal its heat. Anna, grumpy and growling, brushing her hair into submission then pulling it high, with her head ducked and her arms bent up behind her as she twisted a ring of colourful elastic around the thick mass to keep the ponytail in place.

Finn had to suppress a shudder of need, still thinking about Anna as Tony, from the departing day crew, brought him the drug book to sign for the morphine.

'You're driving 117 tonight, right? With Diane?' Tony said.

'Right.'

'Brought your earplugs?'

Everyone joked about Diane's tirades, even in her hearing, as now.

'Guys, I'm sorry, I just *have* to!' she said, backing out of the rear of vehicle 117, parked two metres away. She had understood the earplug comment at once. 'We need a couple of masks for the oxygen kit, Finn. Other than that, we're checked out and ready to go.'

'Let's hope we don't have to.'

'You can drive if you want to,' Diane offered. 'Only I haven't done it for four shifts now, and—'

'Wonder why,' Tony interjected.

'It's fine, Diane, really,' Finn said.

'OK, good.' She nodded, just as the hotline clanged, echoing all through the vehicle bay.

During the day, emergency calls from the central dispatcher were picked up by the receptionist and crews were paged, either over the loudspeaker or on their personal pagers. After hours, the phone was everyone's responsibility, and there were two distinct rings, the loud 'hotline', which indicated a call-out, or the normal ring, dubbed 'friendly fire' by the ambulance officers.

The latter could mean a personal call or some non-urgent administrative matter. It didn't take long to realise which ring was which, and this insistent sound pealing out right now *wasn't* 'friendly fire'.

'We're first cab off the rank,' Diane told Finn, and picked up the phone in the small office which adjoined the vehicle bay.

They left half a minute later, to a reported road traffic accident some distance out of town. Since RTAs were an automatic priority one, Diane hit the lights and sirens as soon as they were through the doors.

So much for seeing Anna. Finn had barely got a chance to say a quick, 'Hello.'

'Bloody idiot. Come on, I do have my indicators *on*. Could you get out of my lane, you stupid great galoot. Lady, let's not *cause* an accident here! Oh...' Diane descended into a string of colourful oaths which she would have been horrified to hear her children use, punctuated by a quick 'Sorry, Finn,' before she lowered the volume and muttered some more impatient suggestions to her fellow road-users.

Finn just shut it all out, turned to the window and thought about Anna as they veered round two corners in quick succession and gained the highway, heading west.

He had never felt like this about a woman before, not even at the height of the best affairs he'd ever had. And 'affairs' was the right word, he could now see. At the time he'd dutifully called them 'relationships,' taken them seriously, and a couple of them he'd really tried to make work.

He'd met two sets of parents over the years. For ten months, a few years back, he'd tried extremely hard for Trudy's sake to get interested in the grooming and showing of a certain breed of miniature dog, about which Trudy had been passionate. Some people might have said she was obsessive, in fact, far more so than any of the other very pleasant dog enthusiasts he had met through her, and in the end he just hadn't been able to stand it. Sorry, but did a dog really need that many kinds of grooming brush?

For a far briefer time before that he had been engaged, but before the half-carat diamond solitaire ring had even been paid for, Simone had started thumbing through a truly enormous stack of bride magazines, talking about engraved swizzle sticks and professional calligraphy on the 250 invitations.

That had been scary enough, but when she had, with excruciating tact, suggested that Finn take a course in etiquette for businessmen, and had confessed that she hoped he'd soon join her father's extremely successful appliance manufacturing enterprise as a junior executive... Well, it really had been a very short engagement!

Anna was different. So different!

He wasn't at all sure that he could put it into words, but it was like...oh, like tasting thick King Island cream on a hot peach pie, after you'd been fobbed off for years with insipid trickles of milk pumped up with gelatine. Or like that glorious wind-swept beach the other day, after half a lifetime of paddling in artificial ponds.

It wasn't just physical. He knew about physical. Physical was what made a man put up with entire, stress-filled, detail-obsessed weekends dedicated to two over-pampered, snappy little pedigreed dogs, when he much preferred mongrels with happily muddied paws. Physical was what had made him briefly consider trying to masquerade as something he wasn't—i.e. born with a silver spoon in his mouth—because if a woman looked as gorgeous as Simone did, then she'd eventually lose that stiffness and repugnance when he tried to kiss her, wouldn't she?

A lot of men were like that, he knew, particularly when they were still wet behind the ears. If they liked the packaging enough, they tricked themselves into thinking they liked its contents as well. The unlucky ones never realised their mistake.

Oh, Lord, I feel so damned lucky today!

Finn knew it wasn't just the packaging with Anna. They shared so much. Their difficult backgrounds, which didn't necessarily matter. Their criteria for what made a satisfying career, which mattered more. Their relaxed approach to leisure time, which was absolutely crucial.

And their physical response to each other…the way his every sense had been awakened by her, the way they set each other aflame, melted together, sparked fireworks… Well, that was the rich, thick, gooey, flavour-filled icing on a very well-made cake.

CHAPTER SEVEN

'CHECK the map for me, can you, Finn?' Diane said.

'Yep.'

'What were the details again?'

'Intersection of Route B51 and Route C735.'

'Should be coming up, right?'

'Yeah...' He looked at the map and at the odometer. 'Another two or three k's.'

He had already filled in the initial details on the patient care report. Priority number. Time received. Time of departure. Location. There were still a lot of blank spaces left, and if this turned out to be a major emergency, the rest of the details might have to wait their turn.

The possibility of this being the case increased as further details came in from Cathy, who was on dispatch tonight. The police were already on scene, and had relayed information about what they had found.

Single occupant, injured and trapped inside the vehicle.

Diane was slowing, and they could both see the site of the accident now. Finn could have judged just from the state of the vehicle that their skills would be needed, even without Cathy's radioed update.

The car's driver, probably either drunk, tired or distracted, possibly as the result of a mechanical problem with the vehicle, had lost control on a bend and had hit a tree at some speed. A passing motorist had called in the accident on his mobile phone, then had disappeared before the police had been able to talk to him, claiming 'an important appointment'.

The police car's blue lights were flashing, and as Diane drew to a halt Finn could hear more sirens behind him. It would be the road rescue crew from their own service.

Luck.

Finn had reflected just a short while earlier on his own feeling of luckiness today. He shared it with the female patient he and Diane delivered to Teymouth Hospital an hour later. Distraction had turned out to be the culprit, not drunkenness, fatigue or mechanical failure.

Lesley Palmer, aged thirty-two, was afraid of spiders, and a very large and very hairy—though harmless—specimen of the huntsman variety had somehow infiltrated the car and crawled across the inside of the windscreen just a half metre from her terrified gaze. She had remained in control enough to slow down, but when it had crawled rapidly around to the door and disappeared somewhere near her thigh, she'd panicked, missed the left-curving bend and crumpled the right side of the vehicle against a tree.

Only the fact that she'd already lost considerable speed had kept her alive and in good shape. There was evidence of mild concussion, a lacerated shoulder and a broken right leg.

Lesley's first words to the police, and then to Finn, Diane and the rescue crew were, 'Can you see the spider? Where's it gone?' She remained almost more shaken about her close encounter with eight hairy legs than about the accident itself.

Finn and Diane satisfied themselves that her airway, breathing and circulation were secure and that her head injury wasn't dangerous, put in an intravenous line con-

taining morphine for pain, and splinted her leg before
sliding the stretcher into the ambulance. It clunked into
place like a freight car shunting into a siding, and Lesley
said again, 'It didn't come in here, did it? Could you
check before we drive off?'

'The spider?'

'Yes, please!' Her teeth were chattering, and Finn had
already taken precautions to maintain her body temperature. She was covered in a blanket, and the small fan
heater in the back of the ambulance was warming the
air.

'You're really scared of them, aren't you?' he said.

'Phobic,' Lesley agreed. 'They're such a hideous
combination of hairiness and unpredictability.'

'Like a lot of men.'

She tried to laugh, but her jaw just chattered merci-
lessly. Her limbs were shaking, too.

'There are courses you can take to overcome various
phobias,' Finn offered.

But Lesley shuddered. 'Do you think I want *not* to be
scared? The very thought…'

He made a note on the form under 'History of
Previous Problems'. 'Patient's arachnophobia was life-
threatening on this occasion and could be again. Follow-
up should steer towards therapy, if patient can be persuaded.'

There was plenty of time to fill in the rest of the form
as well, since Lesley had soon calmed down consider-
ably. The morphine was acting as a sedative as well as
containing the pain from her fractured leg. The hand-
over at Teymouth's Casualty entrance was uneventful,
with some grimaces and raised eyebrows about the spider, and Finn and Diane were back at headquarters just
before nine o'clock.

Diane hadn't sworn once on the final leg of the journey, but said in a rather uneasy voice, 'I'm not all that keen on large, hairy spiders myself.'

'Would you panic in the same situation?'

'No, I'd do my usual and swear my bloody head off!'

Anna turned out to be scared of spiders, too. She was sitting at the table in the staffroom with her crewing partner, Ron, and an off-duty paramedic, Dave Thorburn. The latter had dropped in to report a win for the night-time touch football team in which several of the paramedics played. He was also trying to arrange a roster swap with Anna, but without much success.

Finn hid a grin at this. He knew…*hoped* he knew…why she didn't want to change. She was rostered with him again more than once over the next few weeks, before she returned to flight crewing.

He sat down next to her, deliberately brushing her thigh with his own beneath the table as Diane raised the spider question once more.

'Makes you think,' she said.

'Wouldn't worry me at all,' Dave claimed. 'I could have one crawling all over my hand and I wouldn't raise a sweat.'

Ron admitted to an initial jump of the heart when he'd had a similar experience a year or two earlier, while Anna said, 'I'd do a Diane and scare the thing back.' Everyone laughed.

Ah, this was nice, Finn thought. Much nicer than last week. Then he'd only imagined how it would feel to kiss her. Now he knew, and he could tell she was thinking of it, too. Their eyes met when she got up from the table briefly to make tea. Her thigh was returning the pressure of his. It was a secret they shared, although a part of him wanted to shout it to the world.

The interlude didn't last. She and Ron were called out to a patient with chest pain, Dave left and Diane settled in front of the television with some knitting. She loved her American police dramas on a Monday night. For Finn, some of the images reminded him too closely of a bad day at work. He prowled around, ate some supper and almost wasn't sorry when the hotline cut across the quiet night-time atmosphere.

This time, two ambulances were required, and he knew he'd see Anna when they got there. Not that he'd have wished it on her, because it turned out to be an ugly scene…could have come straight out of the police show he'd just avoided.

There had been a fight outside a pub, and two people were injured. There was still a crew of uneasy, half-plastered men and a couple of women hanging around, with only one or two of them having a clue about what to do. Anna and Ron were already at work over the most seriously injured patient, while the police had just arrived as well and were asking questions, to which they were getting sullen, unwilling responses.

The second patient, Finn and Diane's responsibility, had been propped up against a wall with a makeshift wad of jackets and sweaters to cushion him. He was bleeding from a wound on his temple, had several angry red bruises and was holding two teeth and a mouthful of blood in a handkerchief in the palm of his hand. Diane crouched beside him, ordered everyone to clear away and began to ask him some questions.

'He's lost consciousness,' Anna reported urgently to Finn about her patient. He was beside Diane, and Anna had come straight over, looking for another opinion to confirm her sense of what was going on. There was a young policeman hovering, too.

'He was groggy when we got here,' she went on. 'We talked to him and got a couple of details. He knew his name. But now he's slipping deeper, so we're going to make tracks as fast as we can.'

'I don't like the sound of that.'

'No, I know,' she agreed. 'But isn't it just wasting time to stabilise him here?'

'Can you intubate a patient in a moving vehicle?'

'Intubate?' she echoed blankly. 'I don't intubate at all. It's against protocol.'

'Hell, that's right! Vern said it's still a controversial area down here. He's expecting that will change, right?'

'That's why we carry the equipment. He'd like it to change.'

'But I guess it hasn't yet.'

'Anna, let's go,' Ron said with a snap in his voice. 'His breathing sounds bad. Very bad. I'm going to put in an airway and set him up with a mask. Let's get him in the back.'

But even as he said it, the patient's breathing was deteriorating further, to a low, irregular and laboured gurgle.

'That's not going to be enough,' Finn said. 'You'll lose him before you get there.'

'We have to try,' Ron argued. 'Unless you've got something else to suggest?'

They were all talking in rapid mumbles. The crowd around the scene was thinning, but several people still stood by, and the police presence had coloured their mood. This was serious now, and charges would be laid. Two women were crying, and there was a young man raving on incoherently as his friends attempted to calm him.

'I'll intubate,' Finn answered. 'Or you'll lose him.

You will! Listen to that! He's going deeper every second.'

'On your head, mate,' Ron pointed out accurately.

'I'll take the risk. Let's move him into the car. I don't need this lot as an audience.'

'Diane, what have you got?' Ron turned to her as she talked to the other patient.

'Needs hospital treatment, but not critical. I'll get him in the back and clean him up a bit, Finn.'

'Police want to talk to him at some point,' Anna came in.

'If you want to intubate, Finn,' Diane went on, 'if you feel confident, then do it. I agree it's that or arrive at the hospital with…'

A deceased patient. None of them said it, but they all understood. They had the training to recognise the signs of progressively deepening unconsciousness, and it was happening fast.

Anna and Ron got out their stretcher and moved the patient onto it, then slid it efficiently into the back of their vehicle, where it clicked into place. Finn had already climbed inside to get out the equipment he needed from the respiratory kit. He had the oxygen supply ready, as well as tubing and tape, by the time the patient was inside.

It wasn't a difficult job. Took practice, and you had to know what to feel and listen for. Measure the length of tubing, tape it at the mouth, check that it had gone down the right pipe. No good having it lead into the stomach. Finn usually managed to get it right first time, and tonight was no exception. It felt good when he set the respirator going and heard the regular rhythm start, instead of the dangerously erratic and laboured sounds of a moment ago.

This wasn't the end of the road for this patient, of course, but it was the vital first step. If you couldn't keep them breathing, nothing else mattered. His heart rate was acceptable at least. Blood pressure low but livable. No fractures other than that skull. Several facial bruises, like his sparring partner.

Would the injury to the brain resolve, or leave a lasting legacy? As usual, Finn himself might never know. Although on this occasion, he amended, when there might be professional repercussions, he might know the outcome in every detail.

'OK,' he said to Anna and Ron, 'he's yours again. Might see you there.'

He jumped out of the back of the car and went to help Diane, who was having a hard time persuading the other injured party that he needed a ride. Anna started up her lights and sirens and car 118 disappeared off into the night.

'I feel fine,' Diane's patient was insisting expansively, a night of drinking still colouring his perception. 'Just needed to catch my breath. Thanks for mopping up my face.'

'It's still bleeding, Joe,' Diane told him. 'It needs stitches.'

'Can't you do that?'

'Not our job, mate,' Finn came in. 'Let's go, shall we?'

'What about my mates? We were celebrating, till that idiot came and insulted my girlfriend.'

'Leave your mates, Joe,' Finn said. 'But if there's one of them who hasn't been drinking…'

'We had Geoff as designated driver.'

'He can bring your girlfriend, then, to hold your hand when you get there.'

'All right.' Joe shrugged. He only looked about nineteen. 'Guess I'll go, then. That other idiot, is he going to be all right? Didn't hit him that hard, but he went down weird against the wall.'

'You're going to have to tell all that to the police.' Finn didn't point out how serious the issue might become if Anna and Ron's patient sustained permanent brain damage or, worse, if he didn't survive.

'The police? Yeah, I guess,' the man said vaguely, as if noticing their uniformed presence for the first time. 'That's awkward, isn't it?'

'One way of putting it,' Finn agreed.

They met up with Anna and Ron again in the ambulance entrance at the hospital. Their patient had been raced off to surgery, with the expectation that there was a build-up of pressure in the brain which would need to be relieved at once. After he and Diane had handed over their own patient to the accident and emergency staff, Finn saw that Anna and Ron hadn't left yet, though they'd pulled their vehicle ahead so that they weren't blocking the bay.

'Feeling OK about that?' Ron wanted to know, approaching Finn.

Anna didn't speak, but her eyes did it for her. She was even more interested in Finn's answer than Ron was.

'Don't know,' Finn said. 'Did what felt right, I know that. Pretty confident he wouldn't have made it otherwise. I mean, we all were, weren't we? I'll let you know what sort of a reaction I get from higher up. You think it'll be bad?'

'I'd say it completely depends on the outcome for the patient, if you want the truth, Finn,' Ron answered bluntly. 'You could be in deep…uh, shampoo, let's call it. He's young, and he's probably got parents, who are about to get the worst news of their lives, and—' He stopped and shrugged.

'Well, at least they still have a bedside to come to, and a warm hand to hold,' Finn pointed out. He didn't plan to spend the next few days regretting the fact that he'd saved a man's life.

Seeing Anna's wide, worried eyes still on him, he was sure he'd done the right thing, and he'd rather spend his spare moments thinking about her. Oh, yes! Thinking about her in enormous and very pleasurable detail.

Something was trying to drag Anna out of sleep. Her subconscious fought it, tried to incorporate it into a dream, but finally she realised what it was.

The phone, ringing insistently.

Her first thought was that it had to be Finn, but when she looked at the clock and saw it was two in the afternoon she was less sure. Would he call her at this time of the day when they were both in the middle of two night shifts? Unlikely for a fellow paramedic to make that mistake unless it was urgent.

The continuing ring suggested that it might be, and she stumbled crookedly from the bed, through the doorway and lunged for the instrument, parked on the coffee-table.

'Hi, Anna!'

'Kendra?'

'Yeah, is this a bad time? You sound—'

'I had a night shift.'

'Oh, so-o-rry!' Kendra moaned. 'I woke you up! Shall I hang up?'

'It's all right. I'm awake now. It's fine,' Anna answered her, perhaps a little too impatiently.

Guilty conscience?

Kendra was carrying Finn's child. That was staking your claim on a man in no uncertain terms. And yet when Anna and Finn were together it just didn't feel like that. The painful caving sensation in the pit of Anna's stomach told her that she had to face up to a harsh truth, however. The good, easy feeling about her love for Finn was wrong. There were issues to be dealt with. Issues she'd had an inkling of from the beginning, which meant it was high time she tackled them head on.

'How are you, Kendra?' she asked cautiously.

'Oh, revolting. That's why I'm ringing.'

'I can't do much for you at this distance.' Anna laughed awkwardly. 'You should see your doctor.'

'No, not that kind of revolting. Well, partly. I'm getting so big. Just feeling a bit down, that's all. No one to talk to. Mum's driving me crazy. Says *she* never put on that much weight, and *she* never had food cravings and *she* would never have got herself into my situation anyway. Trouble is...' she laughed '...I'm such an easy target. It's all true!'

Kendra gave another laugh that was more like a sob, and there was a long, snuffly silence at the far end of the phone.

'Ah, Kendra,' Anna soothed.

Suddenly she was miserable. At heart, she cared a lot about Kendra. They were very different, but they had always been allies, plotting their escape from Fryerstown in their teens. Life was an upside-down sort of thing sometimes. Kendra was the one who had planned on nursing as a career, but that hadn't been creative enough for her. Anna had seen herself as an artist, yet had ended up in a profession that was closely allied to nursing.

'Have a good cry and you'll feel better,' she said inadequately. 'I wish I was there to help.'

The words weren't even out of her mouth before she knew what she had to do. 'In fact,' she added, 'Come and stay, Kendra. You turned me down before, I know, but think about it again, please! It'd be...well, good for you, and...you know. I'd love to see you. Molly-coddle you a bit. Sounds like you need it.'

'Oh, Anna, I don't know if—'

'Please, Kendra. You could even have the baby here. Teymouth has a good hospital, you know that. I have a sofa-bed in the lounge-room. With my hours we'd get to spend time together, but you'd still have privacy when I'm at work, particularly on nights.'

'I've got no money.'

'Don't worry about that. I'll take care of the bus ticket. Or you could even fly...'

Kendra raised several more objections, but from her changing tone Anna could hear the idea catching hold in her mind, like flame beginning to lick around the edges of paper.

Aware that she wasn't offering even a hint of the most compelling reason for Kendra to come to Teymouth—to settle things with Finn—Anna held her breath in hope, and was rewarded with, 'I'll think about it. I'll ring you again in a couple of days, OK?'

'OK, Kendra. But take it seriously, won't you?'

When she had put down the phone, Anna felt churned up to the point of nausea. She had to go and lean over the kitchen sink and take some deep breaths, then pour herself a large glass of water and drink it very slowly.

She knew she had done the right thing, but it hadn't been easy. There was still a nagging temptation inside her to hope like crazy that Kendra would decide not to come. Or at least not until after the baby was born, by which time she and Finn would have cemented their relationship into something strong and unbreakable and—

No. *No!* You couldn't build something strong if it had no foundations, and a relationship between herself and Finn as things stood would be a relationship built on quicksand. Finn had to know about Kendra's baby. Anna didn't know what a difference it would make to him— to his plans and goals, to how he felt about herself, to his feelings for Kendra.

But it wasn't her place to second-guess any of that. In fact, she only had one simple task right now, and that was to step aside, take herself out of the equation so that Finn and Kendra could resolve things on their own.

And I may never be able to step back in! she knew. It might already be over before it's even truly begun.

'Not hanging out with us tonight?' Finn said to Anna that evening, after various dinners had disappeared into various hungry mouths.

There had only been one call-out so far, an elderly woman taken to hospital after a fall.

'Not tonight,' Anna said, trying to make it light. 'Too tired! I'm going to snooze in front of telly.'

'Didn't sleep today? Bad girl!' he teased.

There was a little light of curiosity and uncertainty in his eyes, which Anna could read very clearly and didn't blame him for. She knew she was sending out strange signals, in contrast to the private but unmistakable heat of the past couple of days. They could read each other so clearly. He wasn't certain that something was wrong, but he was wary all the same. She wondered, too, if last night's lifesaving breach of protocol was on his mind.

They hadn't heard anything about the outcome of that yet, but at some point they would.

She took a deep breath and said deliberately, 'My cousin Kendra phoned at two o'clock, right in the middle of my sleep, and I couldn't fall back afterwards.'

'Kendra?' he said in surprise, picking up at once on the unusual name. 'Not Kendra Phillips?'

'Yes.' She nodded, refusing to feign any surprise. 'You know her from Melbourne, don't you?'

'Knew,' he corrected quickly, frowning. 'I wouldn't say "know". I haven't seen her for months. I had no idea you two were cousins.'

'There's no reason why you should have,' she told him.

'Then how did you know that I knew her?'

'She mentioned you once or twice.'

'Right…'

He raised his eyebrows briefly, then clicked his tongue before turning to nod affirmatively to Diane's offer of coffee. Anna could see he was trying to dismiss the apparently unimportant exchange, but that he couldn't quite do it. It set her even further on edge than she already was…and that was saying something!

She was so tempted to tell him the truth. *I know you had a fling with Kendra. She's pregnant with your child. She still wants you, but she's waiting until the baby is born because she doesn't trust you to care when she's so big and bloated, with bad skin, and when the baby is just a cloud of imminent burden on the horizon.*

I trust you to care. I know if there's anything still possible between you and Kendra it wouldn't make a scrap of difference to you how she looks and how much of a responsibility the baby would be, but she…doesn't know you as well as I do, I guess, and she doesn't have that faith.

But she had already decided that it wouldn't be fair of her to say any of this. She had no right. Telling him had to remain Kendra's prerogative, and her choice. Anna could exercise her powers of persuasion over her cousin, but couldn't take matters into her own hands.

She was under no illusions about how painful it was going to be. If Kendra didn't ring again by Thursday, Friday at the latest...

She did, however, on Wednesday at one-thirty in the afternoon, when Anna had had even less sleep than the day before.

'Oh, no, did I wake you *again*?'

'It really isn't a good time to phone, Kendra,' Anna said wearily. 'Anyone who works night shifts will tell you that.'

Most people took a while to wind down after they came off duty at seven-thirty. They would run errands and have something to eat, then subside into a sleep that was almost like being drugged at around lunchtime.

'But it doesn't matter,' she went on. 'Just tell me what you've decided.'

'I'm coming down.'

'Great! When?' The sooner, the better.

'The Tuesday after next. I have a pre-natal on the Friday, and then some friends will be in town over the weekend. I'll get the bus on Tuesday morning.'

'I could arrange a pre-natal appointment here,' Anna offered.

'Well, no, I really want to see Rob and Linda. You don't have to worry about me. I mean, I really, *really* want to come. Talking to you made a huge difference yesterday. But now that I know I have, like, an escape valve, I'd rather wait.'

She talked on for several more minutes, asked about Anna's life and made her laugh once or twice with a deliberately exaggerated account of her pregnancy trials and tribulations, then rang off.

Anna then had to sit on the bed and mutter aloud, 'Heaven help me, I had no idea I was such a brilliant actress!' She'd somehow managed to hide just how excruciating the prospect was of almost two weeks of waiting for even the hope of a resolution, especially since she was expected to go to dinner at Finn's on Friday night.

CHAPTER EIGHT

ANNA would have cancelled dinner if she'd had any reason to believe that Finn would have let her do it without a fight. But she knew he wouldn't.

He still had that same light in his eyes when he met her in the doorway of his little farm cottage on Friday night at eight. It contained a mixture of apprehension, uncertainty, anger, desire and sheer fight that flickered back and forth like a candle flame in a brisk breeze.

'You found the place a'right, then?' he said.

'I drive an ambulance, remember? We're trained to make sense of garbled directions.'

'Which mine weren't.'

'Exactly. So of course I found it all right. It's a great spot, Finn, and a great little place.'

'I like it,' he agreed. 'I didn't want something in town. Never lived on a farm before, though.'

'Ah, the smell of the pigs, the sound of the roosters crowing at dawn,' she teased.

'Love it,' he agreed, and he was ninety per cent serious.

'Seems a piece of luck that this place was for rent. It's the old farmhouse, right?'

'Right. The farm people now live in that well-maintained but pretty characterless new place at the top of the hill. They rented this house out to tourists for a few years, but they're getting old now, and felt a steady tenant would be less work, if not as lucrative.'

'As I said, lucky for you.'

'Have a good look,' he invited.

'If you don't mind.'

'Well…hope you'll soon feel right at home here, so of course I don't mind,' he said lightly.

Anna ignored the opening he was offering her. They hadn't touched, yet, which was her fault. Without making it obvious, she'd sidestepped his relaxed attempts to get near her. She had slipped past him to put the bottle of wine she'd brought on the dining table, and now she was diligently going over the house, taking inventory of the old-fashioned fireplace, the modernised bathroom, the two neatly furnished bedrooms.

It wasn't easy. She would have loved to fold herself into his arms, and knew exactly how good it would feel.

But conversation and curiosity seemed like the best ways to distance herself, so she kept them up relentlessly. Peering out of the kitchen window to the view of poppy fields slanted with late golden sunlight, she asked, 'Planning to stay here long?'

'I'm saving to buy a place eventually. Preferably with a little bit of land. I should be ready to start looking in a few months, but I wanted to settle into the work first, take my time with it. How about you? Do you feel as if you're in Teymouth for good?'

'I'm happy here,' she hedged. 'And it's the only place in Tasmania where I can use my flight training.'

'Not the helicopter service out of Hobart?'

'Hate helicopters!' She shuddered. 'I tried going up in one a couple of times to see if I'd like it, but I get motion sickness the way I never have in a plane.'

Finn poured some wine, checked the chicken that was roasting in the oven and they waded through another half-hour of this sort of conversation while they waited to eat.

Well, 'waded' was the wrong word. It was nice. Pleasant. They learned things about each other—factual details, past history, a few more tastes and preferences—but it wasn't the sort of conversation they should have been having, and they both knew it.

The simple roast chicken he'd stuffed with two whole lemons was delicious. Anna complimented him on it as they cleared away, and was about to launch into some trivial and relentlessly upbeat question about what other hidden domestic talents he possessed.

Before she could frame the words, however, he turned to her with a pained, intense expression on his face and asked quietly, 'How much longer are you going to put us both through this torture, Anna?'

'I didn't—'

'Yes, you did.' He reached out, took Anna by the waist with both hands and pulled her against him with one fluid, magnetic motion.

'You've been doing it quite deliberately. I went along with it because—hell, because I don't rush a woman if she doesn't want to be rushed, but it's more than that, isn't it? What's wrong? *What's wrong?*' he repeated softly and urgently. 'Didn't we get over the problem you thought you had about me when we first met? That seemed to disappear for a while, but now it's back. Or maybe it's something different, but it matters just as much. Or even more.'

He had her right up against him, length to length, and he was tracing the line and shape of her lips with his fingertips, back and forth, as he spoke. He was frowning, exploring her lips, watching them gradually part as if it was the most hypnotic sight in the world.

The kitchen where they stood was silent except for the guttural tick of an ancient electric clock, and Anna could hardly breathe. Her heart ached. Chest pain. Priority one call-out. Ha ha. There was no medicine you could give for *this* ache. Not yet. Everything she felt, every explanation she wanted to give, had to hang fire until Kendra arrived, eleven days from now, and the prospect of waiting, and of keeping silent, seemed intolerable.

'Don't ask me about it, Finn,' she croaked at last. 'Please!'

Weakly, she tilted her face forward and just…sort of…leaned her forehead against his mouth, knowing she was inviting a kiss…a very long kiss…but unable to stop herself.

He took it incredibly slowly, as if giving her chance after chance to change her mind. First there was that firm mouth, imprinting itself on her forehead over and over, then the fingers of one hand, scooping and stroking along her jaw, lifting her face once more so that his lips could trail down across her closed lids, past her cheekbones and the side of her nose to her mouth—oh, yes, her mouth—where they rested, played, supped.

'Why can't I ask you about it?' he demanded at last, his own voice croaking now, and his mouth hardly taking the trouble to lift from hers.

'Because it's not something I—' She broke off.

How could she even begin to explain the reason for this barrier between them without usurping Kendra's right to tell Finn about the baby?

'Oh, this is hopeless!' she exclaimed, and turned herself abruptly out of his arms. 'Do you think I want to be going through this? Do you think I want it to be this hard?'

Wild questions, blurted without stopping for thought. They were unfair.

'Thanks for clarifying the situation,' Finn said, the bite of his sarcasm tightening up his face.

'I told you, Finn, I—'

'You've told me absolutely nothing.'

'I know. That's the whole point. I can't. I'm sorry. I know I'm not making any sense. I should go.'

'Should you? Wouldn't it be better if we tried to communicate a little better? I'm not a quitter, Anna, and when I have a strong vision about possibilities, about the future—'

'I can't,' she repeated.

She was fighting her own will as much as she was fighting him. She knew how close she was to giving in to him. Wouldn't it be easy...perfect...just to snuggle into his arms and confess everything?

You're going to share a baby with my cousin, but you don't care about her, do you? You care about me.

If she said that, here, now, she would win this. She was almost sure of it. But if she did that, she would be aware for ever afterwards of the layer of poison lying against the bedrock of their relationship, like the poisoned layers of soil around the copper mine in Fryerstown.

'I'm going home, Finn. Thanks for dinner. I mean that.' She blinked back tears. 'But I don't think we ought to see each other for a while. Let things settle.'

'Not see each other? We're rostered together for two shifts next week and another two the week after that.'

'You know what I mean. We can keep it separate, can't we?'

'Can we?'

'We'll have to.'

Finn nodded briefly. Anna knew he wasn't giving up—*hoped* he wasn't, heaven help her—and wondered frantically, Do I trust myself? I've got eleven days left to ruin this totally before Kendra gets here.

They stumbled through another minute or two of awkward phrases, then she gained the relative safety and peace of her small car and went home to a sleepless night, wishing she'd cancelled the evening with him and not gone to his place at all.

'I'm obliged to convey to you in fairly strong terms that you went against protocol by intubating that patient, Finn,' Vern Land said, facing Finn across the large desk in his private office.

'I'm aware of that, but the patient survived, and I understand he's looking set to make a full recovery,' Finn pointed out.

'So I hear. Congratulations. It's always a good feeling, isn't it?'

'I'm getting mixed signals here, Vern.'

'I'm giving out mixed signals here, Finn,' the older man parodied deliberately. There was a twinkle in his dark eyes, and a crooked little twist of ironic amusement at the corner of his mouth, both of which belied the formality of his uniform and his tidy desk.

'You know the situation we're in,' he went on. 'But just in case it's unclear, I'll say it again. There's a move to change the protocols of the service regarding the intubation of patients by our paramedics. One of the reasons I recruited you was because I knew you were well versed in the technique and took care to keep your experience current.'

'Spent a day in the operating theatre just before I left Melbourne, keeping my hand in,' Finn confirmed.

'It's a mechanical skill,' Vern agreed. 'Gets better with practice. But, yes, I'm patting you on the back with one hand and slapping your wrist with the other. I'd like to see the protocol officially changed, but until it does I have to remind you that, had there been a poor outcome for the patient concerned, and had the patient's family chosen to pursue the issue, your failure to adhere to protocol would have left you without the official umbrella of the service's protection.'

'I take your point,' Finn said. 'I knew it at the time, and I should stress that Ron, Anna and Diane all reminded me about the fact. It was my decision to go ahead and, to be honest, in the heat of the moment the immediate survival of the patient was the only thing I wanted to consider. But, yes,' he repeated, 'I do take your point.'

'Good,' Vern said, 'because it's not one I enjoy having to repeat. We all have to go through the motions sometimes.'

A few minutes later, Finn left Vern's office, knowing he'd been let off rather lightly. He and Vern had both spoken of 'mixed signals'. It seemed to be the story of his life at the moment, both professionally and personally, and he was in no doubt that it was the personal signals which were the biggest headache.

He'd worked day shifts on Saturday and Sunday, and had had Monday, Tuesday and Wednesday off. Now it was Thursday, a warm February morning, and he was rostered to crew with Anna both today and tomorrow. The way he felt about this fact, it seemed impossible that they'd only known each other a month.

The day started off uneventfully, with the usual checking and cleaning of their vehicle. Finn liked the steadier energy of a day shift after the high drama of night-time call-outs and low ebb of fitful sleep in the stand-down rooms. There were more people about during the day.

The crews driving non-urgent patient transport vehicles came and went. The office staff had queries about leave application forms and pay-slips. Sometimes there were training sessions in progress in the conference room.

Unfortunately, none of it was enough to distract him from the fact that he and Anna were paired together. It was too hot for overalls, so they both wore their navy pants and short-sleeved shirts, and Anna probably wouldn't have liked it if she'd known how his gaze kept getting caught by the faintest outline of a pale blue bra beneath the crisp white.

Or would she? he wondered, helplessly angry, helplessly ready to forgive. Maybe she'd like it a lot.

This chemistry in the air wasn't just emanating from him. Her whole body changed when he came within touching range. Brushing past her to check the oxygen kit, he both saw and felt the little shudder of need and awareness she gave. He watched her deliberately with his peripheral vision and saw an unmistakable softening in her limbs and a new light in her face.

He almost, *almost* reached out to snatch a kiss by pulling her head towards his, but at the last minute the tingle of anger replaced the sizzle of desire and he pushed the hot physical need back down into his gut and let it go.

What are you doing to me, Anna Brewster? What are you doing to both of us?

They started the day with a P1 call-out. As so often happened, it was 'chest pain', and didn't look like a false alarm on this occasion. The patient was an elderly man, grey and scared and in pain, and his wife was darting about like a tame park pigeon, flappy and annoying and relentless.

She kept giving them details they didn't need, and

didn't stop talking long enough for them to ask questions about the details that they *did* need, and both he and Anna had to battle to do their job efficiently.

He knew the wife couldn't help her reaction. She was plain, damn terrified, and some people reacted to fear that way, but it was a relief when her daughter arrived to drive her to the hospital in the wake of the ambulance, and a bigger relief once they were on their way, with Finn at the wheel and Anna tackling things cheerfully in the back.

They had only just arrived back at headquarters when they were dispatched again. This time, it was an elderly Alzheimer's patient, aged ninety-one, who had wandered away from his home and fallen in the street. He was extremely suspicious of the young man who had found him and called the ambulance on a mobile phone, and then he didn't recognise his daughter-in-law. She had spent the past fifteen minutes frantically driving around the neighbourhood in search of him, and was in a state.

Although his physical injuries didn't appear very serious, Finn and Anna decided to bring him to hospital just to make sure. He seemed too agitated for his daughter-in-law to handle on her own, and in the ambulance, with Anna driving this time, he was convinced for most of the journey that he was being kidnapped.

Although he had settled down and regained some lucidity by the time they reached the hospital, it was distressing for everyone involved, and Finn and Anna were both in need of a break when they headed back to headquarters once more. Typically, they didn't get one, and were diverted to another P1 call-out before they'd even got halfway back.

'Caller very agitated,' reported Cathy Tyndale, who was on dispatch today. 'Patient is a three-year-old boy pulled from the family pool and they can't revive him. Caller is the patient's mother. There's also a neighbour present, and I'm relaying instructions.'

Anna activated the lights and sirens and tightened her grip on the wheel, while Finn responded to the dispatcher. It was an address in West Teymouth, near where Anna lived, and they were only a few minutes away.

But when they arrived, the little boy was still unresponsive and, after giving it everything they had, on the spot, for fifteen minutes—for most of them Finn knew it was beyond hope—they gave up, and just had to take the little body away. Death would be pronounced officially by a doctor at the hospital.

'Where was the mother?' Anna asked, breaking a long silence, as they neared headquarters once more.

'On the phone,' Finn answered, then summarised tersely, 'His ball went over the pool fence. She didn't realise he was strong enough to drag an outdoor chair over and climb on it to reach the child-lock on the pool gate. The ball was in the pool when they found him. He must have been stretching out for it and lost his balance.'

Anna nodded but didn't speak. She had been too involved in attempting to resuscitate the boy to take in the ragged explanations of the mother and the neighbour, and Finn understood that now she needed to know. It would all go down on the report form as well.

They both felt terrible. Fate didn't always give you the opportunity to pull out a miracle, the way he had with the young man he'd intubated outside the pub ten days ago. In this case, they knew, it had been too late from the moment the little boy had been lifted from the pool.

There was another silence, until headquarters loomed

into view. Finn took the opportunity to say gruffly, 'Are you going to be all right?'

'Yes,' Anna answered. 'But, oh, it *burns*, doesn't it?'

'I know, like a big, hot rock in your stomach,' Finn agreed.

'Makes me want to take out a full page ad in the newspaper or something, saying "Parents, don't trust pools. Don't trust fenced pools. Don't trust locked gates. Teach your kids to swim and, still, *never* take your eye off them when there's a pool." That poor mother…'

'Shake it off, Anna.'

'Why, will *you*?'

'No, not for a while,' he admitted.

What he didn't admit to was the effect it had on him in regard to Anna. How it made him want to hold her. Not say anything. No more words of wisdom and comfort. Just hold her and talk carefully about other things, because a reality in this job was that you had to see people die. Kids sometimes.

They had a late, quiet lunch together in the staffroom, reporting the difficult details of their morning to another crew and getting nods of sympathy and understanding. Then the place began to empty out. Another crew went to a peak-hour RTA which turned out to be minor, and it looked as if the drama of this shift might be over.

Nope. Not yet.

Another urgent call-out, at six-fifteen. They were due to finish at seven. Finn was at the wheel this time, and they arrived at a modest little house in the suburb of Garside to find their patient, Jill Haley, deep in the throes of transitional labour. A taxi had just pulled up outside, Jill's husband had screeched to a halt in the driveway, and two young children were clinging to their poor mother, quite unable to understand why their cuddling and comforting weren't wanted. Under the griller, sausages were burning.

'Think you can make it to the hospital?' Finn asked. 'Or should we try and do it here?'

'Here?' Jill Haley thew up her hands in horror, then stormed raggedly at her husband to deal with the sausages and the children *now*, and not waste time trying to get her to do her stupid breathing techniques, which hadn't been any help with the last two and certainly wouldn't be any help this time.

In fact, however, as each contraction came with scarcely a pause in between, she was breathing more or less as she should—great, desperate lungfuls of air.

She couldn't walk through the contractions. Anna and Finn had to use the stretcher to get her into the back of the vehicle, and Finn found himself saying to his partner, 'Can you handle it? I'm not convinced she's going to make it as far as the emergency entrance, let alone the delivery suite.'

'I know.' Anna nodded. 'But I can understand why she wants to try. Too chaotic at home. I'll be fine, Finn. I've done it before.'

'I'll drive fast anyway,' he promised.

Not fast enough, though. He was barely out of the driveway when he heard an urgent screech and bellow coming from the back, 'I've got to push.'

This was followed by Anna's voice saying steadily, 'All right, then, Jill. Let's get you into a position that works for you. Do you want us to stop the car?'

'No.'

'Then I think it's going to have to be on your back. Is that OK?'

'It's how I did the others.'

'Keep panting, that's great.'

From the front, as Finn drove, it was like listening to a radio play. Lots of dialogue and hair-raising sound effects, with a lot of work for the imagination. He couldn't give it too much attention, had to focus on the road and on *not* rocketing around corners in case it threw Anna and Jill off balance at a critical moment.

Once more he heard, 'Let's stop the ambulance, Jill.'

This was followed by, 'No, I want to get to the hospital!'

'You're not going to make it.'

'Don't care. Keep going.'

Finn was just about to override the patient's decision—it really would be easier to have the actual delivery occur in a stationary vehicle, with his input as well—when Anna called forward to him, 'Confirming that, Finn. Keep going, please.' Her tone, he realised, wasn't quite natural.

'Everything OK?' he tossed back to her in a breezy sort of a way.

'Everything's fine.'

It wasn't.

He felt the hairs on the back of his neck prickle to attention, and his whole scalp tightened. Everything *wasn't* fine. He called back once more, 'Don't forget you have another pair of trained hands in front here.'

'I've...uh...heard that some of the hands at the hospital aren't bad either,' she said in a joking way.

Yep, everything was a long way from being fine. It was obvious, however, that Anna didn't want to worry Jill, who had begun to strain and push through a contraction, making the side rails of the stretcher rattle as she gripped them in her effort.

Finn essayed another cautious, encoded enquiry to Anna. 'Any particular hands you're thinking of?'

'Older hands,' she called back, and he couldn't think about what the cryptic words might mean, because he was just about to scream through a red light at a large intersection and there was still a fair bit of traffic on the road.

He was sweating now, but made it through to a quieter street and could relax a bit. Three minutes from the hospital. They were expecting him.

In the back, he heard, 'OK, you're doing really well, Jill. I can see the baby and you're nearly there… Fantastic… Great, keep it coming… Keep it— No! Stop! Pant, Jill. Don't push, OK? Just for a minute? Pant. Hold it. Hold it.'

Hell, what was happening? What was she doing?

'This…doesn't…feel…right!' Jill said, then echoed Finn's own thoughts. 'What's happening? What are you doing?'

'It's… All right, it's fine now.' Palpable relief in Anna's tone. 'Go ahead and push again on the next contraction, OK?'

'Ah-h-h!' Jill gave some huge, panting bellows. 'What was that?'

'It's fine,' Anna repeated. 'Keep going now.'

'What *was* it?'

But the inexorable grip of a new contraction meant that Anna didn't have to answer. Jill was bearing down once more, and Anna was coaching, 'All right, easy bit, now. Yes! Fantastic! He's looking great. Contraction ebbing? Take a break. Now, get ready, last push. Last push. Really, really good push, please, Jill. Everything you've got, with this one. Big breath. Now…'

'Nnnnnhhh!'

The hospital came into view, a big, cream brick building, whose ambulance entrance Finn could have driven into blindfolded even after just a few weeks on the job. He heard a newborn cry, above the repeated, drained and delighted sound of 'Oh, oh, oh,' coming from Jill's shaking body.

'You have another boy, Jill, and he's gorgeous. He's healthy, he's fine. We did it!'

'And we're here,' Finn announced, slowing to the smoothest halt he could manage.

The hospital staff took over at once. They had a warming unit ready just in case, and began to suction the baby's nose and throat, although he was already breathing, and screaming, beautifully. Jill was able to hold him on her stomach, right there in the entrance, and within a minute both mother and child had been wheeled inside.

A strange quiet descended, broken by Finn, finally voicing his suspicions aloud. 'Anna, was that baby *breech*?'

'Yes.' She nodded, then gusted a large sigh. 'And I did it, Finn. I delivered him, and I didn't panic, and Jill didn't panic.'

'Because you didn't tell her.'

'She knew something was strange.'

'So did I. That's what you meant about older hands.'

'A nice, old-fashioned doctor who'd delivered dozens of breech babies before they started doing routine Caesareans for breech presentations,' she confirmed.

'But you did it.'

'Had no choice. That little guy wasn't prepared to wait. When I saw a little bottom, instead of a head…! That's why I didn't want you to stop, though. In case the baby got stuck halfway and we really needed help.'

'I knew something was up, but I didn't realise exactly

what until you said she had to give it everything she'd got when I knew the baby was already halfway out.'

'Normally, after the head and shoulders they pop out on their own,' she agreed. 'Oh, Finn, I did it! And I was so scared it was going to go wrong. That last bit with the head... But it didn't, and she has a beautiful, healthy boy!'

He didn't think about it, didn't waste any more time, just took her in his arms and gave her a huge hug. It was a hug he'd have given her even if she'd been Diane or Louise or any of the other female paramedics but, of course, since it was Anna, it felt very different.

She was a mess. Her hair was damp at the temples and there was a large wet patch all across the front of her shirt, showing him that pale blue bra he'd been interested in all day. The shirt had got twisted and untucked at the waist, too, so that a smooth triangular shape of pale skin showed at her side. With his arms around her, Finn felt it, warm and silky against his fingers.

He had an urge he'd never experienced with a woman before—to *tidy* her. He gave in to it without question, supporting her back with one hand while he brushed the damp strands of hair away from her face with the other. She held herself very still, but didn't protest.

Next, he dropped his hands to her waist and straightened the shirt. No point in trying to tuck it into that snug waistband, so he pulled it all the way out and smoothed its tail back over her hips, loving the taut, rounded feel of her shape there. Again, during the few seconds it took, she said nothing.

'You should be proud of yourself,' he told her finally.

'I am. But relieved, I suppose, more than anything. Hadn't dared to hope earlier, after this morning, that there could be a good end to the day.'

'I know,' he said softly. 'Neither had I.'

The kiss was a mistake.

It shouldn't have been, damn it, but it was. As he bent towards her mouth, he saw the alarm in her eyes, replacing the glow of what she'd called 'relief', which he knew was really a very well-deserved sense of triumph and accomplishment.

Given what Anna deserved to feel at this moment, and what he and she had both felt with each other so recently, Finn didn't want to recognise anything remotely like alarm. It made him angry, and he compounded the initial mistake of the kiss by making it deeper, more commanding and imperious and ruthless and unstoppable.

Far more than he had intended. Oh, yes. He'd meant just to paint his touch on her lips, taste her quickly. Instead, he found himself ravishing her mouth, compelling her response and stealing the warm flavour of her scent.

She responded with a tightly coiled intensity that told him there was a battle going on inside her. It angered him further. This whole thing angered him. The fact that he didn't have the control to leave her alone when she'd essentially asked him to. The fact that she wouldn't explain.

Couldn't he have it easy for once in his life? He'd really thought he'd found something here. In Anna. *With* Anna.

But apparently not. She was pulling away, her face flushed, her grey eyes blazing, and she looked as if she was about to yell at him. Or cry.

He got in first, too quickly to be in full control of what he said. 'Don't pretend you didn't enjoy that.'

'All right. I won't.'

And at that moment a nurse came out from the main desk to ask if they needed anything, the subtext being, Why are you still here?

Because I was kissing her, that's why we're still here.

'Bit of analysis,' he explained to the well-padded, frowning woman. 'We're off now, though. This super-woman just delivered a breech baby in the back of a moving ambulance.'

He squeezed Anna's shoulders automatically, then dropped his arm again as he felt her stiffen, and they hardly spoke on their way back to headquarters. Exhausted, both of them, after a day which had pulled them emotionally one way and then the other so dramatically. But there was far more to their silence than that, of course, and they both knew it.

I was so sure that we had something, he thought in frustration and more pain than he'd felt since he could remember. I really did. And now, somehow, it's all messed up and I'll be damned if it's my fault. I hate this.

CHAPTER NINE

'DON'T say it, Anna,' Kendra threatened the moment she stepped off the bus, at six-thirty on Tuesday evening.

'Say what?'

'That I look awful.'

'You look pregnant, that's all,' Anna soothed, aware that she was being more tactful than truthful.

She had seen a lot of pregnant women who looked better, including Jill Haley at the height of her labour! Jill had dropped into ambulance headquarters this morning with new baby Daniel, a bottle of wine for Finn and a big bunch of flowers for Anna. Pat, at Reception, had phoned Anna at home as it was her day off.

She had driven straight in to see the baby and collect her flowers, and was thrilled about the happy outcome of the dramatic birth for the Haley family. Little Daniel was just gorgeous, sleepy and pink, with a fuzz of golden hair, and entirely unaffected by his less than orthodox entry into the world.

Finn had been off work today, too, and she hadn't seen him.

'Yeah, a pregnant walrus,' Kendra was saying. She groaned and rubbed her back as she waddled to the side of the bus to collect her dilapidated backpack.

'Not twins, is it?' Anna teased, then wished she hadn't. Finn's twins. And twins ran in his family.

'I've asked the doctor that,' Kendra said. 'But he reckons not.'

'How was your appointment on Friday?'

'Oh, I didn't go in the end. Rob and Linda showed up early and we got talking and I completely forgot.'

'Kendra, you really shouldn't miss them!'

'I know.' She shrugged. 'Except, I mean, every time it's the same thing. Dr Little measures my stomach, he listens to the heartbeat, he weighs me, he asks the same questions.'

'Still...'

'I have another one in two weeks. He's always running late. He was probably glad I didn't show.'

Anna collected Kendra's backpack for her and carried it to the car, then they drove to her flat through the mellow light of the late summer day. She had a casserole and salad waiting, with strawberries and ice cream for dessert, and she was determined to spoil her cousin like an invalid who needed fattening up. No matter how much weight they had already gained, pregnant women needed their nourishment at a point when the baby was growing so rapidly.

They needed their rest, too. Kendra looked tired, and her hands and feet were swollen.

'It's only from the bus ride,' she said. 'Six hours of fluid draining into my ankles and fingers. The heat doesn't help either.'

'Did you get up and move around the bus?'

'Too tired, and too scared I'd fall over if we hit a bend. I'm so clumsy! And I warn you, I'll be in bed by nine. I overdid it on the weekend.'

'You'll have to let me pamper you,' Anna soothed once more.

'No arguments there!' Kendra agreed. 'Thanks so much for all this, Anna. I really appreciate it. You've no idea.'

Anna didn't mention what else she had in mind for

Kendra's open-ended visit. A meeting—or possibly con-frontation—with Finn. She had to struggle to avoid the subject tonight, but forced herself to do so, knowing that Kendra was far too tired. Too absorbed in her own dis-comfort as well, which was understandable.

Kendra wolfed down the meal, took some medicine for indigestion, had a shower and was in bed, as she had threatened to be, by nine o'clock. This left Anna with a sense of anticlimax which she knew was both unfair and illogical. Had she really expected that things might mag-ically fall into place the moment Kendra arrived in Teymouth?

Anna was back at work the next morning, and left Kendra to a lazy day, with food and cool drinks in the fridge and a lounging chair in Judy's back garden for a bit of sun-soaking if desired. Finn wasn't rostered on today, and she didn't know whether to be glad or sorry about that.

'He asked if you'd got wine from the Haleys as well, and I told him about the flowers,' Pat reported.

Finn himself phoned that night, just after she arrived home, to say, 'If you think it's sexist, we can swap.'

Growing hot at once at the sound of his voice, Anna didn't understand at first, and he apologised. 'Sorry, is my humour too obscure? I meant the wine and the flow-ers from the Haleys. I've come up with a plan for a fair split of the goodies. I'll come round with the wine and some take-aways, and you can set the table like a five-star restaurant, with the flowers in the middle.'

The suggestion at once plunged Anna into the realis-ation that she could deal with the problem between her-self, Kendra and Finn *tonight*, if she had the courage. Unknowingly, he was handing it to her on a plate. All she had to do was say yes to his half-teasing plan, but it seemed too unfair to both Kendra and Finn to spring it on them unawares.

Hearing his upbeat tone on the phone, Anna knew that for once he wasn't being fully honest about how he felt. He was trying to go ahead as if everything was all right between them, but they both knew it wasn't.

Over the past two weeks, she truly hadn't known whether to try and plan any of this or not. In the end, she had shied away from planning as being too calculating and cold-blooded, but now it seemed that improvisation might turn out to be even worse.

'I—I can't tonight,' she stammered. 'I've…got someone here. Can we make it tomorrow?'

'When those flowers will be past their best? You really want to keep them to yourself, don't you?'

'It's not the flowers.'

'Damn it, Anna, I *know* it's not the flowers!' he exploded. 'Do you think I care one iota about the flowers? But is it really that you're giving me the brush off? Don't you think a man's capable of feeling—?' He broke off. 'Look, if you want to end it, then end it, OK? I can deal with that.'

'I don't want to end it,' she said desperately, through clenched teeth.

Kendra had just walked into the living room after a late nap. She had a red mark across her blotchy face from a crease in the pillow, and she looked heavy, groggy and listless. She was massaging her temples with one hand.

'I told you, I…have something on tonight,' Anna said. 'Let's make it tomorrow.'

By which time she'd better have thought of a way of preparing both Kendra and Finn for the emotional scene that lay ahead of them.

'Tomorrow,' Finn echoed heavily. 'Sure. A'right. See you then.'

And he had put down the phone before she could say anything to soften the awkward exchange.

'Do you have any painkillers, Anna?' Kendra asked. 'I have a truly revolting headache.'

'Yes, in the bathroom cabinet,' Anna answered absently, still stewing over Finn.

Kendra disappeared for a minute, and Anna heard the mirror door of the cabinet sliding open, the rattle and pop of tablets being squeezed from a blister pack and the sound of the tap running. Kendra reappeared, looking a tiny bit better, in anticipation of the painkillers having their effect soon.

'Sounded interesting just now,' she commented.

She was obviously talking about Anna's end of the phone conversation, which was fair enough, since it wouldn't have been remotely convincing for her to pretend that she hadn't heard.

'Yes, look, it's something we badly need to talk about, actually,' Anna said. 'But first let's scramble some eggs, or something, and…and…I want to hear about *you*. Come into the kitchen while I cook, and tell me. Have you…made any decisions about the future, Kendra? After the baby's born,' she added unnecessarily.

Kendra laughed. 'The future? What's that? Can't think beyond the edge of my own stomach at the moment.'

'But you *have* to! You can't live like this, and when it affects other people…'

'Who does it affect? It's my life.'

'Finn, Kendra! It affects Finn. And anyone else who might be important in *his* life. I know it's hard for you to look beyond what's happening to your body, and beyond the birth. That's scary, giving birth for the first time. I've heard people say it's the Great Divide. B.C. and A.C., some people call it. Before Children, and After Children. But you *need* to!'

'Why, what's happening to him? Has he said something to you?'

'How could he, when he doesn't even know about the baby?'

'I mean, about someone else. Is he involved with someone else?'

'I don't know,' Anna answered, and this was closer to the truth than she wanted it to be. 'But that's why you need to tell him now, while you're here in Teymouth. Give him the chance to make things right between you. Or just to work something out. If you want me to smooth the way for you, I can invite him round here so the two of you can talk. Or take you over to his place. Tell him at work that you're in town and you'd like to see him. I want to *help* with this, Kendra!'

Kendra listened in silence to all this, then insisted stubbornly, 'It's not as simple as that.'

Anna gave up, her frustration and turmoil bringing her so close to tears that she could practically taste the salt. In the face of Kendra's attitude she had only two choices left. She could tell Finn about the baby, or she could tell Kendra, 'I'm in love with the father of your child.'

Both possibilities held all the appeal of having a tooth pulled without anaesthesia.

Ten minutes later, just as two plates of cheesy scrambled eggs on toast sat steaming on the kitchen table, the problem was taken out of her hands.

Finn arrived.

As the evening was still warm, Anna had left the outer screen door closed and the inner wooden door open, and he scarcely waited for an answer to his rattling knock on the screen door's metal frame.

Kendra was slumped at the kitchen table, looking at her nourishing dinner with a jaundiced eye, and Finn didn't see her at first. He came straight up to Anna. Didn't touch her, but obviously wanted to. Seize her by the shoulders, perhaps? His hands opened, then clenched, then opened again.

'I'm not satisfied, Anna,' he began, then stopped abruptly as Kendra rose unsteadily from the table and he caught sight of her for the first time.

'Finn!' she said in a wobbly voice. 'Uh… Hi! Lord, I feel wretched,' she added, and Anna, feeling that way herself, in spades, didn't question the statement.

'Hello, Kendra. Good to see you again.' One sweep of Finn's dark eyes took in the fact of her advanced pregnancy, but he didn't comment, and any self-consciousness that Kendra felt was overtaken by the more urgent concern of her physical state.

'Look, Anna, I feel awful,' she said. 'My headache's getting worse, and I'm seeing double. There's two of you, Finn, and one of them's *not* Craig!' She gave a dry giggle. 'That's not right, is it?'

Finn and Anna looked at each other. Anna was hot all over. Whatever she might have expected in the way of emotions filling the room, it wasn't happening, because Kendra was clearly ill, and dealing with that was the only thing that mattered right now.

'Toxaemia, it sounds like,' Finn said, and Anna nodded.

'You've been swollen in your hands and feet, haven't you, Kendra? You put it down to the bus ride and the heat, and I accepted that. I shouldn't have. Call the dispatcher, Finn?'

'Let's take her ourselves,' he said decisively. 'We know what to do if…'

She starts convulsing.

He didn't say it, but Anna understood.

'Hospital?' Kendra came in.

'You need to, Kendra,' Anna told her gently. 'This could be serious.'

Was already serious, actually, if Kendra had reached the point of having double vision.

'We'll take my car,' Finn decided. 'I brought the Holden.'

'Yes, more room in the back,' Anna agreed. 'Kendra, we're going to have you lying down in the back, OK?'

She grabbed the quilt from the bed and a couple of pillows, and Finn helped Kendra out of the flat. His car was parked in Judy's driveway, unlocked, and Anna quickly arranged the quilt and pillows in the rear seat so that Kendra could lie on her left side with her feet elevated. This should be of some help in maintaining a good blood supply to the baby and to the dangerously overloaded kidneys as well.

I should have realised, Anna was telling herself remorsefully. *I should have at least done what the doctor would have done and taken her blood pressure. It must be sky-high by now. That would have told me something was wrong, but I've been so preoccupied with the issue of the baby, and Kendra telling Finn, and…*

Finn was looking grim now. His mouth was set in a hard line and his eyes blazed with cold fire. It could have been just his concern over Kendra's physical condition, but Anna knew it wasn't.

No, of course it wasn't. That steely expression belonged to a man who had just realised he would imminently become a father, although the mother-to-be hadn't cared to inform him of the fact.

When Kendra was as comfortable as they could make her, Anna climbed into the front passenger seat and Finn reversed rapidly out of the driveway. He drove within the law but made better time to the hospital than an untrained driver would have done. His knuckles were tight on the wheel, and he didn't look sideways at Anna once.

In the back seat, Kendra was clearly feeling too ill to speak, and lay with her eyes closed and a hand cupped over her mouth. Anna encouraged her once or twice with updates on how close they were to the hospital, but didn't want to disturb her with any questions that required a reply.

This gave her time to feel every nuance of Finn's mood, emanating very clearly from the seat beside her. 'I know this must be a bolt from the blue, Finn,' she ventured.

'You're not wrong! You've known about this, presumably.'

'Since just before Christmas.'

'All along, in other words. From the beginning.'

'Yes. But what I didn't realise at first was—'

'Don't,' he cut in. 'It's too crazy. I don't want to hear it, a'right?'

'All right,' she agreed in a strained tone, very aware of poor Kendra in the back.

Lord, Anna had known a confrontation was brewing, and she had tried to bring it about in the best way she could, but fate was well and truly mocking her efforts now. To have it happen like this, when none of them were able to follow through.

Finn certainly didn't look pleased. Kendra didn't look

as if anything mattered at all, and Anna herself felt as if the whole thing, from day one—whenever *that* had been—was her fault.

Finn seemed to think so, too. He hadn't looked at her once. Not once. Did he think *she* should have told him?

They reached the hospital, and he pulled into the ambulance bay automatically, then swore and jerked the car forward several metres, in three erratic lurches. He swore again, and Kendra moaned. An ambulance was keening just behind them, and he couldn't block the bay.

Anna raced inside for a wheelchair and a nurse, gabbled her certainty that Kendra was in severe danger of suffering an eclamptic seizure, and led the way back to Finn's car, where he was helping Kendra to sit up and swivel her legs out to the ground. Clearly, the tablets she had taken had done nothing for her head, and she was clutching her swollen abdomen now as well.

Behind them, Anna saw Diane and Ron taking out a patient on a stretcher. They acknowledged each other briefly, and Diane pulled a face that said, What's happening?

But Anna didn't want to go into any sort of an explanation now.

'We'll admit her upstairs straight away,' said a doctor a few minutes later, after he had examined Kendra on a trolley and confirmed what Anna and Finn both knew. High blood pressure, severe swelling of hands and feet, protein in the urine and unusually brisk tendon reflexes.

'Which one of you is staying?' the doctor added. His intelligent face betrayed his uncertainty on the issue of the exact relationship between the three of them. The awkwardness in the atmosphere was palpable, even to an outsider.

'Anna?' Finn asked, his voice dry and hard. 'Since you're cousins.'

'No, *you* should,' she insisted.

'Both of you?' Dr Peter Sharpe queried hopefully.

Finn gave a brief bark of laughter, and muttered something that no one understood.

'Kendra?' Anna said gently, touching her shoulder.

'By myself,' Kendra croaked.

But that wasn't on.

'You're so stubborn, aren't you?' Anna whispered.

'Have to be.' She lapsed into silence.

'Well, for now she's coming upstairs,' Dr Sharpe said, visibly impatient now. 'The two of you work it out.'

'What's going to happen?' Anna blurted. 'Kendra needs to know.'

He frowned once more. 'Of course. I was getting to that. Kendra, we're going to monitor your condition, try and bring your symptoms under control. If we can't, you may need a Caesarean delivery. In fact, I have to say it's highly likely your baby will be born tonight. He or she will be premature, but we have the facilities here to take care of babies born at thirty-four weeks gestation and up, so you and your baby are both in very safe hands.'

Kendra managed a faint reply, and was wheeled towards the large lift. Finn and Anna were both left staring helplessly, the issue of who should go with her still unresolved. Kendra herself had said that she wanted to be alone, but—

'I'll stay, then,' Anna said coldly.

Finn simply shrugged as if indifferent to the entire issue, and Anna was so angry she would have exploded at him in any other circumstances.

Was this really what she had wanted? To find that

Finn felt so free of any connection to Kendra and the baby that he didn't even want to be present at the birth? Couldn't even manage to stay and hold Kendra's hand?

No, it wasn't what she'd wanted. It hurt. She had believed completely in Finn's decency. Those qualities of honesty and kindness had seemed apparent to her from so early on. She'd loved him for those things. Where were they now? And where did that leave the way she felt?

In a horrible, empty hole!

'This is unbelievable!' he muttered.

'Isn't it, though?' she agreed tightly.

'I'm going to go home and make some phone calls.'

'You do that.'

'Tell Kendra…'

'Yes?'

'That I'm thinking of her. Praying for her. And the baby.'

Well, at least he'd said it.

'All right.' She nodded, then she couldn't bear it any longer and turned from him to go to the lift and follow Kendra upstairs to the maternity unit on the fourth floor.

Kendra was having her observations taken and going through her medical history when Anna reached her. She already had an IV line hooked up, the fluid containing a drug which, it was hoped, would lower her blood pressure.

But obstetrician Patricia Keyes soon decided that Kendra's symptoms weren't responding to treatment and that it was dangerous for both mother and baby to wait any longer. Kendra made no protest about the imminent reality of a Caesarean delivery.

'Whatever it takes,' she said. 'What's best and safest for the baby.'

She seemed very subdued and sober, as if only now that there was a problem was she able to understand the reality of her impending motherhood.

After this, everything happened very fast. Anna was able to accompany her cousin as far as the operating theatre, but was then asked to wait outside in a small room containing a television that she didn't feel like watching and an anxious father-to-be whose wife was also undergoing an emergency Caesarean.

He looked exhausted as his wife's labour had been long and frustrating, and he'd supported her through it for nearly thirty hours before the baby's health required more dramatic action. He was summoned to meet his happy wife and new daughter while Anna was still waiting, so then she had the place to herself.

She felt ill with tension. Kendra's safety, the baby's condition, Finn's attitude. She had been so afraid of losing him to Kendra when he found out about the baby, but his apparent indifference...hostility, even...was almost worse.

She was summoned after half an hour of waiting, and the news from Dr Keyes was mixed.

'Your cousin is going to be fine. She's in Recovery now, and emerging from the anaesthesia just as she should. We'll monitor her with extra care, as problems can show up in the first twenty-four hours post-partum, but her symptoms have already subsided.'

'That's great—and the baby—?'

'She has a baby boy, and he's giving us a little more cause for concern, I'm afraid.'

'Oh, no!'

'He's smaller than we would have liked, and he has a heart murmur. We don't know how significant that's going to be at this stage, but it may need treatment in a more specialised unit.'

'Melbourne Children's?'

'You know it?'

'I'm a flight paramedic with the TAS,' Anna explained. 'I've transferred babies and children there from all over Tasmania.'

'Then you'll know he'll be in good hands if that eventuates.'

'I may even be the one who flies him there!'

'It's good that you have some experience in this area. It will help your cousin, I'm sure, to feel confident about her baby's treatment. That's great. One thing we're hoping you can clarify for us is the next of kin. The baby's father. Is he in the picture?'

'I don't know,' Anna had to say. 'I...assumed he would be, but that's in doubt now. It might take a while until they work things out.'

The obstetrician nodded. She had encountered situations like this before. So had Anna. It didn't help on this occasion. She swallowed what she felt and asked if she could see Kendra and the baby.

'Of course. Try and reassure her if you can. The baby's long-term outlook is good, but it may not be an easy road.'

Kendra was very groggy after the general anaesthesia, and in pain from the surgery, despite medication.

'When will they let me see him?' she wanted to know, her voice fuzzy.

'They'll take you down to the premmie unit in an hour or two,' Anna said, squeezing Kendra's hand.

'What's he like? Have you seen him?'

'Not yet. I will in a minute, but I'll just have to peer

through the window, I expect. I'll come and tell you about him, shall I?'

'Yes, please. I can't... I mean, he doesn't feel real yet. But I miss him. It's weird. I don't like it. I want him.'

'Do you have a name for him?'

Kendra hesitated. 'After our grandfather, I thought, Anna.'

'Stephen.' She nodded. 'Your mum will like that.' So would Anna's.

Anna wanted to mention Finn, but knew that the subject was too emotional for both of them.

After ten minutes she went to look at baby Stephen, who was frighteningly small but safely under the watchful care of a fully trained nurse in the special care baby unit. He had silky black hair all over his head, a red face, no eyebrows and a further fuzz of downy dark hair over his shoulders and back, which would soon wear away. Somehow he didn't quite look finished. 'Not quite cooked yet,' some of the special care nurses would say of their tiny charges.

And yet, somehow, what she told Kendra when she returned to the recovery ward was absolutely true.

'He's beautiful!'

It was ten-thirty.

It felt as if it should have been much later but, in fact, everything had happened very fast. As she left the hospital, Anna found herself wishing it was two in the morning, then she might have had an excuse for *not* doing what she knew she had to do.

She took a taxi home, paid the driver, then went inside to freshen up a little and dry her parched throat with a drink of cold water. On the kitchen table sat the two plates of cold, congealed scrambled eggs on toast. Anna surveyed them without appetite of any kind and left them alone.

Then she went out to her car and drove to Finn's. The lights were still on, and as she walked past the kitchen window she could see him standing at the sink, rinsing out a plate and a mug.

He must have seen her shadow crossing the rectangle of light thrown by the window because he looked up as she passed and met her at the front door before she'd had time to knock.

'You have a son, Finn,' she told him at once.

'Do I?' There was a black edge to his voice.

'Named Stephen. After Kendra's and my grandfather. I thought you'd like to know.'

'Doing well?' He was leaning one hand heavily on the doorknob, making the open door move and creak a little.

'Better than he could be,' she said. 'Not as well as the doctors want. He's small, and they're talking about a heart defect. He may have to go to Melbourne.'

'That's convenient.'

She took it as sarcasm, and agreed in biting tones, 'Yes, out of sight, out of mind, as far as you're concerned.'

He laughed jerkily as if it hurt his stomach—the way Kendra would be laughing for the next few days. He obviously didn't plan to invite her in, which was good because she wouldn't have gone. She wondered why she had thought it necessary to come in person, instead of delivering a terse report by phone.

'Well, that's all,' she said, falsely bright. 'Sleep well, Finn.'

'I won't.'

'No, neither will I.'

Tear-blinded, she went back to the car and sat at the wheel for several minutes before she was able to start the engine.

Listening to her drive away, aware to the minute of how long she had sat out there in the car, Finn tried to pull apart the strands of feeling inside him, tangled like barbed wire. He discovered anger and pain and a love that he really didn't want to feel at the moment, but felt anyway.

There were questions he couldn't answer. Where did his sense of betrayal come from? And why hadn't he told her the truth? Was he punishing her? Or himself? Or was this really the end between them, and therefore the truth didn't matter?

If she didn't hear it from him, she'd hear it from someone eventually. Sooner rather than later probably. He wondered how she would react then.

He also wondered how he would manage to work with her tomorrow. He thought about trying to change his roster, get himself partnered with someone else, then decided it would be too obvious. If no one at headquarters had yet guessed for certain that he was in love with Anna Brewster, he certainly didn't want them to suspect that their fragile young relationship had failed. They were both professionals. They'd just have to get through it.

And they did, of course. No dramas the next day. An elderly woman with dizzy spells. An even older and very terminal cancer patient to take to the hospice. A child with painful but moderate and easily treatable burns.

Finn and Anna both held themselves together very well, talking politely to each other when necessary, ignoring each other when not, using their patients as chap-

erons, safeguarding themselves against the blurting of
ill-chosen words.

Until the very end of the day, when they were both
preparing to go home and Finn couldn't stand his feelings or Anna's tight, hunted face a moment longer.

She was standing in the little storage room just off the
vehicle bay, the place where they had both stood that
first day, bristling at each other over coffee. She looked
like an animal seeking refuge until she saw him, and
then she looked like a cornered fox.

But she lifted her chin and brazened it out. 'Are you
off now, Finn?'

'Yes. I'll see you tomorrow.'

'Uh-huh.'

Look at the spurt of colour in her cheeks! Look at the
way her grey eyes glittered! He wanted to take her in
his arms and…shake her? Yell at her?

No! *Kiss* her! Tell her how angry he was at her mis-
judgement of him, and at her willingness over the past
few weeks to blunder forward in her relationship with
him, believing what she did.

And then, once again, when he was done with angry
words, kiss her senseless and silly and insist that none
of it mattered. But she looked so simmeringly, *volcani-
cally* furious at him—which she had *absolutely* no right
to be—that all he could do was spit out the simple and
to him blindingly obvious truth.

CHAPTER TEN

WATCHING Finn in the doorway, Anna berated herself silently. What on earth do I want from him? Why does my body have to betray me like this?

The strength had drained from her legs at the sudden sight of him, like ice cream melting in a hot frying-pan, and it made about as much sense as this illogical comparison, too.

He looked as tense and tightly wound as she felt, and yet the smouldering fire of his anger suited him somehow. It emphasised the power in his shoulders, the intelligence in his eyes, the strength of his capacity to feel. Looking at him, she had a sudden image, which she at once tried to block out, of the way his face and body would look in the throes of heartfelt love-making.

And then, while she was still battling with her imagination, he spoke once more, a casual, almost throwaway line that stayed hanging in the air after he disappeared from the doorway, and was punctuated by the rhythm of his departing footsteps.

'By the way, Anna, that baby isn't mine.'

She was too shocked to react or even take it in at first. Not his? But Kendra had said—

What *had* she said, exactly? Anna couldn't remember any of her cousin's actual words, but she knew she wasn't wrong in her certainty that Kendra had intended to claim Finn as her baby's father.

None of it made sense.

In a daze, she went home to change and force down

something to eat. She'd had no appetite for breakfast this morning, and hardly any for lunch, and even though she still didn't actually feel hungry, she knew she couldn't go on giving in to the squeamishness of her churning stomach.

Then she drove to the hospital, wondering how she could possibly confront her cousin less than twenty-four hours after an emergency Caesarean which had only by a narrow squeak saved Kendra's life and her child's.

In the end, however, the question was moot. There, in Kendra's room in the maternity unit, on an upright padded chair beside her bed, sat Finn.

No. *Not* Finn.

A rougher, more awkward-looking and to Anna's eyes infinitely less dear version of Finn—his twin brother Craig. They weren't identical, but the resemblance was very strong.

Embarrassed, Kendra introduced them, then sent Craig away to the special care baby unit to look at what was now unquestionably *his* son.

'Tell me what's going on, Kendra,' Anna said.

'I don't know yet,' Kendra confessed. 'I was amazed to see him. I honestly didn't think he'd want to know.'

'Finn told him?' It was the only thing that made sense.

'Phoned him last night,' Kendra confirmed.

'Then Finn's not—' Anna broke off and started again. 'All this time, when I've been trying to persuade you to talk to him…'

Again, the enormity of it robbed her of words.

Kendra shifted uncomfortably. 'Don't yell at me, Anna,' she said. 'You see, it was just a one-night stand with Craig. I—I wanted Finn. I thought he was interested at first. I…guess I tried to seduce him at that party I told you about, but he sort of turned me down. He was too much of a gentleman about it, that was the trouble.'

'Too much of a...?'

'Too nice about it. You know. Courteous regret, sort of thing. Made me feel like I could get him if I kept trying. If I played my cards right, you know what I mean? Only I stupidly took the consolation prize on offer that night, the one who was up for it.'

'Craig.' Anna nodded, masking her discomfort at Kendra's rather crude terminology.

'We'd both been drinking,' Kendra went on. 'Craig and I,' she clarified, unnecessarily. 'Shouldn't have happened, but it did, and then there I was, pregnant, still wanting Finn. *Thinking* I wanted him, I guess.'

She shrugged.

'And Craig had another relationship he was ending at the time,' she went on. 'He wasn't in the right place to deal with my news, so I didn't tell him. The whole thing was hopeless and, as I said, I didn't have any money or a job, so I just left Melbourne and went back home. I *wanted* my baby to be Finn's. Oh, I did! But I knew being pregnant wasn't the best time to try and hook a man. I thought maybe when I had my figure back, and my skin, and this cute little baby.'

'So you and Craig...'

Kendra shrugged once more. 'He's pretty shocked. About being a father. He wants to be involved in some way, but we're not sure how yet.'

'Kendra...'

'I know.' She closed her eyes. 'You don't have to give a point by point analysis of how I've stuffed up my life.'

'I wasn't going to.'

'You've always been the one who knew where you were going, and made the right decisions and choices.'

'That's not true.'

'Anyway...' Kendra sat up straighter, and there was a new look on her face, more determined and clear-eyed than anything Anna had seen there before. 'You wouldn't believe what I feel about Stephen,' she said. 'Honestly, Anna. I don't know what it means yet. All I know is that for the first time in my life I have a guiding star. His well-being. Hell!' She blinked back tears. 'His *survival*, at the moment. And I'll do whatever it takes.'

She would have said more, Anna knew, but at that moment Craig appeared in the doorway once more, looking gob-smacked and happy at the same time. He plunked himself back down in the chair beside the bed and took Kendra's hand in a tight squeeze between both of his, as if he hardly knew he was doing it.

'He's...he's incredible,' he stammered. 'Brave. A fighter, Kendra, I can see that a'ready.' It was startling to hear Finn's accent emerging from another man's mouth. 'Looks like me,' he went on. 'And you. Your mouth, I think. When will they know? About his heart, I mean.'

'They're monitoring it,' Kendra said. 'They don't want to do anything invasive, you see, so they just have to wait and see how it develops. They might have to send him to Melbourne.'

'Will you go, too?'

Kendra laughed. 'Try suggesting anything else!'

'There's a spare room at my place. You're welcome to stay there.'

'Thanks, Craig.' She returned the pressure of his hand and a smile crept into her face.

'You did really well, Kendra.'

She nodded and then shook her head. 'No, *he* did

really well. He survived, and he's strong and they're going to let me try and feed him soon.'

'Can I stay?' Craig asked.

'If you'd like to.'

They smiled at each other again. Tentatively. Like the sun trying to come out at the end of a dull day.

Anna had to clear her throat before she could say, 'I'm going to head off, Kendra, OK?'

'OK, Anna.'

'Are you staying with Finn, Craig?' Anna asked.

He looked vague. 'I suppose so. Still have my overnight bag here under the bed. I came straight from the airport. I have his address. Might not make it out there till pretty late. Will you be seeing him, or something?'

'Uh, no, I shouldn't think so.'

'Right.' He nodded, not particularly interested.

So she left. Just went home and forced down another meal she didn't want, and waited for something to happen. Some miracle that would ease this aching, queasy feeling in her stomach. But nothing did, and she went to bed that night and got up the next morning with the knowledge that she and Finn had another day of crewing together to get through, while trying to pretend to a whole host of colleagues, patients and their relatives that nothing was wrong.

She wished they had been on a flight crew today, because at least the noise of the aircraft and the necessity for headphones would have masked painful silences somewhat.

Encountering Finn at headquarters, she could see at once that he hadn't softened his attitude, and this fact rekindled her own anger so that it throbbed inside her as painfully as her hurt.

Why was he punishing her like this? Was it her fault

that Kendra had deceived her, as a side-effect to Kendra's own self-deception? Surely it wasn't!

But Finn didn't seem to agree.

They avoided each other around the ambulance station, diligently chatting with other colleagues or catching up on busy work that really didn't need to be done. Car 119 was the cleanest, shiniest and best-equipped vehicle in the fleet today, thanks to a solid hour of meticulous attention from Anna.

They didn't get called out until two, but then the momentum of the day changed quickly, as it was a priority one call-out, in response to the trembling voice of an elderly woman whose husband had had a 'funny turn' in front of his favourite daytime television show, and couldn't get up from the couch.

It was a stroke. They discovered this on arriving at an attractive suburban house, where flowers were a feature both in the lovingly cared-for gardens and the cosy living room.

Mrs Abbott was crying when she met them at the door. 'He's breathing. But he still hasn't moved and his face looks so still. Like stone. He's trying to talk, but he can't.'

Definitely a stroke of some kind. Seventy-eight-year-old Stanley Abbott betrayed several classic symptoms. He was unable to move or speak clearly, and one side of his face was slack. It was too early to predict how he'd fare in the long term, but Mrs Abbott clearly feared the worst.

'If only he'd speak to me,' she sobbed.

Beside her, their patient looked agitated, too. He was making little sounds, and lifting a shoulder inefficiently.

Anna had to calm Mrs Abbott down before she could get her to focus on practicalities, such as packing a bag with things her husband might need and asking a neighbour to drive her to the hospital.

'People often can't speak at first,' she soothed. 'But it's amazing how much speech they can get back later on.'

'But we hadn't spoken to each other all day, you see,' Eileen Abbott explained, still tearful. 'He got cross with me because I forgot to pay the credit card bill, and I said it didn't matter, it'd only cost us a few dollars in interest, and he said I was always wasting money like that, and we both got into a huff and wouldn't talk, and now he might never talk to me again.'

'Of course he will!' Anna said urgently. 'He'll talk to you right now.'

She could see that Mrs Abbott was becoming more agitated, not less, and that every bit of what she felt was reflected in her husband's stroke slackened features. She pulled Mrs Abbott over to sit next to her husband, who would be transferred to a stretcher in a moment, then propped him up and got both of them to hold hands.

'It's all right, isn't it, Mr Abbott?' she said to him very clearly. 'You're not cross with Eileen any more, are you? It was just a little, little thing, and you both blew up, but it's over now and it doesn't matter. Do you want to give her a kiss?'

Another little sound. Anna chose to assume it meant yes. It *looked* as if it meant yes, and Mrs Abbott leaned forward while Mr Abbott managed to press his face to her cheek.

'Uv,' he said very clearly, then again, '*Uv!*' And there were tears in his eyes.

His wife understood. 'I love you, too, Stan,' she said. 'I really do! Now, let's calm down and get ourselves organised, shall we?'

She was on her feet seconds later, untying her apron and bustling about, and both of them looked markedly more at ease.

It was possible…probable…that their marriage had entered a challenging new phase today, but the fact that it had been marked by an open statement of love on both sides was good and important.

Finn and Anna left Mrs Abbott with the companionship of her neighbour, an older woman like herself. Mrs Abbott planned to ring her son and daughter, pack some toiletries and other things for her husband and then follow on to the hospital. In the ambulance, Anna drove and Finn sat with Stan Abbott in the back.

'Some movement returning in your right arm now, Mr Abbott,' Anna heard him say as they reached the hospital. 'You couldn't do that before, could you? When we were getting you onto the stretcher? That's a very good sign.'

Half an hour later, they were back in the big vehicle bay at headquarters after another silent journey. Anna went to jump out of the vehicle in the brisk manner she was hiding behind today, but Finn stopped her with a hand on her arm.

'Don't go in yet,' he said. 'I've got something to say to you, Anna.'

'Yes?' She knew her face had tightened. Couldn't help it. She folded her arms across her front, knowing what a defensive gesture it was but needing it so that her body didn't betray how much it…*she*…needed him.

His eyes were glittering darkly, and there was a brooding energy to him that she still didn't trust. Was this going to be an attack? Or…?

'I guess Mr Abbott summed it up really,' he said.

'Mr Abbott didn't say very much,' Anna answered crisply.

'No, but what he did say…'

'All he said was "Uv".'

'Exactly. And if I could get away with it, that's all I'd say, too, only we've got ourselves into too much of a mess for that, haven't we, Anna?'

'Wouldn't disagree with that,' she answered, still thinking about the 'uv' bit.

'Hell, *how* could you think that baby was mine?' he burst out at last, and the words galvanised her.

'How?' she stormed back. 'Because Kendra as good as told me he was. Barely mentioned Craig. *Only* talked about you, and about protecting *you*, being fair to *you*. What else was I to think, when she was deceiving herself even more than she was deceiving me? Why are you so angry?'

'Not angry,' he growled. 'Disgusted. At myself. For loving a woman who'd go after a man—'

'Did I "go after" you?'

'No. Course you didn't.'

'Then use the right words.'

'Let's get out of this damned ambulance first.'

'And go where?'

'Don't care. Stand-down room with the door shut. Somewhere where I can hold you and kiss you till we're both gasping.'

'But you're disgusted with me? Gee, that makes sense!'

They got out of their respective doors and…well… slammed them, if the truth be told. The sound echoed around the vehicle bay and one or two interested faces looked in their direction.

'Disgusted?' he echoed, then sighed. 'No. It's strange.

Other times I'd just have bailed out if something like this had happened. Said goodbye and meant it. No regrets. This time I didn't even think about it. Knew I wasn't going to do that, knew I was going to have it out with you, but I didn't know when, and how, I was going to get past—'

'Sounds as if you still don't. *We* still don't.' She wasn't going to let him think it was all one-sided, because it wasn't. She was angry and frustrated, too.

He scraped his fingers briefly against her palm as they walked up the stairs towards the stand-down rooms, but the gesture of closeness didn't hold, and when they entered the grey corridor he dropped back and let her walk in front. She was aware of him behind her, the way she'd have been aware of a great thick stormcloud approaching behind her on an open highway.

Inevitably, he was going to catch up, and all hell would break loose. This wasn't over yet, she knew. If too many rash things were said, and not enough said that was right...

The stand-down room seemed very small when he closed the door on the rest of the world. She faced him, her arms folded, and invited tautly, 'Talk, Finn.'

'OK.'

He prowled. Not much room for that, so he fetched up six inches from her and stopped, and she crumpled at the knees and sat on the bed, because she wasn't ready to touch him yet.

'This is what I can't get my head around, Anna,' he said in a more controlled tone. 'That you thought Kendra was carrying my baby, but you were still ready to get involved, without saying anything to me about it.'

'But I *wasn't* ready to get involved!' she pointed out. 'I fought it, Finn. You must have felt that.'

'You didn't fight it for long.'

'OK, so either I'm weak, or what I felt was very strong. Take your pick.'

He was silent, then said, '*Was* very strong?'

'*Is* strong,' she admitted. '*Is*, Finn. Isn't that what you were saying in the car? As soon as I decided to stop fighting it, I knew I had to talk to you about Kendra and the baby. It was on the day we went to the beach together, remember? I was primed to have this big, important talk with you, but then what you said about part-time fatherhood, about not wanting that if you could possibly help it, made me realise something I'd never considered. I was working on all the wrong assumptions, I suddenly thought, because you didn't know. Didn't know about the baby at all.'

'You had thought until then that I was the kind of man who'd turn his back completely on his own child?'

'No!' she burst out in frustration. 'I was quite certain that you *weren't* that kind of a man, and that didn't make sense until I discovered you didn't know, at which point I got hit with a whole new swag of dilemmas.'

'Yeah?'

'Well, one huge dilemma, really. You *had* to know before I could freely go further with what had started to happen, and yet I couldn't be the one to tell you. Kendra had to do it. If she was having your baby, if she was hoping for some kind of shared involvement with the child, she *had* to be the one to tell you. I persuaded her to come down, but that eleven-day wait seemed agonising, and I was still trying to persuade her to talk to you when you showed up the other night and her toxaemia reached crisis point.'

'Which was when it hit me what you thought about Kendra and me,' Finn came in. 'And I was so angry with you for doubting my…my honour, I suppose, since that's one of the things I really wanted to offer you, Anna. I wanted to offer you my honour. I guess that's old-fashioned, isn't it?'

'Not to me.'

'Isn't it?'

'Not at all.'

He sat on the bed beside her, and she looked into his face, which she couldn't read. It was very serious. His brows were lowered and his mouth was tight, with his jaw rigid and square.

'Do you still want to offer me that?' she said quietly after a moment, afraid of the answer. 'I mean, you're right,' she went on before he could reply.

This was the heart of the matter. She groped for the right words, hardly aware that he'd taken her hand and was chafing it with his fingers.

'Knowing you,' she began carefully, looking down now. She added her other hand to the tangle of fingers resting on her thigh and he squeezed it. They gripped each other, as if letting go of the contact would tear them apart. 'And—and loving you,' she went on, 'I should have realised that it made no sense, that if the baby had been yours, you would have behaved very differently from the moment you saw Kendra in my kitchen. I'm sorry, Finn. If sorry is enough.'

She looked up at last, frightened of what she might read in his face, despite what he had said.

'Of course it's enough,' he said gruffly. 'Hell, do you think I'm that much of a fool?'

And his mouth brushed hers, then lingered to set them both on fire. It wasn't the most elegant kiss in the world. Too hungry for that. Too happy and scared and needful. Anna could hardly breathe. Finn had his eyes closed and his hands buried in the fabric of her shirt. When they slid upwards to claim her breasts through the smooth satin of her bra, they both shuddered, tore their mouths apart, pressed their foreheads together, then kissed again.

'I suppose what all this is really telling us,' he said slowly, some time later, 'is that we don't know each other well enough yet.' Then he grinned, and his dark eyes lit up like flame. 'Funny how that doesn't stop me from loving you, though, Anna.'

'Doesn't it?' she said. 'Doesn't it, Finn?' Her heart was beating wildly.

'In the end?' he whispered, sliding his arms around her and crushing her mouth against his once more. 'After we've been angry and yelled at each other? And explained and apologised and all the rest of it?'

'After all that,' she agreed.

'Not one…tiny…bit,' he told her, and pulled her down onto the bed.

EPILOGUE

THE baby was crying.

'The pressure change is as slight as we can make it, but it still might be hurting his ears,' Anna said into her headphones, above the noise of the aircraft. 'Let's try that dummy, Kendra.'

'OK.' Her cousin nodded, and passed it across.

The Kingair had started its descent into Melbourne. On take-off from Teymouth, little Stephen had been soothed with a bottle of Kendra's expressed breast milk, but that was all gone now, and he wouldn't yet be ready for another one.

'He's handling this well,' Finn commented.

He was monitoring the readouts on the equipment. Heartbeat, respiration rate and blood gases all fine.

At three months, Stephen was growing steadily. He'd had some ups and downs at first, and had remained in hospital where his heart defect and its symptoms could be properly treated until he was deemed ready for surgery. That milestone had now been reached, and he was on his way to Melbourne with Kendra, in Anna's and Finn's care, for his surgery.

Craig had remained in Teymouth for several days following his son's birth, but had then returned to Melbourne in order to keep his new job in landscape gardening. He had been able to return to Teymouth for weekends twice more over the past three months, staying with Finn each time, while Kendra was still living at Anna's.

Nothing had yet been said about the future of their tentative relationship, but the signs were good. Both the new parents seemed to have Stephen's welfare at the very top of their priority list, and that was a crucial start.

Stephen was still crying, too upset to take and hold the pacifying dummy in his mouth as he needed to for comfort. Kendra looked worried.

'He might take my finger instead,' she said. 'If I could wipe it first, just to make sure it's clean.'

Anna found a disposable wipe and Kendra very seriously swabbed her little finger with it, then put it in the baby's mouth, stroking it against the sensitive skin of his upper palate. This time he responded, and the strenuous sucking soon did the trick, soothing him into silence.

'Thank goodness,' Kendra said. 'Craig is supposed to be meeting us at the hospital. I bet he's nervous about the surgery. I am...'

'A couple of weeks and Stephen will be flying home again,' Anna said to encourage her cousin's positive thinking.

But Kendra shook her head and confessed self-consciously, 'I'm hoping this is going to be a one-way trip. Craig wants the three of us to find a place together and give Stephen a chance at having two parents. I...kind of have a good feeling about it, too. When he suggested it, I said yes.'

'That's wonderful, Kendra,' Anna exclaimed. 'You hadn't said anything about it until now.'

'Scared to,' Kendra admitted. 'But when we talked on the phone last night, he sounded really sure.'

They were on the ground in Melbourne for over three hours, with the journey to and from the airport to complete, as well as the transfer from plane to ambulance, and then from ambulance to paediatric unit. As promised, Craig was at the hospital already, and when he and Kendra stood together beside their baby's high-tech hospital cot, the three of them looked like a family.

Back on the plane, Finn said to Anna, 'That took a bit longer than I thought it would.'

'Usually does, to Melbourne,' she replied. 'The ground time and preparation for take-off eat up the time.'

'Hope we're not going to be late back.'

'I'm feeling positive today,' she told him softly.

'I'm not,' he growled, and leaned closer, threatening a kiss. 'And if everyone decides we're not going to show, and gives up and goes home…'

Anna rediscovered something she'd learned already when it came to Finn. When he felt something, she caught it. By the time the plane landed in Teymouth, and they'd gone through the final flight protocols, she was a bundle of impatience and nerves. They each had precisely forty minutes to get home, shower and dress for a three-o'clock wedding.

Their own.

The conflicting demands of both family and working lives had meant that this was their best opportunity, short of waiting until next spring, and they had seized on it, even though it meant that Kendra and Craig and baby Stephen wouldn't be present.

It was a simple and intimate occasion, just the way both of them wanted it, and was to be held in the park near Anna's flat. Present would be both sets of parents, Anna's brother Rod, Judy Lawton, Vern Land, some more friends from work and elsewhere. There would be a short yet romantic ceremony, conducted by a civil marriage celebrant. They'd each chosen a poem to add to the traditional vows. Finally, a late afternoon picnic meal of champagne and hot and cold savouries and petits fours was scheduled, to be finished off by a cake decorated with ivory sugar lace.

Their autumn honeymoon would be a lazy two weeks of driving in Finn's classic Holden around Tasmania, and they planned on going just where whim took them. They both wanted it that way. No flying, please. No hectic schedules. Who needed any of that? Certainly not two flight paramedics.

The past three months had unfolded like the unfurling of a perfect flower, their relationship deepening into the full intimacy of love-making and the certainty that they wanted to share their future for a whole lifetime.

Strangely, this inner certainty didn't stop the bridal nerves, Anna found.

With the minutes ticking by, no bride had ever donned a white silk slip and simply cut silk overdress with greater speed or shakier fingers, and it was fortunate that Judy Lawton had once trained as a hairdresser. She helped Anna to achieve a piled-up look with combs and pins in precisely three minutes.

And when they reached the park, Finn was waiting in front of the gathering of guests, with Vern at his side as best man. Finn had dressed with shaky fingers, too, Anna guessed. His dark grey tie was half a centimetre crooked, against the background of a steel-coloured shirt and darker suit.

Did it matter about the tie? Not a bit. Anna straightened it anyway, immediately after the ceremony. It was her first act as his bride.

'You haven't even kissed me,' Finn began in an indignant whisper as her fingers reached for the knot at his throat.

But Anna had remedied the objection before the

words were even out of his mouth. She leaned close, her hand still at his neck, and lifted her face to his. She had a moment in which to see the flare of desire and love that brightened the depths of his eyes, then he held her and found her mouth.

They stood together in the late, gentle sunlight, wrapped motionless in each other's arms for quite a bit longer than was customary. Finn's down-to-earth and gruff-voiced father had to resort to ironic applause to end the moment, and everyone laughed. For Anna's mother, the laughter came through tears.

'Never mind. There's more where that one came from,' Anna murmured to her new husband, tangling her fingers in his as they went to receive a barrage of hugs and congratulations.

Rod was beaming down from his gangly height. There were tears in Judy's eyes. Dad had his sinewy arm around Mum's comfortable waist. Finn's mother had her hands clasped together over her heart.

'Hope so...' Finn said, and tested her claim straight away by nuzzling against her ear. 'I want a whole lifetime more of this.'

By five o'clock that evening, they were happily driving west, into a golden autumn sunset, still dressed in their simple wedding clothes and covered in confetti. Finn's yellow car rattled loudly, a cacophony of joyous noise made by two dozen tin cans which Vern and Judy had conspired to attach at the back, giggling more during the process than two divorcees in their forties should have done.

At a superficial glance, they made a pair of unlikely conspirators, but Anna and Finn had their suspicions.

'You know, I have a very good feeling about those two,' Finn said as he and Anna drove away.

'Yeah?' She glanced back through the rear window and watched the pair clapping and grinning gleefully. 'You might be right.'

'Of course I'm right. I have an intuition about these things,' he said smugly.

'Men always do, of course,' she agreed, humouring him.

'They do!' he argued. 'Men are much more romantic than women, when it comes to the crunch.'

'Finn—'

'Honestly. We just don't believe in showing it.'

'Hmm.' Sliding closer to him on the bench seat and leaning her head on his confetti-covered shoulder, Anna remained sceptical, but looked forward to the possibility of being convinced.

And behind them, as the sound of their car faded into the distance, Vern was saying to Judy, with a misty sort of smile and a far-away look in his eyes, 'You know, I have a very good feeling about those two.'

Judy, who was very tired of being divorced and extremely impressed with Vern, simply smiled at him, nodded energetically and sighed.

POLICE DOCTOR

by

Laura MacDonald

Laura MacDonald was born and bred in the Isle of Wight where she still lives with her husband. The island is a place of great natural beauty and forms the backdrop for many of Laura's books. She has been writing fiction since she was a child, her first book was published in the 1980's and she has been writing full time since 1991, during which time she has produced over forty books for both adults and children. When she isn't writing, her hobbies include painting, reading and researching family history.

**Don't miss Laura MacDonald's
exciting new novel
The Doctors' New-Found Family
out in October 2006 from Mills & Boon
Medical Romance™**

CHAPTER ONE

'ADELE, it's good to see you again.' Edward Fletcher stood up, came round his desk and, instead of shaking her hand, which she had expected him to do, kissed her warmly on the cheek. 'Please, do come in and sit down.' The kindly GP indicated a chair alongside his desk. Feeling rather like a cross between one of his patients and some long-lost niece, Adele sat down.

'Did you have a good journey?' Edward asked as he resumed his own seat.

'Yes, it wasn't too bad at all once I got onto the M6.'

'Well, I hope you're going to be happy with us all here in Stourborne Abbas.'

'I'm sure I will be,' Adele replied, looking round at Edward's consulting room as she spoke. She could still hardly believe that she was here, that she'd actually left the familiar world of her home town of Chester and her life as a hospital doctor and started out on the road to becoming a GP.

'Adele, before we go any further I have to tell you that there are one or two things that have changed since you came for your interview.' Suddenly Edward's affable expression had become serious and Adele felt a twinge of unease.

'What sort of things?' she asked.

'Well, for a start, unfortunately I've been diagnosed with angina and high blood pressure which has meant I've had to reduce my workload.'

'I'm sorry to hear that,' said Adele slowly. 'Does this

mean my coming here has caused problems?' She looked at Edward and could see now that he did indeed look tired and rather drawn.

'Not really.' He shook his head. 'But I'm afraid that what it does mean is that I am no longer able to be your trainer. Don't worry,' he added when he saw her look of alarm, 'it isn't going to be as much of a problem as you might think. My partner, Casey, has agreed to take over. Now, Casey wasn't at your interview—he was taking a three-month sabbatical at the time.'

'So is he happy with this new arrangement?' asked Adele dubiously.

'Oh, yes. In fact, it was he who suggested it.'

'Really?' Adele raised her eyebrows in surprise.

'Yes, but he does also happen to be my own GP and having just told me to slow down…'

'He didn't have a lot of choice—is that what you're saying?'

'Something like that.' Edward laughed, seeming to like her direct manner. Growing serious again, he said, 'But you mustn't worry, Adele, your training year isn't in any jeopardy at all. Apart from the fact that it won't be me who is your trainer everything else is as it stood at your interview and your flat is available upstairs. And there is also just one thing that I think might even be to your advantage.'

'Oh?' said Adele, trying to show some enthusiasm. Suddenly she felt rather flat, as if her arrival at the practice in Stourborne Abbas was some dreadful sort of anticlimax. 'And what is that?'

'At your interview you said that you were interested in forensics and police work.'

'Yes, that's right,' Adele agreed. 'I've always felt that's an area I might like to explore further in the future.'

'Well, Casey happens to be the police surgeon for Stourborne Abbas.'

'Really?' Suddenly there seemed possibilities in this new arrangement, which, if she was honest, had thrown her slightly. She had prepared herself to spend a year under the tuition and guidance of this kind and easygoing man and now it seemed that crucial year was to be spent with a man she hadn't even met. 'Tell me,' she said looking up, her gaze meeting that of Edward's, 'what is Casey's surname?'

Edward chuckled. 'Casey is his surname,' he said. 'He likes it that way,' he added when he saw her look of surprise. 'Now,' he went on briskly, 'back to basics.' Opening a drawer in his desk, he took out a set of keys and handed them to her. 'These are the keys to your flat,' he said, adding as an afterthought, 'What have you done with your car?'

'It's on the forecourt,' Adele replied. 'Is that all right?' she added.

'Yes, but I suggest you bring it round to the rear of the building. There's a small car park round there reserved just for the doctors. When you've done that I'll get one of the girls to take you upstairs to your flat. I'd do it myself but...' he pulled a face '...stairs and I don't seem terribly compatible these days.'

Moments later Adele was back in her car and reversing out of the forecourt in front of Woolverton House— Stourborne Abbas's medical centre. It was a large house, over two hundred years old and occupying a prime position in the high street of the busy market town. The house had, in its time, as Adele had already found out, been the family home of a wealthy cloth merchant, a small private school for the children of gentlefolk and for a long period of time a hotel, but more recently had been taken over by the local group practice as its health centre.

Following Edward's instructions, Adele turned the car into an entrance to the right of the building, driving beneath an archway and into a cobbled courtyard where she found three cars already parked and spaces for three more. Carefully she reversed into one of the spaces—it took some manoeuvering as the space was tight but at last, with a sigh of relief, she was able to switch off her engine. Leaning forward, she looked up at the old, mews-type buildings with their gables and attics under the eaves that formed the rear of the house, and just for a moment found herself wondering about the people who had lived there in times gone by, imagining the merchant's children playing in the courtyard or the servants going about their daily tasks. History was one of Adele's passions and it was Woolverton House itself that had been the deciding factor in her reaching her decision to come to Stourborne Abbas for this crucial year of her training.

Opening the car door, she had just stepped out onto the cobbles when she jumped as a sudden roar filled the air, shattering the peace of the quiet courtyard as a large, powerful motorbike swept under the archway, circled then drove into the space opposite Adele. For a moment she felt irritated that her musings of the past had been so violently interrupted by such an acute reminder of the modern world and she found herself glaring indignantly at the rider. Clad almost entirely in black leather, his face— at least, Adele presumed it was a he, there seemed little chance that the powerful figure before her could belong to a woman—was hidden behind the visor of a shiny black crash helmet. Quite suddenly and irrationally her irritability spilled over. Later she was to wonder exactly why, but at the time it had been nothing more than the fact that he had disturbed her moment of peace or maybe it had been something to do with his attitude. First he surveyed her from astride his machine and then as he dismounted, the action in itself suggested an arrogance, which touched a raw nerve.

'You can't park there,' she stated flatly, her voice rising slightly. 'It's reserved for doctors' cars.'

Carefully he unfastened his crash helmet and removed it, shaking his head slightly as he did so, and Adele found herself looking into a pair of eyes that were neither entirely grey nor green but somewhere in between, their expression unreadable as he stared at her, not exactly hostile, just indefinable, which did little to relieve the jangling of her nerves. His hair was dark, cropped close to his head, his features rugged, not handsome, maybe attractive to a certain kind of woman but not handsome, certainly not handsome like Nigel.

But she mustn't think of Nigel now, she told herself firmly, she mustn't think about Nigel at all, it was too dangerous for that was a road that led to despair and depression. Nigel had classical good looks with his blue eyes and fair skin, his blond hair and aristocratic features and the man before her resembled a bandit from a bad Hollywood movie. Why, he even had a scar on his face which ran from the centre of his left eyebrow to the edge of his jaw, acquired, no doubt, in some drunken brawl. She found herself imagining the body beneath the black leathers to be covered in tattoos and expected, as he unfastened the collar of his jacket, to catch the gleam of gold from at least one earring. But there was none and as, without speaking, he removed his gauntlets and unzipped his jacket it was obvious he intended disregarding Adele and staying where he was.

'Did you hear what I said?' she demanded.

'Yes,' he replied calmly, 'you said these spaces were reserved for doctors' cars, in which case I could question what *you* are doing parked there.' He glanced beyond her towards her car as he spoke.

'I am a doctor.' She tilted her chin defiantly, still irritated by the man's whole demeanour.

'Really?' His tone held a suggestion that he doubted the fact. 'I don't think we've met.'

Something in his manner compelled Adele to answer. 'I'm Dr Brooks,' she said, as haughtily as she could, 'Adele Brooks.' She paused and when he still didn't offer any information as to his identity, in the same tone she said, 'And you are?'

'I also am a doctor,' he stated quietly. 'The name's Casey.'

She felt such a fool, but how could she have known that this man who had managed to irritate her for no apparent reason and in such a short space of time was not only one of the partners but also the man who was now to be her trainer for the next year?

'I'm sorry,' she found herself muttering, 'I didn't think you were a doctor. You don't look like a doctor...' she added in her defence.

'And what are doctors supposed to look like?' There was a mocking expression in Casey's eyes now, which only served to irritate Adele even further.

'Well, I don't know too many who wear black leathers or who ride high-powered motorbikes,' she retorted.

'What you're saying is that the ones you know drive BMWs or Volvos and wear tweed jackets, is that right?'

'Something like that, yes.' Adele nodded, wishing she could escape from this man whose stare was beginning to make her feel very uncomfortable.

'I find a motorbike more practical for negotiating traffic

and leather is the only sure protection against the elements or sudden contact with the tarmac. I use the practice Land Rover on occasion...' he nodded towards the large vehicle in one corner of the courtyard '...but I much prefer the freedom of the bike.' He paused, his gaze briefly wandering over her, seemingly taking in every detail of her appearance, from her slender figure in the black suit she had chosen to wear because she had fondly believed it might create the right impression on her first day to her long dark hair and the scarlet ribbed top that matched her lipstick. 'So you're Adele Brooks,' he said thoughtfully, and there was no way of telling whether he approved of what he saw or not. Not giving her a chance to answer, he carried on, 'Have you seen Edward yet?'

'I have.' She paused. 'It was he who told me to come and park here,' she added quickly.

'Did he also tell you about the new arrangements?'

Adele nodded, wondering in that instant quite how she was going to endure working for a whole year with this man who, as far as she could tell on such short acquaintance, was as different from Edward Fletcher as it was possible to be.

'Where's your luggage?' He leaned sideways and looked at the boot of her car.

Without a word she turned and walked to the rear of the car, unlocked the boot and began dragging out one of her two large suitcases.

'Let me do that.' He was suddenly beside her, his leather-clad figure alarmingly close in the restricted space between the car and the wall.

'It's all right, I can manage...' she began, but he ignored her, lifting out the second suitcase and setting it briefly down on the ground before picking up both cases and heading for a doorway on the far side of the courtyard, leaving Adele to scoop up the rest of her belongings and follow him. He kicked open the door and disappeared into a long dark passage at the end of which Adele realised he had turned and was climbing a staircase. He only spoke once and that was when they reached the first landing and he looked briefly over his shoulder. 'Did you see your flat when you came for your interview?'

'No. The previous occupant was asleep at the time but I did see the flat that belongs to one of the practice nurses and I was told it's very similar to the one I would have.'

He was silent until they reached the second floor. A corridor stretched out before them but they walked barely half its length before he stopped before a closed door and set down the cases. 'Did Edward give you your keys?' he asked, as if it had only just occurred to him.

'Yes.' Adele would have unlocked the door herself but he took the keys from her and inserted one of them in the lock, pushed open the door then picked up the cases once more and preceded Adele into the room.

Her first impression was one of light, the warm sunlight of the September afternoon that spilled into the room from the tall, sash-cord windows highlighting the sheen on the polished wooden floor.

'You know it's only a studio flat?' He turned towards her after setting the cases down.

'Yes, but I decided as it was just for a year I could probably cope with that.'

'It does have its own bathroom and kitchen.' He crossed the room in his slow, unhurried way and opened a door to which presumably had once been a large bedroom but which now had been converted to accommodate the facilities he had just mentioned. Following him, Adele allowed herself a brief look around and was satisfied by what she saw. 'Is Penny still a neighbour?' she asked at last. Penny

Rudge was the practice nurse whom Adele had met at her interview and whose flat she had seen.

He nodded. 'She is. We've adopted a new policy with these apartments—above the shop so to speak. We now only rent them out to members of staff.'

'Was that not the case before?'

'No, and the previous occupant of this flat turned out to be a bit of a troublemaker. She had to go in the end.'

'Really?' Adele raised her eyebrows.

'I hope you won't be a troublemaker, Dr Brooks.'

It was such an unexpected comment to make that Adele found herself swinging round to protest, then having to bite back her ready retort as she saw the wry smile that hovered around the corners of his mouth and realised that he wasn't serious. 'It depends,' she said lightly, 'on the way I'm treated as to whether or not I make trouble. If I'm treated well I'm the most easygoing person in the world, but if anyone treats me badly, believe me, Dr Casey, I'm more than capable of making trouble.'

'Casey,' he said with a frown.

'Sorry?'

'You said Dr Casey.'

'Isn't that your name?'

'I prefer plain Casey,' he replied.

'As you wish.' She shrugged.

'I'll leave you to get yourself sorted out,' he said. 'You'd better give one of us a shout if there's anything you want.'

'What about food?' Adele glanced around.

'I'm afraid we don't run to room service here.' The mocking expression was back in those rather curious eyes of his and Adele felt herself flush.

'I wasn't suggesting that,' she protested. 'What I meant

was that presumably there's somewhere I can buy something.'

'There's a small supermarket just down the high street, but—'

'That'll be fine, thanks,' she replied crisply, cutting him short. Suddenly she wanted him to go. She wanted to be alone to explore her flat and settle herself down into what was, after all, going to be her home for the next year. And she wanted to do it well away from the gaze of this man who for the moment she didn't really know quite how to take.

'I'll leave you to it, then.' He strolled to the door then stopped and looked back. 'You'll be ready to start tomorrow?'

It was barely a question, rather, Adele felt, an instruction. 'Of course,' she murmured coolly. Unexpectedly, his features softened into the semblance of something that could almost, but not quite, have passed as a smile, and she felt obliged to say, 'Thank you for bringing my cases up.'

'No problem,' he replied, and then ruined it by saying, 'Eight-thirty sharp in the morning. Don't be late—I can't abide unpunctuality.' Then he was gone out of the flat, closing the door behind him and leaving Adele standing in the middle of the room with her belongings at her feet.

Finally able to relax, she looked around the room. It was a very large room, complete with a sofa-bed in a pale mustard colour strewn with huge, comfy-looking cushions. The décor looked fresh, as if it had all recently been painted, with light, wheat-coloured walls, white paintwork and with long, turquoise, muslin curtains that drifted gently in the breeze from the open window. There were a few ornaments, a large vase in the fireplace filled with twigs, seedpods and twisted pieces of tree bark and on the walls a couple of watercolour prints of local views. There were adequate cupboards, drawers and wardrobe space for her belongings and the kitchen and bathroom, though basic, were spotlessly clean and rather disappointingly modern. She would quite have liked to have found an old Victorian claw-foot bath in a house such as this. The rooms themselves were full of character with little nooks and crannies, and between the main room and the bathroom an unexpected window set with tiny panes of stained glass and with a deep sill on which someone had thoughtfully placed a glass bowl of fragrantly scented pot-pourri.

She unpacked her clothes and hung them up in the vast wardrobe then took a shower and was just drying her hair when she heard a tap on her door.

'Who is it?' she called, switching off her hair-dryer and making up her mind that if it was Dr Casey or whatever he called himself she would say she was changing.

'It's Penny. Penny Rudge.'

'Oh, Penny.' Scrambling to her feet, Adele crossed the room and pulled open the door.

'Hi Adele. Welcome to Woolverton House!' Short, round and blonde with large, expressive brown eyes, Penny Rudge stood on the threshold, a bottle of wine clasped in one hand, a bunch of flowers in her arms and a white square box in her other hand.

'Penny, lovely to see you again. Come in, please.' Adele smiled as she stood back to allow Penny to enter the room.

'These are for you—the flowers and wine are from the rest of the staff and this is from me.' As she spoke she thrust the white box into Adele's hands.

'Oh, how kind.' Adele lifted the lid and peeped into the box. 'Wow, that looks wonderful!'

'It's lemon custard tart—made by the bakery next door

and absolutely scrummy. Thought you might be in need of a little spirit-raiser.'

'Oh, thank you…you're so kind. And what lovely flowers! I must see if I can find a vase for them. Please, do come in and sit down.'

'I'm glad Rosie cleaned this place up,' said Penny as she perched on the edge of the sofa and looked around her while Adele hurried into the kitchen.

'Who's Rosie?' called Adele.

'The surgery cleaner, she's a real treasure.'

'So does she clean the flats as well as the surgery?' asked Adele as she came back into the room, a vase full of water in one hand and two wineglasses in the other.

'She will if you come to some agreement with her. This flat was in a bit of a mess after the last occupant left—I'm just glad it's cleaned up all right.'

'I understand there was a bit of trouble with the last tenant,' said Adele as she unwrapped the flowers—yellow rosebuds and amber carnations—and began placing them in the vase.

'You could say that.' Penny pulled a face then, changing the subject, she said, 'Have you seen Dr Fletcher yet?'

'Yes, I saw him when I arrived.'

'How did you find him?'

Adele looked up. 'Well, I was shocked to learn about his heart problems.'

'He's been working far too hard.'

'Hence the reason he's unable to be my trainer.' Lifting the vase, Adele placed it in the sunlight on a low coffee-table by the window. 'There,' she said, 'they look lovely there. Now, I'll cut this tart and pour some wine. You will join me, won't you? A celebration wouldn't be any fun at all on my own.'

'Absolutely,' said Penny with a sigh. 'Any excuse, that's

what I say.' She was silent while Adele went back to the kitchen and found a bottle-opener, plates, a knife and two forks. When Adele returned and opened the bottle of wine, Penny said, 'Are you very disappointed—about Dr Fletcher, I mean?'

Adele paused, the bottle poised over a glass and considered. 'Well, yes,' she said at last, 'I suppose I am. I really took to him when I met him at the interview and in the meantime I suppose I had envisaged what it would be like working alongside him for the next year.'

'I know, he's a real sweetie, but you mustn't be too upset.' Penny took the glass of wine that Adele held out to her. 'Casey is just as good. Cheers!' She lifted her glass.

'Yes, cheers!' Adele lifted her own glass then took a sip. The wine was extremely good. It was on the tip of her tongue to ask whether Dr Casey was also a sweetie but it seemed such a ludicrous question and so obviously not the case that she remained silent. Instead, she set her glass down and set about cutting the lemon custard tart.

'Where is it you've come from?' asked Penny as she settled herself more comfortably on the sofa. 'You probably did tell me before but I can't remember.'

'Chester.' Adele passed a plate across the table then sat down on the rug in front of the fireplace with her own plate.

'That's right, I remember now.' Penny nodded. 'Well, you may find this practice very different from your hospital work but they're a pretty good bunch to work with. We have our ups and downs, same as any place of work, but on the whole we all get on OK. I hope you'll be happy here, Adele.' Her face broke into a wide smile.

'Thanks, Penny, I'm sure I will. I must say I'm glad you're living in the building as well.' She paused. 'You were absolutely right about this tart—it's really delicious.'

'I know.' Penny grinned. 'I should be watching my weight really but I can never resist this.' She popped another forkful into her mouth and closed her eyes in bliss.

'So who else lives in the building?' asked Adele after a moment.

'Well, there are only us two on this floor but there are two larger flats down on the first floor. Toby has one of those—you know, Dr Nash. You met him, didn't you?'

'Yes, I did. He seemed very nice.'

'He is—a bit serious, but nice.'

'And the other flat?' Even as she asked Adele had a premonition and instinctively knew what Penny was about to say.

'Casey is living in that at the moment while he's house-hunting,' she said.

So, not only was she going to have to work with him, Adele thought wryly, it seemed she was going to have to live alongside him as well. She looked up and realised that a flush had touched Penny's cheeks.

'Actually,' said Penny, leaning forward slightly in a conspiratorial manner, 'he and I are a bit of an item at the moment.'

'Really?' Adele was surprised. She would never in a million years have put them together. 'Well, that's nice,' she heard herself say.

'It's only very early days yet.' Penny took a mouthful of wine. 'But I'm hopeful. And, you have to admit, he is gorgeous.' When Adele didn't reply she went on, 'How about you?'

'Me? How do you mean?' Adele frowned. For one moment she thought Penny wanted her to agree with her last remark and she wasn't at all sure she could do that.

'Yes, is there anyone special in your life?'

Adele took a deep breath. Why did it still hurt so much?

'No,' she said at last, 'no, there's no one special in my life at the moment.'

They chatted on for a while, mainly about Stourborne Abbas and the practice, then with a reluctant sigh Penny hauled herself to her feet. 'I must be going,' she said. 'I have some notes to sort out before I finish. I'll see you in the morning,' she added as Adele also scrambled to her feet.

'Yes.' She nodded. 'At eight-thirty sharp.' Seeing Penny's rather curious look, she explained, 'I've already been told that Dr Casey doesn't like to be kept waiting.'

'That's true,' Penny agreed, then as she reached the door she looked over her shoulder. 'He doesn't like that either,' she added.

'What?' Adele frowned.

'Being called "Doctor". He prefers plain Casey.'

'He said that,' said Adele slowly, 'but I wasn't sure he meant it.'

'Oh, he meant it all right,' said Penny with a laugh. 'In fact, you can be sure that anything Casey says he means.'

After Penny had gone Adele was about to take herself off to the local supermarket to stock up on some food but, on opening the fridge to store the remains of the wine, she discovered fresh bread, milk, butter and cheese and decided that any shopping expedition could wait until the following day. No doubt Penny had been the one who had stocked her fridge and her thoughtfulness, together with the warmth of her welcome, did much to raise Adele's flagging spirits. It was, however, with a certain amount of apprehension that she anticipated her first day in the practice because nothing was to be as she had imagined and she had the feeling that life with Casey was going to be vastly different from life with Edward.

CHAPTER TWO

CASEY looked different next morning. The leathers had gone, replaced by a sweater and cords. It was still a far cry from a conventional suit and tie, but Adele had the feeling there was very little about this man that was conventional.

'Good morning.' That level gaze met hers as she paused in the open doorway of his consulting room at two minutes before eight-thirty. 'I trust you slept well.'

'Like a log, thank you.'

'Come in.' He indicated a chair. 'I've been working out a schedule for us. To start with, I want you to familiarise yourself thoroughly with the practice and the way it's run. That means, of course, getting to know the staff and studying the administration side of things and the system for clinics and surgeries. As you know, I wasn't around when you came for your interview so you'll have to enlighten me—did you meet all the other members of staff?'

'I think so.' Adele sat down. 'That's not to say I can remember all their names. There seem to be quite a lot of them.'

'There are,' he agreed. 'Let's recap—the partners include Edward and myself, of course, and Jeanette Maynard and Toby Nash. You did meet Jeanette and Toby?'

'Yes, I did.' Adele nodded. 'They were both very welcoming and seemed to like the idea of a trainee joining the practice. I hope I will be able to contribute something to the practice as well as benefiting from completing my training.' She wasn't sure what had prompted her to say

20

that—probably it was a throwback to the previous day's slightly abrasive first meeting with this man who had seemingly found himself in the unexpected and unwanted position of being her trainer.

'I would think your measure of contribution will be stretched to the limits,' he remarked dryly. 'This is a very busy practice,' he added, 'just in case you weren't aware. We are the only practice in Stourborne Abbas and we serve a large area around the town, including several outlying villages and hamlets.'

'Edward told me that you are also the local police surgeon for the area.'

'That's correct.' He nodded and Adele couldn't help but notice that the scar on his face seemed to stand out even more that morning, prompting her to wonder anew how he had come by it.

'That sort of work interests me,' she said, 'and I was wondering if I could accompany you sometimes?'

'When I'm called out on a case, you mean?' He spoke in a somewhat dramatic fashion, raising his eyebrows, and for a fraction of a second she had the feeling that he was patronising her.

'Yes, not that I imagine you have anything too sensational happening in Stourborne Abbas,' she said coolly.

'You'd be surprised,' he replied. 'This may look like a sleepy little backwater to the casual observer but it has more than its fair share of happenings. But, yes, certainly you can come if it doesn't affect your work here too much—I'll bear it in mind.'

'Maybe I could come with you if you get called out of surgery hours,' said Adele.

'Quite.' He leaned back in his chair and linked his hands behind his head. 'Now, what I propose is that you spend a period of time sitting in on my surgeries—after that we'll do a role reversal and I'll sit in while you take some surgeries.'

'And after that?'

'You'll take your own surgeries. We have more than enough extra patients every day to make up the numbers for an additional surgery. During that time I suggest you report to me, first on a daily basis and then, as you become more accustomed to the work, maybe weekly, unless, of course, you encounter any problems or difficulties, in which case I would expect you to come to me immediately.' He paused and stared intently at her. 'Does that sound reasonable to you?'

'Yes.' Adele nodded. 'But there is one thing I should like to know.'

'And what's that?' His eyes narrowed slightly.

'Somehow I've gained the impression that you were less than happy with the decision to take on a trainee. Am I right?'

He didn't answer immediately and Adele came to the conclusion that he had been taken unawares by her question and that he was considering his answer carefully.

'I was on sabbatical when the arrangements were made,' he said slowly at last.

'But surely your opinion was sought before you went— it is, after all, I would have thought, quite an important issue.'

'It was Edward in the first place who was keen to take on a trainee and he persuaded Jeanette and Toby of the supposed benefits for the practice. As you know, circumstances have changed since then and it was me as Edward's GP who had to point out to him that it was out of the question for him to even think of taking on the responsibilities of a trainee.'

'But before then,' Adele persisted, 'did Edward convince you of the benefits?'

'Let's just say that over this issue I was outnumbered.'

'So if you were the only one who wasn't happy with the situation, wouldn't it have made more sense for one of the other partners to take over as trainer when the circumstances changed?'

'It wasn't practical,' he replied calmly. 'Jeanette has personal problems at the present time and is unable to take on any extra duties and Toby is only a junior partner himself—so as it was unanimously felt that we shouldn't let you down, it was down to me.'

'I'm not sure that I'm happy with that,' said Adele quietly.

'I'm sorry?' Removing his hands from behind his head, Casey sat forward in his chair and stared at her in apparent amazement.

'I said I'm not sure that I'm happy having as my trainer someone who would rather I wasn't here.'

'I didn't say I would rather you weren't here...all I'm saying is that I alone amongst the partners wasn't in favour of having a trainee.'

'Doesn't that amount to the same thing?'

'Not at all. My reason for not wanting a trainee has nothing to do with you personally. I simply didn't feel the practice would benefit from a trainee at this particular time.'

'So you don't think there's enough here for me to do, is that it?'

'No,' he replied crisply, 'there's more than enough—too much, in fact.'

'Then I don't understand...' Adele looked bewildered.

'I said I didn't want a trainee at this time,' he said patiently, 'because I happen to think the practice is in desperate need of another fully trained partner.'

'Oh,' she said. 'Oh, I see…' Suddenly she felt quite deflated again.

'Does that answer your question?'

'Yes…'

'There will be more than enough here for you to do—you mark my words, you'll soon be begging for time off,' he added with a hint of a smile.

'It can't be any worse than the hours I was doing at the hospital…'

'We shall see,' he replied briskly. 'Now, I was telling you about the staff—apart from the partners, we have two full-time practice nurses, Penny Rudge and Fatima Oram, and there are two part-time nurses who cover for them. Our practice manager, as you know, is Rachel Tait. We have four reception staff and our secretary, Frances Drew, who seems to have been here longer than anyone. If there's anything you want to know you only have to ask Frances.' He broke off as there came a knock at the door. 'Come in,' he called.

The door opened and a young woman with red hair and a creamy complexion entered the room. She threw a startled glance at Adele as if she hadn't expected her to be there. 'I'm sorry, Casey,' she said, 'I didn't think you had anyone with you.'

'It's all right, Lizzie.' He indicated Adele and introduced her. 'This is Dr Brooks. Adele, this is Lizzie Vale, one of our receptionists.'

'Oh, I'm sorry, Dr Brooks.' The girl smiled and held out her hand. 'Welcome to Woolverton House.'

'Thank you, Lizzie, and, please, call me Adele.' They shook hands.

'Was there a problem, Lizzie?' Casey asked.

'Afraid so. Mrs Procter phoned and asked for an emergency visit. Mary spoke to her and she's now agreed to settle for an ordinary house call but only on condition that she speaks to you first.'

'When does she want to speak to me?'

'Now?' asked Lizzie fearfully, pulling a face as she spoke.

'She's still on the line?' Casey looked at the telephone on his desk.

''Fraid so.' Lizzie nodded. 'There really isn't any budging her and she's blocking the line, which is pretty desperate at this time of the morning.'

'OK, Lizzie, I'll sort it. Are those my notes?' He nodded at the bundle of patient records that Lizzie was carrying.

'Oh, yes.' She passed them across the desk then looked at Adele. 'Are you sitting in on Casey's surgery this morning?'

'Am I?' Adele glanced at Casey.

'Why not?' He glanced through the records. 'It'll be a baptism of fire, judging by this lot, but it'll be good for you. Perhaps you'd tell the patients that we have a trainee sitting in this morning, Lizzie. But, please, make sure you explain that Adele has already qualified as a doctor and that she most definitely is not a student.'

'Of course.' Lizzie grinned and left the room, and with a barely audible sigh Casey picked up the receiver. 'Flo?' he said. 'It's Casey here. Now, what's all this fuss about this morning?' He listened patiently for several minutes then he said, 'Right, give him some painkillers and tell him to lie flat. OK, if he can't get up the stairs tell him to lie on the floor. Tell Maudie I'll listen to her chest when I come in and if I think it's necessary I'll prescribe another course of antibiotics—and tell her if I find she's been smoking again I'll skin her alive. And I'll have a look at

Stevie at the same time—stomach upset you say. Was he out last night? Probably too much lager. But I'll be over later. Bye, Flo.' He hung up and turned to Adele.

'Flo is quite a character,' he said when he caught sight of her expression, which in spite of herself was one of amazement. 'She's been married three times, divorced once, widowed once and wishes she'd never set eyes on number three, let alone married him. She has eight children, most of whom still live in or around the family home, and her elderly mother, Maudie, also lives there. There's a crisis of some description probably every week. So, are you ready to face the fray?' He reached out his hand to press the buzzer for the first patient.

'Why did you say that to Lizzie about telling the patients that I'm not a student?' asked Adele curiously as they waited for the first patient.

'There is often a curious reaction to a student sitting in and listening to their problems,' he replied. 'They question it and they aren't always too happy about it.'

'And a trainee?'

'Oh, they like that. As soon as they know they have the attention of two doctors…'

'Two for the price of one, you mean?'

'Something like that.' They were still smiling when the first patient knocked on the door and came into the room. Somehow the episode with Flo and her family problems had lightened the atmosphere between them and by the time the patient had sat down and told them all about the pain he was getting from his bunions, Adele found she was feeling less as if she was a nuisance who was simply getting in the way and more like someone who might actually be an asset to the practice.

If Casey's term of 'baptism of fire' was something of an exaggeration, the morning's list nevertheless presented

Adele with an insight into the diversity that an ordinary morning surgery could bring—a young mum with a fractious, teething baby closely followed the patient with the bunions, then a teenager with a tongue piercing that had gone septic preceded an anxious young man whose face was ravaged by acne. They'd barely drawn breath when a middle-aged woman having menopausal problems confronted them, followed by a man who had been bleeding heavily from the rectum and who required an urgent referral for further tests.

At the start of the surgery after the call from Flo Procter, Adele had had decided reservations about Casey's approach to his patients, believing that it was too casual, but as the morning wore on and she witnessed at first hand the response of the patients to his manner she was forced to revise her opinions.

As the surgery ended, Rachel Tait, the practice manager, phoned through to ask Casey and Adele to join the rest of the staff for coffee in the staffroom.

'I think this is by way of a welcome to you,' said Casey as he replaced the receiver. 'And an opportunity for you to meet the staff all together.' He paused. 'Tell me, did you find that list too daunting?'

'My "baptism of fire"?' Adele raised her eyebrows and smiled. 'Not at all. In actual fact, I enjoyed it.'

'Ah, the enthusiasm of the young and uninitiated...' That rare smile touched his rugged features as he stood up and opened the door for her to precede him out of the room.

It was true Adele had enjoyed her morning and she was feeling a lot better about the whole situation than she had the previous evening, in spite of the fact that Casey had admitted that he'd been so against having a trainee in the practice.

The staffroom at the side of Woolverton House was large and overlooked the garden. Adele had not yet had the opportunity of exploring the garden and as through the windows she caught a glimpse of copper beech and a large blue cedar on the lawn she promised herself that was a treat to come. The room was full of people, some she recognised and others she'd never seen before. Rachel came to meet them as they moved into the centre of the room.

'Adele, it's good to see you again,' Rachel said warmly. 'I looked for you this morning but I was told that this slave-driver…' she glanced up at Casey with a grin '…had your nose to the grindstone at eight-thirty sharp.'

'That's true,' Casey agreed. 'No time like the present for these things, in my opinion.'

'Yes, well, I think there's a time and a place for everything,' said Rachel firmly, 'and now is the time to welcome Adele properly to Woolverton House.'

'Hear! Hear!' Suddenly Edward was beside them and must have heard Rachel's comment. 'Adele.' He beamed. 'Did you survive your first surgery?'

'Well, I didn't really have to do anything.' Adele gave a little shrug. 'I just listened.'

'Sometimes that can be pretty daunting in itself,' Edward observed shrewdly. 'Now, let me see,' he went on, looking around the big room, 'whom haven't you met?'

The next half-hour was taken up with Adele meeting those staff members she hadn't met at her interview and renewing acquaintance with those she had. One of these was the practice's female partner. Jeanette Maynard was an attractive woman in her mid-forties and Adele already knew she was a divorcee with a teenage son and daughter.

'We're so pleased to have you aboard,' she told Adele as they spent a few moments together. 'Me, especially. I get hopelessly outnumbered against the men sometimes, it'll be nice to have another woman's point of view at partners' meetings.'

'Do you think they'll listen to what a humble trainee has to say?' asked Adele with a smile.

'Don't worry, I'll make sure they do,' replied Jeanette firmly. 'Now, tell me, are you quite comfortable in the flat?'

'Oh, yes.' Adele nodded. 'I slept very well last night. Mind you, I was dog-tired.'

'But you have everything you need?'

'Oh, yes.' She paused. 'There was even food in the fridge, bread and milk and things like that. I'm not sure who I have to thank for that.'

'I'm afraid it wasn't me,' said Jeanette with a laugh. 'Although I wish I had thought of it.'

'It was probably Penny,' said Adele. 'She came in to welcome me when I arrived. I must thank her later—it certainly saved me having to think about shopping last night.' Looking round, Adele caught sight of Penny. She was standing in the large window bay and was in conversation with Casey, her eyes shining and her expression animated, and just for a moment Adele was reminded that Penny had told her that the two of them were at the start of a relationship. The memory came with a jolt probably because even when she had first heard it, it had seemed improbable, and now that she knew Casey a little better it seemed even more so.

'Hello, Adele.'

She was brought swiftly back to the proceedings by a voice at her elbow. Turning sharply, she realised that Jeanette had turned away and was talking to Frances Drew, the practice secretary, and that it was Toby Nash, the junior partner, who had spoken to her.

'Hello, Toby,' she said, and found that she was relieved

that something had diverted her attention away from the unlikely couple in the window. She couldn't have explained why she was relieved, she only knew she was.

'Sorry, I haven't had a chance to speak to you yet.' Toby's eyes were serious behind his glasses while his mop of black hair flopped over his forehead.

'That's all right. I'm sure there will be plenty of opportunity later,' said Adele. 'After all, I believe we're neighbours as well as colleagues.' As she spoke she was amused to see that Toby's face had grown quite pink at the prospect of deepening their acquaintance.

'Don't you let Casey work you too hard,' he muttered to cover his embarrassment.

'I understand he's something of a slave-driver,' Adele commented wryly.

'He's a workaholic,' said Toby. 'Eats and sleeps work and seems to live solely for his patients.'

'Which I'm sure is very commendable, although maybe tough for others in his life to live with.'

'Oh, he's not married,' said Toby quickly.

'I was meaning more his colleagues,' Adele replied.

'Oh, yes, I see what you mean…' Toby trailed off as Edward suddenly called for quiet and all heads turned to where he was standing in front of the vast fireplace.

'You all know why you're here,' he said, looking round at his partners and the members of his staff, 'and that is to welcome Adele Brooks into the practice. Adele, as you know, is to do her GP training year with us here at Woolverton House. She comes to us from Chester where she did her medical training.' He stopped, looked round again then cleared his throat. 'As I'm sure you are all aware,' he went on after a moment, 'it was originally intended that I was to be Adele's trainer but unfortunately recent events have decreed otherwise. I am indebted to

Casey who has stepped into the breech and who will take over as Adele's trainer.' He paused and looked over his glasses at Casey who inclined his head slightly in response. 'For the rest of you,' Edward continued, 'I would like you to make every effort to give Casey any help you can and, of course, to assist Adele in every possible way. She is new to the area and knows neither the patients nor you, the members of staff. This, I know from experience, can be a daunting situation. Please, all of you, be aware of it and do all you can to make Adele's year amongst us a happy and pleasant one during which she will learn what is necessary to take forward into her life as a GP.'

It was obvious that he had finished and Adele was aware that all eyes had turned to her, compelling her to think that she should say something in response.

Nervously she cleared her throat then, breaking the silence, she said, 'Thank you, Edward, for that kind welcome. I'm sure from what I've seen so far that I'm going to be very happy here at Woolverton House. I would also like to thank Casey for agreeing to take over my training at such short notice and the rest of you for your kind welcome on my arrival—for the flowers and the wine and for whoever prepared the flat so thoughtfully.' She stopped and for a fraction of a second her gaze caught Casey's and for the second time she saw on his face that expression that she'd been unable to define. It had been there the previous day when they had first met and it was there again now as he stood at the window, watching her. It unnerved her slightly and she stumbled over what she intended saying next.

'I…would like…' She trailed off then took a deep breath and started again. 'What Edward said is very true. I am unused to this way of life so I hope you will all help me to find my feet. I am, however, no stranger to hard work so if there's anything you think I may be able to help with, don't be afraid to ask.'

After coffee and biscuits, which were served by Lizzie Vale and another receptionist, Cheryl Burgess, the gathering gradually dispersed and everyone returned to work.

As Adele prepared to leave the room Rachel joined her. 'Adele,' she said, 'would you like to come along to the office? There are a few things I need to go through with you, like tax and insurance details and your terms of contract.'

'All right.' Adele nodded then found herself looking over her shoulder. 'I'd better just tell Casey,' she said.

While Rachel went on Adele waited until Casey and Penny came out of the big room. Penny was still chattering non-stop but for the briefest of moments Adele got the impression that Casey wasn't listening to her, and as they approached it was her he was looking at.

'Were you waiting for me?' he asked and Penny stopped in mid-sentence.

'Only to say that Rachel has asked me to go to the office to sort out my details,' Adele replied.

'Fair enough.' Casey nodded. 'After that we have a house call to make.'

'You want me to come with you?'

'Absolutely. Or maybe my description of the Procter household put you off visiting them?' There was a touch of sarcasm in his voice and Penny grinned.

'No, of course not,' said Adele quickly. 'I'll come to your room when Rachel has finished with me.'

It didn't take too long to go through her personal details and when they had finished, Rachel said, 'Are you getting on all right with Casey?'

'Yes, I think so.' Adele nodded slowly. 'I wasn't quite

sure how to take him at first,' she admitted, 'but I think we'll be OK.'

'He certainly isn't quite like your average GP, is he?' Rachel smiled. 'I always say he missed his vocation and that he should have pursued some sort of action career like the SAS or a stunt man. But, having said that, he's a good doctor so maybe he was right after all. Certainly his patients think the world of him.'

'One thing does intrigue me about him,' said Adele.

'Only one?' Rachel raised an eyebrow then with a chuckle she said, 'What's that?'

'Why does everyone call him Casey?'

'It's his name,' said Rachel with a shrug.

'Yes, I know, but doesn't he have a first name?'

'He does but he hates it. Only Edward and myself know what it is for legal and administrative purposes and we are sworn to secrecy on pain of death. All he will admit to is the initial H which he uses when forced to sign official documents.'

'Oh,' said Adele. 'I see.' The explanation was fair enough but somehow it just seemed to add yet another dimension to the unconventional aura that surrounded the man who was her trainer.

CHAPTER THREE

'WE'D better take the Land Rover,' Casey said, glancing at Adele's short, straight skirt as they walked out of the building into the rear courtyard.

'I don't mind going on the bike if you'd rather,' she offered.

By this time he had unlocked the Land Rover and was behind the wheel. He seemed to hesitate for a moment then he said, 'No, we'll take this.'

She climbed up beside him, remaining silent as he reversed out of the space then inched out of the courtyard to attempt to join the traffic in the high street. It was as busy as ever with constant streams of cars and delivery vehicles and dozens of shoppers milling across the pavements.

'Is it always like this?' she asked, throwing him a sidelong glance.

'Pretty much.' He pulled a face then gave a thumbs-up sign as a tradesman's van gave way, allowing him out of the mews entrance. 'It's one of the reasons I use the bike so often.'

'Maybe in future I'd better change into trousers for house calls.'

'You can wear trousers for surgery as far as I'm concerned.'

She opened her mouth to say that she considered a skirt and jacket more suitable for surgery but then shut it again. How could she talk about such things to this man who himself was so unconventional in his ways? No doubt in the height of summer he would think nothing of conducting surgery wearing shorts and a T-shirt.

They drove in silence through the heavy traffic then as they sat at a set of traffic lights, waiting for the green light, he half turned towards her. 'Everything go all right with Rachel?' he asked.

'Yes.' Adele nodded. 'It was only a chat to sort out tax codes and the terms of my contract.'

'And are you happy with the terms of your contract?'

'Oh, yes. Yes, I think so.' It hadn't occurred to her to question it. Now she wondered if maybe she should have done but at the time everything had seemed more than reasonable with regard to her working hours, time off and holidays.

'Rachel's OK,' he said. 'She'll sort out any admin problems you might have—she's even been known to sort out other sorts of problems,' he added dryly.

'Other sorts of problems?' Adele threw him a startled glance. 'What do you mean?'

'Personal problems—you know, relationship problems, the sort of problems that inevitably arise after boy meets girl.'

'Oh,' said Adele. 'I see.'

'And as I'm sure you can imagine, we have plenty of those with a high proportion of young women on the staff.'

'Are you saying that men don't experience such problems?' she raised her eyebrows.

'Not at all. I'm sure they do. The difference is that they choose not to talk about them.'

'So Rachel is good at helping to sort these things out?'

'I understand she's a good listener, that together with the fact that she has the patience of a saint.' He gave a short laugh. 'We had an episode recently where both Lizzie and Cheryl had boyfriend trouble—they were commiserating with each other until they discovered it was over the same man. After that there was so much flak about you needed a hard hat just to go into Reception.'

Adele laughed. 'They seem friendly enough now.'

'Oh, yes, the boyfriend was sent packing. They've both moved on and I imagine there are new men on the scene—hopefully, this time they will have one each.' He paused and threw Adele a sidelong glance. 'What about you, Dr Brooks?' he asked.

'What about me?' asked Adele.

'Do you have boyfriend trouble?'

'Oh, no, nothing like that, I can assure you.'

There was a long pause. 'Do you mean you don't have trouble with your boyfriend,' he asked at last, 'or that you don't have trouble because you don't have a boyfriend?'

'I don't have trouble because I don't have a boyfriend.' Adele bit her lip. Why did even thinking of it cause a wave of misery to wash over her? She should be over it now after all this time.

'I find that very hard to believe.' He had taken his eyes from the road, albeit briefly, to stare at her in apparent amazement.

'I don't see why,' she retorted.

'I would have thought they would have been beating a path to your door—hordes of them,' he added.

'Hardly.' She gave a little snort of derision. Turning her head, she gazed out of the window. They were travelling out of the town now into a heavily populated residential area.

'So are you saying there's no one?' He was nothing if not persistent and, irritated, she turned back.

'No, there isn't—not now.' She wasn't sure why she added the rider and immediately wished she hadn't. He, of course, seized upon it.

'So there was someone, is that it?'

What was the point in denying it? Talking of it might be painful but it was no secret. 'Yes, there was someone,' she admitted.

'Recently?'

'Until six months ago.'

'Husband? Live-in lover? Boyfriend?' His gaze was straight now as they negotiated several bends in the road and began climbing a hill.

'You want to know an awful lot,' she protested.

He shrugged. 'If we're to work closely together I think it's important we know where we're coming from, and that includes understanding past history.'

'OK.' She took a deep breath, bracing herself. 'He was a live-in lover. We didn't get as far as marriage or even an engagement, although I believed it was heading in that direction.'

'What went wrong?' There was a softer note in his voice now.

Adele hesitated, unsure how much she should be revealing, then it was her turn to shrug. What the hell did it matter? Casey didn't know Nigel and they were never likely to meet. It was all history now, painful history, but history none the less. 'He went home to visit his family one weekend,' she said at last. 'I had to work, but after he'd gone I found I could get away after all so I decided to surprise him by joining him and his family.'

'What happened? Did you get more than you'd bargained for?'

'You could say that.' She pulled a face. 'I knew they were well off, what I hadn't realised was just how well off. We're talking serious money here—a country estate, a London town-house, that sort of thing. The whole thing was a nightmare. It soon became obvious that his family had never even heard of me. His mother was a frightful snob who looked down her nose at me and made it perfectly plain that her son's affections lay elsewhere.'

'And did they?' asked Casey curiously.

'Yes, I think they did. There was a young woman there from another terribly rich family who seemed to think that she and Nigel—that was his name—had some long-standing arrangement.'

'I take it you tackled him about this?' Casey half turned towards her, raising one eyebrow, the gesture while questioning also indicating disgust at what he was hearing.

'Of course,' she retorted.

'And did they—have some long-standing arrangement?'

'Yes, it appears they did. The idea was that they would marry eventually, so merging the two families' wealth.'

'So what was your part in all this?'

'To start with I suppose I was just a diversion—a bit on the side if you like,' she added bitterly. 'Later it got rather more serious and Nigel confessed he hadn't known how to tell me about Lucinda Ratsey-Pemberton.'

'Good grief, was that her name?' Casey looked startled. 'What happened? What did you do?'

'Ended it immediately.' Adele tilted her chin. 'Chucked him out of my flat and got on with my life.'

'Good for you.' Casey brought the Land Rover to a halt and switched off the engine. They sat for a while in silence while Adele stared out of the windscreen with unseeing eyes as she tried desperately to quell the tide of feelings surging inside her as she relived those final days with Nigel.

'Trouble is,' said Casey at last, breaking the silence between them, 'it's never that easy, is it?'

'What?' Wildly she turned head to look at him. He was staring thoughtfully at her through narrowed eyes.

'The end of a long-term relationship. It hurts, whatever the circumstances, and in your case it must have been doubly so because you had been deceived as well.'

'Yes,' she gulped. 'It did hurt—still does, if I'm honest. But I'm getting there.'

'Good for you.' Casey said, then he glanced out of the window. 'After all that do you feel ready to face the Procter brood?'

'After that I think I could face anything,' she said shakily. Surprisingly she found she meant it. She'd hardly talked to anyone about Nigel and why they had parted, but by telling Casey, who hadn't been in any way involved, she seemed to have released something, whether anger or pain she wasn't quite sure. Whatever it was, it had a cathartic effect and made her feel marginally better.

As Casey began to climb out of the vehicle she found herself looking at their surroundings. While they'd been driving she'd become so caught up in her emotions that she hadn't taken any notice of the area but now she realised that they seemed to be in the centre of a vast housing estate. Rows and rows of identical houses stretched for as far as the eye could see while the skyline was only relieved by a few blocks of bleak, high-rise flats. They had parked in front of what had obviously once been a little shopping mall but which now housed only a take-away and a betting shop, the rest of the units being boarded up.

A group of youths lolled against the railings of the mall, eyeing the Land Rover as Casey and Adele climbed out. Casey turned and looked at them. 'Don't even think about it,' he said warningly.

'All right, then, Casey?' called one of the youths.

Adele looked quickly at Casey to see his reaction to such familiarity but he merely nodded.

'Who's your bird?' said another.

'She isn't my bird. This is Dr Brooks.' Casey placed great emphasis on the word 'doctor'. 'You'll be seeing her around for the next year or so.'

'Phwoar!' The response was collective.

'She can feel my bits any time she likes…'

'I think I'm dying, Dr Brooks…'

'Doctor, come and have a look at this…'

Adele was aware of only two things—the fact that her cheeks had flushed and the smile on Casey's face as they crossed the road and approached one of the houses.

'You'll get used to it,' he said. 'They're a rough bunch but the answer is to give as good as you get.'

'What happens if the Land Rover is minus its wheels when we come out?' she remarked dryly.

'I'd have them—and they know it,' he replied grimly. 'Now, let's see what delights the Procters have for us to-day. As you will have noticed, the houses are all the same—three-bedroomed semi-detached. The Procters only differ in that they have two houses knocked into one to accommodate them all.'

The garden resembled a scrap merchant's yard, with the burnt-out shell of an old car and the parts of at least two motorbikes strewn around. There were skateboards, children's scooters, a vast selection of plastic toys, a rusty barbeque, an old television set, a fridge minus its door and two wheelie-bins stuffed to overflowing with rubbish and kitchen waste. A thin, biscuit-coloured mongrel was tied to the broken stumps of what had once been a fence and on the doorstep two small children were playing with a bowl of soapy water and some empty jars. One of them looked up as Casey and Adele approached.

'Hello,' said Casey. 'It's Robbie, isn't it?'

'No,' said the child, 'I'm Ronan.'

'And I'm Madonna,' said the little girl solemnly, looking up at them through a tangle of blonde hair.

'Madonna…?' murmured Adele.

'I should have warned you,' Casey began, then stopped as Ronan suddenly lifted his head and yelled at the top of his lungs.

'Mam! Casey's 'ere!'

A moment later Flo Procter's awesome presence filled the doorway, a woman of vast proportions. Adele found herself wondering whether child number nine might be on the way then decided that it was too difficult to tell.

'Casey.' Flo, nodding curtly, addressed Casey but at the same time eyed Adele speculatively. ''Bout time, we'd almost given you up. Who's this?' she added. She made no attempt to move aside.

'This is Dr Brooks,' Casey explained. 'She's with us for a year while she completes her GP training.'

'Student, then,' said Flo.

'No, not a student, Flo. Adele is a fully qualified doctor. She just needs to gain experience of what it takes to deal with the demands of being a GP.'

'Dealing with the likes of us, you mean?' Flo chuckled suddenly and unexpectedly.

'Something like that, Flo,' Casey agreed. 'Now, are you going to let us in?'

Flo moved aside into the doorway of what was obviously a living room and Adele followed Casey into the hall, which was crammed with coats, bikes, empty bottles and wellington boots.

'He's in here,' said Flo, then as first Adele, then Casey, squeezed past her into the living room she stared intently at Adele. 'You got Irish blood in you, love?'

'Yes, as it happens.' Adele nodded and smiled. 'My grandmother was Irish.'

'I knew it.' Flo grinned with satisfaction. 'Well, there he is,' she added darkly.

The living room was chaotic, with part of a fish and chip meal still in its paper wrapping on the wooden table, which was also littered with what looked like the remains of the previous evening's meal. A huge television set blared out in one corner of the room and piles of old newspapers and magazines covered every surface.

A man was lying on the threadbare carpet, watching the television, his head supported by a couple of thick cushions. He looked up, startled, as Flo picked up the remote control and muted the sound. Catching sight of Casey and Adele, he immediately adopted an expression of intense suffering.

'Hello, Mick,' Casey crouched beside him. 'What's the problem?'

'It's me back again, Casey,' whined Mick Procter. 'It's gone. All I did was bend over and I heard it go. Can't move, I can't.'

'Right, Mick, let's have a look at you.' Adele watched as Casey proceeded to examine Mick. It was no easy matter as it soon became evident that the man was genuinely in a fair amount of pain and found it difficult to move.

'Well,' said Casey at last as he completed his examination by testing the man's reflexes, 'you know the drill. This isn't the first time this disc has played up. You lie flat, so first of all let's get rid of those cushions.' As he spoke he eased the cushions from under Mick's neck 'I'll prescribe some painkillers and a muscle relaxant. I think it's probably also time we organised another X-ray then we'll see about some physiotherapy.'

'Oh, no,' groaned Mick, 'not that again.'

Ignoring him, Casey began scribbling out a prescription.

'So where you living, love?' Flo, seemingly oblivious to her husband's predicament, turned to Adele.

'In one of the flats at Woolverton House,' Adele replied only after a hesitant glance at Casey. She wasn't quite certain how much information she should divulge.

'Oh, yes.' Flo looked interested. 'I knew someone who had one of those flats. Elvira Jackson—is she still there?'

It was Casey who answered, tearing off the prescription and handing it to Flo. 'No,' he said, 'Elvira has moved on.'

'Strange one, that, and no mistake.' Flo folded the prescription and tucked it into her blouse. 'You said you'd take a look at Mum while you're here, Casey—she's in the other room.' Leaving the hapless Mick on the floor, minus his cushions and unable to reach the remote control, they all trooped through the house to a smaller room at the rear where an elderly woman sat in a corner, watching yet another television and wheezing noisily with every breath she took.

'Hello, Maudie,' said Casey cheerfully. 'How are we today?'

'Well, I don't know how you are,' rasped the old woman, 'but I feel blooming awful.'

'In that case we'd better see what we can do about it. Let's have a listen to that chest.' Casey took the stethoscope from his bag then passed it to Adele.

'Me?' she said, startled.

'Why not? You've got to start somewhere,' Casey replied, his gaze meeting hers.

Maudie looked up in sudden alarm. 'Here, wait a minute,' she snapped. 'I'm not having no one practising on me.'

'She's not practising, Mum,' said Flo. 'She's a doctor

same as Casey—she's come to help them out up at
Woolverton House.'

'But he said she had to start somewhere.' Maudie was
obviously still very suspicious and clutched at the front of
her blouse with bony fingers. 'She ain't starting with me
and that's it and all about it.'

'He meant she had to start getting to know people,
didn't you, Casey?'

'That's exactly what I meant,' said Casey. 'Now, come
on, Maudie, be reasonable or I'll start asking the kids how
many cigarettes you've been smoking.'

The old lady began grumbling under her breath but at
last, reluctantly, she opened her blouse and allowed Adele
to listen first to her chest and then her back.

'Took your time, didn't you?' she muttered as Adele
finished her examination and removed the stethoscope
from her ears. 'Casey don't take that long.'

'Well?' Casey looked at Adele.

'There's congestion and base crackles,' Adele replied.

'Another course of antibiotics, Maudie.' Casey sat down
on the arm of a chair took out his prescription pad for the
second time since entering the Procter household.
Balancing it on his knee, he began writing. 'Are you using
your inhalers, Maudie?' he asked without looking up.

'Course I am,' she wheezed. 'I wouldn't get far without
them.'

'Right.' Casey handed the prescription to Flo. 'Another
one for you, Flo.'

'I'll get Elton to pick them up,' she said.

'When you phoned you said something about Stevie,'
said Casey as he stood up. 'Where is he?'

'Don't know.' Flo shrugged. 'He went out. I told him
to wait. I said you wouldn't like it.'

'So was he better?' Casey sounded annoyed and Adele

threw him a wary glance. Casey in a good mood was one thing; Casey in a bad mood, she suspected, would be something else entirely.

'Said he was,' Flo replied. 'You were probably right when you said it was too much lager last night. Mind you, he did have a terrible guts ache this morning. Rolling around he was. I tell you, what with him and Mick…' She didn't finish the sentence but it was pretty obvious that her sentiments towards her family were a little less than sympathetic.

A few moments later Adele found herself, together with Casey, on the pavement outside the Procters' house.

'Phew!' she said.

'What's up?' Casey raised one eyebrow but there was a glint of amusement in his eyes.

'Well, I have to say that was quite an experience. But tell me,' she said, as they made their way back to the Land Rover, 'do all the children have pop-star names?'

'Oh, yes,' Casey replied in a matter-of-fact tone. 'Flo lives in a world of pop stars—she always has done. I think they're her consolation against the reality of her life. The eldest boy is Elvis, by the way, but he's no longer at home.'

'Is he married?' asked Adele, bracing herself to run the gauntlet of the leering youths at the shopping mall. Their numbers seemed to have swelled alarmingly, which led her to wonder if someone had been despatched to round up others in order to gawp at the new doctor.

'No,' said Casey. 'He's in prison for nicking cars.'

There were a few jibes of a suggestive but reasonably good-natured fashion from the youths but Adele was relieved to see that the Land Rover appeared to be in one piece and within minutes they were heading back to Woolverton House.

Casey was silent to start with and then suddenly and totally unexpectedly he resumed their conversation of earlier. 'So, in view of recent events,' he said, 'can I assume that for the present you are off men in general?'

'Sorry?' Adele threw him a startled glance.

'Well, it would be perfectly understandable if you were. Trust takes a terrific bashing in such circumstances and trust is one of those things that's difficult to rebuild.'

'That's true,' she agreed slowly.

'So men are off your immediate agenda?'

'Well, yes, I suppose you could say that,' she admitted at last. She hadn't really thought about it, but now that he put it like that, she guessed it was true. The last thing she wanted was to rush headlong into another relationship after Nigel and, yes, she supposed trust could well be the factor that would prevent her from doing so. She'd thought she'd been able to trust Nigel and it had been a shock when she'd realised he'd been lying to her from the very beginning. Turning her head, she looked at the man at her side and once again she found herself feeling annoyed with him. This time it was because of the number of questions he'd asked her, all the things he seemed to want to know about her private life, and because he seemed to have had the uncanny knack of summing things up pretty accurately.

Thoroughly irritated, she heard herself say, 'So what about you?'

'What about me?' He was frowning now, a deep frown that was almost a scowl.

'Well, it was you who said if we were to work together you thought we should know each other's past history. I've told you mine...' She trailed off, waiting for him to continue.

'I'm also single,' he said after a long silence.

'I suppose you haven't found the right girl yet?' She

gave a short laugh but his sombre expression didn't change by so much as a flicker of an eyelid.

'It hasn't always been that way.'

'Really?' Suddenly she wasn't sure she wanted to know about the conquests in his life after all and was beginning to wish she hadn't asked.

'No,' he said quietly. 'I was married once.'

'Oh.' She stared at him. No one had said anything about an ex-wife.

'It was a long time ago. We were very young—I was still at medical school, actually.'

'I had friends who married while still doing their training. It put a tremendous strain on the marriage and it didn't last very long.'

'I was married for two years,' he said.

'If you don't mind me asking, why did you split up? Couldn't your wife put up with the long hours? Or was she training as well?'

'No, she was nurse.'

'So she should have known what your job entailed.'

'My wife didn't leave me,' he said, and there was an edge now to his voice that was difficult to identify.

'So you left her?'

'No,' he replied quietly. 'She died, giving birth to our baby.'

Adele stared at him in dismay, wishing the floor on her side of the Land Rover would open up and she could just disappear into a black hole. She had just assumed he was divorced, not widowed. How could she have been so insensitive?

'I'm so sorry,' she managed to say at last. 'I had no idea.'

'How could you have known?' He gave a slight shrug.

'It's not the sort of information I volunteer at a first meeting.'

'No, of course not, but I wish one of the others had told me and prevented me from putting my foot in it so terribly.'

'Like I say, it all happened a long time ago, long before I came to Stourborne Abbas. I don't suppose all the staff are even aware of it. Edward and Jeanette know, of course, and presumably Toby and Rachel, but I don't know about the others.'

She didn't know what else to say but in desperation felt she couldn't simply leave it there. 'But your child…the baby?'

'A little girl,' he replied, and his voice had softened again. 'She didn't stand a chance, she was just too premature—a little scrap of a thing. I had her baptised and she was buried with her mother.'

'That is just so sad.' Adele felt her eyes fill with tears. 'I really am very sorry, you know.'

'It's OK, really. You weren't to know.'

By this time they had reached Woolverton House and Casey drove into the courtyard. 'Lunchtime, I think,' he said, looking at his watch. 'I'll see you at two for afternoon surgery.'

'Yes, of course.' Adele nodded and made her way into the house, heading for the stairs, while Casey disappeared in the direction of his surgery. She was still reeling from all that he had told her. It somehow seemed inconceivable that he should have suffered so much tragedy.

It wasn't until later when she was eating her lunch that it occurred to her that while he had told her of his past life and his brief, tragic marriage he'd said nothing of the present and his relationship with Penny. If, as they'd agreed, they were coming clean over relationships, that seemed to her rather odd.

CHAPTER FOUR

ADELE met Casey promptly at two o'clock for afternoon surgery during which there proved to be every bit as much variety and diversity as there had been in morning surgery. When they finished Casey had house calls and when Adele asked if he wanted her to accompany him he shook his head. 'Not this time,' he said. 'I think you should spend some time in Reception, looking at the filing and appointment systems, and get one of the girls to show you the computer and the software that we use. I'll see you later.' With a wave of his hand he was gone, leaving a slightly bemused Adele standing at the reception desk.

'Are you all right, Adele?'

Adele turned and found Mary Kennington, the senior receptionist, peering at her over the desk.

'Yes, I think so. Dr...er...Casey has just said that I should spend some time getting to know how the system works.'

'Well, in that case you'd better come in here with us.' Mary opened the door beside the desk and Adele went into the office area that housed the patient records and the administration files. The other two receptionists, Cheryl and Lizzie, were working at computers and they both looked up as Adele came in.

'How's your first day going?' asked Cheryl.

'Casey not worked you to death yet?' said Lizzie with a grin.

'I've just finished the day's repeat prescriptions,' Mary explained. 'Maybe you'd like to start with seeing how we deal with them then we'll go on to the appointments system.'

Adele spent the next hour learning as much as she could about how the Woolverton House surgery worked. She was amazed at just how much there was to absorb and when she commented on it Mary suggested that she should come in each day for an hour or so until she was familiar with it all.

'Did you go to the Procters' with Casey?' asked Lizzie a little later as Adele was studying the staff rosters.

'I did indeed,' she replied.

'Nothing like chucking somebody in at the deep end,' remarked Cheryl with a laugh. 'What was wrong with Stevie, by the way?'

'I don't know.' Adele shook her head. 'He wasn't there. Apparently he'd made a miraculous recovery and gone out.'

'After all the fuss his mother made,' said Lizzie with a sigh. 'She made it sound like a matter of life and death on the phone. She was more concerned about him than poor old Mick, or Maudie come to that.'

'Maudie will use any excuse to see Casey,' said Mary. 'I think she's got a soft spot for him.'

'Maudie actually needed more antibiotics,' said Adele.

'Maudie always needs antibiotics,' chorused Mary, Cheryl and Lizzie.

'It's something to do with the number of cigarettes she smokes,' said Mary. 'So what did you think of the Bowscombe Estate?' she added.

'Well, it seemed a pretty tough area,' admitted Adele.

'That's putting it mildly.' Lizzie pulled a face. 'You wouldn't catch me walking through there after dark, I can tell you.'

'I'd think twice about walking there in daylight,' said Mary.

'Casey didn't seem to give it a second thought,' observed Adele. 'In fact, he seemed to know a lot of people there—would they all be registered here?'

'Well some of them are, but Casey probably knows the majority of them from wearing his other hat.'

'His other hat?' Adele frowned then it dawned on her what Mary meant. 'Oh, you mean as a police surgeon?'

'Exactly.' Mary nodded. 'A fair percentage of the population of the Bowscombe Estate spend half their time in police custody.' She paused, eyeing Adele speculatively. 'Are you going to be involved in that, Adele?'

'I hope so. It's an area of medicine that interests me a lot.'

'Rather you than me after hearing about some of the things Casey has to deal with down at the police station.' Cheryl gave a little shudder. At that moment the door opened and Penny came into Reception.

'All finished?' asked Mary.

'Yes, thank goodness.' Penny yawned and stretched then, catching sight of Adele, she said, 'What about you?'

It was Cheryl who answered on Adele's behalf. 'Well, she's survived her first day with Casey which involved a visit to the Bowscombe Estate *and* the Procters, so I say if she can survive that she'll survive anything.'

'Oh, absolutely,' said Penny with a laugh.

'Why don't you call it a day?' Mary turned to Adele. 'I would say you've had quite enough to contend with for your first day.'

'What about Casey?' asked Adele dubiously.

'What *about* Casey?' Mary raised her eyebrows.

'Well, I don't know if he wanted me to do anything

else,' Adele wrinkled her nose. 'He said "See you later" when he went out.'

'You leave Casey to me,' said Penny.

'Yes?' said Adele doubtfully.

'Absolutely,' said Penny firmly. 'You've done quite enough for one day. Besides, I'm sure there must be things you want to do.'

'As a matter of fact, I could do with doing a bit of shopping and getting the flat straight. Which reminds me, was it you, Penny, who stocked up the fridge?'

Penny shook her head, 'No, sorry. I can't lay claim to that. Maybe it was Rosie—she's a little gem like that.'

'Yes, maybe. I'll have to see her and thank her.'

Adele left Reception with her head buzzing with facts and figures. After collecting her jacket and bag, she left Woolverton House by the front entrance and stood for a moment on the steps, enjoying the warmth of the September afternoon. The supermarket was only a stone's throw from the surgery and it didn't take her long to load a trolley with food and other essentials. On her return there was no sign of Casey so, taking the advice of Penny and Mary, Adele made her way up to her flat. The next couple of hours she spent packing everything away and arranging the furniture and her possessions to her satisfaction, after which she lit several scented candles then began preparing the food she had bought for a meal.

While the food was cooking she took a long, leisurely soak in the bath where she found herself going over the events of the day. She was feeling quite exhausted, not from what she'd actually been doing but from all she had been expected to take in. Idly she wondered if Casey was back from his house calls and if he, too, was feeling tired. Somehow she doubted it, deciding it probably took a lot to weary him. She wondered if he and Penny were spending the evening together. Maybe Penny was cooking for him in her flat or perhaps he was doing the cooking if his flat was the more spacious of the two. She frowned as she tried to picture them together, finding it almost impossible. Round, bubbly-natured Penny with her non-stop chatter and Casey who was…well, what was Casey like? Adele found herself hard-pressed to sum him up and in the end gave up the attempt.

She wondered if they slept together and somehow found the idea almost as disturbing as learning about his wife. She'd been shocked and upset and terribly sad when he'd told her about the deaths of his wife and baby daughter but the thought of him sleeping with Penny disturbed her in another way, although she was unable to say why.

She was beginning to regret telling him so much about Nigel, even though in doing so she had felt a little better about the whole thing. What had happened between her and Nigel was private. Why, she hadn't even given the details to her friends or, with the exception of her sister Elaine, to her family, simply that they had decided to part. Somehow she'd doubted whether she could have coped with the utter humiliation if people had found out that Nigel had had someone else right from the beginning, and now she'd told a complete stranger all the gory details. Well, nearly all the details.

She hadn't told him about the terrible confrontation between herself and Nigel when she'd first realised that not only had Lucinda been there in the background of his life throughout the entire time they had been together, but that Lucinda had also been under the impression that they would shortly be married and that Nigel's parents had purchased a home for the happy couple in Cheshire.

Casey had observed that she would find it difficult to trust another man after such a betrayal and he was right.

Adele had found herself wondering in the time since she and Nigel had parted whether she would ever trust anyone again.

So lost had she become in her thoughts that it was with a little shock that when she moved she found that the bath water had grown cold. With a shiver she sat up, released the water then climbed out of the bath, wrapping a large fluffy bath sheet around her.

She ate a solitary meal then, on an impulse no doubt prompted by her reflections on the past, decided to phone her sister. She smiled to herself as she heard the phone ringing at the other end and pictured her sister flapping about in the permanent state of chaos in which she seemed to live. Elaine was four years older than Adele and married with three children. Their mother Jennifer constantly held Elaine up to Adele as an example of motherhood and a state to which she herself should be aspiring. 'But I'm a doctor, Mum,' Adele had protested on more than one occasion. 'It takes time and tremendous effort to become a doctor.'

'That shouldn't stop you from marrying and having children,' had been her mother's ready response. 'My GP is married and she has twin daughters.'

'She's probably a few years older than me,' Adele would reply wearily.

'Hello?'

'Hello, Lainey,' she said at the sound of her sister's voice. 'You sound harassed. Is this a bad time?'

'Is there ever a good time in this house?' Her sister sighed. 'Hi, Del, how are you? How's it going? Is it a nice place? What are the staff like? I've been thinking about you all day and wondering how you were getting on.'

'I'm fine. Exhausted, but fine. The house is beautiful but

I told you about that before, didn't I, after the interview? And so far the staff seem very nice.'

'What's your flat like?' demanded Elaine. 'You didn't see that before, did you?'

'No, it was still occupied then. But I have to say it's lovely. It's a big studio flat but has its own bathroom and kitchen so there's no sharing with anyone else, and the décor and furnishings are really very nice.' She looked around as she spoke, admiring the room suffused in the soft golden light from the lighted candles.

'And what about the staff?' Elaine obviously wanted to know everything. 'Have you made any friends?'

'Well, it's early days yet, of course, but they all seem OK. One girl in particular has gone out of her way to be friendly. Her name's Penny, Penny Rudge—she's one of the practice nurses and she also has one of the four flats above the practice.'

'And the other doctors, are they all right? What about your trainer—Dr Flemming, wasn't it?'

'No, you mean Dr Fletcher, Edward Fletcher—well, unfortunately there's been a bit of a hiccup there. He isn't able to be my trainer after all because he has heart trouble.'

'Well, that's a good start,' said Elaine. 'I hope they have someone else who can do it.'

'Oh, yes, they have someone else all right.'

'I didn't like the way you said that. Who is he and what's wrong with him?'

Adele sighed. She knew there was no hiding anything from Elaine. Her sister had always had the ability to read her like a book. 'His name is Casey—he's one of the partners here. I don't know that there's anything wrong with him exactly—he's just a bit different, that's all.'

'In what way different? You've got me curious now, Del.'

'Well, he's not a bit like Edward and, really, he's nothing like your average GP.'

'Well, go on. You can't leave it there. How's he different?'

'I suppose he comes across as a bit of a rough diamond. For a start he wears leathers and does his house calls on a motorbike.'

'Hmm, tell me more—he sounds intriguing.'

'I wouldn't call him intriguing exactly…'

'Is he good-looking?'

'Not really—sort of tough-looking, the type you wouldn't want to meet in a dark alley at night.'

'Or the type you might want to accompany you in a dark alley at night.' Elaine chuckled.

'Well, yes, I suppose so if you put it like that.'

'Is he spoken for?'

'I think so, at least Penny Rudge told me that he and she have just started a relationship…but…'

'But what?'

'I don't know. They just seem such an unlikely couple that's all. Penny's all lively and bubbly…and Casey, well… Anyway, it's none of my business. I guess I'll just have to get along with my new trainer as best I can. The one good thing—' her voice took on a brighter note '—is that Casey is also a police surgeon and he's said I can go with him sometimes when he's called out.'

'You always were interested in police work, weren't you?' said Elaine. Not waiting for a reply, she went on, 'Why do you call him Casey? Is that his first name?'

'No, his surname—but everyone uses it. No one knows what his first name is, only that it begins with the letter H.'

'It'll be Horace,' said Elaine. 'Remember Horace Barrington at school. He hated his name—we all called him Barry. Oh, by the way, while I'm thinking of it, I saw that rat Nigel the other day in town.'

Adele's heart lurched painfully. 'Did you?' she said in a small voice, wishing it didn't matter and at the same time hating herself that it still did.

'Yes,' said Elaine cheerfully. 'He looked as miserable as sin. Serves him right—he's probably found out that life with lovely Lucinda isn't what he'd thought.'

They talked on for a while and finished with Adele promising to ring their mother in the next couple of days and Elaine promising to ring Adele the next time. Once she'd hung up, tiredness seemed to get the better of her and she decided she may as well have an early night.

She was asleep almost as soon as she closed her eyes.

There was a bell ringing somewhere in Adele's dream. It was shrill and persistent. She wanted to ignore it, didn't want to wake from her deep, satisfying sleep. Maybe if she did nothing it would stop. But it didn't stop, it went on and on until finally she awoke fully and realised it wasn't in her dream at all—it was her phone ringing. For a moment she thought she was in her room at the hospital but there her pager had been beside her bed and had had a kinder, gentler tone than this one. She sat up in bed, thoroughly confused, struggling through the mists of sleep. And then she remembered. She was in the flat at Woolverton House and the phone that was ringing was on the bureau on the far side of the room. Turning her head, she looked at the illuminated display of her clock radio and saw that it was two-fifteen. Whoever could be calling her at that time? With a muttered exclamation she almost fell out of bed then knocked her knee against the edge of a chair as she stumbled across the room and switched on the light on the bureau. She lifted the receiver. 'Hello?' she mumbled.

'Oh, you *are* awake.' Casey's voice was unmistakable.

'Well, I am now,' she snapped irritably.

'You said you'd like to join me if I got a call.'

'A call?' For a moment she thought he meant a house call but she was confused because she'd understood that Toby was on call that night.

'Yes, the police have just phoned. My services are required down at the station. You said you were interested but if you don't want to come...'

Suddenly she was wide awake. 'Oh, yes,' she said hurriedly. 'Yes, of course. Just let me put some clothes on.'

'Five minutes,' he said. 'I'll meet you downstairs. Wear something warm—we'll take the bike.'

Adele quite literally threw on her clothes—a warm sweater and cord trousers, socks, ankle boots and a thick jacket. What Casey had said was true. She *had* wanted to get involved in his police work, she just hadn't thought it would be quite so soon and when she was so exhausted after her first day in the practice. She was about to leave the flat when, as an afterthought, she grabbed a pair of woollen gloves.

The house was silent and Adele crept along the corridor past Penny's door and down the stairs to the first-floor landing. Peering over the banisters, she could just make out the shape of a figure downstairs in the hallway. She sped down the stairs terrified now that he wouldn't wait, knowing how Casey hated to be kept waiting.

She was slightly breathless when she joined him but he made no comment, simply led the way down the passages to the rear of the house where he unbolted the door and they stepped out into the courtyard. There was a moon that peeped intermittently between the ragged dark clouds that raced across its face. The chill in the air was a shock after the warm September day and while Casey wheeled the bike out of its lockup lean-to Adele pulled up the collar of her jacket and thrust her hands into her pockets.

Without a word he handed her a crash helmet then proceeded to push the motorbike out of the courtyard, under the archway and out into the road. After only a moment's hesitation Adele followed him, fastening the helmet as she went. By the time she joined him at the pavement's edge he was astride the bike.

'Hold onto me,' he ordered abruptly after she had mounted and was sitting squarely behind him. 'I don't want you falling off. I haven't time to come back looking for you.'

Taking a deep breath to quell her irritation, Adele slid her arms around his waist as he turned the key in the ignition and with a slight shudder the big machine purred into life.

It wasn't the first time she'd been on a motorbike. When she and Elaine had been growing up, many holidays had been spent with their Irish cousins in Killarney and several of the boys had owned motorbikes. It had been nothing for a large crowd of them to go into the next town to a club and the bikes had been the only available form of transport. She had enjoyed those rides but that had been all of ten years ago and it felt strange now to feel the steady throb of the engine beneath her. But that was probably where the similarity ended, for those bikes belonging to her cousins had been noisy, smelly contraptions which had seemed to spend as much time in pieces in someone's back yard as on the road, and the one on which she now rode pillion through the night was a thoroughbred amongst bikes, so luxurious it was almost like sitting in an armchair with its chrome trim and the deep gold of its bodywork gleaming in the moonlight.

They met no other traffic on the mile or so journey to the police station on the far side of Stourborne Abbas and this, together with the powerful nature of the engine of the machine, meant that they covered the distance in next to no time. Adele found she was quite disappointed when they drew onto the forecourt of the police station as she had just been starting to really enjoy being on a bike again. But as they dismounted she firmly reminded herself why they were there and it had nothing to do with riding about the countryside in the middle of the night on high-powered motorbikes.

'I'm not sure what this is all about,' said Casey as they climbed the steps to the front entrance of the building. 'Something to do with a break-in in a warehouse, I think. I dare say someone has been injured. I thought it might be a good place for you to start.'

Adele nodded. She didn't know what to say. Her body was still trying to adjust to being evicted from sleep and a warm bed in the middle of the night, only to be hurtled through the cold air then deposited on the deserted steps of a police station.

On entering the station, they were greeted by the duty sergeant who, like everyone else Adele had encountered since arriving in Stourborne Abbas, seemed to know Casey very well.

'What have you got for us?' asked Casey, then, realising that the sergeant was staring at Adele with undisguised interest, said, 'Oh, this is Dr Brooks—she's a trainee at the practice but she's also interested in police work. Adele...' He half turned to her. 'This is Sergeant Alan Munro.'

Adele found her hand encased in a paw-like grip as a

huge smile spread across the face of the man behind the desk. 'Well, it's nice to meet you, Dr Brooks. Must say, when I called in our friend Casey I didn't expect him to have such a charming companion—'

'Yes, all right, Alan,' said Casey impatiently. 'Can we just get on with it, please?'

'Of course.' The sergeant winked at Adele who found herself smiling back at him. 'There was a break-in down at the mobile-phone warehouse. We'd luckily had a tip-off and our boys were ready for them. There was a bit of a scuffle and there are a few minor injuries, which need attending to. There is one of them, however, who appears to have something else wrong with him. He's been complaining of stomach pains.'

'Perhaps you'd like to have a look at that one, Adele,' said Casey. 'Don't worry,' he said, catching sight of her anxious expression, 'the sergeant here will arrange for an officer to accompany you.'

Moments later Adele was being escorted by a police officer into one of the remand cells at the rear of the station, while Casey was taken into another farther down the corridor. As the door clanged shut behind them Adele knew a moment of nervous panic—this was so unlike anything she had ever had to do before—then as she caught sight of the young man lying on the narrow bunk, his knees drawn up to his chest, an expression of agony on his face, her professionalism took over and she forgot her apprehension. She was a doctor and this was a patient requiring her help, whatever the circumstances.

'This one's been complaining of stomach pain ever since we brought him in.' The police officer looked to be even younger than the man on the bunk. 'You'd better let the doctor have a look at you,' he added.

The young man briefly raised his head and looked at Adele. 'Where's Casey?' he groaned, 'I want Casey.'

'Dr Casey to you,' said Adele crisply, 'and he's otherwise engaged so you've got me.' She leaned over him and with one hand lifted his wrist and placed her other hand on his forehead. He felt incredibly hot to the touch and his pulse was racing rapidly. 'Where is the pain?' she asked.

'Here.' He indicated the right side of his abdomen. 'And it moves—all over.'

'How long have you had the pain?' Adele perched on the bunk beside him and with his help lifted the grubby T-shirt he was wearing.

'Started this morning,' he muttered. 'Then it went off for a bit. Then it came back during the evening. Since then…it's been agony.'

'Any sickness?'

'Yeah, I threw up in the police van.'

Gently but firmly Adele began examining him, moving her hands across his abdomen. When she reached the lower right side she pressed slightly and as she lifted her hand the young man gave a howl of pain.

'Sorry,' said Adele, 'but I believe I've found what I was looking for.' She glanced up at the police officer standing near the door. 'This man will have to go to hospital,' she said briskly.

'I'll tell the sarge,' he replied dubiously, as if he doubted Adele's authority.

'Yes,' she replied firmly, 'and while you're at it tell him to call an ambulance.' She looked down at the young man again then, seeing the fear in his eyes, gently touched his shoulder. 'It's all right,' she said kindly. 'They'll get you sorted out at the hospital.'

'Can't you give me nothin' for the pain?' he groaned.

'I'm sorry, I can't,' Adele replied. 'You may well be

needing an anaesthetic and if I gave you anything now you would be very sick.' She stood up and as she followed the officer from the room the young man on the bunk curled himself into the foetal position once more. The door shut behind them and as the officer locked it Adele said, 'Was that Flo Procter's son, Stevie, by any chance?'

The officer looked at her in surprise. 'Yes,' he said. 'How did you know that? I thought you were new here.'

'Oh,' she said, 'I am, but there are some situations that don't take a lot of working out.'

CHAPTER FIVE

'IT WAS Flo Procter's son,' Adele told Casey when he emerged from the cells.

'Stevie?' Casey threw her a quick look.

'Yes.' She took a deep breath. 'I've sent for an ambulance or rather I've asked the duty sergeant to send for one.'

'What's wrong with him?' There was a frown on Casey's face now and Adele couldn't help but wonder how he would react to her decision.

'I would say almost certainly appendicitis.'

'I see.' His reply was terse, measured. 'So what led you to that conclusion?'

'He's suffered abdominal pain for most of the day with it eventually settling low down on the right side. He has some fever, pulse is rapid and he's vomited. When I examined him there was rebound pain in the appendix area which was very tender.'

By this time they had reached Reception and the duty sergeant looked up from his desk. 'Ambulance is on its way, Dr Brooks,' he said then he ruined it by throwing a questioning look at Casey and saying, 'That all right with you, Casey?'

'Of course.' To Adele's relief Casey nodded briskly. She wasn't sure what she would have done if he'd questioned her decision or even cancelled the ambulance.

'You don't want to examine him for yourself?'

'Why should I?' Casey gave a light shrug. 'Dr Brooks has made her diagnosis—it's down to A and E now to get

64

him sorted out. One thing we should do, though, is to let Flo Procter know.' He glanced at Adele. 'Maybe you'd like that honour, too?'

'Well…' Adele mentally began bracing herself for such an awesome task.

'Don't worry, I wasn't serious. I wouldn't wish that on anyone.' Casey looked at Alan. 'May I use the phone?'

'Be my guest.' The sergeant indicated the desk phone.

Casey lifted the receiver then paused. 'Has he been charged with anything yet?'

'Not really.' Alan shook his head. 'At this stage he's helping us with our enquiries, although I have to say if he hadn't been taken ill he would have been charged with breaking and entering by now.'

'OK. Fine.' Casey punched out a number and Adele realised he must have known it from memory. As he was waiting for someone in the Procter household to answer the phone, the main doors of the station were flung open and another group of men were marched inside amidst much shouting and swearing and a scuffle that broke out between the men and some of the plain-clothes officers who accompanied them.

'It's like Piccadilly Circus in here tonight,' grumbled Alan. 'And to think this wasn't even my shift. I swapped with Dave Masters because it was his mother-in-law's six-tieth birthday party. He owes me one does our Dave.'

'Flo?' Casey put a hand round his ear to allow him to hear against the noise inside the station. 'It's Casey. I'm down at the station. Stevie's here.' He paused. 'Helping with enquiries is the official line…' He held the phone away from his ear and in spite of the din around them Adele quite clearly heard Flo's shouts of anger.

'There's more, Flo,' Casey went on after a moment. 'I'm afraid Stevie's not well. What? His stomach again. We've sent for an ambulance. No, Dr Brooks examined him. She's pretty certain it's his appendix. They'll be taking him to Stourborne A and E. Can you get there, Flo? Good. OK. I'll speak to you later.' He hung up and turned to Adele. 'Flo and her daughter Tammy are going to get a taxi to the hospital. She said when Stevie's better she's going to kill him.'

'We want him back before that,' said Alan dryly.

Casey turned to Adele. 'Well, I think that's you and me finished here so I guess we'd better salvage what's left of the night. See you, Alan.' He nodded to the desk sergeant.

'Yes, see you, Casey.' Alan paused and looked at Adele. 'Hope we see you again, too, Dr Brooks.'

'I'm sure you will.' It was Casey who answered.

Together they left the building and as they were approaching the bike Casey suddenly chuckled.

'What is it?' Adele threw him a questioning look.

'I was just thinking of poor old Flo.'

'Was she very upset?' asked Adele. By this time they had reached the bike and were securing their helmets once more, and Adele realised she was actually looking forward to the ride home.

'More angry than upset, I think,' Casey replied, pulling on his leather gauntlets. 'Mind you, she should be used to it by now—there's always one or another of her brood in some sort of trouble. I only wish Stevie had stayed around long enough this morning for us to see him. Maybe we could have prevented this.' He mounted the bike and waited for Adele to climb onto the pillion.

'Tell me,' she said, leaning forward slightly over Casey's shoulder so that he could hear her. 'Stevie who?'

He turned his head so that his face was only inches from her own. 'Wonder, I should think,' he murmured then he started the engine.

'Oh, yes, of course.' With a smile Adele slipped her arms around his waist and they purred away into the night.

When they reached Woolverton House Adele waited in the doorway while Casey put the bike away. As he joined her she tried unsuccessfully to hide a yawn.

'Tired?' he said, not unsympathetically.

'Just a bit,' she admitted.

'Well, I guess you've had quite a day. Try and get a bit more sleep now.'

Together they climbed the stairs and when they reached his landing Adele paused for a moment. 'See you later,' she said wearily.

He nodded. 'Goodnight—what's left of it.'

She stumbled up the second flight of stairs, vaguely aware that he stood on his landing, watching her, making no attempt to go to his own flat. At last she reached her own door, opened it, stepped inside then stood for a moment with her back to the door and her eyes closed. Casey was right—it had been quite a day. Opening her eyes, she flicked the light switch and looked at the clock on the wall. The hands stood at four-fifteen. With luck she might be able to grab another three hours of sleep before she need get ready for morning surgery.

It was, however, not to be because, tired as she was, Adele found it incredibly difficult to get back to sleep. Her thoughts were chaotic, ranging from images from the police station—from Stevie's pain to the noise and disruption from the men who had been brought in—to the sensation of riding through the night on that high-powered machine with her arms wrapped tightly around Casey's waist. There had been something so unusual, almost alien about the whole experience that it had stirred something in Adele which now, in retrospect, she recognised as excitement and which, when she thought about it, was ridiculous because it wasn't as if it had been the first time that she'd ridden on a motorbike. If it had been, she would probably have been terrified. So, if it wasn't that, she really couldn't account for this source of excitement.

Maybe, she thought as her digital clock passed five-thirty, it could have been the fact that she was at last being involved in some police work. After all, hadn't that been an ambition for a very long time?

Yes, she thought at last as she tossed and turned, that must be what it was—because really and truly there was nothing else it could have been.

She must have drifted off to sleep at about six o'clock only to be awakened by her alarm at seven. With a groan she buried her head in the pillow, then as thirty seconds later the clock repeated its insistent message she hauled herself out of bed in an attempt to prepare herself to face another day.

News came from the hospital that Stevie had undergone an appendicectomy and Adele suspected that Casey paid a private visit either to the hospital or to see Flo at home.

The remaining days of the week followed a similar pattern to that first day, with Adele sitting in on Casey's surgeries, attending house visits with him and becoming familiar with every aspect of the running of the Woolverton House practice, from nurses' clinics to administration and clerical.

Gradually she was getting to grips with procedures, learning people's names—whether members of staff or patients and their families. Then, at the end of the week, quite casually, as if he were commenting on the weather forecast, Casey informed her without any warning that that afternoon she would be taking her first surgery and that he would be sitting in with her.

She stared at him in astonishment. She had been expecting it to be after the weekend, probably the Monday morning surgery, not the final one on a Friday afternoon.

'Better this one than Monday,' he said, reading her mind. 'This way you won't worry about it all over the weekend.' They had just returned from a couple of house visits and were sitting in the staffroom drinking mugs of coffee. Piles of repeat prescriptions requiring his signature surrounded Casey, while Adele had been leafing through copies of medical magazines, trying to keep abreast of the latest research. 'You happy with that?' he asked as if as an afterthought when Adele remained silent.

'Yes, I suppose so. You just took me by surprise, that's all,' she admitted. 'Like you say, I was expecting Monday…'

'Ah, there's no time like the present. You'll be fine—there's nothing like a fraught Friday afternoon surgery.'

'You make it sound like an ordeal.' Adele looked alarmed.

'Not at all. You wait, it'll be all slight symptoms folk think will exacerbate before Monday.'

In spite of Casey's reassuring words, Adele found she was incredibly nervous as she sat in his consulting room, waiting for her first patient. It was the same room where she had sat beside him on numerous occasions since coming to Stourborne Abbas, the only difference being that now, instead of sitting alongside him, she was sitting at the desk while Casey sat behind her in the corner of the room.

'You're nervous, aren't you?' he said quietly after they had sat in total silence for several minutes.

'Yes,' she admitted at last, 'I suppose I am.'

'You're a doctor, Adele—a fully qualified doctor. You've sat in this room with me for the last week. I promise you, there won't be anything you can't deal with and if there is, don't forget I shall be right here behind you.'

'Maybe that's what scares me.' Adele gave a nervous little laugh, looped her dark hair back behind her ear then looked up sharply as there was a knock at the door. 'Come in,' she called, and the door opened to admit a middle-aged man whose reaction on seeing Adele behind the desk was almost one of suspicion.

Adele took a deep breath. 'Hello,' she said. 'Mr Reynolds, isn't it?'

'That's right.' The man's gaze flickered to Casey.

'I'm Dr Brooks,' Adele went on. 'How can I help you?'

'Well, I've been getting this pain—right here.' The man indicated a point below the centre of his chest at the top of his abdomen, but as he did so he was still looking at Casey.

'What sort of pain is it?' asked Adele.

'I think it's a sort of indigestion pain, but it gets very severe. Last time I had it, which was last night, I was rolling around. My wife gave me some indigestion mixture but it didn't seem to work. In fact, it got worse and went right through to my back. I couldn't seem to get away from it no matter what I did.'

'Does the pain come on after you've eaten?' asked Adele as she turned to the computer screen and studied John Reynolds's medical history.

'Yes, I suppose it does, although sometimes it can be as much as an hour or an hour and a half afterwards.'

'I see from your records you have a history of high blood pressure,' said Adele as she switched to the man's medication chart.

'Yes,' Mr Reynolds nodded. 'I saw Dr Fletcher for that and he prescribed them beta-blockers.'

'I'd like to examine you, Mr Reynolds.' Adele indicated

the adjoining room. 'If you'd like to go into the examination room, take off your jacket and shirt and lie on the couch.'

Casey remained silent as Adele continued to study the patient's records then, taking her stethoscope, she made her way into the examination room where she found John Reynolds lying on the couch. Gently but firmly she carried out a thorough examination of his chest and abdomen, talking to him all the while and asking him to indicate the areas that felt tender to pressure. To complete her examination she checked his heart and blood pressure. When she had finished she straightened up. 'If you would like to get dressed,' she said, 'then come back into the consulting room.'

Casey gave her an enquiring look as she re-entered the room. 'Problems?' he said softly.

'Not really.' She sat down at the desk. 'I'm going to refer him for a gastroscopy and ultrasound but I would also like him to have an ECG today.' She paused, looking at the monitor screen again. 'Can I arrange that on the computer?'

'Yes.' Casey nodded. 'Just go into ''Nurses' Clinics'' and you can see what appointments are available.'

By the time the patient returned to the consulting room Adele had set the chain of events in motion for further investigation of his condition. All that remained was for her to explain to him what would happen.

'Ah, Mr Reynolds, please, come and sit down,' she said gently. 'Now,' she said, 'I would like you to have some tests to try to find out what is causing your pain. I'm going to arrange for you to go to the local hospital to have a gastroscopy.'

'What's that?' John Reynolds frowned, his glance travelling rapidly from Adele to Casey then back to Adele.

'It's a procedure where a tube is passed down into your stomach. Don't worry,' she hastened to add when she saw his expression change from one of suspicion to one of alarm. 'You'll be sedated so you won't know what's going on. I also want you to have an ultrasound, which is a very simple procedure and completely painless but it does tell us anything untoward which may be going on inside you.'

'Will I have to stay in hospital for these?' Mr Reynolds still looked worried.

'No.' Adele hastened to reassure him. 'They can both be carried out in the outpatient department and neither should take very long. I'll write to the hospital and you should receive an appointment through the post. Now, the other thing I would like you to have is an ECG—an electrocardiogram.'

'That's for my heart, isn't it? You don't think it was a heart attack, do you?' The man looked thoroughly alarmed now.

'No,' Adele replied firmly, 'I don't. But in view of your blood-pressure problems I want to make absolutely certain. Don't worry, you can have that done here. I've checked with our nurses' clinic and they have an appointment for later this afternoon at four-fifteen. Could you come back for that?'

'I suppose so.' Mr Reynolds looked bewildered. 'I think I'll go and phone my wife first.'

'I think that's a good idea.' Adele smiled at him. 'And, please, try not to worry. We'll find the problem for you and we'll deal with it. In the meantime I'm going to prescribe a course of tablets that should help to control the symptoms and I would like you to try and stick to a fat-free diet for the time being.'

'What do you mean by fat-free?'

'Animal fats really,' Adele explained. 'Things like butter, cheese, cream or full-fat milk. If you ask at the reception desk on your way out, one of the receptionists will give you a diet sheet which will explain things more fully.' As she finished speaking she tore off the prescription she had just printed out and handed it to him. 'Now, is there anything else you want to ask me?'

'I don't think so, Doctor. I can't think straight at the moment.'

'I'll come along and see you after you've had your ECG,' said Adele with a reassuring smile.

'Right.' John Reynolds nodded. 'Well, thank you, Doctor.'

As the patient left the consulting room Adele glanced at Casey. 'Well, that was hardly a trivial, last-minute Friday afternoon appointment.'

'Absolutely not.' He paused. 'Did you come to any conclusions?'

'I think we're probably looking at gall-bladder disease,' said Adele slowly. 'His abdomen was certainly very tender in that area and the pain and symptoms he was describing seem to point to that, but with his history of hypertension I want to make absolutely certain.'

'You did well.'

It was but slight praise but somehow, and in spite of the fact that she was still acutely aware of Casey's presence in the room, it made her feel more confident to face the next four patients, who ranged from a toddler with severe eczema and a young man with diarrhoea and vomiting to a woman with flu-like symptoms and an elderly man with gout.

By the time she reached the last patient on the list she felt totally at ease with the situation, but as she reached out and pressed the buzzer Casey leaned forward and, peering at the computer screen, sucked in his breath sharply.

'What is it?' Adele frowned.

'Elvira Jackson,' he said. 'Not the easiest way to end a week.'

'Elvira Jackson?' said Adele quickly. 'Where have I heard that name—Elvira?'

'It's OK,' said Casey quickly, as without even the sound of a knock the door was suddenly pushed open 'I'll tell you later.'

A woman stood in the doorway, laden with several bags and plastic carriers. Her age was difficult to determine but she could have been anywhere between thirty-five and forty-five. Her long, straggly, dark hair was streaked with grey, her eyes were strangely light-coloured and in spite of the warmth of the September afternoon she was dressed in a grey, ankle-length knitted coat over a long skirt of the same colour with several dark-coloured scarves wound around her neck.

'Hello, Elvira.' It was Casey who spoke first, which surprised Adele for until then he had remained silent as each new patient had entered the room, allowing her to conduct the consultation.

'Who's she?' Those curiously coloured eyes moved to Adele.

'This is Dr Brooks.' Again it was Casey who spoke and Adele decided it was high time she intervened.

'How can I help you?' she asked firmly.

'I'm pregnant,' the woman declared as she dumped the various bags she was carrying onto the floor and sat heavily down on a chair.

'You know that isn't true, Elvira.' Again Casey intervened.

'I might be. I want a test.'

'Very well,' Adele said soothingly. She was beginning to get a little irritated with Casey's interruptions. Either she was taking this surgery or she wasn't. 'I'll give you a specimen pot and you can bring in an early morning sample and we'll have it tested for you,' she went on firmly, ignoring Casey's apparent attempts to attract her attention.

The woman shot a triumphant expression towards Casey as Adele handed her a specimen pot.

'Now, is there anything else?' asked Adele.

Elvira shook her head then stood up and gathered up her bags. Making no attempt to leave the room, she continued staring at Adele. 'I know you,' she said at last.

'Do you?' Adele was a little taken aback by something in the woman's attitude and at the same time conscious of a sudden, unexpected feeling of discomfort which she immediately tried to dismiss. She was a doctor, wasn't she, for heaven's sake? And if she was going to be a GP she had to get used to all types of people and every possible situation that could present itself.

'You're the one who's living in my flat.' The woman's tone was dull, devoid now of the passion that had been in her voice when she'd announced that she was pregnant. Before Adele could respond she turned and without another word walked out of the room.

Adele turned to Casey. 'What did she mean?' she said uneasily as the door clicked shut.

'She's the one who was living in your flat before you,' Casey replied simply.

'The troublemaker?' Adele raised her eyebrows as she recalled the comments Casey had made when he'd first shown her up the stairs to her flat.

'One and the same.' He gave a little shrug.

'In what way was she a troublemaker?' Suddenly Adele needed to know.

Casey sighed and Adele gained the impression that he was reluctant to talk about Elvira Jackson. 'Let's just say it was a mistake in the first place to allow her to have use of the flat.'

'So who's fault was that? Who was responsible?'

'Unfortunately it was Toby,' Casey admitted. 'Elvira was his patient. She has a long history of psychiatric problems, together with a personality disorder. When she was evicted from her previous flat Toby felt sorry for her and told her she could stay temporarily in the flat, which is now yours. When the local council found alternative accommodation for her she didn't want to move out. We had to get a bit tough in the end.'

'But in what way was she a troublemaker?' Adele frowned.

'She has some very strange ways. For a start she has a fascination with fire. We didn't know that until after she'd moved in and left candles burning which set fire to the curtains and almost burned the whole place down.'

'But surely that could have been an accident,' Adele protested.

'She also developed a fixation with Toby,' Casey went on calmly. 'She followed him everywhere, wouldn't leave him alone. On one occasion she even parked herself in his examination room and stayed there while he took a surgery. He didn't know she was there until a patient went in to get undressed—it quite unnerved him.'

'Yes, I'm sure it did, but—'

'On another occasion she started sending anonymous mail to the reception staff, accusing them of heaven knows what, then sticking up posters in the waiting room listing things they were supposed to be doing.'

'Were the police involved?'

'Only in a very superficial way. Elvira is well known to

the police, unfortunately because of her medical conditions. There seems to be little that can be done apart from warnings...but she appears to be reasonably harmless. Strange maybe, but harmless.'

'Is she still registered with Toby?' asked Adele slowly.

'No, she's with Jeanette now. We thought it for the best to move her. You probably only got her today because I'm duty doctor and she was an extra.' Casey leaned back in his chair. 'Maybe we should have removed her from the list entirely but if we did it would mean she would have to travel miles to another practice.'

'Why did you think she couldn't be pregnant?' asked Adele curiously.

'Because in the past she's had two terminations, which have left her infertile.'

'Oh.' She stared at Casey. 'Why didn't you say? I feel a fool now, telling her to do a specimen.'

Casey shrugged. 'I was going to stop you then I thought it was probably best to humour her—let her have what she wanted.'

'But does she seriously think she could be pregnant?' Adele stared at him in concern. 'If so, I find that incredibly sad.'

'Yes, it is. But with Elvira, who knows? Unfortunately, anything is possible.'

'Doesn't she have a psychiatric social worker?'

'Yes, she does, a young woman by the name of Ruby Felton who monitors Elvira and who on the whole does a good job with her because most of the time she's OK—it's just when she gets some sort of fixation that the trouble starts.'

'Like with Toby, you mean?'

'Yes, poor old Toby—he didn't know what had hit him.'

Casey sighed and stood up. 'Well, that looks like the end of your first surgery,' he said. 'How are you feeling?'

'All right,' Adele replied. 'But I think there's going to be much more to being a GP than I had ever realised...it's going to be a real challenge.'

'Think you'll rise to it?' He raised his eyebrows and the scar on his face stood out sharply, making Adele once again want to ask him how he had got it.

'Oh, yes,' she said firmly. 'I have no doubts about that.'

CHAPTER SIX

'I'VE been called out. Want to come along?'

'Yes, of course.' It was Sunday afternoon and Adele was in her bathroom, having just washed her hair, but she didn't hesitate when she took Casey's call on her mobile phone. 'Give me five minutes,' she said.

As she left her flat she met Penny on the landing.

'Oh, there you are,' said Penny. 'I was just coming to see you. I wondered if you fancied strolling down to the pub for a swift half.'

'Penny, I'm sorry, I can't—' Adele began.

'Never mind,' Penny cut her short. 'How about a quick coffee? It won't take me long, the kettle has just boiled.'

'No, you don't understand,' Adele explained. 'I have to go out right away. Casey has had a call-out.'

'And you're going with him.' It wasn't a question, more a resigned statement.

'Well, yes—he's just phoned and suggested I might like to go.'

'I see.' A tight, almost shuttered expression had come across Penny's face. 'Well, not to worry. Some other time.'

'Yes, some other time,' Adele agreed hastily. 'I'd like that.' Edging past the other woman, she added, 'I'm sorry but I must fly...' She found herself almost apologising for the fact that she was going out with Casey, which was utterly ridiculous because, no matter what there might be between Casey and Penny, Casey was her trainer and this was her job. She fled down the stairs, aware that Penny was still watching her. Hurrying through the house and out into the courtyard, she found Casey sitting in the Land Rover with the engine running.

'It's a police call,' he explained as she climbed in beside him, 'and in view of the fact of where it is I decided the Land Rover would be more sensible than the bike.' They drew out of the courtyard and onto the main road where there was very little traffic as most of the high street shops were closed on a Sunday.

'Your hair is wet,' Casey observed after driving in silence for a while.

'It'll soon dry.' She shrugged.

'You don't have to come with me every time, you know. It isn't compulsory.'

'I know. I want to come. It's the only way I'm going to build up any experience.'

'Fair enough. I just didn't want it said that I was putting you under any undue pressure, that's all.'

'Has anyone said that?' Adele turned and looked at him but his expression as he studied the road ahead was implacable. He was casually dressed today in jeans and a sweatshirt and she was glad that she, too, was similarly clad.

'Penny suggested you might have too much on your plate,' he replied.

Adele frowned, irritated. 'What does it have to do with Penny?' she asked.

'Nothing.' He raised his shoulders. 'I suppose she just knows that I can be a bit of a slave-driver, that's all.'

And Penny would know that, of course. Penny would know him better than most. She took a deep breath, dismissing Penny from her mind but troubled slightly by their recent encounter, although she couldn't say why. She also found once again that even the thought of Penny and Casey together disturbed her. 'Where are we going?' she asked in a concerted effort to change the subject.

'To an old chalk quarry,' he replied. 'It's about five miles out of town up towards Langstone Ridge. It's pretty rough terrain up there.'

'Do we know what it's all about?'

He nodded. 'The police have recovered a body.' He said it in the same matter-of-fact tone he might have used if he'd been asked to comment on the weather.

'Oh.' She threw him a startled glance. Somehow it was the last thing she'd expected to hear.

'I am needed to certify the death.'

'I see.' She fell silent, reflecting on what he had just said. After a while she said, 'Do you think this could be anything to do with the missing girl that has been on the news in the last few days?'

'It's possible,' Casey replied. 'But one of the things that I've learnt in this business is never to jump to conclusions.'

They travelled in silence for some distance then as if he, too, was attempting to change the subject, he said, 'Have you heard about Edward's and Celia's dinner party?'

'Yes,' Adele dragged her mind from missing girls and bodies being found in chalk quarries. 'Celia phoned last night and invited me. She said it was by way of a welcome to me.'

Casey gave a sound, which could have been a grunt.

'Will you go?' she asked him curiously.

'Dinner parties are definitely not my cup of tea but I guess on this occasion I will have to make an exception.'

'Do you think all the staff will be there?'

'I shouldn't think so—just the partners and their spouses, I would imagine, and possibly Rachel and her husband.'

'I see.' Adele wondered if that included Penny because, although not a spouse, at staff social events she well could be included as Casey's partner. She could have asked him, she supposed, but found she didn't want to. Turning her head, she gazed out of the window. The sky was darkening, with rain clouds rolling in from the west and a light drizzle already beginning to mist the windscreen. She wished she'd had the sense to check the weather and to take a rain jacket instead of rushing headlong from the flat. They had left the town far behind now. Travelling in the opposite direction from the Bowscombe Estate, they seemed to be climbing steadily through a thickly wooded area where the closeness of the trees made the afternoon light appear darker than it already was.

'This is a pretty isolated area up here,' observed Casey as they emerged from the trees. 'In the summer it can be quite spectacular with a chance to see plenty of wildlife, but on a day like this it's grim to say the least.' As if to reinforce his words, great gusts of rain began driving across the vast open area of scrubland, obscuring their vision and making driving conditions hazardous.

'The quarries are somewhere over there.' Casey narrowed his eyes and peered across to their left where amidst a mass of rocks and bushes a flashing blue light could be seen. 'Yes, this is it. There are the police. Hold tight, this could get bumpy.' Leaving the road, they drove across the rough, rocky ground and as they entered the bushes a policeman appeared in front of the vehicle indicating for them to stop.

Casey wound down the window and the rain lashed through the opening, spraying both him and Adele.

'Hello, Casey.' The officer nodded. 'I thought that was you.'

'Julian.' Casey nodded in reply. 'Who's in charge?'

'Detective Inspector Daniels,' the officer replied, peering past Casey at Adele.

'It's OK,' Casey said. 'This is Dr Brooks, my trainee.'

'Right. I'll take you down there. You'd better walk from here. It's very rough going.'

Casey turned to Adele. 'Have you got a coat?' he asked.

'No.' She was almost ashamed to admit that she had been foolish enough not to come prepared for any eventuality. Anticipating his disdain, she added, 'It doesn't matter—I'll just get wet.'

'Don't be ridiculous,' he snapped. 'You'll catch your death. Here, take this.' Leaning back, he retrieved his waxed jacket from the rear of the vehicle and tossed it to her.

'But what about you?' she asked helplessly.

'There's an old oilskin there—I'll use that,' he muttered. 'What have you got on your feet?'

Fortunately she had pulled on a pair of boots before leaving the flat so was able to say, 'It's OK, I'm wearing boots.'

He made a noise that could have been a grunt of approval and when she jumped down from the vehicle she saw that he, too, was wearing stout leather walking boots. The rain hit them immediately, taking Adele's breath away, and as they began following the policeman across the wild scrubland the only sound to be heard was the moaning of the wind in the distant trees. If Adele's hair had started to dry since leaving the flat it was wet again in seconds, sticking to her head as the rain ran down her face in rivulets.

Two police recovery vehicles were parked amongst the bushes around the edge of the quarry, and a green tarpaulin had been erected behind the vehicles to form a makeshift tent. Uniformed police, accompanied by Alsatian dogs, were searching the area while the plain-clothes officers in the back of one of the vehicles emerged only when they caught sight of Casey and Adele.

'Hello, Melvin.' Casey nodded to one of the officers, a tall, thin man with red hair and a pale, freckled complexion who looked as if he'd rather have been anywhere else in the world than at this rain-swept quarry on a Sunday afternoon, dealing with whatever tragedy lay beyond the green tarpaulin.

'Afternoon, Casey.' DI Daniels glanced at Adele.

'This is Dr Brooks,' Casey explained. 'She's my trainee.'

'Does she want to be in on this?' DI Daniels eyed Adele doubtfully.

'Of course.' It was Adele who briskly replied.

'As you wish.' The detective gave a slight shrug as if to say that it was up to her but that she'd been warned.

'What have we got?' asked Casey as they began to follow the detective towards the tarpaulin.

'The body of a young girl,' Melvin Daniels replied. 'And before you ask, yes, it does look very much like it's the teenager who's been missing for the last couple of weeks.' Lifting the flap of the tent, he stood back to allow them to enter ahead of him.

It would have been gloomy in the tent but the police had set up an arc light, which cast a pool of light directly onto a shockingly small bundle on the ground. The body was lying beneath a plastic sheet and as DI Daniels crouched down and lifted the sheet, Adele braced herself for whatever she might be about to see. In her work as a hospital doctor she had seen death on many occasions but usually it had been as a result of illness, of natural causes or from an accident. She had never seen death as the result of violence or murder.

The girl was lying on her side almost in the foetal position and looked young, very young, little more than a child really with her pale, blue-tinged face and her wispy blonde hair matted and caked with mud. Taking over from the detective, Casey gently drew back the plastic sheet that covered her body and Adele caught a glimpse of a pink and orange striped T-shirt. The sight of it struck a chord with her and she realised it was identical to one she had bought for Elaine's daughter Holly on her last birthday. As her stomach lurched in revolt Adele's gaze flew again to the girl's face. This girl was fair; Holly was dark. It wasn't Holly but the thought that it might have been and that she was someone's daughter, someone's niece, was Adele's undoing.

Gagging, she turned abruptly away, leaving Casey to do what he had to do. Stumbling outside, past DI Daniels, she collided with one of the officers.

'Are you all right, miss?' He was an older man, big, burly and somehow reassuring as he held her by her arms, steadying her.

'Yes,' Adele gasped. 'Yes, thanks, I'm fine.' She wasn't fine, she felt dreadful, but she could hardly say as much.

'Not pleasant, is it?' The officer jerked his head in the direction of the tarpaulin that concealed its tragic burden.

'No.' Adele gulped, breathing in great breaths of the cold damp air in an effort to steady herself. 'No, it isn't.'

'Your first time, is it?' asked the officer sympathetically.

Adele nodded, suddenly unable to trust her voice. Thrusting her hands into the pockets of her jacket, it took her a full minute to realise that this was, in fact, not her jacket but Casey's, and that the objects inside, the scraps of paper, the pen, the set of keys, weren't hers. Almost guiltily she withdrew her hands.

Casey emerged a few minutes later and Adele found she

was unable to meet his gaze. She waited in the gusting rain as he climbed into the back of one of the police vehicles, presumably to complete essential paperwork. By the time he joined her she had managed to pull herself together at least enough to face the somewhat uncompromising stare of the detective inspector.

'Thanks, Casey.' Melvin Daniels nodded then glanced at Adele. 'You OK, Dr Brooks?'

'Yes, fine,' Adele lied. She was far from fine but she didn't want him or any of his men or even Casey, come to that, to know just how badly she had been affected.

In silence they walked back to the Land Rover, and as Casey unlocked her door she almost fell inside and thankfully sank down into her seat. It was a relief to get out of the wind and the rain but more than that it was as if the familiarity of the vehicle offered some sanctuary from the grim reality of what had happened.

Casey sat for a moment with his hands resting on the steering-wheel, making no attempt to start the engine as if he, too, had been deeply affected by what he had witnessed. 'I'm sorry,' he said at last, turning his head to look at Adele.

'Wh-what d-do you m-mean?' To her horror her teeth were chattering as she tried to speak.

'I shouldn't have taken you there. It was too much, too soon. I should have realised what it might have been.'

'Y-you said you c-can't take anything f-for g-granted.'

'I know, but I should have anticipated.'

'She'd b-been murdered, hadn't she?' In her anxiety Adele began twisting her cold wet hands together.

'It looked that way.' Casey took a deep breath and started the engine.

'How?' Adele's voice was little more than a whisper

and for a moment she thought he might not have heard her above the sound of the engine.

But as they bumped over the rough terrain and the windscreen wipers began to whirr again he shook his head. 'That wasn't for me to say. The post-mortem will determine that.'

'But—' Adele wanted to say that he must have seen signs, must have known or suspected, but he cut her short.

'My job was simply to certify the death. It's best not to speculate, Adele. Believe me, I know. If you start speculating you'll drive yourself mad.'

They were silent after that as Casey drove through the wind and the rain back to Woolverton House. By the time they arrived it was almost dark, and after Casey had parked the Land Rover they made their way through the house and up the stairs. As they reached the first-floor landing Adele would have left Casey and carried on up to her own floor but he touched her arm, stopping her.

'Oh,' she said. 'Your coat—sorry.'

'No, it isn't that.' He indicated the closed door to his flat. 'Come in for a moment.'

She didn't want to. She wanted to get back to her own flat, peel off her wet clothes and step into a hot bath, but somehow he didn't give her the chance to refuse and she found herself meekly waiting as he unlocked the door. As the door swung open Adele glanced up the stairs, wondering what Penny would think if she saw her going into Casey's flat with him, but to her relief there was no sign of Penny and the door to her flat was firmly closed.

The door swung open then Casey flicked the light switch and stood back, allowing Adele to precede him into the flat. It was larger than her apartment, she could see that at a glance, but it was tastefully furnished if in a rather minimalist masculine way with dark wood furniture and a large, glass-topped coffee-table between two leather sofas.

'Let me relieve you of that coat.' Casey slipped the waxed jacket from her shoulders and, together with the oilskin he was wearing, took it through to what appeared to be the kitchen. He reappeared almost immediately, carrying a large, white towel. 'Here,' he said, handing it to her. 'Get yourself dry.'

She stared at him and for the moment it seemed as if she was rooted to the spot, incapable of action.

'Adele...?' he said gently, bending his head slightly to look into her face. To her horror her eyes filled with tears and she was forced to press one hand to her mouth to quell the sob that suddenly threatened to erupt. With a quiet exclamation he reached out and, putting his hand beneath her chin, tilted her face up to his. 'Hey,' he said softly, his eyes curiously tender. 'What is this...?'

'I'm sorry,' she whispered as the tears began to run unchecked down her face. 'It's just that...the girl...she was wearing a T-shirt identical to one that I gave my niece for her birthday...' She gulped, the tears suddenly choking her. 'She...she didn't look much older than Holly... I keep thinking it could have been her. And it was so awful up there, so wet and wild...and...and so lonely...' She shook her head in distress, unable to blot out the pictures that filled her head.

Without a word Casey stepped forward and before Adele had a chance to even think what he was doing he put his arms around her and held her close, so close that all she could hear was the steady beating of his heart through the damp fabric of his sweatshirt as he allowed her tears to flow.

It felt safe, warm and secure in the shelter of his arms and at that moment, if she'd been asked, Adele quite easily could have said that she was happy to stay there indefinitely. But gradually, inevitably, common sense began to return and Adele was the first to move.

'I'm sorry,' she muttered as she fumbled for a tissue, wiping both her eyes and blowing her nose. 'That was very unprofessional of me.'

'Not at all.' He didn't release her, just moved back a bit so he could look into her face again while keeping his arms around her. He really should let her go, she thought, albeit half-heartedly, but he didn't. Instead, he said, 'It wasn't unprofessional at all. It was a perfectly normal, human reaction to tragedy and violence. I just wish I'd thought it through before I allowed you to go in there.'

'I have to get used to that sort of thing if I'm going to be involved in police work,' Adele protested weakly.

'That's true,' he admitted, 'but there are ways of preparing you and I guess I neglected them.'

Still he made no attempt to release her and by this time Adele was beginning to feel not only embarrassed at the way she had shown her weakness and her vulnerability but also uncomfortable at the way she must look. She was cold and wet and could feel that her hair was plastered to her head. And if that wasn't enough, she had been crying—her nose always turned red when she cried. And as it finally dawned on her just how unattractive she must appear she finally managed to pull away from him. Picking up the towel which had somehow fallen to the floor, she began to dry her hair and face while Casey, after watching her for a moment, disappeared into the kitchen then returned to stand in the doorway, vigorously drying his own hair with a dark red towel.

'Are your clothes wet?' he asked after a few moments.

'No,' she replied hastily. 'They're fine.' Her jeans, in fact, were quite damp but she had no doubt that if she'd said yes he would have had no qualms in telling her to take them off so that he could dry them. 'That jacket kept me really dry.'

With the red towel draped casually around his neck, Casey strolled back into the room, crouched down in front of the fireplace and lit the gas fire. 'Come and get warm,' he said as the comforting glow from the flames flickered around the room.

Adele perched on the edge of one of the leather sofas while Casey crossed to a cabinet on the far side of the room, opened it and took out two glasses and a bottle.

A moment later he returned with the glasses and handed one to her. 'Brandy,' he said firmly. 'It'll do you good. You've had a shock.'

She didn't drink spirits very often, preferring to stick to wine, but on this occasion she made no protest and as she sipped the amber-coloured liquid and the combined warmth from that and the fire began to steal through her veins she slowly felt herself begin to recover.

Casey sat opposite her and, taking a mouthful of his own brandy, cradled the glass in his hand. 'Tell me about your niece,' he said after a while.

'Her name is Holly,' Adele replied, setting her glass down on the coffee-table. 'She's my sister Elaine's oldest child and she's twelve years old. She's…she's great,' she added, 'and I love her to bits.'

'You say she's your sister's eldest child?'

'Yes, Elaine has two other children—Katy who's nine and Harry who's five.'

'So is Elaine your only sister?' He sounded as if he was really interested, as if he wanted to know, and suddenly Adele felt something wash over her that could only be described as homesickness. Maybe it was a direct result of the events of the afternoon, she didn't know, but whatever it was she found herself moving farther back on the sofa, settling herself more comfortably, at ease now as she talked of her family.

'Yes,' she said, 'there are just the two of us. Elaine is four years older than me.'

'So she started her family when she was very young,' he observed.

'She did,' Adele agreed. 'She started training to be a teacher, then she met Rod—he's a solicitor—they married within a year and Elaine very soon found she liked having babies.'

'And what about you?' He raised an eyebrow, the one split by the scar, which in the subdued lighting of the room somehow gave him a slightly demonic look.

'What about me?' she said quickly, wondering to what he was referring.

'Don't you think you would like having babies?'

'I don't know.' She shrugged. 'I knew first and foremost I wanted to be a doctor and I guess that took precedence.'

'You can have both these days,' he observed.

'You sound like my mother.' Adele wrinkled her nose. 'She's always going on about the fact that being a doctor shouldn't automatically bar me from settling down and having a family, thus presenting her with more grandchildren, of course.'

'And I guess that could well have happened if everything had gone according to plan with Nigel,' said Casey quietly.

'What?' She looked up sharply, slightly shocked at the sound of Nigel's name on Casey's lips. 'Oh, yes,' she said slowly, remembering that he knew about Nigel because it had been her who had told him. 'Yes, I guess so. I think my mother thought Nigel was a highly suitable prospective son-in-law. Just shows how wrong she was, doesn't it?'

she added. There was a hint of bitterness in her tone but to her surprise not as much as there once had been. Maybe she was becoming immune to the pain she'd once felt whenever she'd thought of Nigel.

Fortified by this thought, she took another sip of brandy. Looking across at Casey, she said, 'How about you? Does your mother go on at you to settle down again and have a family?'

He didn't answer and abruptly Adele set her glass down. 'Oh, heavens,' she said, 'I've done it again. Your mother isn't alive, is she?'

'No, as it happens, she isn't,' he admitted, then as her expression changed, he said, 'But don't go apologising again. It happened a long time ago, when I was in my early teens, in fact.'

'So what happened to you afterwards? Did your father bring you up?'

'My parents had divorced but, yes, after my mother died my brother and I went to live with our father. We lived in a very tough neighbourhood and most of the time we lived by our wits.'

'So when did you decide you wanted to be a doctor?' Suddenly Adele was curious. As she knew only too well, it took time, money and dedication to become a doctor and it didn't sound as if Casey's background was indicative of any of these.

'It had been my mother's dream that I should become a doctor and that my brother should study law. For a long time I simply wasn't interested—it all seemed too much like hard work and I was far happier hanging out with a local gang and getting up to Lord knows what rather than applying myself to study. The school I attended wasn't much use either and there was no real encouragement to try to better myself.'

'So what changed?' asked Adele.

'Ironically it was my mother's death that did it. She was only in her thirties. It was breast cancer—they didn't have the facilities or resources that they do today and she died within a year.' He paused and stared down into his glass. 'It gutted me, I don't mind telling you,' he went on after a while. 'I was rebellious, I didn't want to go and live with my dad, didn't want to leave my mates. I even said I didn't want to leave the school I was going to, even though I hated it, but the alternative would have been going into care, and I didn't want that either, so in the end I didn't really have a lot of choice.'

'So was it not as bad as you thought in the end?'

'Oh, it was tough, make no mistake about that—a father I hardly knew, a stepmother I viewed with distrust and a new school where I was viewed with distrust because I was an outsider. As you can imagine, it wasn't exactly a picnic.'

'So what happened?' She was intensely curious now. 'How did you get from that to where you are today as a partner in a firm of GPs in a county market town?'

He allowed that rare smile to touch his features as he considered his reply. 'Two things,' he said. 'A teacher began to take an interest in me and led me to believe that if I wanted something enough I could have it.'

'And the second?' she asked quietly, somehow knowing what was coming.

'I suppose if I'm honest,' he said, 'I knew deep down that I could do it and I decided I owed it to my mum to do so.'

CHAPTER SEVEN

'SHE would have been proud of you,' said Adele softly.

'I hope so.' Casey took another mouthful of his drink and stared into the fire as if lost in memories from his past. To Adele he suddenly looked vulnerable, not a bit like the tough-guy image she had come to associate with Casey, and she had to fight an urge to sink down onto her knees beside him and put her arms around him.

Instead, as the urge subsided, gently she said, 'And what about your family now?'

'How do you mean?' He raised his head and looked at her.

'Well, your father—where is he?'

'He's in a residential home—I visit him when I can.'

'And his wife?'

'The marriage didn't last.' His reply was brief, abrupt almost, and Adele sensed this was an area he didn't want to talk about.

'And what about your brother—did he study law?'

'Oh, yes,' said Casey softly, peering into his glass as he spoke, 'he studied law.'

'So your mum would have been proud of him as well.'

'Well, that's debatable.' He looked up and his gaze met Adele's. 'The way he studied the law ended up with a spell in prison.'

'Oh, dear.' She paused. 'And now?'

'We've rather lost touch but it would never surprise me to hear he's back behind bars.'

Adele remained silent for a while because there really

didn't seem any more to say on the subject. In the end it was Casey who broke the silence.

'Are you feeling better?' he asked.

'Yes, much, thank you. In fact, I really should think about going...'

'Why?'

'Well, I'm sure you have things to do, and I, well, I—'

'Are you warm?' he asked interrupting her.

'Yes.'

'And comfortable?'

'Oh, yes.'

'Then stay awhile. There's no need to rush off.'

'All right,' she said weakly. She knew she should go really. She had things to do. On the other hand, what she'd just told Casey was true—she was warm and comfortable sitting there on his sofa in front of the fire, sipping brandy and talking about their families, their lives. But there was more than that. There was the lingering memory of how it had been when his arms had gone around her and she'd felt safe and protected. And maybe that was the most telling reason why she should go. It had felt good in his arms but she had had no right to feel that way any more than she'd had any right to be there in the first place. No, there really were no two ways about it—she should go.

But still she sat there, relaxed and contented, as it grew darker outside, the rain lashed against the windows and the wind howled in the chimney.

'The girl,' she said at last. 'Was she one of our patients?'

Casey shook his head. 'No, she wasn't registered here. And I have to say I'm relieved about that. Probably at this very moment some other poor GP is having to deal with hysterical parents.'

'I don't know how people recover from something like that,' said Adele slowly.

'I don't think people ever do fully recover from the death of a child,' he replied. 'I guess they simply learn to live with the pain.' He paused. 'I never knew my daughter,' he went on after a moment, 'but when she was born, I saw her and held her and I can honestly say I don't think a day goes by that I don't think about her…' He shook his head and as Adele caught the glint of unshed tears in his eyes she had the distinct impression that this was the first time that he'd spoken like this to anyone and once again she had to fight the urge to put her arms around him.

'But this…' he went on after a moment, 'this is different. To lose a child in this terrible way as the result of violence…well, that's something else…' He gave a gesture of hopelessness that implied the whole thing would be beyond him. Then, in an obvious attempt to change the subject and at the same time supposedly to regain his composure, he hauled himself to his feet. 'Let me make you some coffee,' he said.

'No, really.' Adele also rose to her feet. 'I must be going. I have things to do before tomorrow. Why…' She managed a weak smile. 'Before I know where I am it'll be time for morning surgery and I shall be behind that desk again.'

She began to make her way to the door but somehow he got there before her and stood there barring her way.

She looked up at him, trying to read the expression in his eyes as he looked steadily back at her, but found it impossible. All she knew was that she'd seen the expression before on several occasions but most notably at the moment when they'd first met.

'Casey…?' she said softly, and all she could think of then was that the last time she had been this close to him he had put his arms around her and held her, and quite suddenly she knew that was exactly what she wanted to happen again. She found herself carefully scrutinising his face, from those dark, brooding eyes, the rugged features and the scar to the dark shadow of stubble on his jaw.

'Casey...?' she whispered again. As she became aware of some battle that seemed to be raging behind his eyes she reached out her hand and with the tips of her fingers gently traced the line of the scar all the way from where it divided his eyebrow down the side of his face to where it ended at the corner of his jawbone. 'Tell me,' she said, about to ask him how he had come by such a scar, but that was as far as she got for with a sound that could quite easily have been a groan, and for the second time that evening, he put his arms around her.

It felt the same, just as good, safe, warm and comforting as before. The smell of him was the same, a slightly woody smell, and he felt the same, the same hard muscular body through the fabric of his sweatshirt. But that was where the similarities ended, for on the previous occasion his motive had presumably been simply to console, to comfort. This time there was urgency, almost a roughness about the way his arms tightened around her, which touched a chord somewhere deep inside and she found herself spontaneously lifting her face to his.

His kiss was hard and firm and so full of passion it took Adele's breath away, leaving her gasping and at first yearning for more. Then, as his hands became entangled in her hair and his kiss grew deeper and more demanding, she felt shocked at her own response.

In the end it was she who drew away. 'Casey,' she murmured. 'We mustn't...'

He appeared not to hear her at first as if so driven by passion and desire that he was oblivious to any sort of reason, and it was only when she put her hands on his chest and gently pushed him away from her that he appeared to return to his senses.

'What...?' He stared at her, confusion in his eyes as desire ebbed away.

'I said...we mustn't,' she said shakily.

And then as it seemed to dawn on him for the first time what they had done he appeared to visibly shake himself. 'No,' he said abruptly, 'no, of course not. I'm sorry, Adele. That shouldn't have happened.'

'It's all right.' She attempted to straighten her hair, to push it back from her face. 'I really think I should go.'

'Yes, of course.' Casey stood aside, running a hand over his own short dark hair, the gesture helpless and yet at the same time somehow boyish.

'I...I'll see you in the morning,' said Adele, her voice husky, not like her voice at all. He nodded, seeming now to be incapable of speech. Putting her head down, suddenly unable to face what might be in his eyes, she tugged open the door and fled out of his flat and up the stairs.

Mercifully there was no sign of Penny. Adele really didn't think she could have coped if she'd met her on the landing and been forced to answer questions about where she and Casey had been. Once in her own flat she ran a bath, added a generous amount of bath foam and, peeling off her clothes, stepped into the comforting warmth of the water.

She was still in a state of turmoil over what had happened between herself and Casey and it was a turmoil that was to last for the rest of the evening, long after she'd had her bath, prepared supper—only to find that she had lost her appetite—watched some television, without being able to say what she had seen, then finally taken herself off to bed. What had happened had been a shock and yet, on the other hand, there had been a sort of inevitability about it—almost as if, now that she looked back on it, both of them had somehow been waiting for it to happen and that it had only been a matter of time before it had.

But it had been wrong. They both knew that and there was no telling where it might have ended, although Adele had a pretty shrewd suspicion. She had protested, not because she didn't find him attractive but because of his involvement with Penny, and Casey himself had said it shouldn't have happened.

So why had he let it happen? If he had restrained himself she wouldn't now be feeling as wretched as she did. Was it quite simply that all men were the same and when it came to restraint they were incapable, or to fidelity where they thought that if no one found out it didn't matter? That had happened with Nigel. He had thought as long as Adele and Lucinda didn't find out about each other no one would get hurt. He had calmly assumed he could have his cake and eat it as well. Was that what Casey thought, too?

Maybe it was, maybe it wasn't. All Adele knew was that he wasn't going to get the chance to find out. She finally fell asleep that night after firmly resolving to ignore the powerful emotions he had stirred in her, emotions all the more disturbing because they had surfaced so abruptly after recently having lain dormant. But more disquieting than all of that, and uppermost in her mind before sleep claimed her, was the fact that the emotions and desires evoked by Casey made a pale shadow out of what she'd felt for Nigel.

The following morning found Adele very apprehensive about taking surgery with Casey but in the end she need have had no such worries for he acted as if nothing had happened between them, bidding her good morning and taking his place slightly behind her in his consulting room as Lizzie brought in the bundle of patient records and placed them on the desk.

She, however, was acutely aware of him—the sight of him in the casual chinos and sweater that he invariably chose to wear for surgery, his hair still damp from the shower, that woody smell that must be the aftershave he used and his very presence that seemed to fill the small room. In spite of her strong resolutions of the night before, she found herself longing for him to take her into his arms again just as he had then, for those strong hands resting now on the computer keyboard to touch her and for his mouth to take control of hers…

But, of course, he did nothing of the sort—that would never happen again.

'Good morning, Doctor.'

Shaken from her reverie, Adele looked up sharply at the woman who had just come into the room and who was lowering herself gingerly onto the chair.

'Good morning…Mrs…er…Mrs Bletchford. How can I help you?'

'Well, Doctor, I keep getting this funny pain…'

Within minutes Adele was drawn into the complexities of yet another daily surgery, but in spite of the fact that she was required to use every ounce of her concentration she remained only too aware of the presence of the man at her side.

As the surgery wore on she found herself wondering what Casey would say when the surgery ended and they were alone. Would he make any reference to what had happened between them, would he maybe attempt to apologise or explain his actions? But she was destined never to know because as she was printing out a prescription for the morning's last patient a telephone call came through.

Handing the patient the prescription and bidding him good-bye, Adele lifted the receiver, noting as she did so that it was an internal call.

'Adele—it's Penny. We have a lady in the clinic—Marion Kendry—whom I'm very concerned about. She has a history of heart problems. She came in for a routine ECG but she's complaining of feeling unwell. She's Casey's patient—is he there?'

'Yes, he is.'

'Can you ask him to come along to the clinic, please?'

'Of course.' Adele looked at the receiver as Penny cut her short and hung up.

'What is it?' Casey raised his eyebrows. The one bisected by the scar looked ruffled and suddenly, irrationally, she longed to touch it, to smooth it as she had before. But even if that was permitted, which now quite obviously it wasn't, there were other, more pressing matters to attend to.

'Penny wants you in the clinic,' she said. 'A patient of yours, Marion Kendry…?'

Casey nodded. 'Yes, what about her?'

'She's feeling unwell. Penny is worried about her in view of her heart problems.'

'Well, you'd better get along there, then, hadn't you?'

'Me?' Adele looked startled. 'But Penny asked for you.'

'I was under the impression that you were attending to my patients this morning.' His reply was calm, unruffled.

'Well, yes, but—'

'You'd better hurry up—you don't want a fatality on your hands, do you?'

'Heavens, no!' Adele leapt to her feet and without a backward glance hurried from the room, leaving Casey stretched out in his chair with his hands linked behind his head as if he hadn't a care in the world.

She dashed through Reception, ignoring the startled glances of the receptionists behind the desk, past the waiting room then down the passage to one of the surgery's two treatment rooms where the nurses held their clinics. Not even pausing to knock, she flung open the door and hurried inside, letting the door swing shut behind her.

A woman was lying on the examination couch and Penny was checking her blood pressure. Penny's anxious gaze met Adele's then flickered past her towards the door.

'Where's Casey?' Penny demanded.

'He said for me to assess—'

Penny drew in her breath. 'I'm not happy,' she muttered. 'Her ECG gave cause for concern and now her blood pressure is dropping.'

Adele looked down at the woman on the couch who was about fifty years of age. Her appearance was pale, her breathing shallow and she appeared to have slipped into unconsciousness. 'I'll draw up an injection,' she said. Turning away to the drug cupboards, she began taking out packs containing a syringe and drugs for heart stimulation but before she had the chance to even open the packs there was an urgent shout from Penny.

'She's arrested!'

'The defib?'

'It's in the other treatment room,' said Penny. 'I'll press the alarm button and someone will bring it.'

'There's no sign of a pulse,' said Adele as she checked that the woman was lying flat and that her airway was clear. 'We'll start resuscitation.'

Penny placed a gauze square over the patient's mouth and Adele dragged a footstool to the side of the couch in order to give herself the necessary space to start heart massage. Together they commenced the resuscitation routine—Adele with her hands linked administering five thumps to the patient's chest followed by a short sharp breath into her mouth from Penny, then five more thumps and another breath and so on.

For a moment it was as if Adele had been transported back to her days as a junior doctor in Casualty where this routine had been something of a common occurrence on victims of road accidents who were brought in.

While they were pausing to check for a pulse the door was flung open and Mary appeared with the mobile defibrillator, closely followed by Casey who must have heard the alarm bell and decided to investigate after all.

'There's nothing,' said Penny.

'Keep going,' instructed Adele.

'The defib?'

'While they're setting it up.'

They resumed the mouth-to-mouth resuscitation and the heart massage while Mary and Casey set up the defibrillator, then Casey moved forward with the pads.

'Anything?' he asked, and they all paused again.

'Nothing.' Adele shook her head and then, suddenly mindful that she was only the trainee, stepped from the stool in order to let Casey take over. He, however, calmly passed her the pads. Her gaze flew to his face but his expression was implacable. She was vaguely aware of a look of surprise on Penny's face as if she, too, had assumed that Casey as the senior member of staff present would automatically take over.

Gripping the pads tightly, Adele took a deep breath. 'Stand clear!' she ordered, and as the others stood back she applied the pads, producing the required shock.

The patient's body jumped and arched then Casey checked for a response. 'No,' he said, shaking his head. 'Nothing. Try again.'

Rapidly Adele repeated the procedure—the command

and the application, followed by the moment of anticipation—and this time there was no disappointment for Casey said, 'We have a pulse. Welcome back, Marion.' Gently he smoothed his patient's forehead, brushing her hair from her eyes.

Amidst sighs of relief from Adele, Penny and Mary, Casey looked round at each of them. 'Well done,' he said quietly. 'Thankfully we don't need that procedure here very often but when we do it's nice to know it works so efficiently. I take it…' he glanced at Mary '…there's also an ambulance on the way?'

Mary nodded. 'Yes, Lizzie phoned for one as soon as we heard the alarm bell.'

Casey looked down at Marion again. 'We're going to get you into hospital, Marion,' he said gently as her eyes opened and she looked up at him in bewilderment.

'Hospital…?' she murmured.

'Yes, a little spell in the coronary care unit,' Casey replied. 'You had a cardiac arrest, Marion. Your heart stopped beating but fortunately Dr Brooks and Sister Rudge were on hand to make sure that normal service was resumed.'

'We've let your husband know, Marion,' said Mary. 'Cheryl phoned him at work and he's on his way here.'

'So there you are, Marion, you've nothing to worry about,' said Casey. 'All you have to do is to rest and let others wait on you for a while.'

The ambulance arrived a few minutes later and while Adele was giving details of Marion's treatment and medical condition to the paramedics, Brian Kendry arrived and was shown straight into the treatment room by Lizzie.

After Marion had been taken to hospital, with her husband following the ambulance in his car, Casey was called away to Frances Drew's office to sign a batch of referrals and Adele found herself alone with Penny.

'Well, that was a drama I could have done without on a Monday morning,' said Penny as she set about clearing up.

'It seems to have been all high drama in the last couple of days,' said Adele. She spoke without thinking then immediately wished she'd been more careful as Penny looked up from the couch where she was collecting up the paper sheeting.

'Did Casey get called out to certify that girl's death yesterday? It's all right,' she added, catching sight of Adele's expression. 'I heard it on the news this morning.'

Adele nodded. 'Yes, he did.'

'Was that where you went with him?' Penny's brown eyes narrowed slightly.

'Yes, he asked me to. It…it was pretty harrowing,' she added.

'I dare say it was.' Penny was silent for a moment then she said, 'I'm rather surprised that Casey asked you to go. He's an old hand at that sort of thing but, let's face it, it's all new to you and something like that…well…'

'I have to get used to things like that,' said Adele. 'Especially if I want to be involved in police work. And, after all, I am a doctor.'

'I know.' Penny nodded. 'But you have to admit that yesterday wasn't your usual run-of-the-mill street brawl or pub punch-up, was it?'

'No, it wasn't,' Adele agreed. 'It was pretty ghastly if you must know,' she added after a moment.

'Did it affect you badly?' Penny looked up.

'Yes, it did, actually,' she admitted. 'I'm ashamed to say I needed a brandy afterwards to steady my nerves.'

'Nothing to be ashamed of in that,' said Penny. 'I would probably have needed a couple if it had been me.'

'Apart from the horror of it all and the sadness of that poor girl's death in such a manner and in such a desolate, lonely place, it was also all the implications behind it that made me feel so bad.'

'How do you mean?' Penny tore a length of paper from a large roll and placed it on the couch.

'Well, for a moment there she reminded me of my niece,' said Adele slowly, 'and from that it's only a short leap of imagination to thinking that it could have actually been her. And then I got to thinking of the girl's family and how they must be feeling as they try to come to terms with it all.'

'I know.' Penny gave a little shudder. 'It hardly bears thinking about.'

They were silent for a moment then Adele looked round the treatment room. 'This won't do,' she said. 'I suppose I'd better go and get on.'

'Have you finished surgery?' asked Penny.

'Yes, I'd just seen the last one when you phoned through, but I've no doubt Casey has something else lined up for me—either some house calls or helping him tackle the ever-growing mountain of paperwork.'

'Not working you too hard, is he?' asked Penny casually.

By this time Adele had started walking towards the door but she paused and looked over her shoulder. 'Not really,' she said with a little laugh.

'I hope he bought you the brandy.'

'I'm sorry…?'

'You said you were in need of a brandy last evening—I hope it was Casey who bought it for you.'

'Er, well, yes…sort of.' Suddenly she didn't know quite

what to say. Penny quite obviously thought they had gone to a pub on the way home but if she allowed her to go on thinking that and Penny then mentioned it to Casey who would deny it, she would be made to look very silly. On the other hand, she wasn't too sure she wanted Penny knowing that she had gone to Casey's flat to drink brandy and she certainly didn't want her knowing what else had taken place.

'What do you mean, "sort of"?' Penny wrinkled her nose. 'Either he did or he didn't.'

'Well, we didn't go to the pub,' said Adele. Taking a deep breath and deciding there was nothing else for it, she said, 'He gave me a brandy when we got back here.'

'Really?' Penny had turned away so Adele couldn't see her expression. 'Well, I suppose that was something.'

'Yes, quite.' Adele went then, suddenly unable to cope with any more of that particular conversation. The last thing she wanted was for Penny to think that she was trying to come between her and Casey, but as she left the treatment room she had the feeling that that was exactly what was starting to happen.

CHAPTER EIGHT

DURING the next few days Adele found herself increasingly on edge whenever she was in Casey's company. Whenever she knew she was going to see him, either to do a surgery together or to go on house calls, a kind of anxious tension would set in, followed by anticipation that seemed to build and build until it reached overwhelming proportions.

She was at a loss to explain why this should be—she only knew it had something to do with what had happened between them the night of the police call. She wasn't even sure why. Maybe it was quite simply because what had happened shouldn't have happened and the forbidden element carried an added edge of excitement, but somehow she doubted it was only that. Deep down she knew it had more to do with how she had felt that night, how she had responded to Casey and of how little it had had in common with the way she'd felt about Nigel.

Towards the end of the week Casey told her he felt she was ready to take her own surgeries.

'You'll be fine,' he reassured her, catching sight of her dubious expression. 'And don't forget, at least to start with you'll simply be taking extra surgeries which in theory should only consist of acute situations, urgent things that have just happened that need immediate treatment and can't wait for an appointment.'

'But we all know that isn't always the case,' she observed dryly. 'There will always be the patient who uses the emergency surgery for an update or a second opinion on a chronic situation…'

'True,' Casey agreed, 'and likewise there will be the patient who has put up with a condition for a long time then suddenly snaps and can't bear it a moment longer. Don't forget, you always have options in these situations. If, for example, you don't feel able to deal with something that's more complex than it first appears, you can give temporary relief and ensure that the patient returns to see his or her own GP at a later date.'

'What about referrals?'

'You can, of course, make referrals or if you wish you could leave a memo to the patient's GP about the condition, leaving them to make the decision. You'll find you'll be authorising tests all the time—blood, urine, liver function, thyroid function and so on. In these situations, again it would be courteous to leave a note for the GP concerned, bringing them up to date with what's happening with their patient.'

They had been talking in the treatment room at the end of a cervical smear clinic, and as Casey finished Adele posed the question that had intrigued her since coming to Woolverton House. 'Where will I take these extra surgeries?' she asked, knowing full well there was no spare consulting room.

'Good point.' Casey nodded. Out of the corner of her eye Adele was aware that Penny had come into the treatment room. 'The only spare rooms in the house are the rooms that are used as storerooms and neither of them is suitable at the present time so we've agreed that as one of the partners is off duty on a different day of the week, theirs should be the room you use. Does that sound all right to you?'

'I suppose so.' Adele wrinkled her nose. 'I shall feel like a bit of a nomad but I guess it can't be helped.'

Penny, who had obviously come in on the conversation and had overheard, suddenly spoke. 'What would happen here, Casey, if you took on another partner?'

'As I wanted to do in the first place, you mean?' he asked, looking over his shoulder at Penny.

'Yes, that's right,' she agreed, leaving Adele to believe that she and Casey had discussed the situation at length, probably before her arrival. It suddenly made her feel vulnerable and uneasy.

'Well, I imagine one of the storerooms would be converted,' said Casey. 'Failing that, I guess we might look at planning permission to build on, but I foresee problems there, with this being a listed building. Anyway, that would all be for discussion in the future, but that's the situation at the moment. I've just told Adele, Penny, that I feel she's ready to start taking her own surgeries.'

'Well, that's great.' Penny smiled. 'It'll certainly ease the appointment situation—the reception staff will be delighted,' she added. As Casey began to move towards the door, she said quickly, 'Oh, Casey, don't run away. Could I have a quick word, please?'

'All right, but it'll have to be quick.' Casey looked at his watch. 'I have house calls then a surgery.'

'I know.' Penny moved closer to show him some notes, and as she looked up into his face Adele slipped unnoticed out of the treatment room, leaving the two of them together.

She still found it extremely difficult thinking of Casey and Penny as an item, maybe because there seemed to be so little evidence of it. Knowing Casey as she now did, Adele could imagine him being quite firm about them keeping their relationship very low-key while they were at work, but more strange was that there seemed no sign of very much happening away from work either. But Adele put that down to the fact that perhaps she'd simply not been around at the appropriate times and hadn't seen the pair of them together.

No doubt, she thought as she made her way back to Reception after leaving the treatment room, Penny would seize this opportunity to speak to Casey alone. Suddenly she found herself envying Penny, wishing that she could again talk intimately to Casey as they had done briefly before. She'd been interested in hearing about his family and his background and longed to know more, just as she'd found herself wanting to tell him about her own family and even about her failed relationship with Nigel. For a moment her envy of Penny threatened to spiral out of control as she imagined her and Casey sharing not only intimate details of their families and friends but also every other aspect of their lives, from meals and outings together to possibly holidays, and…sex. Of course, sex. She couldn't imagine Casey being in a relationship and sex not playing an important part. There was something so masculine and intensely virile about him… She shivered slightly, goose-bumps standing up on her skin as she recalled that moment he'd pulled her into his arms. There had been an urgency about it—a sort of raw passion. But she had to stop thinking like this. Casey wasn't hers and was never likely to be. Not, of course, that she even wanted him to be… Did she?

Of course she didn't, she told herself firmly as she walked into the chaotic mass of people that thronged Reception.

At the end of that week was the dinner party to be held by Edward and Celia.

'What will you wear?' asked Cheryl as Adele returned

a batch of notes to Reception after the final surgery.

'I've bought a new top,' Adele replied. 'I thought I could wear it with my black evening trousers.'

'What colour is it?' asked Cheryl, leaning over the reception desk.

'A sort of burnt orange,' said Adele.

'That'll look nice with your colouring,' Lizzie chipped in. 'I've got a new top I'm wearing tonight as well.'

'Are you going to the dinner party?' Adele asked in surprise. She had understood it was only to be for the doctors but maybe she'd been wrong. A peal of laughter from Cheryl soon clarified the position, however.

'Us? To one of Celia Fletcher's dinner parties? You've got to be joking!'

'I just wondered, that's all,' said Adele weakly, then with a surreptitious little glance over her shoulder, she said, 'Why, what's wrong with them?'

'Oh, I'm not saying there's anything wrong with them exactly,' said Cheryl. 'Although, having said that, I can think of better ways of spending a Friday night...'

'Too true,' muttered Lizzie.

'No, it isn't that.' Cheryl flashed a grin at Lizzie. 'It's just that we wouldn't be invited in the first place.'

'Oh.' Adele frowned then asked, 'Isn't there any socialising between the partners and the rest of the staff?'

'Not really.' Cheryl shrugged and shook her head. 'They take us out for a meal at Christmas but that's about it. We girls go out together from time to time—you know, for an Indian or a Chinese or something like that.'

'I think that's a shame,' said Adele slowly. 'I think there should be more social contact. There were masses of social events at the hospital where I worked.'

'Adele's right.' Mary stood up from behind the computer where she had been sitting and from where she had obviously heard every word. 'I think I'll organise something—maybe a cheese and wine party would be nice. I'll see what Rachel thinks.' With that she bustled away towards the practice manager's office.

'Now see what you've done,' groaned Lizzie.

'Sorry!' Adele chuckled, turning as Toby came out of his consulting room.

'Have I missed a joke?' he asked, blinking and looking round.

'Not really. We were just talking about socialising and about tonight's dinner party,' said Adele.

'Oh, Lord, yes,' said Toby. 'I'd forgotten about that for a while.'

'Sounds like you're not too keen on going,' said Adele quietly as she fell into step beside him and they began to make their way out of the front of the building and round to the courtyard and the entrance to the flats.

'Oh, it'll be all right when we get there,' said Toby. 'It's one of those things it's difficult to drum up any enthusiasm over, but I have to say Celia really does go to a lot of trouble and she's an excellent cook—the food is always superb at these dos.'

'Do they have many of them?' asked Adele curiously as they began to climb the stairs.

'A couple or so a year,' Toby replied. 'I gather this one is in your honour.'

'So I believe.' Adele nodded. By this time they had reached the first-floor landing where Toby paused for a moment. 'Would you like a lift there?' he asked.

'That's kind of you,' said Adele. 'But I can take my car.'

'Wouldn't hear of it,' said Toby. 'Can't have the guest

of honour unable to have a drink. I'll meet you down here…what, about seven?'

'Yes, all right, thanks, Toby.'

Adele found herself getting ready with extra care that evening, taking more trouble than usual over her make-up, hair and nails. When she had finished she carefully stepped into the pair of black crêpe trousers she had bought in Chester, and which had cost her nearly a week's wages, but when she went to put on the new top she had told the girls about she was unable to find it. She had only bought it a few days previously in one of the local high street shops especially to wear at the dinner party. She searched her wardrobe and the chest of drawers, and even went through the rubbish bag, fearing it may have got caught up with things she had thrown away, but there was no sign of it. In the end, in desperation she took from the wardrobe a gold sleeveless top with a roll neck, and by the time she had pulled it over her head and rearranged her hair it was time for her to meet Toby.

He was waiting for her on the landing looking somehow very boyish in evening dress, almost like a student going to a freshers' ball. He had obviously just washed his hair, which still flopped across his forehead and over his glasses. 'You look nice,' he said admiringly as together they made their way down to the courtyard.

'Thank you.' Adele smiled. 'You don't look so bad yourself.' She was amused to see the colour touch his cheeks as if he wasn't used to compliments.

'I was going to ask Casey if he wanted to come with us,' he said as he opened the passenger door of his car for Adele, 'but there was no reply when I knocked on his door. Either he's already left or he's been called out. Knowing Casey, anything's possible.' He started the engine and they drew out of the courtyard onto the high street. 'Have you been to the Fletchers' home?' he asked as he joined the flow of traffic.

'No.' Adele shook her head. 'Do they live far away?'

'About a mile and a half. It's west of the town up at Jacob's Rise. It's an exclusive area that has been developed in the last ten years or so. As you'll see, there are some pretty impressive properties up there.'

'What's Celia like?' asked Adele after a moment.

'Celia?' Toby gave a rare chuckle. 'Oh, she's all right really, I suppose. But she does have the tendency to want to organise things which, I guess, is fine to a point, but unfortunately she includes other people's lives in that as well. She's notorious as a matchmaker,' he said, throwing Adele a sidelong glance. 'To be honest with you, I've been dreading tonight,' he admitted, 'because I'm sure she'll have someone lined up for me. On the other hand, I dare say she may have given up on me by now. She must think I'm a dead loss.'

'I'm sure that isn't true,' protested Adele. Casting him a sidelong glance she said, 'But would she do that? Have someone lined up, I mean?'

'She's done it before,' Toby replied darkly. 'The last one she lined up for me was impossible. I felt obliged to take her home and she kept ringing me for weeks afterwards.'

'Oh, poor old you,' said Adele sympathetically. 'What a nightmare! I say,' she added in sudden alarm, 'I hope she hasn't lined anyone up for me.'

'I expect you'll escape this time as she hasn't yet met you,' said Toby solemnly, 'but be warned for the future.'

'The answer, I suppose,' said Adele thoughtfully 'is to ask if you can bring someone along or, failing that, to at least say that you're seeing someone even if you aren't.'

'I was going to do that tonight,' admitted Toby sheepishly. 'I was going to ask Penny then if...if she agreed I would have checked it out with Celia. But, then, I don't know, I chickened out.'

'Penny?' Adele turned to him. The surprise in her voice must have been obvious.

'I know, pathetic, isn't it?' Toby must have thought her surprise was over his lack of courage rather than his choice of partner. 'I'm afraid I'm always chickening out over things like that.'

'No,' said Adele quickly, 'I didn't mean that. I was surprised that you were thinking of asking Penny, because of Casey. After all, she wouldn't want anyone to think that you and she—'

'What about Casey?' Toby cut her short. He threw her a startled glance, taking his eyes from the road then, as the car swerved slightly to the left, being forced to concentrate again.

'Well, they're an item,' said Adele weakly.

'Are they? I didn't know that.' Toby looked shattered, leaving Adele in no doubt that he hadn't only been wanting Penny as an escort to fend off Celia's matchmaking. Suddenly she felt guilty at being the one to impart news that had obviously had such an impact. He risked another glance in her direction. 'How did *you* know?' he asked.

'Penny herself told me,' said Adele. 'The day I arrived. She said she and Casey were an item, that it was early days but that she was very hopeful.'

'Good heavens!' said Toby. 'I had no idea.' He paused, as if allowing the news to sink in, then he said, 'Well, I have to say Casey's a dark horse—he's said nothing.'

'I know,' said Adele. 'I thought that, then I came to the conclusion that it was probably because he didn't want a lot of gossip and speculation amongst the staff.'

'Yes,' agreed Toby miserably. 'I dare say.'

They travelled on in silence for a while, each apparently lost in their own thoughts. It had been a beautiful day, slightly autumnal but still with the warmth of late summer, and as they climbed the hill out of the town, before them in a spectacular crimson sky the sun was sinking into great banks of gold-edged clouds.

'I'm sorry,' said Adele at last, breaking the silence, 'that I had to be the one to tell you.'

'Don't worry,' said Toby gloomily. 'It's the story of my life. I always leave things until they're too late. It's my own fault. I've been plucking up courage for ages to ask Penny out...' He trailed off with a shrug. 'I had no idea she was seeing anyone else.' He paused then shook his head. 'But Casey,' he went on after a moment, 'that does surprise me. I wouldn't have thought Casey was her type at all. In fact, I would have thought that Casey was perhaps more your type...'

'My type? Oh, no,' she said quickly, 'not me. Besides, I'm off men at the moment. Present company excepted, of course,' she added.

'In that case,' said Toby, suddenly brightening up, 'why don't we pretend we are an item this evening—just to thwart any plans that Celia might have?'

'What an excellent idea,' agreed Adele with a laugh.

They arrived at the Fletchers' residence a few minutes later, only to find that the practice Land Rover was already parked on the drive alongside Edward's Jaguar and Rachel's VW.

'Casey's here,' observed Toby as they climbed out of the car. 'Let's hope if he's come straight from a call-out that he changed first. I wouldn't put it past him to turn up wearing jeans and a sweater.'

'And what would Celia make of that?' murmured Adele

as they approached the house, an imposing mock-Georgian residence.

'He would be forgiven—simply because he's Casey,' Toby reached out and rang the doorbell. 'In Celia's eyes Casey can do no wrong.'

'I have a feeling we could be in for an interesting evening—' Adele began, breaking off as the front door opened.

Edward stood on the threshold, immaculate and distinguished-looking in evening dress but with a drawn tiredness around his eyes that reminded his two young colleagues of his present medical problems. 'Adele! Toby! Come on in.' He stood aside, allowing them both to enter the spacious hallway. As he closed the front door behind them a tall, exquisitely groomed woman came through into the hall. Her blonde, almost white hair was cut into a fashionable, jaw-length bob and she was dressed in a close-fitting, ankle-length black dress. She wore a minimum of jewellery—pearl studs in her ears, a pearl choker at her throat and a single gold bracelet on one of her slim wrists—but the overall effect was stunning. Adele found herself thinking that Celia Fletcher must have been a very beautiful woman in her youth, but as her gaze met that of her hostess she was momentarily puzzled by the expression in her cool grey eyes. If asked, she would have sworn that Celia Fletcher's reaction on seeing her for the first time was one of shock, but later she would question that for it was swiftly replaced by other fleeting expressions—recognition, puzzlement? Adele couldn't be sure, and as the older woman came forward to greet her she even wondered if she might have been mistaken.

'Adele, my dear.' Not waiting for her husband to make the introductions, Celia took Adele's hands in hers. 'How good to meet you at last. I've heard so much about you.'

'It is kind of you to invite me,' said Adele, surprisingly touched by the warmth of the older woman's welcome.

'Toby, hello, how charming you look.' Briefly Celia touched Toby's arm. 'Come into the drawing room. We are all here now except Jeanette. She called to say she was running late but she'll be here shortly.'

As Celia led the way into the drawing room Adele had to fight a sudden overwhelming urge to giggle as Toby suddenly offered her his arm. In order to keep up the pretence they had agreed upon she took it, but as they entered the room all such notions of hilarity flew as she caught sight of Casey. He was standing by a magnificent Adam fireplace, a drink in one hand, talking to Rachel's husband Matt. He must have seen a flicker of interest in Matt's eyes for he turned and looked towards the door, his gaze immediately meeting Adele's as she and Toby entered the room.

She wasn't certain whether it was the sight of that powerful body in a tuxedo or whether it was the expression in his eyes that caused her heart to miss a beat, but, whatever it was, for a moment it threw her and she was glad that Edward caused a diversion by asking Toby and herself what they would like to drink.

But that moment seemed to set the tone for the evening for with every movement, every glance Adele was excruciatingly aware of Casey.

Jeanette eventually arrived, apologising profusely for her lateness, full of stories of a difficult patient and her even more difficult teenage children—her daughter, whom she'd reluctantly allowed to go on a sleep-over at a friend's, and her son, who had just dropped out of his college course in order to hitchhike to Morocco.

'Lord,' said Toby with feeling, 'I don't think I ever want kids.'

'Well, ours are still small,' said Rachel. 'And I have to say we don't seem to have had too much trouble yet.'

'You wait until they leave home,' said Edward darkly. 'That's when your problems really start. At least when they're small you know where they are.'

Gradually they drifted into the dining room, to a table bathed in candlelight, gleaming with silver and cut glass and dotted with ivy leaves and fresh cream rosebuds. Once again Toby was at Adele's side and once again she took his arm, only to find that Celia had almost pre-empted their motives and seated them together.

'Do you think *we* could have been the object of her matchmaking this time?' murmured Adele under cover of them taking their seats.

'Who knows?' Toby murmured in her ear as he eased her into her chair. 'But let's not disappoint her.'

'No, quite.' Adele smiled dazzlingly up into his face, only to find when looking across the table that Casey's gaze was upon her again—and this time there was no mistaking the scowl on his face.

Toby had certainly been quite right when he'd said that Celia went to a lot of trouble when she gave a dinner party. Smoked salmon and goat's cheese preceded succulent rack of lamb with rosemary sauce and tender vegetables, followed by summer pudding and whipped cream.

The conversation around the table ranged from shop talk—everything from staffing problems to the NHS—to some amusing incidents about local characters. Then Celia drew attention to her with a question about her home and family.

'Adele was at a hospital in Chester, weren't you, Adele?' It was Toby who replied. A slightly flushed, unusually animated Toby whose condition must be attributed to the circumstances rather than the mineral water he was drinking.

'Yes,' Adele agreed, 'that's right. I was an SHO.'

'No desire to specialise?' asked Jeanette, leaning forward slightly to peer down the table at Adele.

'For a time maybe,' Adele replied. 'But general practice had long been an ambition, as had police work. Stourborne Abbas has presented an opportunity to combine both.' As she spoke, once again her gaze met Casey's but still his expression was set without so much as a flicker of emotion or amusement, leaving her feeling suddenly rather nervous.

At Celia's suggestion they moved into the drawing room for coffee, with Toby once again taking Adele's arm and cosily seating himself by her side on one of the two vast sofas. And it was while sipping her coffee that Adele realised that Casey wasn't there. Idly she was wondering where he was when suddenly he strode into the room, his mobile phone in one hand.

'Celia,' he said, 'I'm so sorry but I have to go.'

'Oh, no,' said Celia, 'not the police again. Can't they leave you alone for one evening?'

'That's the way it goes, I'm afraid.' He turned and looked at Adele and she suddenly found herself holding her breath. 'I'd like Adele to come with me on this one.'

'Oh, surely not,' protested Celia. 'After all—'

'She has much to learn,' said Casey firmly. 'And this is the only way.'

'I'll come,' said Adele, setting her coffee-cup down and rising to her feet. 'Of course I will.' She turned briefly to her hosts. 'Thank you, Celia, and you, Edward, for a truly delightful evening,' she said, and then she fled, following Casey out of the room.

CHAPTER NINE

'WHAT the hell was all that about?'

They had left the house in silence but no sooner had they climbed into the Land Rover than Casey almost exploded.

Adele, who was more concerned about her expensive black crêpe trousers and what might befall them in the rather dubious interior of the staff vehicle, threw him a startled glance. 'All what?' She frowned, wondering what on earth he meant.

'All that rubbish between you and Toby, that's what!' He positively growled in response and for a moment she still didn't understand to what he was referring. 'He's been drooling all over you like some lovesick puppy since the moment you arrived.'

'Oh, that!' Adele chuckled as at last it dawned on her what he was getting at. 'Actually,' she explained, 'we travelled together—'

'Why did you do that?' Casey demanded as he started the engine and with a squeal of tyres on the loose gravel path drove out onto the main road.

'Well, Toby suggested it...'

'I bet he did.'

'He said as I was the guest of honour it would be nice for me to be able to have a drink,' she carried on, ignoring his interruption and at the same time fastening her seat belt. 'I thought it was very kind of him. Obviously he thought it was silly taking so many cars when we were all going from the same place. He even knocked on your door,' she added, 'to see if you wanted a lift, but you weren't there.'

'That would have cramped his style a bit,' muttered Casey.

'So where were you?' Adele shot him a puzzled glance, wondering just what the reason was for his surly mood.

'I had a police call-out.'

'And you didn't call me?' Adele raised her eyebrows.

'I thought you'd be getting ready,' he said abruptly. 'I was already dressed.'

'Well, yes, actually, I suppose I was getting ready but...but I have to say I feel a bit bad about Toby now.'

'Why? Why should you feel bad?' There was a contemptuous air about Casey now that somehow irritated Adele even further.

'Well, he was good enough to bring me and now...well, now I feel as if I've just dumped him.'

'We can go back if you like.' Casey eased his foot off the accelerator. 'I'll turn around and drop you off.'

'No, of course not,' said Adele hastily. 'I have to go with you now. You made it plain enough to everyone that you felt I should go.'

He didn't answer and after travelling in silence for a while at what seemed to Adele like a speed bordering on the dangerous she said, 'So what is it?'

'What is what?' His voice was tight now, controlled, but his gaze was directed firmly at the road ahead.

'This call-out.' She struggled to keep the impatience out of her tone for increasingly there was something about Casey that night that was downright infuriating. 'Did the police say what it was? Was it anything to do with the first call-out or was it something new?'

'I've no idea,' he replied tightly.

'What do you mean, you've no idea?' She frowned.

'Didn't the police give any idea why they were calling you out? They usually do, don't they?'

'Yes,' he agreed, 'they do. But on this occasion they didn't, mainly, I suppose, because they didn't phone.'

Slowly she turned to look at him but his expression was still fixed, giving away nothing. 'I don't understand,' she said. 'You say the police didn't phone you but back there at the Fletchers', you went out of the room and came back some considerable time later with your phone in your hand, saying you had to go.'

He made no comment, neither agreeing with her nor contradicting her.

'You said it was the police…'

'No,' he interrupted calmly. 'Celia assumed that.'

'But then you said you wanted me to go with you.'

'That's true.' He nodded.

'You led everyone to believe that you thought I should go because it would be of benefit to me.'

'Again that is what they chose to believe.' He shrugged.

'So if there's no police call-out, why did we leave?' asked Adele in bewilderment. Suddenly all this seemed to be getting beyond her—maybe it was something to do with Edward's excellent wine that had been served with dinner.

'Because I'd had enough.' His reply was so terse that for a moment Adele thought she'd misheard him.

'I'm sorry,' she said. 'You'd what?'

'I said it was because I'd had enough. I told you dinner parties quite definitely are not my cup of tea.'

'I know you did but… but…don't you think that was…rude?' She had been about to say outrageous, so flabbergasted was she by his admission, but she changed her mind after another glance at his scowling, uncompromising profile.

'Why was it rude?' he demanded.

'Well…Edward…Celia…they went to a lot of trouble and, well, Edward is your friend, your partner…'

'I know that,' he snapped. 'And in spite of what you might now believe, I am very fond of both of them and just as a matter of interest I don't think what I did was rude at all. If I'd done it in the middle of dinner that may have been different. The meal was long over, everyone had finished their coffee. All that would have happened—all that is happening now—is more gossip, probably more brandy for those fortunate enough not to be driving, and yet more gossip.'

'Well, yes, maybe,' Adele agreed, 'but I still think…well, I mean what made you think I might have had enough? What gave you the right to decide for me?' Suddenly she was angry. Angry at what she had perceived as his apparent rudeness, but even more angry that in his arrogance he should have assumed that she was of the same frame of mind as himself and for including her in his scheme.

'Hadn't you had enough?' He threw her a cynical, side-long glance. 'Go on, be honest.'

'Actually, no, I was enjoying my evening if you must know.'

'You seemed more than willing to come with me when I suggested it,' he replied. 'In fact, I would say "eager" is the word that springs to mind.'

'That was because I thought we were going to a police call,' Adele protested.

'So you feel that would have justified us leaving when we did?' he asked coolly.

'Well, yes, obviously…' She trailed off, still having to struggle to control her temper. 'As it is,' she went on after a moment, 'you've put me in an impossible situation. What will I say if anyone asks me what the police call was about?'

'Who's likely to ask you that?' His lip curled slightly and she couldn't help noticing that his scar stood out more than usual, making him look tougher than ever and somehow even more incongruous in his tuxedo and black tie.

'Well, Edward might...or Jeanette, even Rachel... and...and Toby. Toby is sure to.'

There was another squeal of tyres as Casey slammed on the brakes then reversed the Land Rover for several yards before swinging it into a sharp left turn.

'Where are we going now?' asked Adele in alarm.

'The police station,' snapped Casey. 'Isn't that where you want to go?'

'Well, yes, but...if there isn't anything to go there for...'

'If it'll make you feel less guilty, we'll go there and check on the patient I saw earlier this evening.'

Adele remained silent after that as they hurtled through the night to the police station. She was silent because she couldn't think what else to say with Casey in this strange, almost belligerent mood. As they drew up sharply on the police forecourt and Casey switched off the engine, she threw him a tentative glance. 'This patient...' she began.

He'd been about to climb out of the Land Rover but he paused and looked over his shoulder at her. 'What about him?'

'Don't you think I should know what it's all about—if I'm to go in with you, I mean...'

'He'd been in a fight—usual stuff. Two gangs clashed and our client got bashed over the head with a baseball bat. He's suffered slight concussion but not enough for him to be hospitalised. Is that enough?'

'Yes. I suppose so.' Miserably Adele climbed out of the

vehicle, pulling on her black jacket as she did so. She didn't like Casey being this way with her, so abrupt and offhand, but even more to the point she couldn't think of any reason why he was. He'd been fine at work that day, easygoing and relaxed, even joking with her about taking solo surgeries the following week. And now he was in a really foul mood which, when she really thought about it, seemed to have started at some point during the dinner party. Maybe someone had said something to upset him or maybe it was quite simply that he really did loathe dinner parties, but whatever it was Adele wished it wasn't happening.

She almost had to run to keep up with him as he strode ahead of her into the police station. Alan Munro was behind the desk and he looked up in surprise as they almost erupted into Reception.

'Good grief!' he said. 'If that's not telepathy I don't know what is. I've just phoned for the paramedics.' Disbelievingly he glanced at the telephone receiver in his hand.

'The concussion?' said Casey.

'No, he's fine.' Alan shook his head. 'This is a young girl who was brought in with a crowd of youngsters after neighbours complained of a loud party. These kids were out of their minds on booze and there were no adults present. Since they've been here this particular girl seems to have taken a turn for the worse.'

'We'd better take a look at her, then,' said Casey.

As Alan led them through Reception he glanced back at them both, taking in their attire. 'Been somewhere special?' he asked.

'Dinner party,' Casey muttered.

'Good time?' asked Alan conversationally.

'Yes.' Adele quickly intervened, thinking it was probably better that she should answer that particular question. 'Yes, very good, thanks.'

They were led into a room where a WPC was supervising two teenage girls. One was curled up on a bunk and the other was vomiting into a bucket.

'Some of the parents have been to collect their offspring,' said Alan. 'But we haven't even managed to get names out of these two. We suspect they are both minors so we've called the social worker. But this is the one we've been the most concerned about.' He indicated the girl on the bunk who had her back to the door and who was partly covered by a grey blanket.

Casey had stopped briefly beside the girl with her head in the bucket, and it was Adele who crouched beside the bunk and gently lifted back the blanket. 'Hello,' she said gently. 'Can you tell me your name?'

At first there was no movement from the girl then with a low moan she turned onto her back, flinging one arm above her head, and in the harsh overhead lighting Adele saw her face. It was deathly pale, her eyes circled with kohl, lashes matted with mascara, while her black hair was tangled. She was an absolute mess, but none of this prevented Adele from recognising her from the time she had come into the surgery during the previous week to wait for her mother after missing her school bus.

'Casey.' Adele looked over her shoulder and as Casey looked up, she said, 'It's Jeanette's daughter, Lara. And yes, she is a minor,' she added to the police sergeant. 'She's only fourteen and her name is Lara Maynard.'

With a muttered exclamation Casey moved across the cell and crouched down beside her, taking the girl's wrist as he did so. 'She's very dehydrated,' he said after a moment. Looking across at the other girl, he said, 'Has Lara been taking anything other than alcohol?'

The girl, her damp blonde hair hanging over her face and around her shoulders, looked up.

'We have to know,' Casey added urgently.

'Ecstasy,' muttered the girl. 'Only one,' she added defiantly.

'And you,' he said. 'Have you taken any?'

'Yeah, the same,' she said, before retching helplessly again into the bucket.

'This is exactly what I suspected,' said Alan grimly. 'The ambulance should be here shortly.'

'I'll get my bag,' said Casey. 'I want to put a drip up right away.'

'Shall I get it for you?' asked Adele.

'No,' said Casey briefly. 'I want you to phone Jeanette and tell her what's happening.'

Adele's heart sank. How did you phone a woman, a colleague and friend at that, and tell her that her fourteen-year-old daughter was in police custody and about to be transported to hospital suffering from the effects of drugs and alcohol? But it had to be done. Taking her mobile phone from her pocket, she decided first to try the Fletchers' and see if Jeanette was still there. Celia answered the phone.

'Celia, it's Adele. I'm so sorry to bother you but is Jeanette still with you?'

'Yes, she's here. I'll fetch her for you.' Celia paused. 'Is there anything wrong, Adele?'

'I think I'd better speak to Jeanette,' she replied.

'Very well. Hold on.'

A minute later Jeanette came to the phone. 'Adele?' she said.

'Jeanette, I'm sorry but there's no easy way to say this. We're at the police station. I'm afraid your daughter, Lara, is here—'

'Lara? She can't be, she's sleeping over at a friend's house…'

'It appears there was a complaint about a loud party going on,' Adele continued. 'The police were called and several of the youngsters were brought into the station.'

'So are they in trouble?' demanded Jeanette. She sighed crossly. 'I'd better come down there.'

'Actually, Jeanette, I think there's rather more to it than that.'

'What do you mean?' There was real alarm in Jeanette's voice now.

'Well, they had all been drinking and…some had been taking drugs.'

'Drugs? Oh, my God! But listen, Lara wouldn't have taken drugs. She knows all the dangers—I've drummed it into her often enough.'

'I'm sorry, Jeanette,' said Adele gently. 'But I'm afraid she has. Casey is worried about her—there's an ambulance on the way…'

'I'll go straight to A and E,' said Jeanette. She was suddenly in professional mode—the anguish of parenthood for the time being put aside.

'Have you got anyone to go with you?' asked Adele.

'Yes, my son Nick is at home. I'll phone him.' Jeanette hung up then and Adele made her way back to the cell where she found Casey in the process of setting up an infusion after inserting a cannula in the back of Lara's hand.

The other girl, whose name turned out to be Chloe, had stopped retching and was sitting on a chair with her head in her hands, watched by the WPC.

'Are you feeling any better?' Adele crouched down in front of her.

'No.' The girl shook her head. 'I feel terrible.'

'So where were you?' asked Adele gently.

'We went to a party at the house of a boy from school. My dad thought I was on a sleep-over at Lara's house—he's going to kill us.'

'Only if he gets there before Lara's mother,' said Casey dryly. Looking up at Adele, he said, 'Did you get hold of Jeanette?'

'Yes, she was still at the Fletchers'. I told her what was happening. She's going straight to the hospital.'

'Good idea. Was anyone going with her?'

'Her son, I believe.' Adele looked down at Lara who now had her eyes closed and was lying very still. 'How is she?' she said.

'She's unconscious.' Casey shook his head. At that moment there were sounds of activity in the corridor outside the cell and a second later Alan opened the door and admitted the paramedics.

Lara was immediately given oxygen to assist her breathing and the paramedics took her to the waiting ambulance. Casey went with them while Adele stayed with Chloe, and when the paramedics returned for Chloe, Adele accompanied them out of the police station.

Casey was in the back of the ambulance, still attending to Lara, checking her pulse, blood pressure and breathing, but once Chloe was settled on the opposite couch to Lara he looked at the attendant paramedic. 'They're all yours,' he said.

Jumping from the back of the ambulance, he stood alongside Adele and Alan as the WPC climbed into the ambulance and the driver closed the doors.

A couple of minutes later the ambulance swept out of the police forecourt with its blue light flashing, and the three of them made their way back into the station.

'So that was Dr Maynard's daughter?' said Alan. 'Do you think she'll be OK?'

'Hard to say at this stage,' said Casey grimly. 'Her heartbeat was very erratic. The worrying part is that even those who get through this acute phase can sometimes be left with brain damage.'

'Why do they do it?' Sadly Alan shook his head then, looking from Casey to Adele, he said, 'Well, I think that just about winds things up for the time being. Bit of luck, you coming in like that when you did.'

'Yes, quite.' Casey nodded but he didn't look at Adele. 'But now we're here,' he added, 'it won't do any harm to look at the concussion case again.'

'As you wish.' Alan nodded and led the way once again back to the cells.

They left the station a little later after Casey had checked that his concussion patient was indeed all right. In silence they climbed into the Land Rover, and as Casey put his key into the ignition Adele spoke. 'I felt sorry for Jeanette,' she said.

'She's certainly got her hands full with those offspring of hers,' Casey agreed.

'What happened to her husband?'

'They separated years ago then divorced. I don't think he's played much of a part in his children's upbringing.'

'It can't be easy, bringing up children in today's climate,' said Adele slowly. 'And it seems to me it doesn't make much difference whether they are brought up in an environment like the Procters' or in the supposedly privileged background of a doctor's home.'

'I'm sure you're right.' Casey paused then, drawing out onto the main road, he said, 'How did Jeanette take it?'

'She was shocked, I think, naturally—after all, she thought her daughter was simply at a sleep-over at a friend's house. It must have been pretty shattering to hear where she'd ended up. I only hope her son will be more supportive. Didn't she say he'd dropped out of his college course?'

'Apparently, yes.' Casey nodded. 'At least Celia knows we were at the police station,' he said dryly. After a pause and with a touch of curiosity in his voice he said, 'What did you think of Celia?'

Adele considered for a moment. 'Charming,' she said at last, 'very elegant, but, I have to say there was something in the way she greeted me that left me wondering.'

'What do you mean?' In the darkness of the vehicle's interior Adele knew he was frowning.

'She looked startled. I almost felt that she thought she recognised me—but it couldn't have been that because we certainly haven't met before.' She paused. 'Have you known her for long?'

Casey didn't reply immediately, instead concentrating on negotiating a traffic roundabout. As the Land Rover gathered sped once more on a straight stretch of road, he said, 'Celia and I go back a long way.'

'Really?' Adele was faintly surprised and at the same time intrigued. There must, after all, be a twenty-year age difference between Celia Fletcher and Casey, which surely ruled out any sort of romantic attachment. But on the other hand, with Casey, who knew? With his chequered past anything was possible.

'We worked at the same hospital,' he said. 'I was doing my training and Celia was secretary to one of the consultants.'

'Was she married to Edward then?'

'Oh, yes. She had returned to work after her family had grown up.'

'And what about now—does she still work now?'

Casey shook his head. 'No, she retired when they moved here to Stourborne Abbas and Edward founded the practice. It's Celia whom I have to thank for me being here. It was her who suggested to Edward that he contact me as a prospective partner.' He paused. 'Celia has a knack for that sort of thing—fitting a person into the right situation.'

'Toby said something like that, too,' said Adele wryly.

'What do you mean?' That irritable edge was back in Casey's tone—the one that had been there earlier when they'd first left the Fletchers' home.

'Toby wasn't quite so polite about it as you—he said Celia was too fond of organising other people's lives.'

'I suppose some might see it that way,' replied Casey tightly.

'He also said she was very fond of matchmaking. Apparently, once in the past she lined up some dreadful woman for Toby who clung to him like a limpet and who continued to pester him for ages afterwards. I'm afraid it's made him very wary of Celia's dinner parties.'

'He didn't seem to have any such worries tonight.' Casey spoke in the same clipped tone. 'He was all over you like a rash.'

'He wasn't!' protested Adele.

'Well, it certainly looked that way from where I was sitting,' muttered Casey, 'and I'm sure it didn't go unnoticed by the others either.'

'Oh, heavens! Do you really think so?' Adele stared at him in dismay. 'I'll have to tell Toby he overdid it.'

There was silence for a moment then slowly Casey said, 'What do you mean, tell him he overdid it?'

'Well, we arranged it.' In the darkness Adele turned to look at him. 'We decided rather than risk Celia having lined anyone up for us we would pretend we were an item.' In the sudden silence Adele heard Casey sharply draw in his breath. 'As it happened,' she went on, 'we gradually came to the conclusion that she had lined us up for each other anyway…'

'So you aren't an item?' He almost barked the question, making Adele jump.

'Well, no. No, of course not.' She paused and looked at him again but he was staring straight ahead as by this time they had turned into the high street and he was preparing to enter the courtyard of Woolverton House. 'Surely,' she said incredulously, 'you didn't think that?'

Casey brought the vehicle to a halt and switched off the engine. 'I didn't know quite what to think,' he growled.

'But I'd told you that I'm not into relationships at the moment.'

'I know,' he said abruptly. 'I suppose that was why I was surprised by tonight's performance.'

They were silent for a while then in a small voice, Adele said, 'I guess I'd better tell Toby that we came across as a little too convincing.'

'Yes, maybe you had, if you don't want staff gossip and speculation,' Casey agreed tersely. 'If it fooled me it will have fooled others and there's a good chance that it might have given Toby himself a few ideas.'

Adele wanted to tell him that he was wrong on that score, that Toby certainly wasn't interested in her, that it was Penny he wanted—but how could she when it was Casey himself who was involved with Penny? She could just imagine the ensuing scene. Casey's reaction to the little subterfuge between herself and Toby had been bad enough, let alone what it would be like if he thought Toby was interested in Penny. She shuddered at the thought as she stepped down from the Land Rover. She would have walked straight round and entered the house but found Casey barring her way.

'Casey…?' she looked up at him.

'Adele…' he murmured.

There was something about the sound of her name on his lips that was almost Adele's undoing, and in spite of all her previous resolutions she suddenly wanted him to take her in his arms again the way he had before. She wanted everyone else to go away—Penny, Nigel, Toby, everyone—leaving just herself and Casey here in the darkness, safe in a world of their own. And for a moment it would seem that theirs was but a single thought and of mutual intent for he took a step closer and held out his hand.

There was no telling what would have happened next for there was a slight movement behind them and Penny herself suddenly appeared out of the shadows of the doorway.

'Hello,' she said, her eyes on Casey. 'I wondered where you had got to. Toby was back ages ago. He said you'd had a call-out and that Jeanette's daughter was involved. I wondered what it was all about.'

Leaving Casey to explain, Adele fled into the house and up the stairs to her flat, suddenly unable to cope with anything else that night.

CHAPTER TEN

EXHAUSTED from the evening's events both physically and mentally, Adele fell asleep almost as soon as her head touched the pillow but her dreams were troubled and she awoke suddenly to find it was only three o'clock and she'd slept for barely two hours. Turning over, she attempted to go back to sleep but was so wide awake she knew sleep was now going to be impossible.

Slipping out of bed, she padded to the kitchen, poured a glass of milk and took it back to bed where she sat for a long time going over the events of the evening. If she was honest, the aspect that had intrigued and puzzled her had been Casey's mood, which from the moment she and Toby had arrived at the dinner party had been less than friendly and which as the evening had progressed had grown into something bordering on hostile. She'd been annoyed when he'd used the pretext of a police call-out as an excuse to get not only himself but her as well away from the party and then later he'd admitted he'd assumed that her and Toby's pretence at togetherness had been genuine.

So had that been the reason for his surly behaviour? It had certainly seemed that way. In fact, if she hadn't known better she would have said that he'd seemed jealous by the attention that she and Toby had been paying each other. But that was ridiculous—why would he be jealous? Irritated maybe, in view of her having told him that she wasn't ready for another relationship, although even that didn't give him the right to question her actions, but cer-

tainly not jealous. After all, he had Penny so why would
he be jealous of someone paying her, Adele, some attention?

The only reason for that would be if he had feelings for
her himself and surely there wasn't the remotest possibility
of that. Was there?

Adele shifted her position, disturbed even by the
thought. They had shared those intimate moments in his
flat, it was true, but surely that had been no more than him
comforting her after the traumatic nature of the case they
had just attended. Then again that very night there had
been that moment when there had been no telling what
might have happened if Penny hadn't appeared. But the
fact was, Penny *had* appeared and she was the woman in
Casey's life.

But, a perverse little voice persisted at the back of her
mind, supposing there was no woman in his life, supposing
Casey and Penny weren't an item and he was free, what
then? How would she feel if he wanted to start a relationship with her? She had been adamant that she wanted no
involvement with anyone—that it was too soon following
her break-up with Nigel, but that had been then, before
she'd got to know Casey. What about now? Did it make
a difference now that Casey had come into her life?

Somewhere deep inside she felt a quick, fierce throb of
desire. There was something intensely exciting about the
idea of herself and Casey being together. Then deliberately
she tried to dismiss the thought. It would never happen.
For a start Casey was her trainer and she couldn't imagine
that Edward or the other partners would look upon any
such relationship kindly and even if they did, there was
still Penny.

It always came back to Penny. Deliberately Adele set
her empty glass down on her bedside table. Penny had

shown her nothing but kindness ever since her arrival and she knew she could never do anything to hurt her.

All she could do in the future, she told herself firmly, was to keep Casey at arm's length, especially if he was weak enough to believe that he could have her while he was with Penny. Was that his intention? She'd been down that road before with Nigel and it had led to nothing but heartbreak—she certainly didn't intend letting it happen again.

In this new, resolute frame of mind she finally settled down again and attempted to go back to sleep, but just as she was on the point of dropping off an image of Penny and Casey in bed together—which, no doubt, they were—came into her mind. It tormented her so much that it was another hour before finally she slept.

It had already been decided that Adele should start taking surgeries on her own the following week. From her point of view it couldn't have come at a better time for it would mean that she and Casey would see much less of each other. She would, of course, still be expected to report to him on a routine daily basis or if any matter arose that was beyond her capabilities, but the main part of her days would be spent alone, dealing with extra surgeries and home visits for whichever of the partners was off duty.

When she arrived in Reception in readiness for her first solo surgery on Monday morning she wasn't surprised to find the whole place abuzz with speculation about Jeanette's family troubles.

'You were there, weren't you?' demanded Lizzie when she caught sight of Adele. 'At the police station?'

'Yes,' Adele admitted guardedly. 'I was.'

'What did Lara look like?'

'I should say a reason to put anyone off experimenting with drugs,' Adele replied firmly.

'It's Dr Maynard I feel sorry for,' said Cheryl. 'She's had nothing but worry from those kids of hers—ungrateful little devils.'

'That's enough,' Mary intervened. 'We have work to do. Dr Brooks, needless to say, Dr Maynard isn't in this morning so if you would like to take surgery in her room.'

'Of course.' Adele nodded. 'Have we heard how Lara is by the way?'

Mary nodded. 'Yes, Rachel phoned the hospital and they said she's stable and comfortable.'

'Well, I guess that's something,' said Adele with a sigh. She knew she would carry in her mind for some considerable time the image of Lara lying in the police cell with her ashen face and her eyes rolling.

'At least she's alive,' said Lizzie. 'I heard on the news this morning that the police in Bath have arrested someone for the murder of that girl.'

'I bet it was the mother's boyfriend,' said Cheryl. 'He looked a nasty piece of work in those press interviews.'

'Can we, please, get on with some work?' pleaded Mary with a sigh of exasperation. 'Dr Brooks, these are Dr Maynard's notes.'

'Thanks.' Adele took the bundle of notes. 'I'd better go and get started.'

It felt strange, going into Jeanette's consulting room and preparing to take surgery on her own, but she'd barely sat down at the desk and started to read the first patient's notes when there came a tap on the door and it opened to reveal Casey on the threshold. Her heart turned over.

'Just thought I'd check that you're OK,' he said.

Briefly she allowed her eyes to meet his then at something she saw there she looked quickly away, mindful of her resolve not to encourage him in any way. 'I'm fine, thank you,' she replied crisply.

She was aware of an air of puzzlement about him as if he couldn't quite fathom this new approach of hers.

'Quite happy to go solo?' he asked.

'Quite,' she replied, then in a moment of weakness added, 'Thank you.'

'Well, you know where I am if you need me.' He turned and left the room.

If you need me, he'd said. She stared at the door. If only he knew. But she mustn't let her mind go off down that avenue again. She had a surgery to take—her first solo surgery—and suddenly she was overcome by an attack of nerves as the full weight of responsibility hit her. In an attempt to overcome her fears she pressed the buzzer for her first patient.

The list was long and varied, mainly made up of Jeanette's patients who had come expecting to see their regular GP. One or two, she gathered from the receptionists, had made other appointments when they'd found Jeanette wasn't there, others were desperate and didn't mind who they saw as their symptoms required immediate relief, and yet others, whose condition was neither serious nor who wanted to make other appointments, came out of sheer curiosity—perhaps in the vague hope that this new young doctor might shed fresh light on a chronic ailment.

The conditions in that first surgery ranged from a young woman suffering from frequent and painful bouts of cystitis to an elderly man with chronic bronchitis, from a child with an ear infection to a teenage girl with period pains and finally a distraught woman whose husband had just left her and their young children to set up home with her best friend.

After surgery and a quick coffee in the staffroom to

steady her nerves after the anguish of her last patient, Adele took several of Jeanette's home visits, the remainder being shared between Casey and Toby. One of these visits was up on the Bowscombe Estate, a prospect that filled Adele with apprehension. Her fears proved to be unfounded, however, for when she parked her car in front of the same seedy shopping mall which she had visited with Casey and faced the same group of youths lolling against the railings, it was to find that two of Flo Procter's boys were part of the group. She wasn't sure which two they were but they recognised her and when the inevitable jeers and catcalls began they intervened.

'Leave 'er alone,' called one of them, Robbie maybe or perhaps it was Elton. 'She's OK, she is. That's Dr Brooks—she's Casey's bird and she saw to our Stevie.'

'Yeah,' said the other. 'He were banged up but she saw he were bad and got 'im to 'ospital, didn't you, Doc?'

'That's right.' Adele managed a nervous smile, deciding not to correct the status he had bestowed on her. 'I did. So how is Stevie now?' she added bravely as her courage grew.

'He's all right,' said the first youth. 'He's 'ome now. He'll be in court soon,' he added proudly.

'Oh, really?' Adele swallowed but as she walked across to the block of flats she was visiting she suddenly had a rather satisfying feeling of having been accepted by this community, partly because of having been the one to spot Stevie's condition and partly—and she suspected the greater part—because she was Casey's trainee. But whatever it was, it added to her confidence, leaving her with a certainty that when she emerged from the flats after seeing her patient, her car would not only still be there but would also be in one piece.

'How did your day go?' asked Casey later, after she had

completed her second surgery and was wading through a mountain of paperwork.

'All right—I think.' She was exhausted but she didn't want to let him know that.

'Any problems?'

'No, I don't think so.' She shook her head. 'It was all pretty much routine. I'll leave a list of notes and referrals for Jeanette to see.' She paused. 'Have we heard any more about Lara?'

'She's holding her own apparently,' Casey replied. 'I spoke to Jeanette earlier. She said Lara is still only semi-conscious and they won't know if there's been any lasting brain damage until after they've done a scan, which should be some time tomorrow.'

'And the other girl?'

'She's OK. She was discharged from hospital last night. I just wish—' his jaw tightened '—they could catch the lowlifes who supply the stuff to these kids.' He paused. 'Oh, by the way, did you know the police have made an arrest in connection with the murder case?'

'Yes.' Adele nodded. 'They were saying something about it in Reception. Was it the mother's boyfriend?'

'No, that's what people assumed but the guy they've arrested was a boyfriend of the girl herself—someone in his twenties who had been seeing her for some months.'

'But she was barely fifteen,' protested Adele as an image of the girl came into her mind as she had seen her lying beneath that makeshift tent on the edge of a rain-swept quarry.

'I know.' Casey took a deep breath. 'But it bears out what I said about not jumping to the obvious conclusion.' He paused and after a moment said, 'Do you fancy going for a drink somewhere?'

Her immediate reaction was to say yes, that there was

nothing she'd like better, but something stopped her. 'No, thanks,' she heard herself say. 'I have things to do.'

That look of puzzlement was back on his face as if he simply couldn't understand the new coolness that was suddenly between them. Then he shrugged and left her to her paperwork.

This coolness, probably imperceptible to anyone else, seemed to grow between Adele and Casey as the week progressed and Adele continued to take Jeanette's surgeries. It saddened her that it had to be so, leaving an ache in her heart that surprisingly bore no resemblance to the ache that Nigel had left there.

And then, with no hint of warning, a chain of events began which was to change everything. It started at the end of the week during an afternoon surgery when Cheryl phoned through to ask Adele if she would see Elvira Jackson.

'Does she have an appointment?' asked Adele, her heart sinking at the thought of what she might be asked to deal with, given Elvira's unpredictable nature.

'No, she doesn't,' Cheryl replied. 'She just wandered in like she always does, demanding to see a doctor. I explained that Dr Maynard isn't here but she didn't seem bothered. Normally I would ask Casey to see her but he's out on a call. I can't ask Toby because it's been agreed that Toby doesn't see Elvira and that only leaves Dr Fletcher or yourself. Dr Fletcher has only just started his surgery…'

'And I've nearly finished,' said Adele. 'OK, I'll see her. Let me see a couple more on my list then send her in.'

'Thanks, Doctor.' The relief in Cheryl's voice was only too obvious.

The following two patients were routine appointments, one for a blood-pressure check and the other for a follow-up prescription, and as the second patient left the room Adele pressed the buzzer, mentally bracing herself.

As on the previous occasion that Elvira had come to the surgery, she came straight into the room without knocking. She still had the same rather wild-looking appearance, with her flowing dark hair, her layers of drab grey clothing and the strange expression in those pale eyes.

'Hello, Elvira,' said Adele.

Elvira sank down onto a chair without answering, dumping her various bags and carriers onto the floor beside her, and as the grey knitted coat fell open Adele noticed that beneath the scarves there was a glimmer of some orange material.

'How can I help you, Elvira?' she asked, folding her hands together on the desk and hoping desperately that Elvira wasn't going to demand more pregnancy tests.

'I want you to make sure the baby's all right,' said Elvira.

'The baby...?' Adele frowned.

'Yes. This baby.' Elvira patted her stomach. 'I need you to listen with one of those trumpet things.'

For a moment Adele was thrown. There was no baby, neither was there likely to be in view of what Casey had told her concerning Elvira's infertility, but he'd also said they'd had many problems in the past with Elvira and that it was probably best to humour her. While she was still struggling over the best approach to take, Elvira stood up, picked up her bags and walked towards the examination room, tugging open the door then disappearing inside. Adele hesitated for a moment then, rising to her feet, took an obstetric trumpet from Jeanette's cupboard and followed her. No doubt humouring her was by far the best way right now. Later maybe she could have a word with

Elvira's psychiatric social worker warning her that it seemed Elvira had another of her fixations.

Still fully clothed, Elvira had hauled herself onto the examination couch and was lying there, staring at the ceiling. As Adele approached the couch Elvira pulled aside her coat and scarves and fumbled with the silky material of her orange top. It suddenly struck Adele that the top was very similar to the one she had bought for the Fletchers' dinner party, the one she had been unable to find either at the time or since. In fact, it was identical, with its pleated neckline edged with tiny crystal beads. No doubt Elvira had bought herself one from the same high street shop.

Pulling up the top, Elvira exposed her smooth, white stomach. 'Listen in there,' she demanded.

Dutifully Adele put the trumpet to Elvira's abdomen and listened, at the same time wondering what Casey would have done. Probably he would have refused, being quite adamant that there was no baby. On the other hand, it had been he who had said it best to humour Elvira.

'What can you hear?' demanded Elvira.

'Actually,' said Adele, straightening up, 'I can't hear anything, Elvira.'

'What are you saying?' Elvira struggled into a sitting position.

'Only that I can't hear anything,' Adele replied truthfully.

'You're saying there isn't a baby,' said Elvira. Pulling her clothes around her, she slid from the couch, gathered up her various bags and plastic carriers and stalked out of the examination room and then out of the consulting room.

Adele followed her to the door. 'Elvira…' she called after the woman's retreating figure, but Elvira failed even to turn and with a sigh Adele went back into the room and sat down once more at the desk.

She was far from satisfied with how she had dealt with the situation but she wasn't quite sure what else she could have done, given the circumstances. Lifting the telephone receiver, she asked Cheryl if Elvira had left the surgery.

'Yes,' Cheryl answered, 'she's just swept out. Did you have a problem with her?'

'Not exactly, but I think I'd like a word with her psychiatric social worker. Could you get her for me, please?'

'Yes, of course,' Cheryl replied. 'That'll be Ruby Felton.'

Adele held the line and Ruby came on within a couple of minutes. 'Dr Brooks?' she said. 'How may I help you?'

'It's probably nothing, Ruby,' said Adele. 'But I've just had Elvira Jackson in.'

'Do we have a problem looming?' asked Ruby.

'I think we might,' Adele replied. 'Unfortunately Elvira thinks she's pregnant.'

'Oh, dear, no, not again,' sighed Ruby.

'I had heard this has happened before.'

'Yes, about a year ago. Elvira will have quite long stretches of time where she's absolutely fine—that's when she remembers to take her medication. If she forgets or refuses to take it we usually have a problem, more often than not some sort of fixation. If it gets out of hand Elvira could then become a danger to herself and to others.'

'Where is she living these days?' asked Adele.

'She's in a hostel. I think I'll call in later today and check up on her medication.'

'Thanks, Ruby, I'd appreciate that.' Adele was relieved.

'Not at all. It should be me thanking you. You've probably tipped me off in good time before things get out of hand.'

Adele put the phone down, feeling decidedly better than she had when Elvira had stalked out of the room, and by the time she'd finished her surgery she'd almost managed to put Elvira out of her mind.

On returning to Reception with the patients' records, she found a debate going on between Penny, Cheryl and Lizzie over what Penny was going to wear that evening.

'I think the black for where you're going,' said Cheryl, standing back and eyeing Penny up and down as if she were wearing the garment she had in mind instead of her nursing uniform.

'But I think it makes me look fat!' wailed Penny.

'No, it doesn't,' said Cheryl. 'Black is slimming, isn't it?' she added, looking at Adele for support.

'Er, yes, I suppose it is,' Adele agreed.

'Not that she'd know,' said Lizzie with a sniff. 'I'll bet she's never had to lose weight in her life.'

'No, not really,' Adele admitted. 'In fact, at one time when I was in my teens I was actually trying to put a little weight on.'

'Doesn't it just make you sick?' sighed Penny. 'I know after tonight I shall probably have to go back to my slimming club. Honestly, I only have to look at a slice of cheesecake and it settles on my hips. Which makes me wonder whether I should wear the cream trousers. They do make my hips look thinner…whereas the black…'

Suddenly Adele couldn't bear to listen to any more. It was pretty obvious that Penny had a date that evening and it stood to reason that date was with Casey. She didn't want to hear about it, about what Penny intended wearing or where they were going, because if she did, she knew that for the rest of the night she would carry in her head

images of a romantic, intimate meal for two in some se-
cluded restaurant together with what would inevitably follow.

Out of the corner of her eye she saw Casey coming
through the front entrance and with a muttered excuse she
hurried out of Reception, passing Casey with barely more
than a nod as she made her way outside and round the
building to the entrance to the flats.

Wearily she trailed up the stairs, angry with herself for
feeling the way she did. She should be happy for Penny
and Casey—and she was, wasn't she? she asked herself
firmly as she inserted her key in the lock and opened the
door of her flat.

The first thing that struck her was that something was
different. It was darker than usual—the muslin curtains
drawn together, shutting out the light. Surely she hadn't
left them like that when she'd left the flat that morning?
The second thing, to her amazement, was that there were
candles burning—on the coffee-table, the mantelpiece and
the bureau. Although she often lit candles, she knew for
certain she hadn't left any burning that day and even if
she had, they would have burnt out in the time she had
been away.

With a muttered exclamation she started forward and as
she did so the door shut behind her with a loud click,
which caused her to turn sharply. A figure was sitting in
the chair behind the door. In shock Adele saw that it was
Elvira.

CHAPTER ELEVEN

'ELVIRA!' Adele's mouth suddenly went dry. 'What are you doing here?'

Elvira stared steadily back at her. 'I live here,' she said. 'This is my flat.'

'No, Elvira.' Adele struggled to stay calm. 'This is my flat. It used to be yours,' she added hastily when she saw Elvira's nostrils flare, 'but it's mine now. You live at the hostel.'

'I live here,' said Elvira, deliberately emphasising each word.

'How did you get in?' Adele frowned, knowing for a fact that she'd locked the door that morning as she did every morning when she left the flat.

'With my key, of course.' Elvira's lip curled in derision. 'How d'you think I got in?'

'I didn't know you had a key.'

'Of course I have. I had a spare one cut.'

Adele stared at her. 'But didn't you hand it over with the other keys when you left?' she asked at last.

'Why should I?' Elvira demanded. 'It's mine. I paid for it. I needed it to get into my flat.'

For a moment Adele was speechless. An awful possibility began to form in her mind and she said, 'Have you been in here before, Elvira? Since you've been staying at the hostel?'

'Oh, yes.' Elvira's strange, pale eyes shone in the candlelight. 'I can't get in at night because they lock the out-

side door, but during the day when you're all busy downstairs I come up here.'

Suddenly the hairs at the back of Adele's neck stood on
end as it became clear what Elvira was saying, and at the
same moment she knew with indisputable certainty that
the orange top Elvira was wearing was the one she herself
had bought and been unable to find. From what Elvira had
just said, it sounded as if she'd let herself into the flat,
rummaged through her possessions and taken the top. And
it seemed as if that hadn't been the only occasion. If what
she'd said was true, it would appear she had been here in
the flat many times while Adele had been working.

Fighting a sudden wave of rising panic, Adele somehow
hung onto her sanity, knowing the only way out of this
was to humour the woman. 'I think,' she said, her gaze
flickering briefly to the door, 'I'll just pop down to the
surgery again. I left some notes down there—'

'No, you won't.' Elvira's voice was like a whiplash.
'You'll tell them I'm here and they'll make me go back
to the hostel. I'm not going back,' she said determinedly,
'and you're not going anywhere either. I need you here to
deliver my baby.'

'Your baby…?' Adele swallowed, wondering how on
earth she could get out of this desperate situation.

'It'll be born soon.' Elvira nodded. 'See, I've started to
get ready. I've lit all the candles…you'll have to boil the
water. They always have boiling water.'

Adele stared at her. 'Yes, of course…the water,' she
said at last. Turning, she moved into the kitchen.

With shaking hands she filled the kettle, plugged it in
and flicked the switch. There was no sound from the main
room and as she waited for the water to boil she leaned
across the sink unit and peered out of the window. The
kitchen overlooked the courtyard—maybe, if she was care-

ful, she could attract someone's attention. Even as the possibility entered her head Toby's car drew into the courtyard. Adele sucked in her breath then as quietly as she could she gently lifted the window catch and pushed open the window.

As Toby stepped out of his car she braced herself to shout.

'Get away from that window!' She turned sharply to find Elvira behind her, and in that instant while she was thrown off her guard Elvira leaned forward and pulled the window shut. It made a noise and from where Adele was standing she could see that Toby glanced up before disappearing from their view into the house. Even now he would be making his way up the stairs to his own flat on the first floor, totally unaware of the drama being played out above him.

With a little gasp of despair Adele turned to find Elvira so close that her face was only inches from her own. She was vaguely aware that she had something in her hand but she was so close that for a moment she was unable to see what it was.

'Don't even think about any funny business!' hissed Elvira. 'You have a job to do.'

There was a click and a flame flared in Adele's face. As she felt the heat she recoiled in horror as she realised that the object in Elvira's hand was a cigarette lighter.

'If you make any trouble I'll set fire to your hair.' Elvira spoke quietly but with so much menace that Adele in a moment of sheer terror didn't for one moment doubt that she would carry out her threat if the desire took her to do so.

Humour her, she heard Casey say in her mind. Humour her. That might have been relatively easy in a crowded surgery—it was something else entirely up here, alone, at the top of the house with a disturbed woman who had a tendency towards pyromania.

'We're not leaving here till you deliver my baby.' Elvira extinguished the flame but the light in her eyes burned as fiercely as ever. 'So you might as well get that into your head now.'

In a desperate effort to pull herself together Adele took a deep breath. She knew that everything depended on how she handled the situation with this very disturbed woman. Slowly she followed Elvira back into the living room where the other woman resumed her position on the seat behind the door. Gingerly Adele perched herself on the edge of the sofa and for a period of time, the length of which she found impossible to determine—and as all around them the candles flickered and burned lower—they remained that way, waiting presumably for Elvira to announce the imminent arrival of her baby.

And then, slowly at first but gathering momentum and in a more determined fashion, Elvira began rocking herself back and forth in her chair and muttering under her breath. Once or twice Adele caught the word 'Nash' and remembered that Casey had told her that Elvira had had a fixation with Toby in the past. She wondered if in her own mind Elvira thought that Toby was the father of the baby she believed she was carrying.

Adele knew that if she didn't do something the situation could well go on all night, but the only other way to attract attention would be by phone. She had already ruled out using the main phone, which was in full view of Elvira, but in her pocket she carried her mobile phone. Maybe, if she could get away from Elvira's gaze for just a few moments, she could text a message to Casey whose own mobile number was programmed into her phone. But getting away from Elvira was going to be the biggest problem.

Humour her, Casey had said. Previously, Adele had doubted the wisdom of going along with the pretence of the baby. Now, as she gradually reached the conclusion that it could offer the solution she needed, she had no such qualms.

'Do you have a name for the baby?' she asked after a while. She struggled to keep her tone casual, matter-of-fact, just as if she were talking to a patient in the antenatal clinic.

Elvira, however, chose not to answer, instead increasing the momentum of her rocking action. Adele decided to continue with the strategy she had chosen.

'I was just wondering,' she said, looking around the room, 'where we'll put baby after it's born. I could clear out a drawer, or on second thoughts the bed might be better—the sheets were clean on this morning and we do have to make sure everything is clean. Speaking of which, I'll need to scrub up if I'm to deliver a baby.' She stood up and, keeping a wary eye on Elvira, moved towards the bathroom. Elvira seemed oblivious to her and carried on with her rocking movement, all the while muttering to herself.

Once inside the bathroom Adele didn't dare to shut the door, let alone lock it, afraid if she did so that Elvira's mood might change again and she might see fit to set fire to goodness knows what, endangering the safety of them both in this top-floor flat. Instead, she turned on both taps and, picking up a nailbrush in her left hand, began a scrubbing movement against her leg. With her right hand she carefully withdrew her mobile phone from her pocket and under cover of the sound of scrubbing and of running water she compiled a text message to Casey. All she put was, 'Elvira. My flat. Dangerous.' Then she sent the message, slipped the phone back into her pocket and washed her hands before turning the taps off.

When she returned to the living area she was wiping her hands on a towel. Elvira was in exactly the same position but her gaze very briefly flickered in Adele's direction. Adele noticed that one of the candles had gone out and another two were flickering wildly. She wondered whether she should offer to light more. The last thing she wanted was for Elvira to start waving her lighter around again, but in the end she thought better of it. While being attracted to fire herself, Elvira might well resent anyone else's control over it.

'Well,' Adele said brightly, resuming her seat on the sofa, 'that's that. We're all ready now for baby's arrival.'

Elvira stopped rocking and looked levelly at Adele, and Adele found herself holding her breath. 'What baby?' she almost snarled the words.

'Your baby, of course, Elvira,' said Adele, endeavouring to keep a smile on her face but she feared, failing miserably as she felt it degenerate into a grimace. 'The baby you're expecting.'

'You silly cat!' spat Elvira. 'I'm not having a baby.'

'You're not?' said Adele weakly.

'Course I'm not. How dare you say I'm having a baby? That's filthy, that is. I never let no one touch me.' Elvira's voice began to rise hysterically.

'All right, Elvira,' said Adele more calmly than she was feeling. 'You're not going to have a baby.'

Desperately she wished Casey would come. Had he got her message? Had he gone out with Penny already or had she caught him before they went? The clock read ten past seven which meant she had been here with Elvira for just over an hour. It seemed longer than that—much longer. Supposing Casey hadn't got the message, what then?

Would they be here all night? She shuddered at the thought and as Elvira began to get increasingly restless and Adele was on the edge of despair, wondering what on earth she could do next, the door was suddenly flung back on its hinges and the room was full of people.

Casey was there in his battered leather jacket, there were policemen in uniform and Ruby Felton, Elvira's social worker, was with them. What happened next was to become a blur in Adele's mind. She was vaguely aware that Elvira was being examined by Casey who gave her an injection then, accompanied by Ruby, she was led away by the police until in the end there was only herself and Casey left in the flat together with one policeman.

'Are you all right, Dr Brooks?' The policeman crouched down in front of Adele who was still sitting on the sofa.

'Yes, I'm fine, thanks,' Adele lied automatically. She wasn't really fine. She had started to shake, her throat was dry and her stomach was churning.

'Can you tell me exactly what happened here?' The policeman was very young and not one whom she'd seen at the police station.

'She was here when I came up to the flat.' Adele clenched her hands, digging her nails into her palms in an attempt to stop them shaking.

'So had she broken in?' The policeman was writing now in a spiral-bound notebook.

'She said she had a key.' Adele swallowed. 'She said she had one cut.' Casey drew in his breath sharply and Adele threw him a quick glance. His expression was grim, his jaw taut and his mouth set in an uncompromising line.

'Will you be wanting to bring any charges?' asked the policeman.

Adele shook her head. 'I shouldn't think so,' she said. 'She's a patient and she was very disturbed.'

'Can we discuss this later?' said Casey.

'Yes, of course.' The policeman straightened up and closed his notebook. 'We'll be wanting a statement from you, Dr Brooks, next time you're down at the station.'

He departed, leaving Adele and Casey alone.

'Are you really all right?' Casey turned to Adele as the door shut behind the policeman.

'Yes, I think so…' She attempted to stand up and as her legs threatened to give out, she would have stumbled if Casey hadn't steadied her.

'Hey,' he said softly, 'you're not all right, are you?' He continued to hold her.

'I seem to be making a habit of this sort of thing,' she said shakily. 'Last time it was certifying a death, this time it's…well, I don't really know what you'd call this. All I know is that she frightened me to death.'

'You say she had a key?' Casey lowered his head slightly to look into her face.

'Yes.' Adele nodded. 'She said she'd had one cut when she was living here.'

Casey looked quite stricken. 'We should have changed the locks. So what happened?' Slowly he sat down on the sofa and drew Adele down beside him, all the while keeping one arm around her.

'She came to surgery,' Adele explained slowly. 'I was the only one available so I told Cheryl I would see her. She was still fixed on the fact that she was having a baby— she wanted me to listen for the heartbeat.'

'So did you?' Casey's eyes narrowed.

'Yes, but I told her I couldn't hear anything,' Adele replied. When Casey nodded, as if in approval, she went on, 'But that seemed to annoy her. She walked out of the surgery. I was concerned about her state of mind so I rang Ruby Felton. Ruby said to leave it with her and that she would call at the hostel where Elvira is living and check that she's taking her medication. I was happy with that but later after surgery when I came up to the flat I found that—' her voice wavered as she relived that awful moment '—Elvira had let herself in.'

'What state of mind was she in at that point?' asked Casey.

Briefly Adele told him about how Elvira had thought that this was still her flat, of how she wanted her, Adele, to stay there and deliver her baby and of how she had lit all the candles in the flat.

He interrupted her only once. 'Did she threaten you?'

Adele took a deep breath then nodded. 'Yes, when I tried to attract Toby's attention out of the window. She'd followed me into the kitchen and she threatened to set fire…to my hair.' She turned and looked at him as she spoke and saw the brief look of horror that passed across his features.

'Did she have matches?' His arm tightened around her.

'No, a cigarette lighter.' Adele shuddered at the memory. 'I don't doubt she would have done it but I managed to get her back in here and we sat for ages, but when I started talking about the baby again…you know, to try and humour her, she didn't seem to know what I was talking about. It was pretty scary, I can tell you…'

'I'm sure it was.' Casey ran a hand over his hair in a distracted fashion. 'Hell, it must have been a nightmare.'

'It was…rather,' Adele gulped. 'And another thing, and I have to say this really freaked me out—she was wearing one of my tops.'

'What?' Casey frowned. 'You mean she went through your things before you came up here?'

'No.' Adele shook her head. 'It was worse than that. She'd been in here before and taken it. She was wearing it when she came to the surgery. At that point, even though mine had gone missing I thought it was just a similar one, but after finding her here and realising that she'd had a key all this time I knew it was mine and that she'd been here before. I...I don't know how many times...but I tell you, it's really scary, thinking back over and just wondering when she might have been in here.' She paused, reflecting.

'She said she would come here while we were working during the day,' she continued after a while. 'Presumably she couldn't get in at night because the outer door would have been locked and bolted.' She clenched her hands again. 'That's something, I suppose—the thought of her getting in here at night simply doesn't bear thinking about.' Falling silent again, she dwelt on the awful possibility of that then after a while she went on, 'It's made me wonder about other things. Like when I first moved in, I found food in the fridge. I thought at the time that it might have been Penny or Rosie but when I asked them neither of them knew anything about it. I guess that must have been Elvira as well. Goodness knows what other things she did. She probably went through all my things— my letters, my clothes, everything...'

Casey, while continuing to hold her closely against him, had grown very quiet and when she turned towards him questioningly, he said, 'Actually, I have a bit of a confession to make...'

'A confession?' She frowned.

'Yes.' He hesitated, as if uncertain how to continue, then he said, 'It wasn't Elvira who put the food in the fridge— it was me.'

'You!' She stared at him in amazement.

'Yes.' He nodded in an embarrassed sort of way. 'I thought, well, I thought it would be by way of a welcome,

I suppose. I guess I was feeling a bit guilty. I'd opposed the idea of a trainee and in the end I'd been forced into being the one to take on your training. I wasn't too happy about that and I knew I would have to make a real effort if I wasn't to let my attitude show…'

'And there was me being really off with you when I first arrived,' said Adele slowly, 'saying you didn't look like a doctor and telling you that you couldn't park in the courtyard…'

'Yes, you were a bit uppity,' agreed Casey with a sudden grin. As always the smile transformed his features, giving a brief glimpse of the man beneath the tough exterior he presented to the world.

While they'd been talking they'd gradually relaxed, moving farther back into the comfort of the sofa's many cushions, and all the while Casey's arm had remained protectively around her. It had felt good, warm and safe, and she'd had not the slightest desire to push him away, but now, as the terrors of her ordeal faded a little and the reality sank in that the danger was over, the incongruity of their situation finally hit her.

Very gradually Adele began to ease herself away from him, but even though she succeeded in putting a little distance between them his arm remained along the back of the sofa.

'I'm all right now, Casey,' she said at last, a little uneasily. 'I mustn't keep you any longer.' Really, there wasn't anything she would have liked better—for him to stay there with her for the rest of the evening, or even the night. But, no, she mustn't even entertain such thoughts, intriguing as they might be.

'I'm not in any hurry.' Casey leaned back on the sofa, stretching out his legs before him and linking his hands behind his head.

'But aren't you going to be late?' Adele half turned and looked at him, surprised at his apparent lack of urgency. She wasn't sure what time his date with Penny was but it had to be soon.

'Late for what?' He'd closed his eyes and he answered without opening them.

'Well, your date,' she said uncertainly, wondering whether in the heat of the moment he might have simply forgotten. Surely now he would leap up and beat a hasty retreat to his own flat to change into appropriate wear to take Penny to the restaurant she had been talking about earlier?

'I wasn't aware I had a date.' He opened one eye and looked at her.

'But I thought…I thought you and Penny had a date this evening…'

'I can't imagine why you would have thought that.'

'Well, I thought… Penny was talking to the girls earlier about what she was going to wear for her date this evening.'

'So why should you have thought her date was with me?' He'd opened both eyes now and, lowering his arms and easing himself into an upright position, he stared at her.

'Well, you and Penny are an item…aren't you?' Adele felt she was rapidly in danger of losing the plot.

'Do you know,' he said, 'you're the second person recently who was under that same impression.'

'Am I?' she asked faintly.

'Yes.' He nodded. 'Toby thought the same thing.'

'Toby…?' Suddenly this whole conversation seemed in danger of spiralling right out of control.

'Yes. Toby seemed to think that Penny and I had a thing going. I can't imagine how these rumours start.' He shook his head as if the whole thing was beyond him. 'And then,' he went on, 'when I put Toby right he seemed not only amazed but utterly delighted. It appears he had wanted to ask Penny out but hadn't because he thought she was seeing me. In fact, I think you'll find it's Toby who has the date with Penny tonight.'

'I don't understand.' Adele stared at him but somewhere deep inside a little throb of excitement had begun. 'I thought you and Penny were an item. I've thought it ever since I arrived. It was me who told Toby that you were—'

'Ah, so it was you who started the rumour.' There was a look of exasperated amusement on his face now. 'But I have to say I can't think why. Whatever gave you that impression?'

'It was Penny herself who told me.' Adele was thoroughly bewildered now. 'The day I arrived she came in here to welcome me and she confided in me that you and she were a bit of an item. She said it was only early days but that she was hopeful that it was going somewhere.' She paused and saw that Casey had grown very still. 'So what was all that about?' she asked. 'Why would Penny have thought that?'

'I can only think,' he said at last, 'that it was something to do with the fact that I took her out to dinner.'

'You took Penny out to dinner?'

'Yes,' he said. 'It was by way of showing appreciation. She'd given me a hand when I moved in here—cooked me a couple of meals, that sort of thing—and I just thought it was a gesture, that's all. I had no idea she'd misconstrued it. When Toby mentioned it, I just thought he'd been mistaken and when he said that he'd fancied Penny for a long time I told him to go ahead and ask her out. But now that you've said this I wonder if perhaps I'd better speak to Penny and clear up any misunderstanding.'

'So there was never anything between you?' asked Adele softly.

'Of course not.' He stared at her then in further exasperation he said, 'Don't get me wrong. Penny's a lovely girl but she isn't my type—it's as simple as that.'

Suddenly Adele longed to ask him just exactly what was his type but she didn't quite dare and in the end she didn't have to, for right out of the blue Casey suddenly leaned forward and said, 'You're my type, Adele.'

'Am I?' she said, delighted but startled by his bluntness.

'I thought I'd made that only too obvious,' he said ruefully. 'In the end I backed off because I thought you weren't ready for another relationship yet.'

'And I kept you at arm's length because I thought you were two-timing Penny,' said Adele incredulously.

'You mean…you, too?' he said, his eyes widening.

'Oh, yes,' she replied softly.

A variety of emotions passed across his features and after a moment he said, 'I couldn't believe it when you turned up with Toby at Celia's party, especially after you'd made it plain to me that you weren't into relationships at the moment.'

'You acted as if you were jealous.' Adele raised one eyebrow.

'Maybe I was at that,' he said quietly, and suddenly the idea of him being jealous of Toby stirred some basic emotion deep inside her.

They were silent for a while, each reflecting on what had happened, then Casey rose to his feet and, taking her hands, drew her up beside him. 'I have a suggestion to make,' he said.

Adele looked up at him and her heart lurched at the expression she saw in his eyes.

'What's that?' she whispered.

'I suggest we start again—as if we'd just met. I'll speak to Penny and make sure there are no misunderstandings. I want you to be sure you're over Nigel and happy about starting another relationship, and I'll have a word with Edward and make sure there are no ethical complications with a trainer and his trainee becoming an item. How does that sound to you?'

'It sounds wonderful,' she said simply. 'Just let me know when you've sorted it all out.'

Slowly he leaned forward and very gently touched her lips with his. It had none of the fire or passion of that last time but it carried tenderness beyond her wildest dreams and more than the hint of a promise of what might be to come.

CHAPTER TWELVE

AT FIRST Adele could hardly believe it was happening. 'We'll take it slowly,' Casey had said, and they did, allowing their initial attraction for each other to grow into a delicious awareness of one another. For Adele, the fact that Casey and Penny weren't an item, and furthermore never had been, had come as a wonderful revelation. She was anxious at first as to how Penny would react when Casey spoke to her but she needn't have worried.

'She was fine,' he told her in response to her worried questions. 'She'd thought that maybe we could get together after the meal we'd had but she'd realised in the last few weeks that it wasn't going to happen.'

'What about her and Toby?'

'Well, that does look as if it might be going somewhere. Toby's leaping about like a two-year-old and Penny looks, well, I don't know what the word is...'

'Radiant?' suggested Adele.

Casey frowned. 'Yes, I suppose you could call it that,' he agreed at last. 'Radiant.'

Adele smiled. 'And what about us?' she asked softly. They were in Casey's consulting room at the time. She was perched on the edge of the desk and he was seated alongside her in his chair.

'What about us?' he asked, reaching out and covering her knee with his hand. His touch sent shock waves through her body and she was forced to struggle to concentrate on what she was saying when really she would have liked nothing better than to slide along the desk and into his lap.

'Did you tell her about us?' she asked, ignoring the clamouring of her body.

'Yes, I did,' Casey confessed.

'How did she take it?'

'In my experience, those who are in love have nothing but generosity towards others.'

'You mean she didn't mind?'

'On the contrary. She said she wasn't surprised, that she'd suspected it might happen from the moment you arrived.'

'Maybe that was why she warned me off on that very first day,' said Adele slowly.

'Yes, maybe,' Casey agreed, 'but whatever, we needn't worry about that any more.'

'And what about Edward?' Adele leaned forward slightly. 'Have you told him yet?'

'Ah, yes, Edward. Now, that was a bit more of a worry.' Removing his hand from her knee, Casey rubbed his fingers over his forehead, the gesture somehow both boyish and endearing.

'Was there a problem?' asked Adele quickly. 'Did he object?'

'Not object exactly.' Casey shook his head. 'In fact, when I first told him I would have said his initial reaction was one of delight, but since then he's seemed a little more...well, guarded I suppose you'd call it.'

'Has he said why?'

'Not really.' Casey shrugged. 'He did imply that it mustn't affect our work in any way and I suppose he does have a point there. Neither would he want too much gossip...'

'Probably there will only be gossip and speculation

whilst people don't know for sure,' said Adele slowly. 'Maybe once they do know it won't matter to them.'

'Maybe,' Casey agreed, then he added, 'But perhaps at least for the time being it might be an idea to keep it low-key whilst the others are around.' He must have seen her look of disappointment. 'Don't get me wrong,' he added hurriedly, 'I would like to shout it from the housetops, but I don't want anything to compromise your position here.'

'OK.' Adele nodded.

'We'll make up for it behind closed doors,' he added softly.

'Oh, yes,' she murmured. He looked faintly anxious and, reaching out her hand, she gently smoothed his forehead as if to eradicate the lines of tension. At the same time she smoothed his eyebrow which, as ever, was ruffled by the deep line of his scar. 'Tell me,' she said in the same soft tone. 'I've been dying to ask ever since we met. How did you get this?'

'How do you think I might have got it?' There was a hint of amusement in his voice now as his brow cleared.

'I thought probably in those wild days of your youth, in a fight between rival gangs, maybe over a girl...'

He laughed, throwing his head back. 'Nothing so romantic, I can assure you,' he said.

'Then how?'

'I came off a motorbike. Years ago. Wet night, sharp bend.' He shrugged. 'These things happen. There, now, you're disappointed, aren't you?'

'Not exactly. I just thought...' It was her turn to laugh and that was how Cheryl found them as she tapped on the door and opened it without waiting for an answer—Adele sitting on the desk facing Casey, both laughing.

'Oh, I'm sorry.' Cheryl looked from one to the other

with barely concealed interest. 'I just wanted some signatures.'

'So much for keeping it quiet,' said Casey ruefully after Cheryl had gone. 'She couldn't wait to get back to the others to tell them.'

'Well.' Adele slipped down from the desk. 'From now on we'll be models of discretion.'

And they were. During surgery hours anyway, whether in their consulting rooms, in the staffroom, on house calls or if they both attended a police call-out. But when they were off duty it was a different matter as they spent more and more time together. Within a very short space of time Adele knew she was falling deeply in love with Casey.

'Am I always to call you that?' she asked one day as they walked together in the woods behind Stourborne Abbas.

'I would prefer that you do,' he replied.

'So do I get to know the first name you so despise?' She looked up at him from beneath her lashes.

'It isn't so much that I despise it,' he said stiffly. 'It was simply that I got fed up with people's reactions when they hear it for the first time.'

'And what reaction is that?'

'Oh, they laugh,' he said wryly. 'Every time they laugh.'

'So try me,' she said. 'I promise I won't laugh. Neither will I tell.'

He was silent for a moment, as if hesitating over whether to tell her or not. It was a misty, autumn morning and to the accompaniment of distant church bells they had tramped for miles across fields damp with dew before entering the splendid silence of the woods where all around the trees were turning to glorious shades of gold, russet and copper.

'Let me try and guess,' she said playfully at last, tugging at his hand.

'Go on, then.' His eyes were serious but a smile played around the corners of his mouth.

'Well, I know it begins with H,' she began slowly.

'How do you know that?' He sounded indignant and she laughed.

'I just do, that's all. Let me see—is it Horace?'

'Of course not.'

'Oh, well.' She shrugged. That put paid to Elaine's theory. 'How about Hannibal?'

'No!' He gave a barely disguised shudder.

'Hamish, then, or Horatio or Hornblower.'

He didn't answer and she flashed him a quick look. 'Am I right?' she demanded. 'Is it one of those? Hornblower?'

'Not Hornblower.' He shook his head. 'And I have to say I wouldn't have minded if it was Hamish.'

'Horatio?' She raised her eyebrows and he nodded miserably.

'Oh, but, Casey…' She stopped, forcing him to do the same. When he turned to face her she took his other hand and looked up at him. 'There's nothing wrong with Horatio. It's a fine, noble name—the name of a hero!'

'You try explaining that to a classroom full of boys when you have to call out your name,' he said gloomily.

'How did it come about?' she asked.

'My mother had a thing about Nelson and Lady Hamilton.'

'I think that's incredibly romantic.'

'OK.' He shrugged, then with a scowl added, 'Just as long as you carry on calling me Casey.'

'Of course I will.' Reaching up, Adele wound her arms around his neck. His kiss as his lips met hers was gentle, full of tenderness, then as passion flared between them, consuming them in a fierce sense of urgency, it grew deeper and more demanding.

That night for the first time they made love. After returning from their walk, Casey cooked supper for them both in his apartment then they lay together on the sofa, listening to music. They had both known all day what was going to happen and when at last, much later, he stood up and, taking her hand, led her to his bedroom it was with a satisfying sense of inevitability. He undressed her slowly in that calm, unhurried way that she had come to associate with him, savouring each moment as if each action and its revelation were precious beyond price. When she was naked he discarded his own clothes, but rapidly this time, letting them fall to the floor before joining her on the bed.

His love-making was passionate and exciting, just as Adele had imagined it might be, arousing her to fever pitch then showing a tender restraint that rendered her almost helpless with impatience.

'We have all night,' he murmured once, and she was forced to wait.

Finally he took her to a place she had never been, from a plateau of longing and desire to a pinnacle of unutterable fulfilment before a long, slow, shuddering descent to reality.

She knew she called his name then clung to him in the darkness, almost sobbing with relief before finally drifting into a deep, dreamless sleep.

In the morning when Adele awoke to bright sunlight she couldn't for a moment think where she was. As memory came flooding back she turned her head, but Casey was no longer beside her. Suddenly she felt bereft, but even as she wondered he came into the bedroom wearing a white towelling robe and bearing two mugs of tea on a tray.

'Good morning.' His gaze met hers.

'Hello,' she said almost shyly, as she suddenly recalled her uninhibited demands of the night before. She sat up, pushing her hair back from her face.

'I trust you slept well.' He sat beside her, passing her one of the mugs.

'Oh, yes.' She smiled, sipping her tea. It was hot and sweet, exactly the way she liked it.

'I just have time for this,' he said, sipping his own tea, 'then I have a call-out.'

'Do you?' She was disappointed. She'd been hoping he would get back into bed so that they could maybe enjoy another half-hour or so together before going down to the surgery.

'Yes, Maudie isn't too well. I just had a call from Flo. I told her I'd go before surgery.'

'OK.' She set her mug down on the bedside table and stretched. 'Do you want me to come with you?'

'No.' He grinned then gently touched her cheek. 'You get yourself sorted out.'

He was gone almost before she knew it. One moment he was there beside her and it seemed the next he was dressed and gone and she was alone in his apartment. But wasn't that what being a doctor entailed? Wouldn't it always be like that, with one or the other of them constantly at the beck and call of the public? With a little sigh Adele finished her tea then slipped out of bed and headed for the shower.

She had a busy day ahead of her. Jeanette was due back at work following the news that Lara hadn't suffered any brain damage, so she would need to go through all the notes of the patients she had seen in Jeanette's absence. And as if that wasn't enough, Edward had said he wanted a couple of days off so she would be covering his surgeries as well.

The day proved to be every bit as hectic as she had feared and it seemed to set the pattern for the remainder of that week. She and Casey snatched moments together whenever they could, but their special time continued to be the nights, which they spent in one or the other of their flats.

One evening when briefly she was alone Adele had a call from her sister.

'Lainey!' she exclaimed when she heard her sister's voice. 'I've been meaning to call you, but somehow I just don't seem to have got round to it. How are you?'

'I'm fine,' her sister replied brightly. Too brightly, thought Adele, who knew her very well. 'More to the point, how are you?'

'Yes, er, pretty good. What's wrong, Lainey?'

'What do you mean, what's wrong?' Elaine sounded indignant now, on the defensive.

'Well, I always know when there's something wrong, so you might as well get it over and tell me what it is.'

She heard her sister's sigh. 'Well, actually…yes, you're right, there is something. I might as well tell you because you'll find out sooner or later anyway. There's not really any easy way of saying this…'

'Oh, do get on with it, Lainey,' said Adele impatiently. 'You're getting me really worried now. It isn't Mum, is it?'

'No, no, it isn't Mum. Nothing like that,' said Elaine hastily. 'It's just that there's an announcement in this morning's *Times* about Nigel's marriage. Apparently he and Lucinda were married a week ago.'

'Nigel?' Adele said coolly, and she surprised even herself at just how coolly. 'Nigel who?'

There was silence from the other end of the line and

Adele found herself smiling as she imagined her sister's expression.

'Well, Nigel.' Elaine sounded bewildered now. 'Your Nigel, of course.'

'He isn't my Nigel.'

'Well, no, I know he isn't now but, well, he was, wasn't he?' The indignant note was back in Elaine's voice.

'Yes, Lainey, he was,' agreed Adele. 'But that's history now. I wish him well—he and Lucinda were made for each other.'

'Well.' Elaine sounded astonished. 'That's very generous of you, I'm sure. I don't think I could have been so charitable under the circumstances…unless… Del, do I detect the presence of another man in your life?' she demanded suddenly.

'How did you guess?' Adele chuckled.

Elaine gave a shriek and Adele nearly dropped the phone. 'Oh, wonderful!' she cried. 'Who is it? No, don't tell me, let me guess. Is it that hunky trainer of yours—the one with the leathers and the motorbike?'

'Right first time,' said Adele dryly, but her heart had leapt at even her sister's description of Casey.

'Oh, Del, I'm so happy for you!' Elaine was almost babbling now. 'So, do you think this is it?' she asked eagerly.

'Oh, I hope so, Lainey,' Adele replied. 'I do hope so because I've never been so happy in all my life.'

It was perfectly true what Adele had told her sister. She had never been so happy before. Casey had added a new dimension to her life, showing her a love of depth and tenderness that she hadn't even touched on with Nigel. In spite of their agreement to keep their relationship as low-key as possible in front of the other members of staff,

Adele's radiance must have been only too obvious to those around her. To her delight Penny's and Toby's romance also seemed to be flourishing.

'This love lark must be catching,' muttered Cheryl one morning in Reception.

'Oh, I hope so,' said Lizzie, leaning over the desk and watching as Penny and Toby lingered together in the foyer before he went off to do his house calls. 'Because whatever it is those two are on—I'd like some.'

Adele and Casey were behind the desk, signing prescriptions, and they both looked up at the comments. As their gazes met, Adele felt the colour flood her cheeks and Casey's lips twitched.

'What do *you* think, Adele?' Cheryl obviously hadn't finished.

'Me?' Adele's voice came out in a startled squawk. 'Oh, I wouldn't know,' she said hastily.

'Yeah, right.' Cheryl turned to answer the phone and Adele was saved from further embarrassment by the arrival of Ruby.

'Ruby, hello!' It was Casey who hailed the social worker, almost as if he was also glad of a diversion in the direction the conversation was taking. 'What news of Elvira?'

'Elvira is doing well. She's still in hospital but she's responding well to a new drug regime. Oh, and you'll be pleased to know I've sorted out new housing arrangements for her in sheltered accommodation. There will be someone on hand to make sure she takes her medication but she'll still retain a good level of independence.'

'Well, that's a relief,' said Lizzie, 'and I'm sure Adele will agree with that.'

'Absolutely.' Adele nodded.

'Keep us posted on Elvira, Ruby,' said Casey. 'When

she comes out of hospital one of us will visit, either myself or Jeanette.'

A few moments later they moved out of Reception and Casey threw a sidelong glance at Adele. 'Does that suit you?' he asked.

'Oh, yes,' she said. 'I don't want to bring any charges against Elvira but, on the other hand, if it can be avoided I'd rather not have any further dealings with her.'

'That sounds sensible to me.' He paused as they reached his consulting room. 'I have a surgery to do now—how about you?'

'I'm going to grab a quick coffee then I'm doing a couple of house calls for Jeanette. She has a meeting with Ruby about counselling for Lara.'

'OK.' He nodded, and as she would have moved away he lightly touched her arm. 'I'll see you later.' He spoke softly so that only she would hear.

'Yes,' she whispered, with a thrill of anticipation. 'Of course.'

She felt as if she were walking on air as she made her way to the staffroom—she could still hardly believe what was happening to her. This heady feeling, this lurching of her heart whenever she caught sight of Casey, the torment when they were apart and the way he filled her thoughts in every waking moment were so unlike anything she had ever known before that sometimes she found herself dreading that it might all come to an end.

Pushing open the staffroom door, she almost ran into the room then she stopped in surprise because Celia Fletcher was sitting in the big chair by the window. With her long, slender legs crossed, she was flicking through the pages of a glossy magazine. It was so unusual to see the senior partner's wife at Woolverton House that for a moment Adele found herself lost for words.

Celia looked up. 'Adele, my dear!' she exclaimed. 'How are you?'

'I'm well, thank you, Celia.' She paused. 'This is a surprise, seeing you here.'

Celia smiled. 'I know. I have to confess I don't come here very much. I'm just waiting for Edward to finish his surgery. He's promised to take me to lunch.'

'Well, that's nice…'

'Actually, Adele…' Swiftly Celia interrupted her. 'I'm glad I've seen you. There was something I wanted to talk to you about.'

'Really?' Adele wondered what on earth the senior partner's wife and herself could possibly have in common.

'Edward tells me that you and Casey have been seeing each other lately.' Celia came straight to the point.

'Yes, that's true, we have,' Adele agreed. Guessing what might be coming next, she rushed on, 'It's all right. Edward didn't seem to think there would be a problem with Casey being my trainer, provided we're discreet and don't let anything interfere with our work…'

'Oh, I'm not worried about that,' said Celia with a dismissive little wave of her hand.

'No?'

'Not at all, and under normal circumstances I would be delighted for the pair of you. I love it when friends of ours get together. No, my worry is something else altogether. I became concerned when I first saw you, the night you came to dinner, but then I thought that you and Toby had something going and I stopped worrying. Later, however, Edward told me about you and Casey and it was then that I made up my mind I should warn you.'

'Warn me?' Adele frowned. 'Whatever do you mean?' A niggle of fear had started somewhere at the back of her mind, a fear that looked as if it could threaten her newly found happiness with Casey.

'You know that Casey was married before, don't you?' said Celia.

'Yes, of course,' Adele replied, 'and that his wife died—and his baby daughter.'

'I knew Casey at the time. I also knew his wife, Trisha—we all worked at the same hospital. Casey was devastated when it happened.'

'Yes, I'm sure he was.' Adele nodded in agreement, wondering just where this could be leading.

'The thing is, Adele, he hasn't been able to commit to anyone since. You see, he adored Trisha. Oh, there have been others since, one in particular, a lovely girl, another nurse, but Casey couldn't commit himself. He moved on—she was heartbroken.'

'Yes, but—'

'No, hear me out, Adele.' Celia raised her hand. 'This other girl was tall and dark-haired, just like Trisha...'

'Maybe that's simply the type Casey is attracted to.'

'Yes, probably so,' Celia agreed, 'but the thing is, Adele, not only are you that same type but you also happen to be the image of Trisha as well.'

'What?' Adele stared at Celia.

'It struck me the moment I met you. I couldn't believe my eyes. I thought I was seeing a ghost. Even your mannerisms are the same and the sound of your voice. Like I say, I feared for the situation then but when you appeared to be so taken with Toby I thought my fears were unfounded. But now I know the truth I really feel I should warn you before you get too attached to Casey. I would hate you to get hurt and, believe me, that's what will happen when Casey moves on again—because he will, make no mistake about that.'

*   *   *

'Before you get too attached to Casey,' Celia had said. If only she knew. Already it was too late. Adele was in as deep as it was possible to be. She loved him and she'd hoped he felt the same way about her. Celia's revelations had come as a shock and Adele knew she needed time to think. Pleading a headache that evening, she told Casey she intended having an early night. He seemed disappointed but so concerned about her that she ended up feeling guilty about lying to him.

In the time that she had known him Casey hadn't given the slightest indication that she resembled his late wife, but what Celia had told her offered a possible explanation for the strange expression on Casey's face when they'd first met and on other numerous occasions when she'd found him watching her. It also explained Celia's strange reaction on meeting her. But more worrying than that was that Celia had said Casey would use her as he had used others in some desperate quest to reconstruct the past then, when that failed, he would leave her and move on.

If that was how it was going to be, Adele knew deep in her heart that she should end the relationship now. After Nigel, she had vowed never to allow herself to become so involved with a man again unless the relationship carried some promise of commitment.

And had there been any such promise from Casey? With a little jolt she was forced to admit there hadn't. Caught up in the thrill of the affair, it had been easy to imagine a glorious future ahead of them, but when she really thought about it she had to accept the stark truth, and that was that Casey hadn't as much as mentioned the future.

Could it really be, as Celia had suggested, that he was living purely for the moment? Since his wife's death did he really find it impossible to love anyone else and was this why he'd wanted to keep their relationship as low-key as possible—because he knew it wasn't going to last?

He'd told her he loved her. Mostly, deep in the night as he made wonderful love to her, as they soared together or afterwards when he tenderly held her, he would tell her he loved her. But when he did so, was it her he was talking to or was it Trisha? Because she looked so like his dead wife, did he imagine it was Trisha he was making love to once more? The thought made her blood run cold and by the end of a sleepless night spent tossing and turning Adele knew she would have to confront Casey. If her fears proved to be true, she knew she would have no other choice but to end the relationship even though it would break her heart to do so.

The following day was extremely busy and she saw Casey only once in passing when he asked briefly if she was feeling better. Later, just as she was finishing her late afternoon surgery, her phone rang.

'Adele, it's me.' There was no need for him to explain—she would have known that voice anywhere. 'I have a police call-out. Care to come along?'

'Er, yes, of course.'

'You hesitate. Are you sure?'

'Yes, I'm sure.' She couldn't let her personal feelings stand in the way of her training, even though she wondered how she would cope in the future, working alongside Casey, if their relationship came to an end.

'We'll take the bike,' he said shortly. 'I'll meet you outside in five minutes.'

She flew up to her flat and changed into warm trousers and a thick sweater. Pulling on a padded jacket and gloves, she hurried down to the courtyard where she found Casey already astride the bike with its engine running. The spare crash helmet was on the pillion seat ready for her and within seconds she had put it on, secured it and had mounted the bike behind him. Then they were away and instinctively Adele wrapped her arms around Casey's waist, holding him tight as they sped to the police station. She could feel the warmth of his body through his jacket and beneath her the deep throbbing of the engine. It felt good to be there, good to be alive and good to be Casey's woman, and it was with a sudden painful pang that she remembered this could be about to come to end, for while the motorbike journeys might well continue, she might soon no longer be Casey's woman.

At the police station a harassed-looking Alan was on duty and briefly outlined the problem as he escorted them to an interview room. It appeared that a woman had been caught shoplifting by a store detective and the police had been called. The woman had been brought to the station where she had been charged, but during the bail process she had been taken ill.

'She looks pretty groggy,' said Alan.

'What age is she?' asked Casey.

'Sixty-five,' Alan replied.

'Does she have anyone with her?' asked Adele.

'Yes, her son has arrived but he seems more concerned with the shame and embarrassment of his mother having been arrested for shoplifting than over the fact that there might be something wrong with her.' As he finished outlining the details, Alan pushed open the door, allowing Casey and Adele to precede him into the interview room.

A grey-haired woman was seated in a chair with a red blanket around her shoulders. She looked pale and dazed and the right side of her face looked as if it had dropped, giving her a curiously lopsided appearance. A police-woman was crouched on one side of her and a man of around forty, dressed in an immaculate pinstriped suit, was pacing around the room. As the door opened he stopped pacing and spun round.

'Are you the doctor?' he demanded.

'Yes. The name's Casey and this is my assistant, Dr Brooks.'

'This is my mother,' the man went on. 'There must have been some dreadful mistake. They're saying she was caught shoplifting but that's impossible—she wouldn't do anything like that. The last thing she would want is to bring shame on the family—on me, in my position.'

'And what is your position, Mr...Mr...?' asked Adele as Casey crouched down in front of the woman in the chair.

'Lauder. Robert Lauder. I'm chairman of the local council. I also have my own firm of accountants. I tell you, all this is simply ludicrous.'

Casey spoke quietly to the woman in the chair. 'Mrs Lauder, can you tell me what happened?'

The woman stared at him but when she attempted to speak her words sounded garbled.

'Good Lord!' Robert Lauder, who had been staring down at his mother, now ran one hand over his head in distraction. 'You haven't been drinking again, have you, Mother? Heaven help us!' He rolled his eyes then turned to Adele. 'She's always been a bit partial to the sherry bottle, but I didn't think she'd get into this state. On the other hand, I suppose it might account for her actions in the store. I mean...if she was drunk...'

By this time Casey had checked Mrs Lauder's pulse and shone his torch into her eyes.

'Is that it, Doctor? Is she drunk?' demanded Robert. He sounded hopeful now, as if it had just occurred to him that this possibility could be by far the lesser of two evils.

'I just want to check your mother's blood pressure,' re-

plied Casey. Adele recognised the cool note in his voice
and knew he didn't think much of the man's attitude. As
Casey took a sphygmomanometer from his bag, she helped
him to expose the patient's arm and secure the cuff. As he
checked the pressure she looked up at the patient's son
once more.

'Does your mother live alone?' she asked.

'Yes, since my father died—that was two years ago.'
Robert spoke as if that should have been a sufficient length
of time for his mother to be over her bereavement. 'So…'
He looked at Casey who had removed the cuff and
straightened up. 'Am I right? Too much sherry?'

'No, Mr Lauder,' Casey replied. 'Your mother has suffered a stroke.'

'A stroke!' Robert looked astounded.

'Yes, it has affected her right side and she's suffered
some paralysis and loss of speech. I want to get her admitted to hospital right away.' He turned to Alan who was
still standing by the door. 'Can you arrange an ambulance,
please, Sergeant?'

'Of course, Doctor,' Alan replied.

'He's a bit of a monster, the son,' said Adele as they stood
on the forecourt and watched the ambulance draw away,
bearing Robert Lauder and his mother.

'We mustn't judge him too harshly,' said Casey as he
put on his crash helmet and passed Adele hers. 'All he
could see was his life becoming complicated.'

'But she's his mother!' protested Adele.

'I know, and on the face of it his treatment of her did
seem pretty uncaring, but we don't know all the facts,
Adele, and ours is not to reason why.'

In silence Adele mounted the bike, but as they drew
away from the station inside she was still seething.

They had travelled for several miles before she realised that they were nowhere near Woolverton House. She leaned forward. 'Where are we going?' she shouted. When Casey didn't answer she thought her words must have been whipped away by the speed at which they were travelling, but a few moment later he pulled into what seemed to be a lay-by and switched off the engine.

Looking around, Adele saw they were on a fairly deserted road high above the town. By now it was late afternoon and the sun was sinking fast in the glorious blush of a mackerel sky while below them smoke from several fires drifted upwards in long thin columns.

Casey indicated for her to dismount. Doing the same himself, he took her hand and said, 'I want to show you something.'

Mystified, she allowed him to lead her through a gap in the hedge and into a field. Below them against the dramatic skyline were the ruins of the once magnificent Stourborne Abbey, to their left lay the town, slumbering in the last of the day's sunlight, and beyond the sweep of the distant hills.

'That,' said Casey as he slipped his arm around her, 'is one magnificent view, do you not agree?'

'Yes,' Adele agreed, 'it is.'

'I've always wanted to live somewhere with such a view,' Casey went on.

'It would be marvellous.' Adele nodded, wondering why Casey had brought her here.

'Actually,' he said after a moment, 'some of this land up here is about to be developed and I'm thinking of putting a deposit on one of the plots. But if I'm to do so I need to move fast—I imagine they'll be snapped up immediately.'

'Yes, I imagine they would.' This didn't come as any

great surprise—Adele had known that Casey was only staying in his flat at Woolverton House until he found a new property.

'The thing is, Adele…' his arm tightened around her. 'I don't want to do so unless I'm sure that it's what you would want as well.'

'Me?' Slowly she half turned to him, for a moment unable to take in what he was saying.

'Yes.' Suddenly his voice sounded husky. 'I'm sorry, I didn't mean to rush you over this. I know we said we'd take things slowly but this opportunity has come up…' He trailed off.

'You mean you want to have a house built up here and you want me to move in with you?' She could hardly believe what she was hearing. This sounded nothing like the Casey who wouldn't allow himself to commit to anyone.

'What I would really like is for us to be married,' he said softly. Turning to face her, he looked down into her eyes. 'There… I've said it and I really am rushing you now, I know, so maybe if you'd prefer it we could live together first…'

'No, oh, no!'

'No?' His face fell.

'Oh, what I mean is yes.' She stared up at him as a wave of pure happiness washed over her. 'Oh, Casey, of course I'll marry you.'

'You will?' He looked astounded and delighted at the same time. 'I thought it was far too soon but I have to say I was getting fed up with keeping it quiet from everyone.'

'What about Edward, and you being my trainer and everything?'

'I shouldn't think there will be any objection. Fiancée has a much more respectable, if old-fashioned ring to it than live-in lover. And when your training is over I imagine the others will finally see the need for another partner—always supposing that's what you want, of course,' he added hastily.

'I may want to concentrate on police work.'

'Whatever.' He shrugged.

'Or have lots of babies.'

'Wonderful.' His arm tightened around her. 'Even better. And I don't think we need have any fears about Edward. I'm sure he will be delighted. Celia, too,' he added with a chuckle.

'Celia?' Adele looked up at him quickly. She had planned to confront him over what Celia had told her but now she wondered whether it was necessary. Celia's fear had been that he would be incapable of committing to her, but surely there was no greater commitment than a proposal of marriage?

'Celia has been wanting me to settle down again for years. But I kept telling her you can only settle down with the right person.' He paused and lightly touched her cheek. 'After I lost Trisha I despaired of ever finding that right person again. I tried dating one or two but I think it must have been too soon after Trisha…and then…and then you walked into my life, Adele, and I knew instantly. The moment I met you, I knew you were the person I wanted to spend the rest of my life with.'

'Am I like Trisha at all?' She spoke lightly but her heart was thumping as she waited for his reply.

Casey frowned. 'A bit, I suppose,' he said at last, 'in some ways, but in others not at all. You are you, Adele, and it's you who I want for my wife.' Lowering his head, his lips covered hers in a kiss both tender and full of passion. Her earlier fears melted away, leaving her in no doubt about his intentions or the depth of his love.

'There is just one question,' she said as at last she drew away from him.

'Oh?' he murmured. 'And what's that?'

'While this house is being built, while I'm your fiancée, can we be live-in lovers?'

'Oh,' he said, his arms tightening around her, 'I'm sure that can be arranged.'

'Well, that's all right, then.' She gave a little sigh of pure contentment and, lifting her arms, wound them around his neck. 'Because I'm not sure I could wait for as long as it takes to build a house.'

FIRE RESCUE

by

Abigail Gordon

Abigail Gordon loves to write about the fascinating combination of medicine and romance from her home in a Cheshire village. She is active in local affairs and is even called upon to write the script for the annual village pantomime!

Her eldest son is a hospital manager and helps with all her medical research. As part of a close knit family, she treasures having two of her sons living close by and the third one not too far away. This also gives her the added pleasure of being able to watch her delightful grandchildren growing up.

With grateful thanks to the men of
Marple Fire Station

CHAPTER ONE

ZOEY eyed the man in charge dubiously when he heaved himself out of the removal van. He was overweight, florid of face and wouldn't see sixty again.

His companion was a youth with a vacant face, spiked hair and an earring, which increased rather than detracted from her uneasy lack of confidence in the one-man firm that she'd employed to transport her belongings from a studio flat in the city to a more superior residence in the countryside.

But they seemed to be managing all right with a lot of puffing and panting from the big guy, and soon she was locking her door and preparing to follow the van to pastures new.

Pastures new in more ways than one, and her spirits were at their lowest.

Normally bright and bouncy, Zoey Lawrence had asked to be transferred from the job she loved in the bustling city to the quieter confines of a rural fire station.

Twelve months ago she would have scoffed at the idea, but life with its twists and turns had changed all that.

First of all there'd been the finish of her relationship with Damien. Damien the smiling charmer. A firefighter colleague who'd told her he loved her, while all the time he'd been doing the rounds of some of the young and attractive teachers they'd met during talks on fire safety in the schools.

She'd given the impression that she didn't care when

5

she'd ended the affair, but his deceit had hurt…a lot…and having to carry on working with him hadn't been easy. Especially as he'd been acting as if he'd been the injured party. She'd vowed grimly that another time she would be more wary of smiles and soft talk.

But that hadn't been the end of it. There had been worse misery to come…much worse…and it had made the break-up with Damien seem like just a passing cloud.

Two years ago her widower father had taken himself a new young wife and a few months ago they'd had a child. But sadly, with the baby only a few weeks old, he had collapsed and died from an embolism, leaving mother and baby to fend for themselves.

But Zoey had soon found that hadn't been happening. Mandy hadn't been coping at all. She'd spent the days bemoaning her loss and doing little else and Zoey had found herself going backwards and forwards between her job and Mandy's house like a yo-yo, offering comfort and making sure that baby Rosie wasn't being neglected.

It had all become too much and now she was about to move in with Mandy and the baby, while at the same time pursuing her career as a trauma technician in the fire service at a much smaller station than where she'd been employed before.

She was having to put her own life on hold because of the needs of her young stepmother and was happy to do it for her father's sake as much as anything, but sometimes she wondered where it would all end.

During the last traumatic weeks there hadn't been a moment to call her own, and as she followed the removal van in the Nissan Micra that had transported her from town to country so many times the future didn't look exactly bright.

*   *   *

They had arrived. Mandy was at the gate to greet them with a grizzling Rosie in her arms, and as Zoey reached out for her tiny stepsister she eyed Mandy's pale face.

'How are you?' she asked.

'Feeling better now you're here,' she replied tonelessly.

'Good,' Zoey told her bracingly as she cuddled the baby, adding with a vestige of the smile that could have charmed ducks out of the water when she was on top form, 'We're going to be just fine...the three of us. You'll see.'

The man had unlocked the van and he and his assistant were lifting out her wardrobe when the youth suddenly yelled, 'The boss ain't well, miss!'

As Zoey turned round she saw the wardrobe tilt forward, and as the lad frantically held onto it his companion slowly sank to the ground, clutching at his chest as he did so.

Passing Rosie quickly back to her mother, Zoey raced down the path and took the other end of the wardrobe to prevent it falling on the man. When they'd righted it she dropped down beside him and loosened his collar.

His skin was clammy, his breathing shallow, and the amount of chest pain he was experiencing indicated a heart attack.

Then she was racing past a dumbstruck Mandy to phone for an ambulance, giving the voice at the other end precise details of the man's condition and where he was to be found.

As she ran back to him Zoey saw that a car had stopped at the house facing Mandy's and a man was getting out of it. Would he come across to help? she wondered as she checked her patient's pulse.

Yet it would make no odds if he did. She knew what she was doing. It was vital that the patient was taken into Coronary Care as soon as possible, and if his heart stopped beating before the ambulance arrived she would have to try to resuscitate.

'What's the problem?' a cool authoritative voice asked from somewhere above her head, and Zoey looked up to see the man from across the road observing her.

'Suspected heart attack,' she said briefly.

He quickly knelt beside her and observed the removal man.

'I'm ready to resuscitate if he stops breathing,' she told him, 'but at the moment he's just about holding on.'

'I'll take over,' he said in that same cool voice. 'In this sort of situation amateurs can do more harm than good. So if you'll just give me some space...'

'I know exactly what I'm doing,' she told him, equally coolly. 'In any case, the ambulance will be here any second.' And because she was totally frazzled with one thing on top of another, she added, 'They'll be treating it as a red alert.'

That would show him that she knew what she was about!

'A-agh!' the man cried as the pain attacked him again, and Zoey thought contritely that this poor fellow wouldn't care who looked after him as long as somebody did.

Within the next few seconds the ambulance came screeching into the quiet cul-de-sac and Zoey and the stranger moved to one side to let the paramedics take over.

As it speeded off into the chilly autumn night, Zoey breathed a sigh of relief. The coronary unit was where he needed to be. There was little that she could have done for him in the circumstances, except to be there, ready to act if the worst had happened.

The lad, who'd been agog while it had all been happening, was now facing up to his predicament as he said, 'I can't carry this stuff in on me own.'

'No, of course not,' she agreed. 'I'll help you. We'll manage somehow.'

'I take it that you're in the process of moving in,' the stranger said.

'Er...yes. I am,' she said awkwardly.

Why didn't he go away? She had enough to cope with at the moment without having to make polite conversation with this rather patronising man.

His glance was on Mandy and Rosie.

'If you'd both like to go inside before the baby gets cold, I'll help this young fellow to bring in your stuff.'

Zoey wanted to tell him that they would manage, but she was tired, and devastated at what had just happened to the removal man.

So she nodded meekly and said, 'Thanks for the offer...and then I'll have to see about getting the lad home and the van back to where it belongs.'

'One thing at a time,' he said calmly, and again she was irritated by his manner. It was almost as if he thought that here was some female who wasn't coping very well and he'd better sort her out.

In a short space of time her bed, dressing-table and wardrobe had been placed in a bedroom at the front of the house, her clothes had been brought in ready to be hung up and her computer placed in the room that her father had used as an office.

Then the man told her, 'I'm going to take the lad home and will call to see the sick man's family on the

way to tell them what's happened…if that's all right
with you.'

Instead of being appropriately grateful, she muttered,
'Yes, of course,' and thought that maybe he'd like to
tell her what time to go to bed and what time to get up
in the morning, too.

He smiled for the first time.

'Nothing in this life is ever as simple as we would
like it to be, is it?' And off he went, taking the spike-
haired youth across the road to where his car was parked.

'Thank goodness for that,' she breathed when they'd
gone. Turning to Mandy, she gave a tired smile. 'What
a catastrophe! Maybe now we can settle down.' As her
young stepmother led the way into the house, Zoey
asked her how her day had been.

Mandy shrugged her thin shoulders.

'The same as always…awful.'

Zoey groaned inwardly. It was hard to cope with
Mandy's constant depression. She was grieving herself.
But most of the time she had to contain it while she
cheered up the young widow.

They'd had a meal of sorts and Zoey had taken over
Rosie's bathtime so that Mandy could have an early
night. Now, much as she would have liked to have been
able to fall into bed herself, she felt that she couldn't do
that until the man who'd helped them came back.

She'd been churlish and snappy with him and felt that
she should make amends, if only by thanking him properly. The fact that he'd seemed out to rub her up the
wrong way would have to be ignored.

At last she saw his car draw up outside the house
opposite and, not wanting to accost him on the road, she
waited until he'd gone inside.

When he opened the door to her ring on the bell she was able to take stock of him properly for the first time, and she caught her breath as unreadable dark eyes above a firm jawline met hers.

The hair matched the eyes. Almost black…in a stylish cut that accentuated the strong stem of his neck and lay smoothly above his brow.

Wow! she thought. I must have been really wound up earlier not to have registered this guy!

But she'd been too engrossed in being irritated by him to have taken note of his physical attractions.

'Ah! It's you,' he said. 'I was going to make my report in the morning as it's late.'

It seemed that he wasn't going to ask her in so Zoey prepared to say her piece on the doorstep.

'I know that, but I had to come across to thank you properly for helping out. I was so stressed earlier I must have seemed inappreciative and I'm sorry.'

He smiled…again.

'No problem. I saw the lad safely home and then went to see the patient's family. Needless to say, they were very upset and I've been wondering since if there was any news of him.'

Zoey nodded.

'Yes. I phoned a short time ago. He's in Coronary Care and responding to treatment. That was all they would tell me.'

'Good,' he said dismissively. 'So maybe we can both now relax and you can forget your somewhat hectic arrival at the house across the way.'

She sighed.

'Yes. I've come to live with my stepmother. She's all alone with little Rosie and needs my help. So I've transferred from the main fire station in the city and moved to the local one here in this country backwater. Where no doubt I'll find Pugh, Pugh, or Barney Magrew maybe.'

He pursed his lips and she realised that he wasn't amused.

'I doubt it,' he said blandly, and then to make her feel even more guilty he looked pointedly at his watch and said, 'If you'll excuse me, I'm about to prepare my belated evening meal.'

'Of course,' she mumbled apologetically. Turning away, she hurried back to her new lodgings.

When he'd closed the door Alex Carradine leant against it and let out a deep breath. So the girl with eyes like sapphires in a pert face framed by a golden bob was Zoey Lawrence, the trauma technician about to join the team at the fire station tomorrow. What a turn-up for the book!

That was his first thought. The second was that it was fortunate that most of the guys there were happily married. With the exception of himself and Leading Fireman Greg Osbourne, who was away on a course.

That one would create havoc if she started swaying those trim hips around the place and flashing those incredible eyes. Having a woman on the staff wasn't unusual. It had happened once or twice before, but they'd been of a more staid appearance than Zoey Lawrence.

Her tight black trousers, skimpy white top and shoes that lifted her a good three inches off the ground were fashionable to say the least. But thankfully tomorrow she would be dressed more soberly in the dark blue uniform of the fire services.

It was a pity they'd started off on the wrong foot. It had been one of those days. Lots of red tape to deal with from headquarters in the absence of the station officer who'd suddenly taken early retirement.

Then a call to a false alarm, followed by a distressing house fire in the late afternoon. And as if that hadn't been enough, Gloria had come through on his mobile to say that she would be in the area in the near future and could he put her up for a few days?

He'd said it would be no problem, but had wished that she would stay away now that they were divorced. It had been strange, the way their marriage had foundered. They'd been friends for a long time before they'd decided to marry...even as far back as junior school, which everyone had thought would make their union as solid as a rock.

But maybe they'd known each other too well as it hadn't worked. They'd got on each other's nerves soon after the event, realising that their friendship had endured because there had been no ties to it and that marriage could be an irksome thing.

The break, when it had come, had been amicable enough and now they were going their separate ways with no acrimony on either side. Alex was thankful they'd had no children. He would have stuck it out if they had.

All in all it had been a chastening experience and he had decided that it would be a long time before he made another commitment...if ever.

When he'd seen what had been happening over the road he'd gone across to see what the problem was, and it had gone on from there with the blonde girl and himself becoming reluctant acquaintances.

Gloria and he had moved into the house in the cul-de-sac when they'd got married and he had bought her half from her when they'd divorced, opting to stay there because it was close to the fire station.

It was a requirement of all personnel that they live within a short distance of the place, so as to be able to respond quickly to any emergency when not on site.

Vaguely aware that a young widow with a baby lived opposite, he hadn't taken much notice...until today. And now he had a feeling that, whether he wanted to or not, he was going to get to know the folk in the house opposite a lot better.

While eating his solitary meal, Alex found himself smiling. That young madam with her Pugh, Pugh, Barney Magrew. Did she think they were all yokels in the countryside? It looked as if tomorrow might turn out to be a very interesting day.

As Zoey walked the short distance to the fire station the next morning it seemed strange not to have high-rise buildings around her and the deafening noise of city traffic in her ears.

She could hear birds chirping in the trees and the air smelt fresh and clean. Her step lightened. She had done the right thing, coming here. Mandy seemed brighter already now that she wasn't so alone.

Zoey had given Rosie her early morning bottle and had then tucked her up with her mother, having made Mandy promise that she wouldn't mope all day, and now it was time to get into the swing of things in her new surroundings.

After only a short time amongst her new colleagues she had to admit that she'd been too quick to prejudge them. They were friendly and obviously efficient and well trained if their conversation was anything to go by.

If there were a few warm glances coming her way she chose to ignore them.

The only civilian employee on the station was the cleaner, Dorothea, a plump, motherly being who eyed Zoey's slenderness and commented laughingly that she could do with some flesh on her bones. A suggestion that was immediately vetoed by the crew.

'The station officer has just taken early retirement on the grounds of ill health,' one of them told her. 'He was due to go soon anyway, and we're expecting that Sub-officer Alex Carradine will eventually take over. He's been to a meeting at headquarters this morning, and has just phoned to say that he'll be back any moment.'

As if on cue, the door was opening and as Zoey turned round her jaw went slack.

'Good morning,' the man from the house across the road said. 'If you'd like to step into the office, Zoey, I think we need to have a chat.'

She swallowed hard.

'Yes, of course,' she croaked. Following him meekly, she lowered herself onto a grey plastic chair opposite a big wooden desk.

When he'd seated himself facing her, Alex said smoothly, 'Sorry to disappoint you, but the name is Carradine. Alex Carradine. Not Cuthbert, Dibble or Grubb.'

Zoey bent her head as her cheeks began to burn.

'I'm sorry. I didn't know who I was talking to when I said that.'

'Obviously. How could you?' he murmured.

'Why didn't you tell me who you were when I explained that I was coming to work here?'

'Why should I? It seemed a pity to knock sideways all your preconceived ideas.' His eyes were on the paperwork that he'd just deposited on the desk. 'But shall we get down to business?'

Zoey nodded mutely.

'I had wondered why you were seeking a transfer from the main fire station. What you told me last night gave me the answer,' he said with the smooth tone crisping up. 'I've received details of the training you've received in first aid and at the accident and emergency department of the city's main hospital, and your function here will be the same as before, but on a smaller scale.

'As you will be aware, most stations have a trauma technician on the team to give emergency medical assistance when needed. Either before the ambulance arrives, in conjunction with paramedics, or even instead of them if their help isn't required.

'There's a good atmosphere at this station. We are all friends who meet socially as well as being workmates. There are no disruptive influences and I want it to stay that way.

'I'm aware that you are used to working in a more sophisticated setting than this and you won't find the same sort of night-life here as you would find in the city. You may have to look further afield.'

Zoey eyed him mutinously. What did he think she was? Some pleasure loving sex-pot? Her social life had been non-existent for months while she'd been doing a very demanding job and spending every spare minute with Mandy and the baby. And in any case, what had it got to do with Alex Carradine what she did in her free time?

But not being prepared to let him discover that her evenings were far from pleasure-filled, she said easily, 'I'll find the nightspots when I need them, never fear.'

'Hmm. I'm sure you will,' he agreed unsmilingly. 'I

take it that you've met all the firemen based here with the exception of Leading Fireman Osbourne.'

'Yes, I have,' she told him, now in subdued tones.

Everything had been fine until this man had appeared to dampen her spirits. What did he have against her? He hadn't even seen her in action. But he had, hadn't he, after a fashion? And he'd wanted to know if she knew what she was doing. Well, she would show him just that. That she definitely did know what she was doing.

'We have just the one engine at this station,' he was saying, 'and when a "shout" comes we all go out on it, with myself in charge. Is that clear?'

'Perfectly.'

'Good. As Bonfire Night will soon be here, we will be going to the schools over the next couple of weeks to lecture the pupils about the dangers of fireworks, and a week on Saturday we are doing a charity "pull" for the local hospital's children's ward.'

His glance went to her slim shoulders.

'You may want to think about that before committing yourself. A fire-engine is some weight to pull and the straps over our shoulders can bite a bit.'

Zoey shook her fair mop, brushing away dismal thoughts of what working alongside teaching staff sometimes led to.

'I'd like to take part if you don't mind. It sounds like fun and it's for a good cause.'

'Fine. Just as you wish. You know where to go for a dislocated shoulder, I take it?'

She didn't answer, just glared at him, and he said dismissively, 'I think that's all for now, Zoey. If you have any kind of problems, come to me. I repeat…any kind. Right?'

She nodded obediently, while vowing not to if she could help it.

'Maybe you wouldn't mind asking those guys out there if there's any tea and toast left from the elevenses,' he said, and picked up the top sheet off the papers on the desk.

When she'd gone, Alex leaned back in his chair and gazed pensively through the window. He was treating this bright young woman as if he was dubious about her joining the team. What was the matter with him?

She hadn't put a foot wrong so far, except by being quite stunning. Had his marriage flop really made his attitude towards young attractive women so negative?

The information he'd received about Zoey Lawrence said that she was twenty-four. He wasn't that much older than her, eight years or so, and yet he was laying down the law like some crabby Methuselah. The first opportunity that came along he would show her that he was human...and fair.

Engine and crew were called out at midday. Three youths in a car had crashed on a narrow bend on one of the local hill roads and the police had asked for their assistance in freeing one of them who was still trapped in the car.

Within minutes they were off, wearing their fireproof jackets and yellow helmets, with Zoey displaying a green and white flash on hers to denote she was the trauma technician.

Geoff Baines, an affable, middle-aged father of two, was in the driving seat with Alex beside him. The rest of them were in the back.

Alex turned round and his eyes met hers, yet what he had to say was for all of them, or so she thought.

'Remember,' he warned them, 'don't release the victim too fast without medical help on hand or…what? You tell us, Zoey,' he said in a milder tone than he'd used before.

'Sure,' she said easily. 'The "crush syndrome" can occur. The extensive damage to the muscles causes protein pigments to be released into the bloodstream, causing temporary kidney failure. That causes substances usually excreted in the urine to build up to toxic levels in the blood. Without prompt dialysis the kidney failure will be fatal.'

As the men clapped at the end of her description of the perils awaiting someone who had been severely crushed, Zoey gave a saucy little bow and, watching her, Alex had to smile. Whatever she did, Zoey was certainly going to brighten up the place.

Of the three youths in the car when it had gone out of control on the hill bend, one was standing in a daze, too shocked to comprehend properly what had happened. Another was unconscious by the roadside, with paramedics attending him, and the third was trapped in the car which had overturned when it had hit the stone wall by the roadside.

He was crushed beneath the twisted metal of the seats and the sun-roof, and it was immediately obvious to the fire crew why they'd been called to assist.

His arm was hanging limply through the window and while Zoey ran across to apply pressure on the forearm in an attempt to contain heavy bleeding, Alex and Geoff got out the Combi tools and connected them to the petrol-powered generator that would provide the hydraulic pressure needed for their steel jaws to cut away the framework of the car.

Both men had put on goggles with visors attached to

protect their faces from flying fragments as they worked, and another of the team was holding a teardrop-shaped plastic shield to protect the casualty from a similar hazard.

'Cutting!' the cry went up, to warn anyone close by to stand back. With Alex at the front of the car, beginning to slice through what the men called the 'A' post, which in ordinary jargon was the metal that held the windscreen, and Geoff doing his bit at the 'C' post, the framework at the back of the window area, they began to clear the way to the injured youth.

The noise of the generator and the cutting equipment was deafening, blotting out all other sounds, and when Zoey looked up she saw that the 'smart' team from Accident and Emergency had arrived.

Two doctors and two nurses were spilling out onto the road beside them, which made the turn-out of the emergency services complete. Police, ambulance, fire service and the staff from A and E, who were called out when surgery on the spot might be required, such as amputations.

Amazingly the lad was still alive and as the last piece of metal was cut away there was a sigh of relief from all those present.

He'd been given an injection for pain and as they slowly eased him out onto a spinal board he was drifting in and out of consciousness.

As the fire team prepared to leave the scene, the senior policeman in charge came over.

'Well done, lads,' he said.

Zoey smiled. In the bulky coat and with the helmet on her head she looked no different from the rest. Alex Carradine would be pleased about that.

*   *   *

Later in the day Alex rang to see how the three victims of the car crash were, and as the rest of them waited anxiously for the report Zoey was amazed how she'd settled in so quickly. It was as if she'd never worked anywhere else.

'One lad treated for shock and then discharged,' Alex informed them as he put the phone down. 'The guy who was lying in the road has severe concussion and a fractured arm and leg. And our young friend who came off worst is in Intensive Care with multiple injuries...but they seem to think he'll live. I suggest that some of us call in to see him when he's stabilised. What do you think?'

'Yes, sure thing,' Geoff said, and the rest nodded their agreement.

When Alex saw Zoey's surprised expression he said, 'Sometimes we get a case like today's and it gets to us more than others. Maybe it was the look of silent pleading in the kid's eyes as we tried to free him. Or because they were just reckless youngsters who might have had their lives cut short. I don't know.

'The lad who was trapped lives near one of our guys, which makes it all the more personal. So we'll follow it up. It stands to reason that in an area like this we're much more likely to find it's someone we know when we get a call-out than in one of the bigger stations.'

'Yes, I suppose so,' Zoey said, adding with unconscious wistfulness, 'Though it's not likely to happen to me as I don't know anybody.'

'We'll soon put that right,' one of the men said. 'Meet us in the pub tonight, Zoey. We'll introduce you to our wives.'

Her smile was wry.

'I can't. I'm here to give my young stepmother support and she won't want me to leave her the moment I've arrived.'

'Bring her with you.'

She was conscious of dark, inscrutable eyes watching her as she told them, 'It's not that easy. She has a young baby.'

Remembering Alex Carradine's comments earlier in the day when he'd called her into the office, she thought that he would have expected her to jump at the chance of mixing with the locals as the next best thing to flaunting herself beneath city lights.

When she arrived back at Mandy's place Zoey's face brightened. Mandy had cleaned up the house and in the afternoon had taken Rosie to the baby clinic in the nearby community centre.

Both activities were a step in the right direction as the house had badly needed freshening up and previously Mandy hadn't even bothered to have Rosie weighed.

Zoey gave her a hug.

'Well done, Mandy,' she encouraged her. 'The place looks like a palace. What sort of a report did you get on Rosie?'

'It was all right,' she said with slightly more zest than usual. 'They said she was healthy and putting on weight nicely, but that I must see she gets plenty of fresh air as she's rather pale.'

'Good. The fresh air should be no problem. All it needs is for you to get out a bit more.'

'About getting out more,' Mandy said. 'Some of the mothers from the clinic are going out for a pizza tonight and they asked me to join them. What do you think?'

What did she think?

'I think you should go,' Zoey told her firmly. 'You've

been shut away in this place long enough. I'll see to Rosie.'

Mandy's face lit up and Zoey thought, I don't believe I'm seeing this. Was there a light at the end of the tunnel at last? If Mandy was going to come out of the depression that had swamped her ever since her husband's death, putting her own life on hold would have been well worthwhile, she decided.

When Mandy had gone, looking almost like her old self, and Rosie had been tucked up for the night, Zoey stood looking at the house opposite.

What would Alex be doing at this moment? she wondered. Off to the pub to join the others? Or spending the evening with his family? There'd been no mention of him having a wife but it stood to sense that there would be someone. He was far too attractive to be unattached.

She was tidying up the kitchen after the evening meal when the doorbell rang. When she opened the door he was there. Almost as if she'd willed him to appear.

'Alex!' she said in a voice that wasn't quite steady. 'What brings you here?'

He didn't reply for a moment. If he were to answer truthfully he would have to say that he wasn't sure, and that wouldn't sound much like a man of purpose.

She was stepping back.

'Come in, but, please, don't make a noise as I've just got Rosie to sleep. That little one doesn't know the meaning of slumber.'

He smiled as he stepped over the threshold and this time it was a proper one, not just a relaxing of the face muscles.

'Where's her mother?' he asked in a low voice.

Zoey couldn't resist it.

'Gone gallivanting. I'm baby-minding.'

'So that's why you turned down the invitation to go to the pub.'

She shook her blonde bob.

'No, not exactly. I didn't know what I'd be doing until I got home as Mandy is a bit unpredictable these days. She hasn't got over my father's death. They hadn't been married long.'

'You've lost your father, then,' he said with swift concern. 'I'm sorry to hear that. And what about your grief? Who's helping you through it?'

Zoey stared at him. She could feel tears pricking. He was the first person who'd realised that Mandy wasn't the only one who'd been bereaved.

Then to her horror the tears were spilling down her cheeks. She turned away as the torrent of misery unleashed itself, horrified that this should happen in front of Alex of all people, only to find herself pulled gently round again into a pair of sheltering arms.

'Let it out,' he said quietly. 'Is this the first time you've wept?'

'Yes,' she gulped.

'Then it's overdue. Bottling up emotions never did anyone any good, Zoey. I should know.'

Her sobs were subsiding but she didn't move out of his arms.

'There was never time to grieve,' she choked. 'Mandy and the baby needed me so much.'

He tilted her chin with a gentle finger and as she looked up at him with reddened eyes he told her, 'I only came across to ask if you'd enjoyed your first day.'

She managed a smile.

'Yes. It was great.'

'All of it?'

'Well, apart from the lecture I received at one point.'

'Standard procedure,' he said blandly, but knew it not to be true. He'd acted like he had because he had a gut feeling that the newest member of staff at the small fire station was going to be a disturbing influence.

Zoey was wiping her eyes and moving out of his arms, and Alex knew he didn't want her to do that. She'd felt frail, vulnerable, and her perfume was as light and tantalising as Zoey herself. He couldn't remember when last he'd held a woman as close as this. But he knew she was doing the right thing, or he would be falling into his own trap.

'Thanks for being there for me in a dark moment, Alex,' she croaked. 'I had no intention of burdening you with my problems.'

'I did tell you to come to me if you had any, didn't I?' he told her, not knowing quite what to say. 'Though I didn't think it would be so soon.'

Was that meant to tell her she was being a nuisance? she wondered. That she'd no sooner arrived on the scene than she was demanding his attention?

'Yes, well, it won't happen again,' she told him.

As he began to try to explain what he'd really meant they heard the baby crying up above.

'I'll see you tomorrow,' he said, and as Zoey pointed herself towards the stairs he went.

CHAPTER TWO

As ZOEY soothed Rosie back to sleep again her thoughts were chaotic. She'd really let her grief show for the first time since losing her dad, and whose arms had she ended up in? Those of a tall dark stranger. And what was more, she'd been enough aware of him to enjoy it, in spite of her tears.

It was incredible that he of all people had realised how little time she'd had to come to terms with her own hurt. She hardly knew Alex, was wary of his brusque approach, and yet for an amazing few seconds she'd felt cherished—and that wasn't a feeling she experienced very often.

'Your big sister's going all soppy, and it won't do,' she told the now slumbering Rosie. 'Not with that man anyway. He's not sure what to make of me, but "bimbo" is a word that springs to mind.'

After tonight's incident she wouldn't know how to look him in the face in the morning. Her face softened. Yet he had been kind. And what had he hinted about bottling up one's feelings...that if anybody knew about that, he did?

Maybe she might ask a few questions about him in the morning. Just to get a picture of what made him tick...or otherwise. Merely out of curiosity, of course.

From what she'd seen of him so far, Alex wasn't likely to be attracted to anyone like herself, and for her part she could think of lots of men more appealing than

26

him…couldn't she? In any case, she wasn't looking for romance. She'd recently had her fill of male ego.

Mandy came home from her night out with the young mothers almost animated. Her cheeks were flushed, eyes bright, and Zoey thought, This is what she's short of. Her stepmother was only a few years older than herself. Her father wouldn't have wanted her to waste her young life grieving for him.

'So I take it you enjoyed yourself,' she said, as they sat by the fire with mugs of hot chocolate before going to bed.

'Yes, I did,' Mandy admitted. With heightened colour, she went on, 'I knocked my drink over and the man who owned the place was really nice about it. He came and mopped it up and brought me another one. I felt such a fool, and told him it was a long time since I'd been out socialising. He asked me why and when I told him he was really sorry.'

Zoey's eyes were dancing.

'Not bad for your first foray back into the wicked world.'

Mandy smiled.

'It didn't feel wicked to me. It felt lovely.'

'Mmm,' Zoey agreed. 'It's been a nice night all round.'

'But you haven't been anywhere.'

'True,' Zoey agreed, 'but with a beautiful baby to care for and a neighbourly visit from a most intriguing man, what more could I ask for?'

'You don't mean the good Samaritan from last night?'

'Yes. I do.'

'And?'

'And…nothing. He merely called to see if I'd enjoyed my first day.'

What Mandy would say if she heard the rest was something Zoey wasn't going to risk at that moment, and with a yawn she said, 'I'm off to bed. Sweet dreams of your pizza man.'

Zoey tried not to smile as the young widow went bright red, but her step was lighter as she climbed the stairs. They were an all-female household. Some male blood was needed to level the scales. Whose, though?

The next morning Alex Carradine greeted her as if they hadn't had any contact since leaving the station the night before, and Zoey got the message. He'd obviously decided that if the job brought them together that was fine. But he was going to treat what had happened when he'd called round to see her as a one-off, triggered by circumstances.

All right, she thought rebelliously. What did he think she was going to do? Make something out of a special moment they'd shared?

It was quiet during the morning with little to occupy the staff, but in the early afternoon it all changed. A public house not far away, which had been boarded up prior to demolition at some future date, was on fire.

When they got there it was clear that unless the blaze was brought under control quickly it would spread to neighbouring shops and houses.

'There are no services at this place,' Alex informed them, 'so it looks as if it might be arson. Either kids messing about, or a grudge against the brewery maybe. Whatever it is, let's get it under control.'

At that moment a woman who had just arrived on the scene told them, 'There's been a tramp sleeping in there for the last week.'

'Right,' Alex said decisively as they uncoupled the

hoses, 'it seems that we might have a "persons reported" on our hands. Zoey, get back to Control and tell them what's happening. The rest of you look out for a person somewhere in the building. He might be long gone but we can't take any chances.'

While she was making the call, Alex and two of the team disappeared into the smoke-filled public house wearing breathing apparatus while the others tackled the blaze from the outside. Zoey was about to follow them into the building when it became apparent that the woman's warning had been timely. The tramp had been inside and now he was being carried to safety by the firemen.

They laid him on the ground some distance away from the blaze and Alex said, 'He's barely conscious, Zoey. Get the oxygen to him while I radio for an ambulance.'

As she put the mask over the man's face, she could smell alcohol. That was the last thing he'd needed around him in a burning building. It was a wonder he hadn't gone up in flames, but the fates had been kind and as he began to breathe more easily she thought grimly that but for a comment from a bystander this fellow wouldn't have survived.

Fortunately he had no burns. His main problem was smoke inhalation, and once his breathing had stabilised the tramp would have some questions to answer.

Alex was back and nodding his satisfaction to see the man responding to treatment. Then he turned and said briefly, 'We're going back in there to make sure there was no one else with him. Stay with him until the ambulance arrives, Zoey.'

She didn't need telling. It was her job to give medical assistance. They all had to do it at times, but hers was the role of trauma technician. Yet she did wonder if Alex was keeping her in the background because she was a woman.

It was to be hoped that wasn't the case. She wouldn't be doing the job if she wanted to be treated differently from the men. Whatever she looked like on the outside, she was just as capable as the rest of them. Not as strong maybe, but there were ways to overcome that sort of handicap. Quick thinking and agility always came in handy.

At last the fire was under control. The vagrant had been taken to hospital for observation and it now remained for the fire crew to return to base and the local authority to make a decision on how soon the demolition could begin.

Alex had been right when he'd said there was no gas or electricity supply to the premises. But they hadn't reckoned with an intruder making a fire from rubbish he'd found lying around and then dropping off into a drunken sleep.

Zoey had a feeling that the fire crew wouldn't be following this one up, but she was wrong.

'That fellow needs some proper accommodation when he's discharged from hospital,' Alex said when they got back, 'and if the health authority doesn't do anything about it, I will.'

They hadn't been back at base long when the phone in the rest room rang, and as she was nearest to it Zoey picked it up.

'Put Alex on the line, will you?' an authoritative voice said in her ear.

'Who shall I tell him is calling?' she asked.

The question was answered by another.

'Are you new, or something?'

'Yes,' she answered coolly, suddenly on the defensive.

'And so who are you, then?'

'My name's Zoey Lawrence. I've just been transferred here,' she said levelly. 'And you are?'

'Er, just tell him that Gloria's on the line.'

Alex had come out of the office and was observing her questioningly.

'Someone called Gloria for you,' she told him as she handed him the phone.

'Thanks,' he said briefly, and waited until she'd moved out of earshot before answering.

'Who's Gloria?' she asked of Geoff when Alex went back into the other room. 'And why didn't she ring him on the office phone?'

'Gloria is his ex-wife and she came though on this extension because he's usually in here with us,' he explained. 'Was she coming the queen bee with you?'

'A bit.'

'That's Gloria. She's not a bad sort but inclined to be a bit pushy where Alex is concerned. Normally he would be no pushover in anybody's book, but he always has time for that one.'

'Yet you say they're divorced?'

'Yes. It was an amicable affair. No other persons involved. Not as far as he was concerned anyway.'

'No children, then?'

'No. For which he's truly thankful.'

'You mean that he didn't want any?'

'No. Certainly not that. More because he wouldn't have wanted them to get hurt by a marriage break-up.'

'I see,' she said thoughtfully.

Some of the questions she'd intended asking had been

answered, and now she was curious about the woman who'd taken his name and slept in his bed…and was still in touch.

They were due at the local comprehensive school the next day to talk about fire safety in the forthcoming bonfire season. As they left the station the team was in relaxed mood. On this occasion there would be no hazards awaiting them at the other end. Unless facing a hall full of teenage pupils could be termed as one.

When the youngsters crowded round after the lecture had finished, Zoey found that as usual her presence was creating some interest. With the boys because her youthful glamour was unexpected in such an occupation, and from some of the girls who expressed a desire to join the fire service themselves after meeting her, though whether it was to help the community or to be in the company of a group of macho men, she wasn't sure. Which brought back to mind painful memories of Damien's dallyings with a teacher from one of the schools they'd visited.

Her own decision to become part of the vital emergency service stemmed from when she was twelve years old and a young plumber working at her parent's house had left his wife and child safely at home, only to be told an hour later that she'd tried to light a coal fire with paraffin and had set the place on fire.

Members of the fire service had risked their lives to get the woman and child out of the blazing house, and Zoey had never forgotten their bravery or the young husband's gratitude. She'd known then it was what she wanted to do and had never swerved from her purpose.

The physical fitness tests she'd had to pass had been gruelling, but she'd come through them and soon after being accepted had decided that she wanted to be a trauma technician.

And now here she was. Out of her environment and surprisingly not regretting it. For one thing, Mandy had bucked up almost from the moment of her arrival, and for another...there was Alex Carradine. Everyone had a good word for him except herself.

Yet that wasn't strictly true, was it? She'd acknowledged his kindness when she'd wept in his arms. Admitted that he was extremely high up in the presentable male stakes. But she wasn't too keen on the way he seemed to be dubious about her.

For one thing, he seemed to think that because she was young and liked to be fashionable, she was trouble. He expected her to be pleasure-loving and materialistically minded. If he only knew. It had been months since she'd been anywhere other than work or Mandy's.

The ex-wife sounded as if she was still in the picture. Maybe it wasn't surprising that Alex was a bit edgy. On the other hand, if there'd been no hard feelings maybe he was happy to still have her around.

Every time Alex thought about the break-up of his marriage there was relief in him that it was over. It had been a monumental mistake and he was still plagued by it.

The weird thing was that he and Gloria had always got on so well until they'd lived under the same roof, and then it had all fallen apart.

He'd found that in some ways they'd known each other too well and in others hadn't known each other at all. The marriage had lacked the mystery and magic that made each day something to look forward to and the predictability of life with Gloria had made him realise that he'd made a big mistake.

It would have been awful if they'd been his sentiments only, but she'd felt the same and so the break, when it had come, had been a lot less painful than it might have been. Though he did sometimes feel that she was finding it harder to adjust than he was.

His main problem was regret that they hadn't stayed just friends and looked elsewhere for marriage partners. Because now they'd ended up not anything at all, except maybe polite acquaintances.

Gloria had been a solicitor with a local practice and he'd sometimes wondered if her unimaginative legal approach to the job had spilled over too much into their lives.

She'd moved to the London area after the divorce, taking up a position with a firm of solicitors there, and seemed happy enough with the arrangement. She phoned from time to time, and on the day that Zoey had answered her call had said, 'So you've got a new woman working with you now?'

'Yes.'

'What's she like?'

As he'd glanced through the office window to where Zoey had been chatting to Geoff, with the rays of an autumn sun turning her blonde bob to silver, he'd felt that for some reason he didn't want to discuss Zoey Lawrence with his ex-wife.

So he'd merely said, 'Seems all right, but it's early days yet.' Veering away from any further discussion about her, he'd asked smoothly, 'What can I do for you, Gloria?'

It had been then that she'd asked if she could stay with him for a while and with no real reason to refuse he'd agreed.

*   *   *

In the days that followed Zoey continued to adjust to a more rural lifestyle. In her free time she pushed Rosie in her pram along country lanes and beside the canal that wound its way between woodland and green meadows, enjoying the feeling of space and breathing in the fresh untainted air.

She sometimes thought that Alex Carradine would be surprised if he knew how much pleasure it gave her, being in this place, as for some reason he'd got her labelled as a typical townie.

Her forays into the countryside with the baby gave Mandy the chance to have some time to herself, and their domestic situation was improving all the time.

On a Sunday afternoon she spotted Alex coming towards her with a frisky red setter on the lead. As they drew level Zoey found herself suddenly tongue-tied. It was the first time they'd met outside working hours since the night she'd wept in his arms and she wondered if it was as clear in his memory as it was in hers.

'Hello, there,' he said, and as she stooped to fondle the dog he bent over the pram. 'Beautiful baby. What's her name?'

'Rosie,' she said awkwardly.

'Hmm, nice. I take it that you're very fond of her?'

'I adore her.'

'Yes, but shouldn't you be doing your own thing occasionally instead of constantly being child-minder? You're certainly full of surprises.'

'I'm not sure how to take that comment, but I have a feeling that there is criticism in it somewhere. Are you saying that I'm not living up to your expectations of what a city girl wants?' she said, with a breezy sort of nonchalance now that the first strained moments of meeting had passed.

'Now, why would you think that?' he asked with a smile.

'Because I don't fit into the mould perhaps?'

Alex was serious now.

'There is no mould. We are all what we are, Zoey. Life would be just too boring if we were all the same.'

She waited for him to go on but he was changing the subject.

'How far are you going?' he asked, as the dog pulled at the lead.

'Just to the end of the lane and then I'm turning back,' she told him.

'We'll walk with you, then. Gipsy has had enough exercise for one day.'

'Why Gipsy?'

'Because when I first got him he was roving all over the place, straining to be free.'

'So why not Rover?'

'Too mundane for a livewire such as this dog.'

Their respective dwellings were in sight and when they stopped outside Mandy's house Zoey was loath to end their brief time together.

'Until tomorrow, then,' Alex said, and for a moment she let herself imagine that he was as reluctant to go his own way as she was.

'Yes,' she agreed, 'and regarding your earlier remark that I'm full of surprises, watch this space.'

As dark brows rose questioningly she laughed and, wheeling the pram up the path, left him to ponder.

The men from the station had repeated their invitation to join them one evening in the pub and the next night Zoey took them at their word and turned up at the old inn that was a popular place of refreshment for ramblers, motorists and the local folk.

It had been a stressful day at the fire station. They'd attended a house fire and had brought a young child out just in the nick of time. They'd also been called to a head-on car crash where an elderly man had suffered a heart attack at the wheel and as he'd lost control had swerved into the path of a vehicle going in the opposite direction.

The casualties had been trapped and the fire service had been called out to separate the two cars with a Tifor winch...a steel cable passing through a winding mechanism and operated by a lever.

The elderly motorist had been pronounced dead at the scene, but the woman driver of the other car had miraculously survived, with Zoey putting a temporary splint on a broken leg and administering pain relief until the arrival of the ambulance.

And now, for some light relief, she'd come to The Wheatsheaf Inn.

She was introduced to wives and girlfriends and might have felt out of it if there hadn't been someone else there on his own.

Alex appeared halfway through the evening and after observing her with the same surprised expression as when they'd separated the day before he came across to say, 'So you've taken note of what I said yesterday.'

She smiled, turning the full brilliance of her sapphire gaze upon him.

'Yes, I've been let out for the evening.'

'Good for you. Let me buy you a drink.'

'How about introducing me first?' a voice said from behind her, and as she swung round Zoey found herself looking into a strange face.

'Ah, yes,' Alex said levelly. 'Zoey, this is Greg Osbourne. The only member of the team you haven't already met. Greg's been away on a course.'

'I'd have been back earlier if I'd known what I was missing,' the newcomer remarked smoothly as light hazel eyes looked Zoey over.

He was of medium height with brown hair and a trim physique, and seemed pleasant enough. She might even have given him a second glance if Alex hadn't been around, but he was, and the more she saw of him, the more Zoey liked what she saw.

But she hadn't forgotten Damien. She'd often heard it said that it wasn't a good idea to date the people one worked with, and he'd been a prime example. It was claustrophobic, for one thing. No chance to get away from each other.

Ignoring the comment, Alex said, 'This is Zoey's first visit to The Wheatsheaf. She spends most of her free time baby-minding.'

Greg was eyeing her in disappointment.

'So you're married.'

'No!' she protested laughingly. 'The baby belongs to my stepmother. Rosie is my half-sister.'

'Bet she's as gorgeous as you are,' murmured Greg with a wink.

This one has a smooth tongue, Zoey thought, and saw that she wasn't the only one thinking that. Alex's face had tightened and when someone else claimed Greg's attention Alex steered her to a table in the corner.

'He thinks he can charm the birds out of the trees,' he told her as she settled herself opposite him.

'Well,' she told him breezily, 'some men have it and—'

'Some don't?' he finished off for her. 'Which lot do I come into?'

'Oh, you have it all right,' she said airily, as if the subject was of no particular interest, 'but you keep it well under wraps.'

'I see. So that's what you think of me.'

'Partly. Don't forget you were very abrupt with me when I first came to the station. You still are sometimes. But I make allowances for you.'

She was putting out bait and wondering if he would rise to it. He did.

'Why do you feel you have to do that?' he asked slowly.

'Oh, I don't know. Maybe it's because I sense you're miserable. Did it hurt a lot when your marriage broke up?'

'No, it didn't, as a matter of fact. It was a relief. It had been a big mistake almost from the word go, and as we were both of the same mind there seemed no point in carrying on. It would have been a different matter if we'd had children. But as we hadn't it was a clean break. Or at least it was on my part.'

The door of the old inn opened at that moment and he groaned softly.

'Ugh! Here's Gloria now!'

So this was the woman who hadn't been able to make Alex happy, Zoey thought as the new arrival sighted them at their corner table and came across.

Zoey found that she was bracing herself, yet didn't know why. Gloria looked ordinary enough. Of medium height and build, with light brown hair swept back off a face which was expressing some degree of surprise at seeing Alex with her, she wasn't quite as forbidding as Zoey had expected her to be.

A diversion was taking place. Greg had seen her and was stepping in front of her.

'Hi, Gloria,' Zoey heard him say. 'Nice to see you back amongst us. We've missed you.'

Was he being deliberately tactless? Zoey wondered. Winding up the man who was sitting tensely beside her?

'I've missed all of you, too, Gregory,' Gloria said in a husky voice that made Zoey think of throat pastilles.

He was pointing to a nearby vacant table but Gloria wasn't to be sidetracked any longer.

'I'll see you later,' she promised, and carried on to where Zoey and Alex were sitting.

His face had been completely expressionless while she'd been talking to Greg, and it didn't change when she stood over him and said, 'Aren't you going to introduce me to your young friend, Alex?'

'Yes, of course,' he said flatly, and as he made the introductions Zoey's smile beamed out defiantly.

She felt as if she was being patronised and didn't like it.

'Ah, so you're the girl who answered the phone when I rang that time,' Gloria was saying. 'Zoey, isn't it? Settling in, are you?' She sent a slanting glance at Alex.

'Yes, thank you,' Zoey told her politely, and picked up the jacket that she'd draped across the back of the chair when she and Alex had seated themselves. 'I'll leave you to it. Nice to have met you…Gloria.'

If the other woman had been expecting her to address her as Mrs Carradine, she had another think coming, Zoey decided as she went to join the others. And in any case she wasn't, was she?

When she looked across again Alex was frowning as he listened to what his ex-wife was saying, and Zoey wondered why Gloria didn't leave him alone.

He'd said it had been an amicable divorce, so maybe that was why they were still in touch. Yet Zoey could tell that he hadn't been all that pleased to see Gloria.

He came across a few minutes later and when Zoey eyed him enquiringly he said, 'Gloria's gone round to my place. I've given her the keys to let herself in. She's going to be staying for a few days.'

That was all. No explanation of why the woman he'd been married to had suddenly appeared. Maybe he didn't think it warranted one. After all, she herself was only someone that he worked with.

Yet Alex stayed by Zoey's side for the rest of the evening, and when the crowd from the fire station began the short stroll back to their respective homes he was still there beside her.

There was a full moon in the sky, throwing shadows onto the road as they walked along. Feeling strange, as she always did when they were alone, Zoey said, 'I can't believe how quickly I've got used to this place. I never expected to.'

She could have told him that she couldn't believe how quickly she'd got used to him, too. But that might have been asking for trouble. Especially if he wasn't of a similar mind.

'So you've no regrets?' he questioned casually.

'None. For one thing, I see more of Rosie, even though I was never away from her for long before. I have peace of mind where Mandy's concerned.' She took a deep breath and continued rashly, 'And I've met you.'

That stopped him in his tracks.

'What do you mean by that?'

'Exactly what you think I mean.'

They were facing each other and Zoey thought that

they had all the ingredients to make it into a memorable moment. A harvest moon, the quiet peace of the place, and the two of them alone and unobserved with passions rising. At least hers were. She couldn't vouch for his.

Alex reached out and gripped her arms tightly.

'Listen, Zoey,' he said quietly, 'don't start anything you can't finish. I don't play around with other people's emotions and I don't expect them to play around with mine. If you want to flirt around, fine. But don't do it with me. OK?'

She had stiffened in his grip.

'Yes! OK! But tell me…why do you always expect my feelings to be shallow?'

'I don't.'

'Oh, yes, you do. If you don't like me, say so, and I'll take the hint.'

'How long have you known me?' he asked.

'About a week.'

'So how can you possibly feel as you do?'

'I don't know, as I've had cause to be wary of relationships with those I work with.'

'There you are, then,' he said evenly. 'And I've gone through a marriage break-up that was still very stressful even though there was no acrimony, so we have the answer, don't you think?'

Alex was actually smiling and it really ruffled her feathers as he went on to say, 'But the longer you stand there with moonbeams in your eyes, the more I realise that I want to call your bluff.'

'So why don't you?'

'Because for one thing I hope that you're just teasing.' He touched her cheek fleetingly. 'Go home to your family…and I'll go and see what Gloria is up to.' And before she could protest, he was crossing the road and leaving her no choice but to do as he'd suggested.

As Zoey was about to put her key in the lock, the front door of Mandy's house opened and a strange man stood there, looking at her.

'This is Harry. He's just going,' Mandy said, appearing, red-faced, from behind him. 'He owns the pizza parlour down the road. You remember me telling you about him, Zoey?'

As they shook hands she was taking stock of him. He was fortyish, fair-haired and had a kind mouth. Zoey always looked at people's mouths when assessing their character. It had been only seconds ago that she'd been mesmerised by another mouth, wanting it on hers, and she was still limp with the longing it had aroused in her.

When Harry had gone she asked teasingly, 'And so what is going on, Mandy?'

'I met Harry this morning when I took Rosie to the shops,' she explained uncomfortably. 'He recognised me and we chatted for a while. Then went for coffee as his place doesn't open on a Monday.'

'And?' Zoey probed gently.

'I invited him round this evening. Do you think your dad would have minded?'

Zoey kissed Mandy's pale cheek.

'Of course he wouldn't. I've told you so often that this is what he would want you to do…get on with your life. When are you seeing Harry again?'

'Soon maybe. But tell me what sort of an evening you've had.'

'Thought-provoking.'

'Is that it?'

'Yes, for the moment.' And off Zoey went to bed.

CHAPTER THREE

ALEX found Gloria unpacking when he got back and when he saw the amount of luggage she'd brought with her he eyed it in dismay.

She saw his expression and said quickly, 'I've brought extra clothes as I don't know how long I'll be here.'

He was frowning.

'What's going on, Gloria? Why are you here?'

'Aunt Mary is going into hospital tomorrow for a major heart operation and as she's my only relative I've come back to be near her. And as you said you didn't mind, staying here seemed the logical thing to do.'

'I'm sorry to hear about your aunt,' he said, and meant it.

He knew that Gloria was very fond of the old lady, but he thought ruefully that they were supposed to be going their separate ways. Yet what were a couple of weeks in a lifetime?

'Right, then, I'll leave you to finish your unpacking,' he told her, unable to credit that this was happening. Gloria back under his roof...and Zoey, the young enchantress, just across the road.

The following Saturday was the day of the sponsored 'pull' in aid of the local hospital's children's ward. Everyone was eager to take part in such a good cause and Zoey was amongst them.

Twenty-four fire-service personnel from around the area were going to pull the engine from the nearby town

44

to the city seven miles away. It had been taken there the night before to be suitably decorated.

In two teams of twelve, each person would have nylon webbing straps over one shoulder, attached to a centre strap, and, with a fireman in the driving seat to steer the vehicle, they were going to pull it to its destination.

There was a banner across the front of the engine telling the public what the 'pull' was in aid of, and volunteers were collecting loose change in brightly coloured buckets from the jovial crowd that had gathered.

'I got the impression that Alex wasn't keen for me to take part,' she'd previously told Greg, who always seemed to be hovering near, 'but I intend to.'

'Why not?' he'd said carelessly. 'There'll be enough of us to take the weight. We've done it before and no one came to grief. Mind you, we didn't have any women taking part on those occasions. Maybe he has it in mind for you to be on top of the engine dressed in a bikini,' he'd said with a smirk, 'like some of the floats when there's a carnival.'

'It's more the kind of thing he would expect of me,' she'd said wryly, 'but I'd much rather be with the rest of you, doing my bit for the kids.'

It was a cold, clear morning and Alex, who hadn't raised any objections since his comment when the 'pull' had first been mentioned, had offered to give her a lift.

'There's no point in two of us driving to the starting point,' he'd said. 'I imagine you'll enjoy seeing your old haunts again when you get back to the city. Presuming you've not been back there since you moved in with Mandy.'

Here he was again, she'd thought, expecting her to be pining for the bright lights. With the devil in her, she'd said, 'Yes, I might sign on for a couple of hours' lap dancing if we finish early enough. It's one way of balancing the budget.'

'All right,' he'd conceded. 'Point taken. I'll mind my own business.'

Neither of them had referred to those moments beneath the scudding moon a week ago, and as far as she was concerned that was how it was going to stay. She'd made it clear to Alex that she was attracted to him and what had she got? A lecture. Maybe it was just as well that one of them had some sense.

They were off, with the crowds cheering and waving them on their way. The collectors walked alongside them as they pulled, and a van carrying supplies of food, drink and first-aid equipment brought up the rear.

Zoey had positioned herself at the front of the engine as a gesture to women in the fire service everywhere, and as some wag in the crowd cried, 'Heave ho, blondie,' her smile flashed out.

Alex wasn't far away and after he'd asked her a couple of times if she was all right, he gave up.

Greg had other things on his mind, and when they stopped for a rest he said, 'How about us making a day of it, Zoey, once this is over? A meal and a show perhaps, or we could go clubbing.'

She laughed up at him.

'Why? Have you brought a change of clothes? Or are you intending doing the rounds of the clubs and cafés in your uniform? It's going to be a bit sticky after all this effort.'

He tutted irritably.

'Yes, of course I have. They're inside the engine. I thought that you might have done the same.'

'It never occurred to me,' she told him lightly, and

could have explained that even if it had, she wouldn't have accepted the invitation.

She could also have told him that there was only one man she was interested in. That he was only a few feet away and she couldn't get him out of her mind. That he was a different person away from the fire station and she felt confused and off balance.

Her brief relationship with Damien of the roving eye had left her wary of being too trusting of the opposite sex and she'd had no intentions of getting involved again.

But the way she felt about Alex was different. Losing her father and having to give Mandy and Rosie continual support had taken some of the life out of her. She felt she'd grown up a lot, though she was still the same person underneath, bouncy, generous, imaginative, inclined to be a bit reckless, and incredibly romantic.

And now, since she'd met Alex, it was as if the mantle of maturity had fallen even more firmly upon her. Yet she knew he didn't see her like that. He was all the time expecting her to fulfil the role of dizzy blonde, and it was irksome.

She'd been conscious of his dark watchful gaze upon them while Greg had been chatting her up, and she'd thought wistfully that it would have been nice if he'd had a similar idea.

But she sensed that, no matter how often he might say that his marriage was over, he wasn't finished with Gloria yet. Maybe he still cared more than he was prepared to admit. Or hadn't the heart to desert her completely. There was something. His ex-wife's proprietorial manner was proof of that, and he wasn't a man who would be happy to have loose ends in his life.

By midday the sun was shining strongly and they

stopped again for refreshment. A group of small boys had gathered round the engine and one of them said to Alex, 'Can we see inside, mister?'

He smiled and lifted each one of them up in turn.

'I want to be a fireman when I grow up,' one of them said.

'That's good,' Alex replied with suitable gravity, 'but it can be a dangerous job, you know.' In an aside to Zoey, who was standing near, he said, 'That's what the young guy who was trapped in the car on the hill bend wants to do when he comes out of hospital.'

'What?'

'Join the service.'

'Maybe he feels he owes it to us.'

'Could be, but the poor lad will have to be a lot fitter than he is now to be accepted.'

While they'd been stationary some of the volunteers had dropped out and others had replaced them.

'How about you?' Alex asked Zoey.

Zoey had shaken her head. She was beginning to feel the strain, due to the unseasonably warm weather more than anything. But she was the only woman in the pull and as such felt she was flying the flag for the small contingent of women in the fire service all over the country.

There was a reception committee waiting for them in the city centre with the local press in attendance, and when the engine and those who'd pulled it came into view, cameras began to flash and a cheer went up from those who had been waiting to welcome them.

It was a light-hearted moment, yet Zoey felt tears prick as she thought of why they'd done the charity 'pull'. Some of the children from the hospital had been allowed out to cheer on the firefighters, and the delighted expressions on their faces made a lump rise in her throat.

As she wiped the tears away with the back of her hand, an arm was placed around her shoulders and Alex said, 'They're all such brave kids. I'm glad we can do something for them.'

She nodded and smiled.

'So am I.'

The speeches were over, the money had been handed in and the crowds were dispersing. Alex said to his team, 'Let's go. I don't know about you folks, but I'm ready for a shower and a change of clothes,' and to Zoey, 'The guys can drop us off where I've parked my car before they take the engine back to base.'

Zoey nodded her agreement and within minutes they were leaving the city limits and moving in the direction of home.

Shortly after they'd transferred to his car, Alex said, 'I need fuel.' As a garage loomed up in front of them he turned onto the forecourt.

When he'd gone into the shop to pay, Zoey sat mulling over the day's events. The 'pull' had been a huge success, but what now?

She reckoned that Alex would just drop her off and that would be that. If she hadn't any plans for the hours ahead, it didn't mean that he didn't.

He was having to queue, standing head and shoulders above the rest, and she thought that when he got back into the car she was going to try to make him see how he was affecting her.

There was no guile in her. It wasn't her style. If he told her again to forget it, or something similar, then she would have to accept it. But there was always the chance that he might have changed his mind and her heartbeat quickened at the thought.

He was chatting to the man behind the counter now and she looked around her disinterestedly. There was a block of flats beside the garage, and as she observed them the glass in the window of an apartment on the first floor shattered and smoke started to belch forth.

'It's on fire,' somebody shouted, and she was out of the car in a flash.

Zoey still had her uniform on and she reached inside and grabbed the helmet which was lying on the back seat. Then she was running. Flinging herself towards the entrance of the flats.

'Dial 999,' she told the woman on the pavement who'd alerted everyone to what was happening, and in she went. There was a lift with a sign that said it was out of order, and as Zoey raced up a badly lit staircase doors on the landing above were opening and shrill voices asking what was the matter.

The door of the nearest flat was wide open and a woman was banging frantically on a door at the other end of a cluttered living room.

When Zoey burst in the woman cried, 'Thank God you're here! It's my lad, Connor. He's got fireworks in there. They've gone off and set the place on fire and he's got the door locked.'

Taking in the situation at a glance, Zoey banged on the door and bellowed, 'Open the door, Connor. Now!'

'I can't,' he cried in a muffled voice. 'That's where the fire is.'

'We're going to have to break it down,' Zoey told his terrified mother. 'You'll have to help me. If two of us put our shoulder against it, we might manage it.'

They tried but it didn't budge, and behind it the crackling of the fire was getting louder.

'The air coming in through the shattered window will be making the fire burn faster,' Zoey gasped. 'He's going to have to get out that way.'

'Where's the rest of your lot?' the other woman cried. 'Can't they put ladders up to take him down?'

'They're not here yet,' Zoey told her. 'I'm off duty. I was on the garage forecourt and—'

'Clear the building immediately,' she heard Alex telling the bewildered tenants on the landing, and then he was there, cool, calm and the most welcome sight she'd ever seen.

'Get out of here fast,' he told the woman, adding to Zoey, 'Find me a wet cloth to cover my face.'

As the boy's mother hesitated, Zoey ushered her out. 'Do as he says. We know what we're doing.'

There was a pile of ironing on the kitchen table. Grabbing a couple of towels, Zoey soaked them under the tap and ran back to where Alex had just put his shoulder to the door and had it creaking on its hinges.

He did it again. This time it flew open and with the blast of air that it created, flames and smoke came leaping outwards.

Alex moved back, but only for a second. Then with a towel over his nose and mouth he went in with Zoey close behind him.

'Go back!' he bellowed. 'You have no breathing apparatus.'

'Neither have you,' she said grimly, and followed him into the thick black smoke.

After groping around for precious seconds, they found the boy lying in a crumpled heap in the far corner of the room. Alex bent swiftly and heaved him over his shoulder.

'Come on!' he cried. 'Let's get out of here before the whole place goes up. You first, Zoey. I don't want to have to come back in here looking for you.'

It wasn't a moment to argue, so she did as she was told.

When they got out into the open Alex laid the limp figure of the youth on the grass verge outside the flats and she dropped to her knees beside him.

She'd heard his mother screaming hysterically as they'd brought him out but it had barely registered. The lad was suffering from burns and smoke inhalation and they had no equipment to treat him with.

To her dismay she saw that there was no rising of the chest to indicate he was still breathing. There was no pulse or heartbeat either and she told Alex, who was asking urgently if anyone had phoned the emergency services. 'He's gone! I'm about to resuscitate.'

'Right!' he said briskly. 'Let's see if we can bring him back. In the meantime, pray that help isn't long in coming or we're going to have one dead boy and the whole block of flats on fire.'

It could have only been seconds yet it seemed like a lifetime before paramedics were spilling out of an ambulance and the wail of a fire-engine siren indicated that colleagues from a station other than their own had arrived.

In those brief moments the boy began to breathe again and his mother, who had now relapsed into a shocked silence, grabbed Zoey's arm.

'It's OK,' Zoey told her quietly. 'We've got him back but he still needs urgent medical attention. Once he's in the ambulance they have oxygen and drugs to prevent any further cardiac arrest. They'll take over now.' As two paramedics fell to their knees beside the inert figure of the boy, she briefed them quickly and then got to her feet.

'Can you believe that just happened? That we were there when we were needed?' Alex shook his head and smiled wryly as, smoke-grimed and dishevelled, they set off for home once more. 'I didn't have to look far for you when I found the car empty.'

Zoey gave a tired smile. She was weary now after her exertions in the fire-engine 'pull' and the incident at the flats.

That sort of rescue had been a much more dangerous thing than when they had the back-up of the fire-engine's resources and other crew members to assist.

Luckily they'd been wearing their fireproof uniforms and helmets, but they'd had no breathing apparatus and now her throat felt raw and her eyes were smarting.

'You should have gone to Casualty, along with the boy, when the paramedics suggested it,' Alex said with a quick sideways glance at her blackened face.

'And what about you?' she parried. 'Isn't your throat dry and your eyes smarting?'

'Er...yes, but I'm not you. I don't want to see you suffering from smoke inhalation or any other nasty effects of the fire.'

'I'm all right,' she told him as her eyelids began to droop. 'A bath and a hot drink will put me right. I wish it were as simple for that foolish boy.'

'Yes. But remember he was still breathing and with the care he'll be getting now should make a full recovery.'

'If there's no brain damage,' she commented drowsily, and the next time Alex looked at her he saw she was asleep.

Zoey looked young and defenceless, slumped in the seat beside him, with the firm globes of her breasts rising and falling inside the bulky coat and her soft blonde hair tumbled over her face.

What was she doing in such a dangerous job? he asked himself irritably. Looking at her, he felt that she would look more at home in some kind of fashion outlet…and she'd certainly be at less risk there.

When she'd followed him into that kid's bedroom he'd wanted to bellow at her to obey orders. But they hadn't been on a fire-service 'shout'. It had been a one-off they'd stumbled on and he'd known that she wasn't going to take any notice of his command to stay out of it.

Fortunately she hadn't come to grief and a shudder went through him at the thought of how he would have felt if she had. He was getting involved, he told himself, and it was against his better judgement.

When her head slid sideways and came to rest against his shoulder, he turned and his lips brushed against her dishevelled golden bob.

She smelt of smoke. Not the most appealing of perfumes. Yet it made his blood warm. He smiled. This confident young creature would run a mile if she discovered that she evoked a tenderness in him that made him want to take care of her. The knowledge really would widen the gap between them. She was more in the market for fun and romance.

Zoey was still asleep when he pulled up in front of Mandy's house and Alex sat looking down on her in the shadowed confines of the car. It seemed a shame to rouse her, but the autumn dusk was falling and he couldn't leave her there.

He touched her face gently and she murmured his name.

'Zoey,' he said gently. 'Time to wake up. We're home.'

'Hmm?'

'We're home, Zoey,' he repeated.

She opened her eyes and for a second gazed at him bewilderedly. Then she was straightening up in her seat and raking through her hair with a grubby hand.

'I can't believe I did that,' she groaned.

'What?'

'Went to sleep. What am I?'

'How about someone who's had a very busy day?'

'Mmm. I suppose so. We think that Rosie is teething so it doesn't help, being up in the middle of the night.'

'You mean to say that you've been up with the baby!' he exclaimed. 'Where was her mother?'

'We take turns.'

'But Mandy doesn't have a job.'

'I know, but I am here to help her. She's had a rough time.'

'And you haven't?'

Zoey's smile was wistful.

'Don't start on that again, Alex. Self-pity doesn't suit me.' And because she couldn't resist it, she asked, 'Do you remember last time?'

Did he remember! It had been those moments when he'd held her in his arms that were the cause of his present state of mind. He'd been quite content with his life before she'd appeared on the scene.

His marriage was over without any great amount of rancour on either side, to his great relief, and he'd been planning a woman-free existence. At least until such time as the taste of life with Gloria had left him.

But what had happened? Temptation had appeared in the form of a confident young blonde. Quite stunning in her own way and hardly likely to have the same outlook as a jaded divorcee like himself.

Zoey was waiting for a reply and as he looked into her wide sapphire gaze Alex knew he couldn't lie.

'Of course I remember,' he said stiffly, miffed that she was putting him on the spot like this. 'For some reason I feel that I have to look after you, though goodness knows why as you're one tough cookie.'

It was part of the truth, but not all of it. Alex hadn't told her that once she was in his arms he'd wanted to hold her for ever.

Her expression was telling him that he hadn't said what she wanted to hear and her next remark was in keeping with it.

'I don't need looking after, Alex,' she snapped. 'I've fended for myself since I was eighteen and haven't come to grief yet.'

It was on the tip of her tongue to tell him that there was something that she did need, but that it was connected with passion and desire, not the frailties associated with womankind.

Zoey reached out to open the car door and he knew he didn't want her to go.

'Let's go for a meal when we've washed and changed,' he said quickly. 'That's if you haven't anything else planned.' He gave a teasing smile. 'Or are you too tired?'

She beamed back at him, her temporary irritation banished at the thought of some more prime time together.

'I'd love to…and, no, I'm not tired.'

She would have gone if she'd been dropping in her tracks, she thought. But that short sleep in the car had pepped her up and now she couldn't wait to get inside and into something more alluring than her uniform.

'How long will it take you to get ready?' Alex asked, casual now that he'd managed to prolong their time together.

'An hour?'

'Fine. I'll come across and get you.'

'Zoey!' Mandy exclaimed when she saw her. 'Where've you got all the grime from? I thought it was a pleasure day today.'

'It was…is,' Zoey trilled from halfway up the stairs. 'The grime is from a fire that Alex and I got caught up in on our way home. But the rest of the day has been great and it isn't finished yet. We're going out for a meal.'

'Just the two of you?'

'Mmm.'

'Where to?'

'I don't know. He's the one who knows where to dine out in this area. I don't care where we go…just as long as he's there. What about you?' she asked. 'Is Harry coming round?'

Her stepmother pulled a face.

'Hardly. It's Saturday night, don't forget. But he's taking Rosie and me for a drive tomorrow afternoon, which will be nice.'

As Zoey lay soaking in perfumed water, she was deciding what to wear and smiling as the choice presented itself. It was always a temptation to wear black, but tonight there was the urge in her to dazzle. To let Alex see that amongst the other things that she was, trauma technician and child-minder, she was beautiful in her own special way.

There was a long sleeveless dress in her wardrobe that was the same colour as her eyes. It was plain and understated and yet the moment she put it on everything about her sprang to life. Hair, skin, curving slenderness, the lot.

What effect would it have on Alex? she wondered as she lifted a leg high out of the water and surveyed her toes. Would the day end how she wanted it to?

Don't bank on it, she told herself. He's picking up the pieces after Gloria. The ex-wife who is at present back in the marital home.

She would love to know why. Maybe now that she hadn't got Alex she wanted him back. If that was the case, she should have held onto him when she had him.

'Wow!' Mandy said when she saw her. 'Alex won't be able to take his eyes off you when he sees you in that.'

'I hope you're right,' Zoey sparkled. 'But I feel that he doesn't know what to make of me. Do you know, he didn't want me to be there as back-up when he went into the bedroom where the fire was at those flats? What do you think of that?'

Mandy's face was solemn.

'I can understand that.'

'You can?'

'Yes. You weren't on duty for one thing, and for another neither of you had breathing apparatus.'

'So what difference does it make?'

'I take it that he doesn't fuss when you're out on a call with the fire crew?'

'Er…no. Well, not much anyway.'

'Right. So you were both taking a big risk when you

brought that boy out to safety. Alex wouldn't have wanted your life to be on his conscience. Surely you see that.'

'Yes, but I was first on the scene.'

At that moment the doorbell rang and her stepmother said laughingly, 'Just for once let him be protective if he wants to.'

Alex's step had been light as he'd gone upstairs to shower, but before he'd been able to strip off a voice from down below had brought him to a halt.

'I've just got back from the hospital,' Gloria had said. 'Aunt Mary's surgery is scheduled for Monday.'

He'd looked down at her in some disbelief. For a moment he'd forgotten that she was back on the scene, but not for long. There was a trying time ahead for both Gloria and her elderly aunt and he would do what he could to make it easier. Even though her being back in his life was totally unexpected.

So he said gravely, 'I see. Well, let's hope that it all goes well for the old lady. And now, if you'll excuse me, Gloria, I need a shower. Zoey and I got involved in a fire of all things on the way home and I feel decidedly smoke-blackened.'

'What's going on between you and her?' Gloria asked in her flat legal voice.

Alex sighed. He didn't think for a moment that she was really interested.

'Nothing. We're just getting to know each other. Why do you ask?'

She shrugged.

'No reason. Just curious. She doesn't look your type.'

Alex frowned, irritated that Gloria felt in a position to comment. *She* hadn't been his type. Had she forgotten that?

When Zoey opened the door to him the frown was still there, and she took a step back.

'Ready?' he asked briefly.

She nodded, her bright expectations dimming.

'Yes,' she told him with like brevity, and without wasting any time settled herself into the passenger seat of his car.

'I thought we'd go to the local golf club if that's all right with you,' he said in a lighter tone as they pulled out onto the main road that ran past the fire station. 'The food's excellent.'

'Fine,' she said abruptly, thinking that if she'd dressed in an old sugar sack he couldn't have taken less notice of her.

Alex took his gaze off the road for a second.

'What's wrong, Zoey?'

'Nothing! Nothing at all!'

'Really? Well, I wouldn't like to see you when there is. How can you sit there looking so beautiful and yet be so miserable?'

'Me miserable! I beg your pardon. When I opened the door to you it was like when we first met. You were abrupt and monosyllabic. What have I done?'

'You haven't done anything,' he said levelly. 'If that's how I was, I'm sorry. Gloria was there when I got in, asking questions.'

'So she's still with you?' Zoey said flatly.

'Yes. An elderly aunt of hers is to undergo surgery and she's come to give moral support.'

It was none of her business but she had to ask.

'So how long is she staying?'

'I don't know. As long as it takes, I suppose. She's very close to the old lady and is in some distress.'

'So why didn't you ring me and cancel our arrangement?' Zoey said coolly. 'It would seem that you had more important things to do.'

'Like what?'

'Holding Gloria's hand. You were the first person she came to. Couldn't she stay at her aunt's house?'

'Hardly. She's in a rest home for the elderly.'

Zoey knew she was being unkind but she couldn't bear the thought of Alex being in such close intimacy with his ex-wife.

He was observing her set expression and he said levelly, 'I'm not taking you back. I asked you out for a meal and that is what we're going to do...eat...together...because we've earned it. OK?'

Zoey shrugged as if she couldn't care either way.

'Suit yourself. Just as long as you're not going to be pining to be back home all the time.'

'As if!' He was smiling and her spirits lifted when he went on to say, 'I haven't told you how fabulous you look.'

Not entirely forgiving him, she said, 'Don't follow that comment with the old cliché about how somebody will be a lucky fellow one day.'

'Why not?'

'Because it doesn't apply. I was supposed to be steering clear of love affairs after dating a firefighter who, unknown to me, was sleeping with one of the teachers we'd met during our talks to the schools.'

'And?'

'Oh, for goodness' sake, Alex. Stop pretending that you don't know what I mean.'

'You're crazy,' he said softly. 'I have no intention of

starting another relationship so soon after my divorce. It wouldn't be fair to all concerned.'

Zoey was sitting bolt upright in her seat.

'Including Gloria?'

'Maybe. The divorce wasn't all that long ago.'

'I see.'

He shook his head.

'No, you don't, Zoey. I'm trying to be sensible, if you'll let me.'

He was stopping the car in front of a spacious single-storey building on the edge of parkland, and as she observed him with mutinous eyes Alex said, 'Well? Are you ready to be wined and dined? Let's just concentrate on that, shall we? Enjoy each other's company and forget the rest.'

'All right,' she agreed, with a sinking feeling that if he could put something as serious as her feelings for him to one side so easily, there couldn't be much of a flame burning in return.

But as they were shown to a table Zoey was bouncing back. Why spoil the night with dismal thoughts? If Alex had any doubts about their budding relationship she was going to banish them here and now. She'd wanted to dazzle...and dazzle she would. Even though he had let his ex-wife back into the fold.

CHAPTER FOUR

ALEX watched Zoey with a quizzical smile as the meal progressed. She was obviously out to charm him, with eyes bright and mouth curving into laughter as she regaled him with amusing stories about happenings at the city-centre fire station where she'd worked before.

She talked about life with Mandy and Rosie, too, and it was all upbeat. No mention of the sadness and worry of the time when Mandy hadn't been coping very well and she'd been frantic about Rosie's well-being to the extent that she'd spent every free second with them.

She could discuss it light-heartedly now, as everything was so much better since she'd gone to live with them and Mandy had met Harry who owned the pizzeria. Nothing might come of it, but if having a man friend was making her young stepmother feel less desolate, it had to be good.

When she finally lapsed into silence Zoey sat twirling a wineglass between finger and thumb. She was leaning forward, watching Alex from beneath lowered lids. Alex could see the cleft between her firm, creamy breasts. Her perfume was as tantalising as before.

He was crazy if he thought he was going to resist Zoey Lawrence, he told himself. Intimate meetings of this sort weren't going to keep them out of each other's arms.

'I know what you're up to, you know,' he said in a low voice.

As she slowly raised her head and fixed him with her

challenging sapphire gaze, he called the waiter across to settle the bill. Once that was done he got to his feet. 'Let's go,' he said.

When they reached the shadows outside Alex stopped, and as she turned to face him he reached out and took her in his arms.

'You don't have to put yourself out to attract me,' he murmured against the smooth brightness of her hair. 'You're as enticing in the clumsy gear we wear for work as in this beautiful blue dress.'

'So?' she challenged.

'So this,' he said softly, and like a thirsty man who'd found an oasis he bent his mouth to hers and kissed her.

His lips were firm and warm...and demanding. His arms where she wanted them to be, around her. And his arousal, which she could feel hard against her own inner thighs, was making the moment complete.

This is it, Zoey thought dizzily. Love! We might have only known each other a few weeks, but it's as if I've always known Alex...and he me.

She was presuming too much. Even as the sentiments formed themselves in her mind, Alex was putting her gently away from him.

'I knew it was crazy to bring you out here,' he said with a sigh. 'I should have had more sense. I'm going to take you home, Zoey, before our feelings get the better of us.'

There was no teasing challenge in her eyes now. They were sparking fire.

'What's the matter?' she snapped. 'Have you just remembered there's someone waiting for you at home? Better the devil you know?'

Alex shook his head ruefully.

'You see. You're all upset now. We should have stayed as we were...friendly acquaintances.'

'You have some nerve!' she cried. 'I told you to take me back home in the first place. But you insisted on bringing me here. What had you in mind? The best of both worlds. A quick flirt with me and then back home to Gloria?'

'If that were the case we would have been further along the seduction line by now,' he protested tightly. 'I wouldn't have been considering your best interests.'

'Huh!' she snorted. 'I'll be the judge of what are my best interests...and now...yes...I would like to go home. I can't think of anything I would prefer more.'

They were both silent on the way back and when Alex pulled up in front of their respective houses Zoey was out of the car in a flash.

'Goodnight. Thanks for the meal,' she said stonily. As he would have spoken, she added, 'I don't want to hear it, Alex.'

On that parting note she walked up the drive with head held high and spirits as low as the hem of the blue dress around her ankles.

After Saturday night's dampener Sunday was a no-day as far as Zoey was concerned. She helped Mandy with household chores, did some lukewarm tidying up in the garden and was leaving the house with Rosie in her pram when she saw Gloria coming out of the house across the way.

She averted her head, having nothing to say to her, but irritatingly Gloria caught her up as she pointed the pram towards the main road. Of Alex there was no sign.

'You're the girl from the fire station, aren't you?' Gloria said as she drew level.

'Yes.'

'And you have a child, I see.'

'The baby isn't mine.'

'Oh. Whose is it?'

'Rosie is my stepsister.'

'Rather a big age gap.'

'That's right.'

Suddenly Zoey felt ashamed. She had no quarrel with this woman. No need to be so abrupt. It wasn't Gloria's fault that she was falling in love with her ex-husband.

'I'm turning off here,' she said, forcing a smile. 'Nice to have met you again.'

It wasn't strictly true but she had to say something to get away from her, but Gloria didn't seem to have any particular destination in view.

'I might as well do the same,' she said. 'I've come out mainly for some fresh air. Alex would have come with me but he'd arranged to go to hospital to visit some young fellow who was in a car crash on the hill road.'

And so why have you latched onto me? Zoey thought. We hardly know each other.

Daylight was fading. Another chilly autumn evening was approaching and when a car pulled up at the side of them and the driver opened the door on the passenger side, Gloria perked up.

'Hello, there, ladies,' Greg said. 'Anyone fancy a trip to the cinema?'

Zoey shook her head.

'No, thanks. As you can see, I've got my hands full.'

'How about you, Gloria?'

'Er…yes…why not?' she said. 'I spend most of my time visiting my aunt. It will make a nice change.'

'Absolutely,' Zoey agreed, with a fervour that

stemmed from a mixture of surprise and relief. She turned the pram and headed for home.

As she walked the last few yards back to the house she was wondering why it couldn't have been Alex wanting to walk with her instead of Gloria. But that wasn't likely after her snappy farewell of the night before, was it?

Another thought presented itself. What would Alex have to say when he discovered that Gloria had gone to the cinema with the smooth-tongued Greg?

When Alex saw Gloria fall in step beside Zoey he groaned. The two women in his life out for a stroll together!

One of them should by now be in the past, yet she wasn't. And the other? Beautiful Zoey. Like a proud young colt. Confident and outspoken when it came to what she wanted.

And what was wrong with that? He ought to be over the moon that she wanted him. But he'd rushed into marriage once. Not given it enough thought. It wasn't going to happen again.

As they disappeared round the corner of the cul-de-sac he got into his car. He was committed to visiting the lad in hospital, and a promise made was a promise kept as far as he was concerned. But he would have dearly liked to know what sort of a conversation Zoey and Gloria were having.

When Zoey turned up at the station on Monday morning Geoff said, 'We've got a suggestion.'

There were smiles all round and a few nudges and she observed them warily.

'Oh, yes?'

'Yeah. The guy that you replaced used to be the mo-rale officer. He kept us cheerful when things weren't so good. It's hard not to be affected when there's been a "shout" and there are bodies to be brought out of a burning building or untangled from what's left of a car.

'It's happened to all of us at one time or another and we don't always manage to get it in perspective. But if one of the team is there to do a bit of counselling and cheering up, it can make a lot of difference to whether we sleep at night.'

'And so what are you saying?' she asked slowly.

'That you take his place, Zoey. Even on a normal day, just looking at you makes us feel better. What do you say?'

'I'd like to know what Alex thinks first.'

'It was his suggestion.'

'Really?'

That was surprising! Especially as she was in just as much need of cheering up as anyone at the moment. Maybe he thought that if she had to spread herself around a bit more, she would forget her fixation about him.

'All right, I'll do it,' she agreed. 'Just as long as I don't end up being a perpetual hand-holder or shoulder to cry on. Or…' with a mischievous glance at Alex who'd just come out of the office '…asked to organise sing-songs.'

She was making a joke of it, but she knew that there were times when the impersonality that the emergency services strove for to keep them sane fell apart in times of great stress, and a calm word or a friendly gesture could make all the difference.

At that moment she had no means of knowing that in the very near future the morale of the fire crew would be at its lowest ebb.

It was Friday afternoon and the end of a long and uneventful week. Zoey was feeling restless and on edge and had thought a few times that the role of morale-booster might be sitting on the wrong shoulders.

She would have felt better if Alex had made some mention of their brief passionate encounter outside the golf club, but he was putting up a barrier of bland politeness between them and, still sore at the way she'd been brought down to earth so abruptly, she'd decided that if that was how he wanted it to be, it was all right by her.

Yet if there was pretence between them now, she knew that it hadn't been like that when he'd held her in his arms and they'd leapt to answer each other's need.

There had been wonder in the moment. A magic unlike anything she'd ever experienced before. And what had he done? Cheapened it into a casual encounter.

She'd caught him watching her a few times with a sort of guarded thoughtfulness and it had taken all her time not to go up to him and demand that they talk it through.

Yet something always held her back. Pride? Uncertainty? She didn't know, as now she wasn't the confident person that he'd described her as.

If Mandy had noticed that she was in the doldrums, she hadn't commented. Her own life was coming together again because of her friendship with Harry, and as she began to sparkle so Zoey's zest faltered.

The 'shout', when it came in the last hour of Friday's shift, was for engine and crew to turn out to a blaze in the science laboratory at the nearby comprehensive school, attended by some of the older children of the firefighters.

A police presence was already on the scene when they got there, and after having a quick word with the officer in charge Alex told them in their own familiar jargon, 'It's a persons reported. We don't know how many. Most of the pupils and staff had gone home when there was an explosion in the lab. But there were still one or two stragglers on the premises and the head teacher and caretaker were seen running in this direction. Neither of them have been seen since.'

While he was speaking they'd been attaching the hoses and donning breathing apparatus and were almost ready to go into the single-storey building where the blaze was.

'We don't know what caused the explosion,' the police officer told them tersely. 'There might be another if the fire spreads to other equipment.'

'Great!' one of the men said dolefully. 'That's all we need, with gas taps all over the place. It'll have been kids messing about. You'll see.'

The school's laboratory was much bigger inside than they'd expected, and as the fire crew groped their way through the dense smoke and rising flames Alex was in the forefront, with Zoey and the others close behind.

'Spread out,' he called over his shoulder, and almost fell over the body of a woman lying at his feet.

Zoey was by his side in a flash and she saw immediately that the disappearance of the headmistress had been solved. Who would they find next?

There was no time to ponder on that score. They were bringing her out, and if the ambulance services hadn't yet arrived, she would be needed to treat the woman...if it wasn't too late.

It seemed that it might be. When they laid her down at a safe distance from the burning building Zoey found that there was no heartbeat or pulse. The woman's lips were blue, her skin cold and clammy, and as Zoey desperately tried to resuscitate her it became clear that the headmistress had suffered a cardiac arrest as she'd run into the building to check that none of her pupils were inside.

Paramedics were on the scene now and as it became obvious that life was not going to return to the still form in front of them, their faces were sombre.

As Zoey got slowly to her feet, Alex and the others were bringing out the caretaker and a teenage boy. The youth was badly burned, the man suffering from smoke inhalation. As if the moment wasn't horrendous enough, Alex told her tightly, 'It's Geoff's lad. We found him by one of the workbenches.'

'Oh, no!' Zoey breathed. 'How awful! Where is Geoff?'

'Over there, vomiting. He was the one who found him.'

The ambulance crews had taken over the casualties. One lot were giving the caretaker oxygen and the others preparing to wrap the injured youth in a water gel blanket to stop the skin tightening before they got him to the burns unit.

Geoff was beginning to absorb the shock of finding his son in the lab and was now hurrying to be by his side.

'I never expected this,' he said hoarsely as he prepared to board the ambulance that was taking the lad to hospital. He cast an anguished look at the still form of the headmistress. 'Dead?'

'Afraid so,' Alex told him.

Geoff groaned.

'That woman lived for the school.'

'And now she's died for it,' Zoey said quietly. 'Let's pray that she's the only one.'

The rest of the men were working to get the blaze under control now that the casualties had been brought out, and the atmosphere was grim.

It was one of their own close-knit band who was suffering from the results of this fire, and as most of them had children of their own, they could comprehend what Geoff was going through.

'Let me tell Geoff's wife,' Alex told the police. 'She'll take it better from one of us. They live right next to the station, so as soon as we get back one of us will take her to hospital.'

It was late that night and Zoey had been on edge ever since arriving home. Alex had left them abruptly while they'd been putting the engine away and had gone to see Mrs Baines.

Within seconds she'd seen his car set off for the hospital with an ashen-faced woman in the passenger seat, and ever since then she'd been waiting for news.

It came at last. At eleven o'clock he rang the doorbell and her first words as she let him in were, 'How's the boy?'

He looked tired, drawn, and had no smiles for her.

'Lost the sight of one eye. Has second-degree burns down one side of his face and on the upper arm that he tried to shield himself with.'

Zoey shook her head sadly.

'Do we know what happened?'

'Yes. Geoff's kid sneaked back after the chemistry lesson to try out an experiment of his own. He was too ill to be properly interviewed, but they did manage to get that out of him.'

'And his parents?'

'What do you think? Devastated.'

She pointed to the sofa.

'Sit down and I'll make you a drink.'

'I won't say no to that,' he said, doing as she'd suggested. 'I'm desperate for a wash and a change of clothes, but those sort of needs seem very unimportant after today's tragedies. That poor woman...Geoff's son...and the caretaker.

'He's come out of it the best of the three. The staff and governors of the school are dumbstruck at what has happened to the head. No one can believe it.'

He yawned and raked his hand tiredly through his dark locks, and by the time Zoey appeared from the kitchen with a steaming mug of hot chocolate he was asleep.

She stood looking down at him tenderly. 'Action man' had given in to human frailty. It was nice to see his vulnerable side for once.

She bent and planted a gentle kiss on his brow. His eyes flew open and she sighed. She should have known better than think that he had really succumbed to weariness.

Reaching out for the drink, he patted the cushions beside him and said, 'Where's Mandy?'

'Out with the new man in her life.'

'You mentioned she had someone—what's his name?'

'He's called Harry and I told you, he owns the local pizzeria. I can hear wedding bells in the distance.'

'Really?' he said, sitting up straighter. 'So that would leave you free to get on with your own life?'

'Er...yes...I suppose so. I hadn't given it much

thought. Though I might have done if a certain person hadn't been so touch-me-not.'

'Me?'

'Who else?'

He put the mug down and turned towards her.

'And you think it's easy…resisting you.'

'It must be. You seem cheerful enough.'

'There's cheerful…and cheerful, Zoey. I haven't felt really light-hearted in years.'

'I've not been exactly on top of the world myself since Dad died,' she said quietly. 'Before that I was having a great time—lots of friends, parties, theatres, the lot—but it all went by the board when I saw the state Mandy was in.'

Her voice thickened.

'I've been so lonely, with no one to turn to, and…'

The words trailed away into silence as she thought, What am I doing? Asking for sympathy again! Alex will think I'm a veritable Miss Whinge.

He put his arm around her shoulders and cuddled her up against him.

'So we're both putting on an act,' he said, with his chin resting on the golden crown of her head. 'Crazy, aren't we? There is a difference, though. Once your step-mother is settled again with someone who cares for her, the way ahead will be clear for you. While I have the legacy of a failed marriage to contend with and an ex-wife who has appeared on the scene again.'

As Zoey swivelled round to face him their eyes were only inches apart.

'So what?' she exclaimed. 'Gloria need only be a problem if you let her. It seems strange to me that she didn't find somewhere else to stay if she wanted to come back here, instead of planting herself on you. If you had nothing in common before, you must have even less now...unless you're both having second thoughts.

'And as for having a failed marriage, so what? Failed...gone...kaput...none of that matters as long as you don't let it spoil things for us.' Her voice had softened. 'Because we are right for each other, aren't we, Alex?'

He wanted to resist the appeal in the sapphire eyes looking into his. Ignore the mouth that was parted in anticipation of the reply that she was begging for. Clamp down on the longing that was making his loins ache. Yet he did none of those things.

When he kissed the mouth that was made for his kisses, and felt the soft mounds of her breasts harden at his touch, reason was a far-away thing, something for others to indulge in. To make love to Zoey Lawrence would be like coming in out of the cold.

A car pulling up on the drive outside brought an end to that fantasy.

'Oh, no!' Zoey breathed. 'Mandy's back. Let's go across to your place.'

He shook his head.

'I've got Gloria staying with me, don't forget.'

'So? She doesn't sleep in your bed, does she?'

Alex was getting to his feet.

'You should know better than to ask that kind of question.'

'In other words, you don't want to answer it,' she said with sudden weariness. 'Mandy coming home has provided you with an escape route. You'll be able to look yourself in the eye tomorrow, knowing that you didn't succumb to the bimbo in the house across the way.'

'I ought to smack your backside for that remark,' he said grimly. 'If Mandy hadn't come back when she did, you might at this moment be regretting losing your virginity. That is, supposing it hasn't already been lost.'

'Yes! Quite so! And that is something for me to know and for you to find out...one day when you've sorted out your affairs.'

'Hello, Alex. Nice to see you.' Mandy was framed in the doorway and he forced a smile.

'Nice to see you, too,' he told her. Ignoring Zoey's stormy gaze, he went on, 'Have you had a pleasant evening?'

'Lovely, thanks. What have you folks been up to?'

'Not a lot,' he said levelly. 'I've been at the hospital most of the evening, giving support to one of the fire crew whose son has been badly burnt. I called here on my way back to let Zoey know how the lad was, and she offered me...er...sustenance.'

Very funny, Zoey thought. They both knew what had been on offer and it hadn't just been a mug of hot chocolate. But he'd reminded her again of the sort of day he'd had and, though Alex had only dozed for a matter of minutes, he must be tired.

So getting off the sofa to stand beside him, she chucked him playfully under the chin and said airily, 'Off you go, then, or your ex will be sending out a search party.'

He laughed, and called her bluff, remarking, 'Gloria will have a pretty good idea where I am, but I will go. It's been a long and trying day.'

When he'd gone Mandy said, 'You seem very perky.'

Zoey groaned.

'Don't you believe it. It would be easier to charm the fish out of the sea than get through to that one.'

In the week that followed Zoey found that spirits at the station were very low, as was to be expected. There had been a post-mortem on the much-respected headmistress, and to no one's surprise the cause of death had been diagnosed as cardiac failure.

The funeral was to take place on the coming Saturday and some of the men at the fire station and their families would be attending.

Geoff's son was still very poorly in the burns unit, but the caretaker had been discharged from hospital. That was the only good thing that had happened since the explosion in the school laboratory.

The lad's distraught parents didn't know whether charges would be brought against their son, but right now it wasn't their main concern.

Given the task of boosting morale in a situation such as the present one, Zoey did her best to put on a cheerful front, but it wasn't easy. The men were all friends. They spent a lot of their free time together, as well as their working hours, and when one of them hurt they all hurt.

It seemed as if Alex had once more put their brief moment of bliss into his file of events to be forgotten. He was pleasant, polite, but far from personal whenever they were in each other's company.

'In some ways I don't feel old enough to be offering counsel to the men,' she told Dorothea the cleaner one afternoon when there'd been more gloom than usual.

'Don't be thinking that,' the older woman said. 'Only this morning one of them was saying that just looking at you cheers them up. Alex is the one I worry about. There's no domestic joy in his life, and here at work he carries everybody's burdens.'

Zoey felt shame wash over her. It was true, and all she had been bothered about were her own plans and desires. The next time they were alone together, if that day ever dawned, she would admit to being a selfish little beast.

Greg was still hovering whenever he got the chance, and Zoey wished he wouldn't. He wasn't her type for one thing, and for another she felt he wasn't cut out for the job.

That was until the morning when they'd been called to a house fire and as it had been a persons reported emergency she'd been one of those searching a rambling old house for possible casualties.

There hadn't been any and she'd turned to grope her way outside when a smouldering beam had fallen and a glancing blow to the shoulder had sent her flying. Greg had been behind her and he'd picked her up and half carried her out of the building.

She'd been shaken by the incident and had let her rescuer hold her longer than had been necessary. When Alex had hurried over to ask if she was all right she'd said, 'Yes, thanks to Greg.' And had flashed the man in question a grateful smile.

It had been a mistake, being too effusive. For the rest of the day he'd hinted that he wouldn't mind seeing her gratitude in a more practical form.

So while Alex had been carrying out his duties tight-lipped and withdrawn, the station Romeo had been doing his best to get her to agree to meeting him that evening.

Zoey had shaken her head and used Mandy and Rosie as her excuse when she'd told him, 'I've too many family commitments at the moment, Greg. Maybe when the baby is older.'

'Suit yourself,' he'd said with surly brevity. 'I know that it's Carradine that you're after.'

'I'm not ''after'' anybody,' she'd flared. 'You make me sound like some sort of scalp hunter.'

'So?' he'd taunted, and she'd decided that enough was enough where Greg Osbourne was concerned.

The funeral of the teacher was over and there was better news about Geoff's son. He would need skin grafts and would have to cope with the loss of an eye, but his general condition was improving. So much so that his father reported for duty on Monday morning.

With his appearance the atmosphere lightened and Zoey gave a sigh of relief. It hadn't been easy keeping up morale, especially as she wasn't feeling on top of the world herself.

But she'd reasoned that being kept at arm's length by the man she was falling in love with was as nothing compared to Geoff's problems and those of the head-mistress's family.

Yet it didn't stop her from fretting inwardly, especially as Gloria's stay with Alex seemed to be going on for ever.

Dark November had replaced a mild October and Zoey wasn't the only one thinking that Gloria was outstaying her welcome. Her aunt had come through the operation satisfactorily but was now very frail and had been admitted to a smaller hospital for post-operative care. Which meant that her niece was still visiting her on a regular basis.

Gloria didn't seem to have any concerns about being away from the law practice where she was employed, and if she was aware that Alex was finding her extended stay irksome she didn't do anything about it.

A few days had become a few weeks. Yet he couldn't just ask her to leave. As long as she was concerned about the old lady he would have to put up with having her around, but the moment her aunt was allowed back to the rest home he was going to suggest that she move out.

For one thing, the stalemate situation that he'd created between Zoey and himself wasn't going to resolve itself with Gloria around. He reckoned that most folk would think it a funny set-up, he and Gloria back together.

Feeling drained and dispirited after a stressful day at the fire station, Zoey was making her way home on a cold winter night when she saw Gloria getting out of her car outside Alex's house.

So the limpet was still in residence, she thought glumly. There had to be a spark of some kind left from their marriage for Alex to put up with her prolonged presence like he was doing.

As she watched the other woman unloading shopping from the boot of the car, there was the sound of running feet and to Zoey's horror she saw a dark figure make a grab at the handbag over Gloria's shoulder.

She screamed and tried to fight him off but he was determined. Without having to think twice, Zoey threw herself across the road and jumped on him from behind.

With an angry roar he left hold of the bag and, turning, he pushed her off him, sending her crashing to the ground. Then he was running off down the road empty-handed, leaving Gloria still screaming hysterically and Zoey horizontal on the pavement with the breath knocked out of her.

As she struggled to a sitting position Alex's voice cried from above, 'Zoey! What's happened?'

As he bent over her she saw horror on his face in the light of the streetlamps. 'Are you hurt?' he asked urgently.

'No. At least I don't think so,' she gasped. 'See to Gloria. She was being robbed and I came across to help fight him off.'

His ex-wife's screams had turned to sobs.

'So what happened, Gloria?' he asked, putting his arms around her.

'I'd just come home from shopping,' she wailed, 'and as I was taking the stuff out of the boot this fellow came up from behind and tried to take my bag.'

'Did you recognise him?'

'Er…no. It was too dark.'

'I saw a guy running along the road as I turned out of the fire-station car park,' he said grimly. 'I guess that would be him. He wouldn't have got far if I'd known what he'd been up to.'

Zoey was standing to one side, watching them. Her face hurt where she'd hit the ground with such force, but what hurt even more was the feeling that Gloria looked as if that was where she belonged…in Alex's arms.

He turned and as their eyes met in the dim light he said, 'Let's get you both inside. Zoey's taken a nasty fall.'

'I'm all right,' she said quickly. 'Mandy will be wondering where I am.'

He'd taken his arms away from Gloria and was propelling them both towards the house.

'You're coming inside with me first,' he said firmly. 'I want to check you over. Make sure there are no broken bones. Then you can phone Mandy. All right?'

She nodded meekly, too miserable to argue.

The side of her face was grazed from when she'd hit the ground and bruising was already showing. No doubt a black eye would be part of the aftermath. Her shoulder

was also hurting where she'd fallen, and even before
Alex suggested it she'd decided that a visit to A and E
was required to make sure that nothing was broken.

Alex was very pale. They all were. But the skin of
his face had a stretched look about it when he said, 'I'm
going to take you to Casualty, Zoey.'

She thought, Surely he isn't looking like that because
I ended up in a heap on the pavement?

'You can't leave me!' Gloria cried. 'He might come
back.'

'That's not likely. He was a street mugger. Not
Burglar Bill,' he told her tersely.

'Can't you just phone for an ambulance to take her?'
she protested, still apprehensive, and Zoey had to smile,
even though her lips were beginning to swell.

No thanks for coming to the rescue. She couldn't even
refer to her by name. Gloria wanted Alex back in her
life. Zoey could feel it in her bones.

'Certainly not,' he said levelly. 'If you're nervous,
you'd better come with us.'

There were plenty of bruises but thankfully no broken
bones, and when in shared relief Alex and Zoey returned
to the waiting room at the hospital, they found Gloria
drinking coffee and leafing through a magazine.

At that moment Zoey decided she'd had enough of
Gloria. For one thing, she was ravenous, not having
eaten since lunchtime. On top of that, she was aching
from the fall. If Alex was prepared to put up with his
ex-wife's lack of sensitivity, she wasn't. So, assuming a
briskness that was far from real, she told them coolly,
'I'd like to go home now for some food and a good hot
bath.'

'Of course,' he said with an anxious glance at her

swollen face. 'It makes me shudder when I think what he might have done to you. As it is, it's bad enough. Promise me that you'll take the painkillers that they've given you. And, Zoey…'

'What?'

'Don't report for duty tomorrow unless you feel up to it.'

She wished she didn't feel that Alex was following some sort of guidelines. She didn't doubt his concern, but after seeing Gloria in his arms she was finding it difficult to forget that he must have held her like that countless times before. Was it surprising if the bond was still there?

CHAPTER FIVE

MANDY had already eaten when Alex dropped Zoey off at the house, and she exclaimed, 'Are you all right? I was worried when I got your phone call. What an awful thing to happen.'

Her eyes widened and her brown ponytail swung to and fro as she shook her head in horror at the sight of the grazes on Zoey's face.

'So tell me?' she cried. 'What happened?'

'I was on the point of coming inside when I looked across and saw Alex's wife being attacked outside the house.'

Mandy was positively goggling now and she glanced uneasily behind her.

'And you got involved?' was her next question.

'Yes. I couldn't not do, could I? I jumped on his back and he knocked me to the ground and ran off.'

'What was he like?' Mandy asked fearfully.

Zoey shrugged aching shoulders.

'I don't know. I only saw him from the back.'

Her stepmother shuddered.

'Did you report it to the police?'

She shook her head. 'No. There seemed no point. None of us saw him properly and he didn't get away with anything. I would imagine that people are reporting those sorts of incidents all the time. Gloria was very shaken, which isn't surprising, but Alex arrived soon after and was there to offer comfort.'

For once in her life she'd wished that she was a clinging vine instead of an independent woman. Then she might have been his first concern instead of the unglorious Gloria.

She ate a solitary meal with her mind still going over what had happened earlier. It had been the last thing she'd expected...or wanted...to be involved with both Alex and Gloria at the same time.

Him yes, but not her. Seeing them together had made her own hopes and longings seem futile. Before tonight his ex-wife's presence in his house had been just an irritating niggle. Now she saw it as a threat to all that she longed for. And unless she wanted to risk being told to mind her own business, there was nothing she could do about it.

Why didn't that woman go back to where she'd come from? She would volunteer to take over ministering to the elderly aunt herself if Gloria would do that.

Alex had said that Gloria had wanted to make a fresh start somewhere else when the divorce had come through and she had done so. But for some reason she was back in the fold. Had she had a change of mind? Was the sick relative angle just a ploy to be near him?

The moment they were back at the house, after dropping Zoey off, Alex turned to Gloria.

'You didn't exactly fall over yourself to thank Zoey for going to your assistance,' he said levelly.

'I don't know what you mean,' she protested.

'Oh, yes, you do. That fellow might have had a gun or a knife and one of you could have been injured or killed. She didn't have to get involved, you know. You behave as you do with her because you think I'm attracted to her, don't you?'

She eyed him coolly.

'Well, you are.'

He sighed. They'd known each other for so long he could almost read her mind.

'And what if I am? I didn't object to you going to the cinema with that smoothie Osbourne.'

'That was nothing.'

'Oh, no? Don't let's have one set of rules for me and another for you, Gloria. And while we're on the subject, how much longer are you going to be here?'

'Not much longer,' she said defiantly. 'You know that I had a very good reason for asking you to accommodate me.'

'Yes, that's true,' he agreed, 'and I'm going along with it, aren't I? But don't make life difficult for Zoey and myself.'

As Alex lay sleepless that night, he told himself that Gloria was just doing a bit of hanging on. She never had liked to lose anything that belonged to her, even though she'd raised no objection to the divorce.

But if she hadn't moved on, he had, and his thoughts turned to Zoey. Beautiful, brave Zoey.

He was accustomed to seeing her take risks. It was part of the job and he always wished her far away when danger was near, but the last thing he wanted to contemplate was her risking life and limb out on the street at the hands of some thug who was attacking Gloria.

If Zoey wished his ex-wife far away, he wished her even farther. He'd thought that once the divorce was through they would be out of each other's hair, but her prolonged presence was intruding into the new life he'd made for himself, and today's episode hadn't helped.

As his restlessness continued, he got up and went to the window. There was a light on at the house across the road so someone was still up, and a sudden desperate need to know that Zoey was all right overwhelmed him.

As he crossed the road Alex thought that he'd been pretty brusque with Gloria but sometimes he felt that he didn't know her at all and at others that he knew her only too well.

'Oh!' he exclaimed when Zoey opened the door to him. 'That really is a shiner. How are you feeling?'

'Unlovely and unloved,' she said wryly. 'Dare I hope that you've come to make me feel better?'

'I couldn't sleep,' he told her, 'and thought that if you were still up I'd come across to see how you were.'

'I was the same,' she said wearily. 'Tossing and turning.'

She had an old towelling robe on and her feet were bare. Her hair looked as if she'd washed it and just left it, as it lay flatly against her head like a lustreless cap. And with the black eye and its surrounding bruising providing a lurid range of colours, she was definitely not looking her best.

Yet she was lovely to him. There was something valiant and feisty about her. Those things, along with her slender golden fairness, made her the most desirable thing he'd ever seen.

As she stepped back to let him in, he said gently, 'Come here, my battered one.' Taking her in his arms, he touched her swollen face gently and told her, 'Don't ever expose yourself to such danger again. It's bad enough on the job, but thinking of you being at the mercy of some thug makes my blood run cold.'

'I know of a way to heat it up again,' she said laughingly. 'Shall I show you?'

He bent his mouth to hers.

'Like this, you mean?'

'Mmm. Just like that…except that it hurts.'

'I'm content to just hold you for as long as you'll let me,' he said softly.

She was smiling but there was a question in her eyes.

'What about Gloria, Alex?'

'What about her?'

'Is it really over between you?'

He sighed.

'Of course.'

'Then why is she living under your roof?'

'I thought I'd told you. She's here because of an elderly aunt who's had surgery. Staying at my place is convenient for visiting.'

'But it's been going on for weeks.'

'The recuperation is taking longer than expected.'

'I see. So you don't mind?'

'I'm prepared to put up with it if that's what you mean, as Gloria and I go back a long way.'

'Unlike ourselves.'

He'd been frowning, but now there was a glint of amusement in his glance.

'Yes…unlike ourselves.'

'Maybe that's why I feel I can't compete.'

'I'm not with you.'

'You know her through and through…and you don't know me at all.'

'And you think I'm unwilling to take a step into the unknown?'

'Yes. Something like that.'

'You'd be surprised how well I feel I know you, Zoey,' he said, back to being serious. 'Any reservations I might have come from somewhere else. The aftermath of divorce, for instance. Lots of people rush into marriage again the moment the divorce is through as if desperate to prove that they are desirable to someone, and often it leads to another catastrophe.'

'Well, thanks for that, Alex,' she said stiffly, moving away from him. 'I thought you'd come across to cheer me up. How wrong I was! So you see the way we feel about each other as the forerunner of a catastrophe. You're not the only one who's discovered that human relationships can be tricky. But they can also be fantastic when the two people concerned really love each other.

'Maybe you still care about Gloria as you seem loath to do anything to upset her. If that's the case, why don't you say so and I'll back off? It seems as if I'm always attracted to the wrong sort of men, those who have other women in their lives and find me all right for a bit of light relief. But when it comes to the crunch...'

Alex's jaw was tightening as he said, 'I would have thought you knew me better than that...and what's this about the ''wrong sort of men''? Who else are you referring to?'

Zoey tossed her head rebelliously, indignation still upon her.

'Why? Did you think you were the first?'

'It would appear that I was mistaken if I did,' he remarked drily. 'I'm just one of a string of conquests, am I?'

'I'm hardly likely to see you as that, am I?' she retaliated. 'You are the most unconquerable man I've ever met.'

He ignored that and in the same flat tone asked, 'And what happened to them all?'

'Oh, this and that,' she told him airily, while beginning to think dismally that in her pique she'd behaved like a spoilt child. Allowing Alex to believe that he was one of many when in truth there'd only been Damien the devious.

What was the matter with her? Was it jealousy? She wanted to throw herself back into his arms and tell him that it wasn't how she'd described it at all, but he was turning to go and she didn't blame him. With what was left of her dignity she picked up the skirt of her robe and began to climb the stairs.

Was anything ever simple? Alex asked himself as he went back to his own house. He didn't blame Zoey for getting worked up about what was going on.

It did look as if he was letting Gloria manipulate him, but although she was living in his house they were leading completely separate lives. The only physical contact they'd had had been when he'd held her in his arms after the attempted mugging, and Zoey seemed to have latched onto that as if it had meant something to him. She wasn't to know that his ex-wife got more satisfaction from reading a legal document than from a close embrace.

Hopefully she would soon depart and then he and Zoey could get to know each other better…explore their feelings. But he already knew how she felt. It was his own feelings that he was going to have to face up to.

As Zoey slipped beneath the bedcovers she was wishing she hadn't been so uptight with Alex. She'd questioned his integrity and made him sound indecisive where Gloria was concerned when she knew very well that he was the least indecisive person she'd ever met.

She had to admit that one reason why she'd been so indignant was because she was jealous of Gloria's place in his life. She was supposed to be part of his past, but she wasn't, was she? At the moment she was well and truly in the present.

Then there'd been the calm logic with which he'd explained his feelings about divorce and its aftermath, making her feel as if she never gave any serious thought to anything.

But Alex could be on the defensive as much as he liked, she thought wearily as she drifted into sleep. One thing he couldn't deny. He wanted her as much as she wanted him, and what had she done when he'd been full of protective concern for her? Berated him and then stalked off to bed. Leaving him to see himself out. If she wasn't careful, the man in her life would be telling her to grow up.

'So what happened to you?' the firefighters wanted to know when Zoey arrived at the station the next morning.

Alex was already there and she glanced at him quickly to see his expression. It was bland, giving nothing away, so she said casually, 'I fell on the pavement.'

It was the truth, but not all of it, and once the interest had died down she followed him into the office.

'I'm sorry about last night,' she said contritely. 'I was tired and aching all over. Do you forgive me?'

He smiled.

'Of course. I shouldn't have disturbed you at such a late hour. Let's forget it, shall we?'

'What, everything? The bit before I got ratty as well?'

'Yes. At least for the time being.'

'I see.'

He sighed.

'If only you did.'

At that moment the police came through to say they were needed at a house fire and the non-productive conversation came to an end.

With Bonfire Night in the past and Christmas approaching, the firework hazard was being replaced by candles. The crew had already been called out to a house fire where there'd been a party and much drinking had taken place. A candle that had been left burning had fallen over and set curtains alight.

Luckily no one had been hurt. Yet it was a warning that candlelit rooms were all very nice, but they could be the forerunner to disaster.

And now here was another house fire, stemming from the same kind of hazard but in very different circumstances. It wasn't the result of jollification. The householder had been using candles because the electricity supply had been cut off for non-payment.

On a gloomy morning in late November, small children playing in a downstairs room had caused a blaze by knocking a candle over onto sheets of paper that they'd been drawing on.

The mother, who had been gossiping with a neighbour at the front door, had sensibly whisked them to safety and then shut off the room until the fire-engine arrived, by which time the sparse furnishings were well alight.

When they got there it was bedlam, with the children screaming and the neighbour having hysterics. Only the young mother was calm and Zoey thought that she must be used to catastrophes. They'd already been living without light and now the house was on fire.

'Maybe they'll rehouse us now,' she said prosaically as she and her family gathered on the pavement. 'Don't be in any rush to put it out.'

'Sorry to disappoint you, but we've already damped

it down,' Alex told her as the hoses were turned off. 'You'll need to get in touch with Social Services. This place won't be fit to live in until it has dried out.'

The woman shrugged.

'It wasn't fit to live in before. They'll have to do something.'

'I'm sure they will,' he said, 'and, please, keep your children away from candles in future.'

As they drove back to the fire station Zoey thought that when they were working there was always harmony between Alex and herself. Possibly because they had the same amount of dedication and were part of a committed team. But away from it was a different matter.

They were deeply attracted to each other, no matter what Alex said to the contrary. Yet it always went wrong when they were alone. Maybe she should try to fix some prime time for them when there was no one else, such as Gloria, to command his attention.

The attempted mugging was still very much to the front of her mind. She wondered how Gloria was feeling today. More gracious, she hoped. The incident could have brought them closer, which could only have been a good thing.

It might have helped her to understand Alex's ex-wife better, as she would very much like to know what was going on in that one's mind. But it hadn't, and she couldn't help but think that, alarming as it had been, Gloria would rather it had been someone else who'd gone to her rescue.

Zoey had booked a day's leave the following week so that she could look after Rosie while Mandy and Harry went out on their own.

She waylaid Alex as they put the fire-engine away and

said casually, 'I'm minding the baby next Wednesday so that Mandy can have some time with Harry. Would you like to come for a meal?'

He stopped in his tracks, waited until the rest of the crew had gone inside and then said, 'What's the occasion?'

'There isn't one. Unless you would call us spending some time together an occasion.'

He looked down on her from the high metal step of the fire-engine and remarked, 'It will be if we can keep the peace.'

'So you'll come?'

'Yes. What time?'

'Half six?'

'Fine. And, Zoey…let it be just about us.'

Her smiled flashed out. 'That's the intention. Unless you want to bring Gloria along to make up a happy little threesome.'

He pursed his lips.

'No. I see enough of Gloria as it is.'

Greg was observing them from the station doorway and there was a knowing smile on his face.

'There's a phone call for you from Area Command,' he told Alex, 'if you can tear yourself away.'

When Alex had gone inside Zoey glowered at the messenger and Greg's smirk widened.

'Alex is back with his wife. You're wasting your time.'

'Really? Ex-wife, I think you mean. And I'll be the best judge of whether I'm wasting my time,' she said coolly, and pushed past him.

But once inside with a mug of hot tea in her hand, Zoey didn't feel so confident. Was what Greg had just said the general opinion, and she was the only one not facing up to it? Yet if that were the case, would Alex have agreed to her suggestion for the coming Wednesday?

She sighed and Geoff, who was seated nearby, said, 'What's dimming your light today, Zoey?'

'Oh, this and that,' she said with a pale smile, 'and none of it as depressing as what you're going through.'

He nodded.

'Yes, it's been a bad time for me and mine, but thankfully the lad is coping...and we've still got him. That's the main thing.'

December had arrived and with it the awareness that Christmas was approaching fast. Zoey expected that Mandy would be spending most of it with Harry, when he wasn't at the pizzeria. As for herself, she had no idea what she would be doing over the festive season.

Whether she enjoyed it or not would depend on the man who lived across the way. Their relationship would have to move on a bit if they were going to see anything of each other over the Christmas period.

But first, as a stepping stone, was the evening they were going to share. Once Rosie was tucked up in her cot the night would be theirs. Every time Zoey thought about it her eyes sparkled.

Alex would be working during the day while she was looking after Rosie and shopping for food, but once he'd been home to change they would be together.

She was no great cook so it was going to be steak and salad, followed by bought apple crumble and cream, with a bottle of good wine to elevate the menu.

The blue dress that he'd admired was going to have another airing, and if they weren't on better terms before the night was out she would be asking herself why.

She heard the fire-engine go past in the middle of the afternoon and wondered where they were off to, but once she became involved in feeding and bathing the baby and preparing the meal she forgot all about it.

Until there was a ring on the doorbell at just after six o'clock and she opened the door to find Geoff on the step.

'Alex has been hurt,' he said without preamble. 'He's in hospital with severe concussion and a head wound. If it hadn't been for his helmet he would have been killed. We were called out to a fire at the old print works and the roof fell in while we were dousing the flames.

'He was unconscious when we pulled him out but he came to in the ambulance for a few seconds and the first thing he said was for me to tell you what had happened.'

Geoff was observing her stricken face and he asked curiously, 'Were you expecting him here, or something?'

'Yes,' Zoey said in a daze as she tried to take in what he'd said. 'I'll go to him, Geoff. Which hospital is he in?'

'The General. Ward fifteen,' he informed her, still a bit nonplussed. 'Two of the guys will be going back to see him when they've had their meal but it will be later in the evening.'

'No problem,' she said hurriedly. 'I've got my little car.'

He nodded.

'Right, then. I'll be off. See you tomorrow, Zoey.'

When he'd gone she stood, frozen, in the hallway. She'd told Geoff that she was all right because she had her small car. That was the good news. What she'd forgotten for the briefest of moments was that she also had something else small in her possession. A sleeping baby!'

She would have to take Rosie with her. There was nothing else she could do. She had to get to Alex, to see for herself how badly hurt he was. Geoff would have played it down. They always did when one of them was injured.

When she got to the ward, breathless and dishevelled, a nurse stopped her and eyed the baby in her arms.

'Are you the firefighter's wife?' she questioned.

Zoey could see him lying quite still with his head heavily bandaged, and her heart missed a beat. She saw something else, too. He wasn't alone. Gloria was sitting beside the bed and on hearing the nurse's question she turned and said coolly, 'No, she isn't. I'm Mrs Carradine.'

The nurse's smile was apologetic as she turned to Zoey.

'I'm afraid that I'll have to ask you to leave, then. The patient is quite ill and only allowed one visitor.'

She stepped back in surprise when she found herself holding the baby and her eyes widened as Zoey walked purposefully towards the bed.

'I know. I won't be a second,' she told the nurse as the woman opened her mouth to protest. 'I have to see for myself how Alex is. Then I'll go.'

He looked pale and battered and would have no knowledge that she'd been. She planted a gentle kiss on top of the bandages and then held out her arms for the baby.

Gazing down on the sleeping Rosie, she told the nurse, 'The baby isn't his, you know. In case that's what you're thinking.' She pointed to a frowning Gloria. 'And neither is she!'

On that note she set off down the corridor, heels

clonking on the shining tiles and mind bogged down with worry and frustration.

The only comfort was that the first words Alex had said when he'd come round for those brief moments had been for her. She would have to hold onto that until there was more news from the hospital.

With Rosie once more in her cot, Zoey sat picking at the food she'd so zealously prepared. If she hadn't been so concerned about Alex she might have laughed at the spectacle of herself turning up at his bedside with the baby, like something out of a Victorian melodrama. And there'd been the expression on the nurse's face when she'd been putting her right about who was who.

But there wasn't a laugh in her at that moment. Supposing something even worse happened to Alex during the night and no one told her. She would go insane.

As if a higher presence was tuned into her anxieties, the two firefighters who'd gone to visit Alex called to see her at ten o'clock and they brought better news.

Gloria had been nowhere to be seen and they'd been allowed to sit by his bed.

'He came round while we were there,' one of them told her 'and although he was still groggy he sent you a message.' He grinned across at her. 'You must be well in there.'

'It's nothing like that,' she told them awkwardly. 'It's just that I'd invited him round for a meal.'

'Well, he says why haven't you been to see him? That he'd rather it had been your face that he saw when he woke up instead of ours, and we can't blame him for that.'

'I've been!' she exclaimed distractedly. 'And the

nurse wouldn't let me see him because Gloria was already there.'

'Go now, then,' he suggested. 'We'll stay to keep an eye on the baby.'

Zoey was on her feet.

'Would you? I'd be really grateful. I only hope I don't meet the same nurse as the one who turned me away.'

The ward was dimly lit when she got there and it was the night staff that she spoke to this time.

'I'm Alex's fiancé,' she fibbed. 'If I could just see him for a moment.'

'Go ahead,' a robust staff nurse told her, 'but don't be too long. He has a nasty head wound.'

Alex was lying with his eyes closed, but almost as if he sensed her presence he opened them the moment she reached his side.

'So you got my message,' he murmured drowsily.

'Yes, I did,' she said softly, taking his hand in hers.

'But you only came because I asked for you.'

'Of course not. Nothing would keep me away. I've been once but they wouldn't let me see you,' she said anxiously.

She waited for his response but there was none forthcoming.

'He's asleep again. Best not to disturb him,' the same nurse said from behind her.

Zoey got to her feet, thankful that he'd been aware of her presence if only for a few moments. How could he have doubted that she would come? she thought tearfully as she drove back home. Did he think she saw him only as someone to play around with?

If he'd been merely a colleague in her scheme of things she would still have gone to see him, but Alex held her heart in those big capable hands of his. Was he ever going to realise that?

The trouble was that Gloria had got in there first, sitting by his bed, staking her claim, as if he still belonged to her.

Zoey hoped that he wouldn't awaken in the morning still thinking she'd only visited him because he'd asked her to. He would have no idea of the state she'd been in ever since hearing about the accident.

Which was perhaps as well. He wouldn't have wanted the guys at the fire station to know that she was crazy about him, and if she wasn't careful that was exactly what they were going to think.

But none of that mattered as long as he made a full recovery. She'd had a quick glance at the chart at the bottom of his bed and seen that there were no skull fractures or suspected haematomas, so that was something to be thankful for. But the fact remained that he had a deep head wound and was far from being his normal self.

CHAPTER SIX

WHEN Alex awoke in the middle of the night the first thing he remembered was Zoey's face when she'd sat by the bed. She'd looked anxious and tearful and he wasn't sure why. Whether it was because she was worried about him, or because of something he'd said, he didn't know. Maybe a bit of both.

He knew he'd said something and although his thought processes were back to normal now, they hadn't been then. He'd felt muzzy and sleepy.

He wondered how she'd felt when he hadn't turned up for the meal. She was his prime concern. Everything about her mattered to him.

It wasn't that simple, though, was it? There was Gloria in the background. They had no future together. That was as sure as night following day, but he couldn't turn his back on her while she was so concerned about her aunt, which left Zoey to think that there were still feelings there.

Raising himself off the pillows, he looked around him. He could see all right and as he flexed himself under the sheets he decided that he could move all right, too. So when the new day appeared he would ask to be discharged.

If he'd known about Zoey's appearance like a rejected mistress by his bedside he might have managed a laugh, but as he didn't he remained in sombre mood. Until some hours later when the consultant came round and reluctantly agreed to discharge him.

'Any unpleasant after-effects or infection in the head wound, I want you back here immediately,' he said, 'and no reporting for duty until I've given you the all-clear.'

Zoey went to bed that night with what felt like a heavy weight inside her chest. When she looked at the bedside clock it seemed incredible that less than six hours ago she'd been planning the meal and been on the point of making herself beautiful for Alex.

And now he was hurt, in hospital, and under the impression that she wasn't all that bothered when in truth she'd visited him twice. Both times with little joy.

But the main thing was that he was alive and not as badly hurt as he might have been. She would go to see him again tomorrow and hope that it would be third time lucky.

It would have to be in the evening as she was on duty at the station all day, which could mean that Gloria or some of the men might be there. But she would have to chance that.

Yet it was a long time to wait for news of him, she thought the next morning and decided to go home at lunchtime to phone the hospital in privacy. She would feel better once she had a report on his progress.

As she walked up the cul-de-sac her step faltered. His car had just pulled up at the front of his house with Gloria in the driving seat. Sitting next to her was Alex, easily recognisable by the bulky bandage around his head.

'I don't believe it!' she said to no one in particular. 'He's home! It's too soon. What are they thinking of?'

He was easing himself out of the car when she reached

it, and as she stood observing him with amazed eyes he gave a quirky smile.

'Hi, Zoey. Surprised to see me?'

'Surprised? I'm appalled! You were comatose when I left you last night and earlier you'd been unconscious. They should have kept you for a few more days at least.'

'It was at my insistence,' he said. 'Don't fuss.'

'You are risking your physical well-being,' she persisted. Turning to Gloria who was gazing around her as if the discussion going on didn't concern her, she said, 'Why did you let Alex discharge himself?'

'It's not for me to tell him what to do,' she said with a shrug, and went on, adding to Zoey's outrage, 'Though you obviously think that you have the right.'

That made Zoey want to lash out.

'It's common sense we're talking about, not rights!'

She knew she was overreacting. Alex's expression told her that. Yet surely he realised that she was behaving like this because she loved him.

A feeling of anticlimax had swept over her when she'd seen him getting out of the car. After all her anxiety, here he was, home, and as cool as a cucumber.

'The doctor wouldn't have let me come home if he'd thought there was any risk,' he said with a restrained kind of patience that did nothing to calm her down.

He looked pale and tired and, immediately contrite, she said, 'I'm sorry. I'm keeping you out here when you should be inside, resting. I'll see you when you come back to work, Alex.' Then she said to Gloria with a steely glare, 'Look after him.' Off she went with outrage and misery vying for first place in her thoughts.

The need to phone the hospital had gone now that Alex was home so she went back to the station and told the others the news.

'Gee whiz!' Greg said. 'That's a quick recovery.'

Zoey turned away. So she wasn't the only one who thought it was a bit too soon for Alex to be out and about. 'Don't fuss,' he'd said. It was like him to play it down, but couldn't he see her point of view for once?

To deepen her gloom, Greg went on, 'So he doesn't want you over there, holding his hand, then? But I'm forgetting, he already has company, hasn't he?'

She glared at him.

'If you're trying to annoy me, you're succeeding. Don't push your luck, Osbourne.'

He laughed and reached for the top piece of toast on the pile that they always made for elevenses and she was left to her thoughts.

'What is the matter with that girl?' Gloria said irritably when they went inside the house. 'You haven't known her five minutes and she's acting as if she owns you.'

Alex gave her a long, level look.

'Don't pretend you're not aware that you're messing up my life, Gloria,' he said coolly. 'It isn't always the length of time one has known a person that counts. Look at you and I. We'd known each other for ever, but it didn't work out.

'Zoey is warm and caring with everyone she meets, and if she's prepared to pass some of it my way I consider myself lucky. But I've recently gone through the demoralising experience of divorce and if it's left you unscathed, it isn't like that for me. I don't want any more hurt for myself...or anyone else.'

'I don't want a lecture, Alexander,' she said huffily.

'All right, then. Just as long as we know where we stand. And regarding Zoey Lawrence...that's my business.'

In the privacy of his room he stood gazing bleakly through the window. Zoey had been horrified when she'd seen that he was home, but instead of taking her in his arms and telling her how much her concern meant to him, he'd told her to stop fussing.

Would they ever get it right? His head was aching. His usual clear thinking absent. If it hadn't been for the previous day's accident they might have reached a better understanding by now, but it was almost as if the Fates were conspiring to test them. Working in the background to complicate their lives.

He'd been looking forward to spending a quiet evening with Zoey. Had thought it might present an opportunity to tell her how he really felt about everything...the divorce, themselves, Gloria's continuing presence. But instead he'd ended up in hospital with his ex-wife on the front row and Zoey fretting on the sidelines.

If Zoey had known that Alex's day was taking its course just as dismally as her own, she might have felt better. But she had no way of knowing and as it dragged on with only one 'shout' to a chip-pan fire that mercifully the householder had dealt with sensibly before they'd got there, she felt her gloom deepen.

But a break was about to appear in the clouds. When she arrived home in the evening a radiant Mandy was waiting for her. She held out her hand and Zoey saw a diamond ring sparkling on her finger.

'What's this, then?' Zoey asked excitedly.

'Harry's asked me to marry him!' Mandy bubbled. 'We're engaged!'

'Fantastic!' Zoey crowed, her own woes forgotten. 'And what does Rosie have to say?'

'Gurgle, gurgle,' her delighted mother said laughingly, and Zoey joined in.

It was marvellous news. Mandy had found someone to love and cherish her, Zoey thought as they chatted excitedly about dates and wedding preparations.

Tonight wasn't the time to be thinking about her own future. Today was Mandy's. She would concern herself about her own affairs some other time.

If Alex and herself had been more in tune she would have wanted to dash across the road to tell him the good news. But did she want to have to impart it beneath Gloria's supercilious gaze? And would he think she had an underlying motive? Such as using it as a reminder that she would soon be free to pursue her own life?

No. That wasn't what she wanted. She would tell him when he was back on the job in more impersonal surroundings.

For the rest of the week Zoey made an effort to put Alex out of her mind. She caught occasional glimpses of him going in and out of the house, which seemed to indicate that he was no worse, and with that knowledge she forced herself to be content.

Mandy was planning a Christmas wedding. The day of Christmas Eve, to be exact, and once the first excitement had died down Zoey had told her, 'I'll move out before the wedding. You won't need me any more and you'll want the house to yourselves.'

As Mandy had opened her mouth to protest Zoey had forestalled her.

'It's true, Mandy. You don't want to start your life together with me around all the time. I'm truly happy for you. Harry is kind, generous and funny. You're a lucky woman...and I know Dad would have approved of what you're doing.'

'You are something else,' Mandy had said chokily. 'You gave up a lot to come here and now you must be wishing you'd stayed where you were.'

'Never!' she affirmed stoutly. 'For one thing, I've met the love of my life. It's taking him a while to get used to the idea, but I'm working on him.'

'We could have a double wedding,' the bride-to-be suggested, laughingly.

Zoey shook her head.

'No way. Alex and I seem to take one step forward and two steps back all the time. It doesn't made for easy communication with Gloria under his feet, but hopefully he'll soon be back on duty and we can make up for lost time.'

She was trying to sound positive, but deep down inside she wasn't quite so confident. It felt as if she was doing all the running. Yet there had been moments when it had seemed as if paradise beckoned. When she'd known beyond doubt that Alex cared. But they'd been few and far between.

There was much more happening in Mandy's life at the moment and Zoey wasn't feeling as calm about finding somewhere else to live as she made out.

She didn't know whether it was going to be easy or not. It would have to be close to the fire station for one thing. Was it time to consider buying a property of her own, or would rental be more in keeping with the uncertainty of her present existence?

With that thought in mind she went into the local estate agent's during her lunch hour to check on the prices and availability of suitable flats or small houses.

As she was leaving she came face to face with Alex.

His glance went immediately to the brochures in her hand, while Zoey's wide gaze was taking in the fact that the bandages had gone, to be replaced by a large sterile dressing.

It was their first meeting since the day he'd been discharged from hospital and it seemed like a lifetime. For some reason she felt tongue-tied and off balance and it was he who spoke first.

'What's with the brochures, Zoey? Not thinking of moving, are you?'

She was beginning to gather her wits and told him breezily, ''Fraid so. Mandy's throwing me out.'

He smiled but it didn't reach his eyes.

'You don't expect me to believe that.'

'You might. One never knows. But, no, the truth of the matter is that she's getting married...on Christmas Eve...and Rosie and I are going to be bridesmaids. Isn't that marvelous?'

'To the guy from the pizza place?'

'Yes, to Harry.'

He was sombre now.

'And so where does that leave you? Amongst the nation's homeless?'

'Not really, but I am looking for a place of my own. Mandy and Harry will need space—it's my choice to move out.'

'It seems a bit unfair that you've uprooted yourself to come here and then find out it was all for nothing.'

Her face had clouded.

'It wasn't for nothing, Alex. My being here gave Mandy the chance to do some socialising. Otherwise she might never have met Harry.'

And I wouldn't have met you, she wanted to tell him, but it was the kind of thing best said when she was in his arms, if that ever happened again, not eyeing him achingly on the main street.

'Your head, how is it?' she asked, changing the subject.

'Fine. I'll be back on the job after the weekend and for various reasons I can't wait.'

That makes two of us, she thought wistfully.

'I've been to see Geoff's son while I've been attending the hospital,' he was saying. 'Has he told you that the lad is being discharged next week?'

'Yes. He's done well to make such a quick recovery under the circumstances, hasn't he?'

Alex nodded.

'He was a crazy young fool, tampering with stuff in the lab, and sadly has paid the price. But as is often the case with that age group, he's bounced back remarkably well. He'll have to keep going back for skin grafts, of course.'

She sighed. What would they be discussing next? The weather? Anything but themselves.

'I have to go, Alex,' she told him abruptly. 'Or they'll be sending out a search party for me.'

He took a step back and she knew he'd got the message. Now it was his turn to sound regretful as he said, 'Yes, of course. Blame me if the guys want to know where you've been.'

As they went their separate ways Alex was fuming for various reasons. Why hadn't he told Zoey how much he was missing her? Told her she could stay at his place if she hadn't found anywhere to live in time? Even though he knew that her young stepmother would never leave her out in the cold.

The two women were close. They had a loving relationship and Zoey, kind and unselfish, would never blame Mandy for letting her move out here, only to find herself surplus to requirements.

Yet he wasn't happy about the set-up. In fact, he wasn't happy about anything at the moment. When he'd met Zoey outside the estate agent's he'd had to take a grip on himself. He'd wanted to reach out for her, take her in his arms and tell her how he ached to be with her. How he was sorry for the way he'd been the last time they'd met and...

But she'd taken the wind out of his sails by telling him about her change in circumstances and now he was putting his own longings to one side in concern for her.

Alex sighed. It was crazy to think of offering Zoey accommodation at his place...with Gloria around. His gloom deepened as another depressing thought reared its head. Would Zoey see this recent turn of events as a reason to go back to the city? To the area's biggest fire station where she'd been based before? He sincerely hoped not.

The eating place belonging to the Harry fellow was just across the way. Maybe he would have a pizza for his lunch and at the same time ask a few searching questions of the man whose life was taking an upward turn, unlike his own.

He didn't have to introduce himself. As he ordered the food the pleasant man behind the counter said, 'You're the officer in charge at the fire station, aren't you? The guy who lives across from Mandy and Zoey?'

Alex smiled.

'Yes, that's me...and...er...it's because Zoey's a member of my team that I've come in to have a word with you.'

So much for subtlety, he thought wryly, but he was in no mood for beating about the bush.

'Go ahead,' the other man said.

'I'm concerned that she may end up with nowhere to live after moving out here to be with Mandy and the baby.'

Harry was looking worried.

'Zoey doesn't have to move out on my account. She was there before I came on the scene and I'd be happy for her to stay. It was her own idea to go. I think she wants to give us some space, but I feel the same as you, that she mustn't be left in a position where she has nowhere to live. If I'd had a house of my own we could have gone there, but there's only a poky flat up above this place and, although it suffices for me, it would be no fit place for a baby.'

'I agree,' Alex told him, 'and I must say I feel happier knowing that you have Zoey's best interests at heart.'

'Just how far does your concern for her extend?' Harry asked quizzically. 'According to what I've heard, Zoey cares for you a lot. Mandy and I thought a double wedding might be on the cards.'

Alex felt his jaw slacken.

'Wha-at?'

'Hmm. It's true.'

'And what did Zoey say to that?'

'Put the dampener on it straight away, from all accounts. Seemed to think you were too engrossed in your ex-wife.'

'And if that turned out not to be true…what then?'

Harry laughed.

'I've no idea. You'll have to ask her yourself.'

'I might just do that,' Alex told him purposefully, and once he'd finished eating he pointed himself in the direction of home. What he had to say to Zoey would have to wait until the evening. He'd no wish to have a discussion with her while all the men were listening in. But once she'd had time to eat her evening meal he would go across and talk to her.

'Alex!' Zoey exclaimed when she saw him on the doorstep. 'This is too much! The pleasure of your company twice in one day.'

'You'll be having that same pleasure all day and every day from next Monday onwards,' he said with a glint in his eye. 'Just look upon today as a breaking in. I want to talk to you, Zoey. Is it convenient?'

She inclined her head graciously and stepped back. As he strode over the threshold he said, 'Are you alone?'

'Yes. Why? Have you come to seduce me?'

He laughed.

'You're very saucy tonight.'

'Aren't I just.'

It was a cover-up, of course. In truth, she was nervous and on edge. What did he want to talk about? As far as she was concerned, nothing had changed since their meeting earlier in the day, but Alex had a look of purpose about him.

She was as beautiful and bouncy as ever, he thought, but she looked tired. There were dark smudges beneath her incredible eyes and she'd lost weight. He hoped he wasn't to blame for either of those things, yet he had a feeling that he might be.

'I want to talk to you about Gloria,' he said gravely.

He watched Zoey stiffen and thought that had been a bad opening.

'I thought you might be here because of us,' she said flatly. 'What about her?'

'I just want you to know that there is nothing between us any more. I know that she was in the forefront when

I was in hospital, but as I was in no fit state to argue I wasn't able to do anything about it.

'I also know that you were hurt and angry because you weren't involved and because I appeared to treat your anxieties too lightly. I certainly didn't mean it to seem like that, Zoey. If I was insensitive, I'm sorry. Maybe I'm out of touch with tender loving care, but I do recognize it when I see it. So will you forgive me?'

She was about to tell him that of course she would when he amazed her by saying lightly, 'I can't promise a double wedding, though.'

Zoey could feel her cheeks starting to burn. How had he found out about Mandy's teasing? As if he'd read her mind, Alex went on, 'Harry told me. I was in his place at lunchtime.'

'It was just a joke,' she gabbled weakly, 'on Mandy's part. It wasn't me rushing in where angels fear to tread. I wasn't presuming anything.'

'No, of course not,' he agreed smoothly, adding to her discomfort.

She'd been delighted to see him, but now she just wanted him to go while she got over her embarrassment, but Alex had other ideas.

'So you do understand that Gloria and I are finished for all time? The only woman I'm interested in is you, and if you would just let me get my breath I might get around to doing something about it.'

Her face had softened.

'Is that a promise?'

'Come here and I'll show you.'

His kisses were gentle and passionless this time. As if he knew she'd been hurting and wanted to take away the pain first. And as she nestled against him Zoey thought, It's going to come right. I can tell.

'We've got a lot of catching up to do,' he murmured against the bright cap of her hair.

She laughed up at him, her embarrassment forgotten.

'I've no objections to that.' As if an imp of mischief was on her shoulder, she added, 'What else did Harry say about me?'

Alex was smiling.

'Oh, that you fancied me like mad and that he wouldn't dream of turning you out onto the streets.'

He was joking, but saw from her expression that she wasn't amused.

'So you think it's funny, discussing my innermost feelings with Harry…and the pair of you talking over where I'm going to live. I'm not exactly an idiot, you know, Alex. I can sort out my own affairs. I'd like to see your face if I told someone about your feelings…and made it known what was going on in your establishment.'

He groaned.

'Here we go again! Me saying the wrong thing and you taking umbrage. You're making a fuss about nothing. Why do you think I went in there?'

'Not to have a pizza, from the sound of it.'

'Correct. If you'll calm down, I'll explain.'

'Don't patronise me!' she hissed.

'I'm not!' he told her, his voice hardening. 'You're as prickly as a hedgehog.'

'Yes, well, they're always getting flattened, too. I think you'd better go,' she said wearily, as her annoyance drained away.

'No!' he said firmly. 'Not until I've imparted a few home truths. You say I'm the love of your life. Well, how about considering my feelings for a change? Do you think I like the idea of being roped in as part of a double wedding without it even being mentioned? It would seem that you're not the only one who gets discussed behind their back.'

'Nobody has roped you into anything,' Zoey protested.

This time he was prepared to go. The tender moments they'd been sharing had turned sour because of an innocent conversation with Harry. He'd gone there because he'd been concerned about Zoey. Because he felt she was getting a raw deal. But it would seem that he'd touched on a sore spot as far as she was concerned.

With his hand on the doorhandle he said, 'This is totally ridiculous, rowing like this. I came over with the very best of intentions and look where it's got me. I'll see you on Monday at the fire station. Maybe by then we'll both be feeling calmer.'

In the process of deflating like a pricked balloon, she turned away. 'Yes, maybe we will, Alex. By then I might be seeing everything more clearly.'

He could have questioned what she'd meant by that, but he felt there'd already been enough lack of communication. No point in risking more, so he went.

During the weekend Zoey viewed a couple of flats and a small cottage, all within a short distance of the fire station. Her interest was lukewarm. Finding somewhere to live was going to be a necessity, but she couldn't work up any enthusiasm after the quarrel with Alex.

She kept telling herself she'd been unreasonable. That she'd flipped because he'd found out about the double marriage suggestion. But there'd also been pique in her because she was being seen as unable to look after herself.

It was a nuisance that she was going to have to find

somewhere else to live. But she was so happy for Mandy that it was a small price to pay, and once she started looking in earnest it shouldn't be a problem. She would find somewhere. There was no reason for Alex and Harry to get involved.

Harry called round on the Sunday night and asked with a twinkle in his eye, 'Have you had a visit from your firefighter friend? When I talked to him earlier in the week I got the impression that he might be going to pop the question.'

Her throat had gone dry. Pop what question? Harry couldn't be serious.

'He's been round, yes,' she told him, 'but it was only to tell me that he has completely finished with his ex-wife. He didn't pop any question.'

Doubts were choking her. She hadn't given him the chance, had she? The moment Alex had opened his mouth she'd jumped down his throat.

'So he's not in favour of the double wedding idea?' Harry persisted.

'It would seem not,' she said tonelessly. 'He was just as annoyed as I was at being discussed by a third party.'

Harry's face clouded.

'Gee, I'm sorry, Zoey. It wasn't meant to be gossip. That bit just slipped out, more as a joke than anything. He came to see me because he was so concerned about you. Worried in case you were going to end up with nowhere to live.'

'Oh, no!' she exclaimed. 'Alex did that? And all he got from me was a tirade of pettish abuse!'

How was she going to face him in the morning?

With that thought still uppermost in her mind, Zoey was in sombre mood as she prepared to leave for work the next morning, but as she opened the door to a blast of cold air Mandy came into the hallway with Rosie in her arms.

'It's through, Zoey!' she crowed. 'The young miss has got her first tooth.'

'Oh, that's lovely,' she said, looking down at her young stepsister's smooth face. There was a bright spot of colour on each of the baby's cheeks. That, along with uncharacteristic fretfulness, had told them that teeth were on the way, and now the first one was through.

And so as Zoey stepped out into the December morning there was a smile on her face and a new lightness in her step. To the man who was about to leave his own home for the same destination it was an indication that the girl of his dreams wasn't feeling anywhere near as despondent as he was.

Maybe it was better to leave things as they were, he thought. If Zoey wasn't bothered about their quarrel, what was the point of trying to put things right?

They arrived simultaneously and it seemed to her that this was the moment to say she was sorry, while they were outside on the fire-station forecourt.

'Good morning,' Alex said coolly. 'I saw you leaving the house looking very happy.'

'Happy?' she echoed blankly, as she tried to control the bone-melting feeling that was always there when she saw him after even the shortest of absences. 'Oh, yes, of course. Rosie cut her first tooth this morning. Just what I needed to cheer me up.'

'Why? Did you feel that you needed cheering up?'

'What do you think, Alex? I spoke to Harry last night and he explained why you'd been to see him. I'm totally contrite and in future will keep my mouth zipped.'

He was laughing as relief coursed through him. So

she had been just as upset as he'd been. Thank goodness for that.

She was bouncing back.

'So we can start catching up on that lost time whenever you like.'

His amusement increased.

'I'll bear that in mind, as I take it that you're not meaning for me to commence at this exact moment.'

Zoey looked around her. Dorothea was attacking the entrance to the fire station with mop and bucket. Greg and one of the other firemen had just driven onto the forecourt. She pretended to consider.

'Er…no. Later maybe. How about the park at lunchtime?'

'Bit fresh for sitting on wooden benches, isn't it?'

Her eyes were sparkling.

'We'll have our love to keep us warm,' she said, adding with unconscious wistfulness, 'Won't we?'

'You are something else, Zoey Lawrence,' he told her in a low voice. 'Will you please stop looking at me like that? Or I'll start now, whether we have an audience or not.'

CHAPTER SEVEN

IT WAS cold in the park. A chill wind nipped Zoey's ankles and lifted what were left of autumn's dry leaves, but she was barely aware of the fact.

Apart from a woman walking a snappy little dog and an old man shuffling along, she and Alex were the only ones there. For a short space of time they were alone, and the trysting place didn't matter as long as Alex was strolling beside her and holding her hand.

She'd thought a couple of times during the morning that they wouldn't be able to get away. The crew had no sooner reported for duty than they'd been called out to a house fire on a nearby council estate where children had been trapped in an upstairs bedroom.

They'd arrived to find the mother screaming hysterically in the back garden and the demented father being held back by neighbours.

'Our two boys are in the bedroom,' the man had cried as the fire-engine had screeched to a halt. Breaking free, he'd ran towards the open back door.

Alex had flung himself off the engine and grabbed him by the arms. 'This is our job. We'll tackle this. Stay back, sir.'

They'd brought them out through the bedroom window. Alex and Greg had gone in and found the children huddled behind one of the beds. As they'd brought them down the ladder to safety a cheer had gone up from the anxious onlookers, and while the rest of the crew had

119

concentrated on putting out the blaze, Zoey had concentrated on the children.

The small boys were both in shock and suffering from some degree of smoke inhalation. They also had minor burns to the upper arms and legs but thankfully they were alive. The elder of the two had prevented it from being much worse by having the presence of mind to slam shut the bedroom door when he'd seen the flames coming from an airing cupboard and engulfing the landing and stairs.

It seemed that the parents, who had just got up, had smelt smoke coming from upstairs while they'd been preparing breakfast. The father had traced its source to the landing and when he'd opened the cupboard door flames had leapt out to such an extent that he hadn't been able to get past them to the bedroom where the children had been getting dressed.

Faulty wiring had been the cause, as it so often was in those sorts of incidents. Once the blaze was under control they went into the premises and inspected what was left of the upstairs electrical wiring. The quality and arrangement of the wires had told its own tale.

She gave the children oxygen, covered the burns with temporary dressings and asked a neighbour to provide some hot sweet tea to counteract shock for both parents and children.

By the time the crew got back to the station the morning was well under way but its events weren't over.

Jeremy, the lad who'd been trapped in the car on the hill bend all those weeks ago, appeared and, after receiving a warm welcome, was shown around the station.

He looked gaunt and, although off crutches, still needed a stick to lean on, but there was nothing frail about his determination to join the force.

'As soon as I'm really fit I'm going to apply,' he told them. 'You guys were the most welcome sight I'd ever seen when I looked up from that mangled mess I was trapped in.'

'You'll have to concentrate on getting back to full health and strength,' Alex told him. 'The fitness tests you have to undergo to join the fire service are very stringent.'

'What's the routine?' the would-be firefighter asked.

'Basic training takes two years. The first fourteen weeks are spent on a residential course at the Brigade Training Building in the city centre and it covers a lot of things.'

'Such as?'

'Handling equipment, first aid, chemistry, physics, hydraulics, building construction, general fire safety...'

'No problem. I'll do it,' the lad told him with the sublime confidence of youth, and for some reason none of them had doubted that he would.

At last a late lunch-break arrived and they were off, separately at first, joining up by the park gates.

'So tell me about the wedding,' Alex said as they walked towards an ornamental lake of cold grey water which was being whipped up by the wind. 'That is, if the subject isn't taboo.'

Zoey smiled up at him.

'Of course it isn't. I wasn't the one who was making a fuss about Mandy's suggestion. Like I said, she was joking.'

He rolled his eyes heavenwards.

'All right. I get the message. So what about the wedding?'

'Mandy is going to wear a long cream brocade dress which will go beautifully with her brown hair and eyes.

Rosie and I are going to be dressed in blue velvet trimmed with white fur—fake, of course.'

'Unless that little one qualifies for the *Guinness Book of Records* as a child who walked at five months, I don't see how she's going to be a bridesmaid at her mother's wedding.'

'I'm going to carry her, of course.'

'I see.'

He would have liked to have told her that it would be totally enchanting to have seen the two of them together, but he had no intention of putting a foot wrong today. He wanted a relationship with Zoey and he fully intended to pursue it, but in his own time. There was still the thought of Gloria hanging over his head like the sword of Damocles.

'I shall come to watch.'

'You might find yourself doing more than that.'

'What do you mean?'

'Mandy wants to know if you'll give her away as she has no male relatives.'

There was surprise in Alex's dark gaze.

'Really? Well...yes...I suppose so. I will if she wants me to.'

'She does...and so do I.'

'Tell me the arrangements, then.'

'The ceremony is at half past three at St James's Church on Monday the twenty-fourth of December, followed by a meal. There will be just the five of us. Mandy, Harry, Rosie, and you and I. Afterwards the bridal couple are going away for a few days.'

'And taking the baby with them?'

'Er...no. I'm taking a week's leave to look after Rosie.'

He was frowning.

'What sort of a Christmas is that going to be for you?'
Zoey had stopped and was looking up at him.

'We could pretend she's ours and play happy families.'

Alex touched her cold cheek gently but didn't take her up on the suggestion.

'So you won't be moving out of Mandy's house until they come back from their honeymoon?'

'Mmm, that's right. Why do you ask?'

'No special reason. I'm just curious.'

Of course, there was a reason, but it didn't seem like the moment to tell her that he hoped to have sorted out his affairs by then and might have some ideas of his own about where she was going to live.

There was peace between them and he didn't want to spoil it, so he changed the subject to one less delicate.

'I'm applying for the Station Officer vacancy,' he told her. 'As I'm virtually doing the job already, it seems logical to seek the proper status. During the coming weeks I'll be taking written and practical examinations and appearing before the selection panel at Command Headquarters.'

Zoey smiled up at him.

'I really will have to behave myself then, won't I? Will I have to call you "sir"?'

'Yes, and bend the knee,' he teased. 'Seriously, the only difference will be that I'll be wearing a white helmet instead of a yellow one.'

It wasn't strictly true. There would be more responsibility with the promotion but the time to concern himself about that was when he got the job.

He checked his watch.

'We're going to have to make tracks, Zoey. The

lunch-break is almost up. Have you enjoyed our stroll in these sub-zero temperatures?'

She pretended to shiver but her glowing cheeks belied the pretence.

'Yes, I have,' she told him, 'but we do have the means to generate some heat of our own, you know. Melt frost with fire.'

He bent his mouth to hers.

'What a good idea.'

'Mmm,' she murmured as his arms went around her, and it was like the other night. Only this time she wasn't going to spoil it. A warm tide of longing was running through her veins.

She could have stayed there for ever in the deserted park. But there was nothing to guarantee that the cold weather meant there would be no fires to attend or accidents on icy roads. As they drew apart, she said softly, 'We'd better go before we're missed.'

Alex nodded.

'Yes. There'll be other times. If we'll let it, life can only get better for us.'

The afternoon was uneventful and as the fire crew left the station in the early evening, after switching the call-out system through to headquarters, Alex caught up with her.

'What have you planned for tonight?' he asked casually.

'Er...nothing really. The lady who's making our dresses for the wedding is coming round for a fitting session but that shouldn't take long. What did you have in mind?'

He smiled, and Zoey saw contentment in his gaze.

'Nothing in particular. Certainly not another sojourn

in the arctic waste that the park has turned into. Maybe we could have a bite somewhere and a nice long chat.'

He saw her expression and his smile wavered.

'Is that not exciting enough for you?'

She looked away, not meeting his glance.

'That would be great. I was only thinking that privacy is a hard thing to come by in our two lives.'

'You mean with Gloria at my place and Mandy and the baby at your end?'

'Yes.'

He didn't take her up on that. The subject of Gloria was like walking on stony ground.

Instead, he said, 'I'll pick you up in an hour if that's all right with you. And, Zoey…'

'Yes?' she breathed.

'Wrap up warmly. There's going to be a keen frost tonight.'

'Is that all?'

She could see his eyes glinting beneath the street-lamps.

'For the moment…yes.'

'Which, interpreted, means don't rush you.'

'Yes, something like that.'

He gave her a gentle push.

'Go on in. Mandy will be thinking you've got lost.'

It seemed that Gloria had been watching them from the window. The moment Alex turned his key in the lock she was there, and he wondered in sudden irritation why she didn't get a life of her own. Unable to help himself, he referred to it in an oblique sort of way.

'How's your aunt?'

'A bit better,' was the abrupt reply, and he sensed that something had ruffled her feathers.

'When is she going to be transferred back to the rest home?'

'Soon, I hope.'

'Your clients must be wondering what's happened to you.'

'Possibly.'

Alex observed her thoughtfully.

'What's wrong, Gloria? Who's upset you?'

She answered the question with another one.

'Are you in love with Zoey Lawrence?'

He smiled. For the first time he was ready to admit it.

'Yes.'

'I see.'

'Good,' he remarked blandly. 'That's all right, then.' When she had nothing further to say he went up to his room to change.

As he came down the stairs she was taking a phone call and he heard her say. 'Right. We'll come straight away.' Then she began to weep.

'Who was that?' he asked quickly.

'The cottage hospital,' she sobbed. 'Aunt Mary's had a stroke. You'll have to take me, Alex. I'm too upset to drive.'

'Yes, of course,' he agreed, and knew that he wasn't going to be able to keep to the arrangements he'd made with Zoey.

When the phone rang Zoey was almost ready, snugly attired in a soft blue angora jumper, trousers and a three-quarter-length black coat with a neat fun-fur collar.

Her eyes were sparkling at the thought of the evening ahead, but the sparkle faded when she heard what he had to say.

'Yes, of course I understand that you have to take her,' she said tonelessly. 'I hope Gloria's aunt isn't too badly affected.'

Alex sighed. He knew Zoey was disappointed. So was he, but he could hardly leave Gloria at such a time. He owed it to her, if only for old times' sake.

'I'll be in touch as soon as I get back,' he promised, 'but we could be there for hours if it's as serious as Gloria seems to think.'

'Yes. I realise that,' Zoey told him. 'You'd better go—we'll see each other soon.'

'What a shame that your evening has been spoilt,' Mandy said when she heard what had happened. 'You look lovely. It's a shame to waste it. Why don't you go to the pub? If Alex can't be there the rest of them will be, and from what you say they're always pleased to see you.'

Zoey hesitated. She knew that Harry was coming round and that he and Mandy would be happy to have the place to themselves for a while. But going to the pub would be a poor replacement for a quiet evening with Alex.

'All right,' she agreed. 'You've persuaded me. If Alex gets back earlier than expected, you can tell him where to find me.'

Greg was at her side within seconds when Zoey arrived at The Wheatsheaf and for the rest of the evening he monopolised her.

Miserable that he was available when Alex wasn't, she didn't object. She'd no illusions about the man. He was a womaniser, conceited and always had an eye to the main chance. He was also getting very drunk. But at least he was someone to talk to as the minutes ticked by and there was no sign of Alex.

When it was time to go home she made no comment when he fell into step beside her, as they both lived in the same direction. When he drunkenly draped his arm around her shoulders as they strolled along beneath a moonlit sky she didn't make a fuss because she was so preoccupied with her own thoughts. She also thought he might fall over without some support.

They were at her gate and the look in his eyes told her that he wasn't in a hurry to get home to his bachelor pad. She reached out for the latch but he pulled her back.

'What's the hurry?' he slurred. 'Don't you want some company now that action man's not here?'

The house was in darkness so it looked as if Harry had gone.

'I don't think so,' she told him firmly, shrugging off the arm that was tightening around her shoulders. 'I'm tired. It's been a long day. And, Greg…'

'What?' he asked, bringing his face close to hers.

'The fact that we chatted in the pub doesn't mean that it's payback time. In fact, it won't ever be that. Do you understand?'

But Greg had had so much to drink, he wasn't listening. Suddenly he grabbed her in a bear hug and kissed her on the lips. Frantically, Zoey tried to avoid his mouth and struggle free from his grip, but it was almost impossible.

Then, as if by magic, Alex was there on the pavement with them, dragging Greg away from her, almost lifting him off his feet in his fury, and she was staggering back against the gate with her hand against her mouth and her legs wilting beneath her.

'Clear off!' Alex told him. 'If you lay a finger on Zoey again you'll have me to deal with.'

Greg had got the message and was backing off, but he wasn't quite finished.

'Ask her who she's been making eyes at all the time we've been in the pub,' he muttered, and with that he went staggering off.

'Thanks for that, Alex,' Zoey said tearfully. 'I should have seen it coming.'

His face was like granite and the words when they came were just as cold.

'Don't apologise. I don't own you…and if I'd thought I did, that little episode would have made me see differently. The next time you feel inclined to tell me how much you care for me, throw in an explanation as to why the moment my back was turned you sought Osbourne out.'

Her hand was still over her mouth, as if she didn't want Alex to see the lips that another man had kissed. Observing it, he said coldly, 'If you have a thick lip in the morning, I'll know why, won't I?'

She opened her mouth to tell him that she was sorry. That she'd only chatted to Greg because she'd been miserable and at a loose end, but he didn't give her the chance. He'd turned on his heel and was striding back to where he'd come from with the set of his shoulders telling their own story.

As she walked wearily up the garden path, Zoey wondered how long he'd been back and how the old lady was, as she hadn't been given the chance to ask.

When Alex went back inside his house he was relieved that Gloria was asleep in the spare room and not around to witness his dejection.

They'd found her aunt unconscious after the stroke and had been told that she wasn't expected to recover. At eleven o'clock they'd left her bedside with a promise from the nursing staff that they would ring if there was any change.

When he'd got home he'd seen that the house across the way had been in darkness and had resigned himself to having to wait until morning before he spoke to Zoey.

He knew that she was impatient for progress in their relationship and all the time was being thwarted by the situation at his end. Tonight had been yet another frustrating postponement of getting to know each other better.

All of that he understood, but to kill time with Osbourne in his absence and let him come on to her like that was trying his own reserves to the limit.

He'd been gazing sombrely across at Mandy's house when he'd seen them walking up the cul-de-sac. Greg's arm had been around her and Zoey hadn't been complaining.

Raw anger had ripped through him to discover that she'd substituted the station Romeo for himself so quickly. Then it had become concern when he'd seen her fighting Osbourne off. So how did he feel right now? That he'd been right to be wary of getting involved in another relationship so soon?

For the rest of that week Greg avoided Zoey and Alex treated her with such glacial indifference that she clung to the breezy, cheerful normality of the rest of the fire crew like a soul in torment, which was what she was.

It wasn't in her nature to be deceitful or immoral, and if she'd expected an escapist night at the pub to turn out like it had she would have stayed in. But the damage had been done. Alex had put her outside the circle of his life and from the looks of it that was where she was going to stay.

But she kept telling herself there was light in the darkness. It was only two weeks to the wedding. He'd agreed to give Mandy away and, even if her own behaviour was unreliable, his wasn't.

Maybe on that occasion they might find a level of understanding that would take away the salt of the tears that she kept shedding. The wedding was the only thing she had to look forward to, as Christmas with just Rosie for company looked like being a non-event.

'I'm going across to have a word with Alex about the wedding,' Mandy said one evening. 'I don't suppose you want to come?'

She knew they'd fallen out, but didn't seem unduly bothered. Probably because Zoey had played down the quarrel, leaving Mandy confident that he would be available to give her away.

Zoey sighed.

'No, thanks. I'm not his favorite person at the moment. I'll bath Rosie while you're gone, if you like.'

As her tiny stepsister gurgled in the bath water, Zoey looked down at her wistfully.

'Why is it that your mummy's romance is so happy and uncomplicated, little rosebud,' she said, 'while mine is like a disaster area? Am I being too defeatist 'cos I'm sick of eating humble pie? But neither can I face a large helping of rebuff.'

She reached for a large white towel and, lifting the baby carefully out of the water, began to pat her dry. As she did so, her mind went back to what she'd said to Alex about the three of them playing happy families.

When she'd said it she'd been thinking that one day

they might have a family of their own. She must have been crazy.

'That ex-wife of his is a pain,' Mandy said when she came back. 'She behaves as if they've never been divorced. She's dug in there, Zoey, and from the looks of it has no intentions of moving, even though her elderly aunt has passed away.'

'Has she? Oh, dear!' Zoey exclaimed. 'That's awful, but maybe Gloria will go now. When did it happen?'

'Early this evening. They'd just got back from the hospital when I got there.'

'So you didn't get the chance to discuss the wedding.'

'Alex and I had a quick word. No problem there. He's going to do the honours.'

'Thank goodness for that!' Zoey breathed. With the wistfulness still upon her, she said, 'Did he mention me?'

'Er…no.'

'Ugh,' she moaned. 'What am I going to do, Mandy? I really do love him.'

'Take each day as it comes,' she advised. 'Alex will come round. You just have to give him time.'

Zoey was taking each day as it came and none of them were bringing much joy. But whatever doldrums the man in charge and the latest member of the team might be wallowing in, the rest of the firefighters made up for it in light-hearted anticipation of the fast-approaching festive season.

One of the men had turned up with a tree. Another had brought decorations to be hung from the ceiling of the station and, in spite of her gloom, Zoey couldn't resist joining in.

She was on top of a step ladder when a 'shout' came

through, and as the men dropped what they were doing and hurried to climb aboard the fire-engine one of them caught the bottom of the ladder and it began to topple.

As it rocked she lost her balance and would have fallen if someone hadn't been there to break her descent.

'For goodness' sake, watch what you're doing,' Alex said as she looked up at him from the circle of his arms. 'You are totally careless.'

'I'm not!' she protested.

'Yes, you are,' he insisted, 'in more ways than one.'

'You're referring to the people I mix with, I suppose,' she breathed as they grabbed their fireproof jackets.

'Possibly.'

'You're an unforgiving soul,' she flared in sudden anger. 'I didn't know that Greg was going to jump on me. He was drunk. All I'd done was chat to him in the pub. Surely there was no crime in that.'

'So you don't see anything wrong in leading someone on without considering the consequences.'

'You can believe what you like,' she snapped as they took their places on the engine. 'But I didn't lead him on. I wish you weren't coming to the wedding.'

There was irony in his smile.

'Well, hard lines. I've promised Mandy, who, I must say, is a far less complicated person than you, that I will give her away and I intend to do just that.'

The blaze they'd been called out to, an area of dry scrubland that had been accidentally set alight, appeared on the skyline and it was time to put aside personal differences. But it didn't stop Zoey from bringing into the light of day a half-formed decision that had been at the back of her mind ever since the aftermath of the Greg Osbourne episode.

She and Alex were going nowhere. She was going to

ask to be transferred back to where she'd come from. There were plenty of flats in the city. It would solve the problem of somewhere to live once Mandy was married, and she could start to pick up the pieces after a disastrous romance. Any further than that she didn't want to think.

'You'll be able to join in the Christmas promotion down on the main street of our community this year,' Mandy said one morning as they breakfasted together.

Zoey observed her doubtfully.

'What do you mean?'

'We all try to do our bit to bring business to the traders on the cobbled street down by the river. There will be a big Christmas tree in the square, and smaller illuminated ones above every shop. At midday one of the local officials turns on the lights and then the fun starts.

'All the shopkeepers are dressed in old-fashioned clothes and they serve those who go into their premises with hot mince pies and mulled wine. There'll be Morris dancers, a carousel for the children, a popcorn stall, various outdoor craft presentations and a brass band, amongst other things.'

'Really!' Zoey exclaimed. 'What a good idea. When is it?'

'Next Saturday.'

'Right. So are we going to be there?'

Mandy smiled.

'I am, certainly. I'll be supporting Harry in his place.'

'Dressed up?'

'Yes, I suppose so…and with regard to yourself, the folk at the post office and general store want to know if you'll help out as they're going to be short-staffed on that day.'

'And what would I be wearing?'

'Oh, you know.'

Zoey laughed. 'No, I don't.'

'A long dress, an apron and a mob-cap.'

She groaned. 'Oh, dear! Not very captivating.'

It was Mandy's turn to laugh. 'I think you'll look lovely in that garb. So, what do you say? Shall I tell them that you'll oblige?'

Zoey sighed. 'Yes. I suppose so. I've nothing else to occupy my time with.'

'So you're still on the outside where Alex is concerned?'

'Mmm. Well and truly.'

'Maybe he'll relent when he sees another side to you,' Mandy teased.

'What? Looking like a character out of Charles Dickens? And who's the bigwig who'll be turning on the lights?'

'It's not a bigwig. Just someone of local prominence. This year they're honouring your lot.'

Zoey's eyes had widened.

'The fire service?'

'Yes.'

'It's not Alex, is it?'

'The same. Our popular fire chief. So, you see, we're all involved.'

'No one's mentioned it at the station.'

'He probably doesn't want a big thing made of it.'

Zoey found herself perking up. Maybe he would come in for a glass of wine or a mince pie, and if he didn't she would go to seek him out, even though the chill would probably still be persisting. At least she would be in his vicinity for part of that weekend.

*   *   *

It was a cold, clear morning, and by midday, when the festivities were due to start, a pale sun was warming the cobblestone street. There was already a festive atmosphere all around, and as Zoey observed herself in the big mirror at the back of the shop she was smiling for two reasons.

Firstly, because she was looking forward to the afternoon ahead and, secondly, because she was almost unrecognisable in the clothes that they'd found for her. With the mob-cap pulled well down over her golden bob, she wouldn't stand out in the crowd when Alex turned on the lights. Not that she was expecting him to be interested if she did.

It was one o'clock. The moment had arrived and when they all went to gather in the square for the 'turn-on' she was filled with pleasurable expectancy...until she saw Gloria beside Alex. It was a week since her aunt's funeral and she was still around. It looked as if Mandy had been right. She was dug in at Alex's place.

Zoey turned away. The day had lost its appeal. Alex's ex-wife was standing beside him looking elegant and relaxed, while she herself was dressed in somebody's grandmother's cast-off clothes.

He was making a short speech, but it was washing over her. Then he was reaching out for the switch and a cheer went up as the lights came on.

Yet in spite of the afternoon's depressing beginning, Zoey found that she was enjoying herself as the crowds came to eat and drink and browse around the shop. Whenever she had a moment to spare, she stood in the doorway and watched the festivities.

There'd been no sign of Alex and she'd concluded that as someone of importance he was with the organisers and those more interesting than the serving maids in the post office.

The light was beginning to fade and winter's chill settling on the street when someone came hurrying into the shop to ask if they would phone for an ambulance.

'What's wrong?' she asked immediately.

'A youngster's fallen off the roundabout and hurt himself badly,' she was told.

As the postmistress began to make the necessary phone call Zoey said urgently, 'Take me to him.'

The child was lying in a crumpled heap on the concrete beside the carousel. He wasn't moving, and as she pushed her way past those gathered around him she heard someone say, 'He's been riding on this thing all afternoon. Must have felt dizzy.'

As she bent over him Zoey was relieved to see his small chest rising and falling, but the gash on his head and the subsequent swelling that was appearing around it were not reassuring.

'Stand back, please,' she heard a familiar voice telling the onlookers, and as if history were repeating itself Alex was saying, 'I'll take over, if you don't mind. The child's injuries are severe for such a short fall. I need to check his pulse and that his tongue isn't—'

'I've already done that,' she said quietly, and as she raised her head his jaw went slack. But he quickly regained his composure and crouched down over the boy.

'We can't move him as there's no way of telling what damage there is to the head,' Zoey continued. 'There could be spinal injuries as well. Will someone ask the folk at the shop for a blanket?' she cried. 'His body temperature is dropping fast in this cold air.'

'Who was he with?' Alex asked of those standing nearby.

'The kid was on his own,' the ashen-faced carousel owner told him. 'Came with a pocket full of coins and stayed on all afternoon.'

Someone came back with a blanket and soon they could hear the sirens of an approaching ambulance. 'I'm going with him. I'll stay until the parents arrive,' Zoey said quickly.

'Me, too,' Alex said briefly.

'How do you mean?'

'I'm coming, too.'

'What about your part in the proceedings here?'

'Done and dusted,' he said drily. 'I was only here to pull a switch.'

'Hadn't you better tell her ladyship?'

'Gloria? She's in the pub with the fire crew. She'll find out eventually.'

As the ambulance sped along the darkening roads Alex said in a low voice, 'Do me a favour, will you, Zoey?'

'What?'

'Take that thing off your head. I feel as if I've been catapulted into the middle of *David Copperfield* or something similar. I do like to be able to see your hair.'

If she hadn't been so worried about the boy she would have been laughing at the thought of what she looked like. The paramedic who was helping her to monitor the young accident victim smiled.

'I thought it was because you were a bit eccentric. I take it that you're the lad's parents.'

Alex shook his head.

'No. We're from the local fire station and were involved in the event.'

As they hung around Accident and Emergency while the boy was being examined, Zoey said flatly, 'Hospital visits seem to be the order of the day where you and I are concerned. It was like going back in time, having you bending over me and bossing the show.'

Alex was eyeing her questioningly.

'I'm not with you.'

'When we first met and the removal man had collapsed.'

'Oh, that. Yes. But on that occasion I soon found out that you knew what you were doing. At least with regard to that.'

'In other words, I make a mess of everything else.'

'If the cap fits.'

'Oh! You make me so angry!' she cried. 'Not a word about having Gloria swanning around beside you when you were doing the celebrity bit.'

'Grow up, Zoey,' he snapped. 'Do you really think that cuts any ice with me?'

At that moment there was a commotion beside the enquiry desk and it became clear that the parents of the injured child had turned up, both of them totally distraught at discovering what had happened.

'We were busy decorating,' the mother was wailing tearfully, 'and didn't know that Grandad had given George his pocket money. We thought that he was still around somewhere until…'

X-rays had shown that there was a subdural haematoma present in the skull and surgery would be required to stop the bleeding.

As Zoey and Alex left them to their own particular nightmare she thought dismally that nothing had changed between Alex and herself. It was still one step forward, two steps back.

* * *

It was Christmas Eve and the day of the wedding, but all the bright expectation Zoey had expected to feel was missing. She didn't have to look far for the reason. It lay with the man who lived in the house across the way.

But it was Mandy's day and she was determined that nothing was going to spoil that, so she prepared to put on an act for her sake.

The ceremony was at half past three and as the two women dressed themselves and the baby the immensity of the changes that were about to take place in her life began to hit the golden-haired bridesmaid.

This time spent with Mandy and Rosie had been the happiest time she'd ever known, she thought wistfully. She'd met Alex here, hadn't she? Alexander the Great! Strong, mesmeric...and unforgiving.

The sight of Mandy in her bridal outfit broke into her reverie and Zoey put aside her yearnings.

'You look lovely,' she breathed. 'Harry will be overcome at the sight of you.'

The bride-to-be smiled as she observed the slender figure in blue velvet, holding the smallest bridesmaid in one arm and a posy of white snowdrops in the other hand.

'You don't look so bad yourself. If a certain person doesn't melt when he sees you, I shall be most surprised.'

Zoey pulled a wry face.

'I wouldn't expect too much from that quarter if I were you.'

When Alex came across Zoey did some melting of her own. The grey suit and pristine white shirt he was wearing emphasised his dark attractiveness to such an extent that she felt her blood heat, even though he was observing her unsmilingly.

She wasn't to know that those dark, unreadable eyes were seeing a vision that was affecting him in a similar manner. In her long blue velvet dress, she was the loveliest thing he'd ever seen. So why was he being so unrelenting?

He wanted to take hold of her and kiss away the doubts in those beautiful eyes, but he wasn't here to make love to Zoey. Mandy had asked a favour of him and he'd been only too happy to oblige, even though the golden girl was going to be left out on a limb once her stepmother was married.

They were all going to the church together—Mandy, Zoey, the baby and himself. Harry would meet them there. Afterwards the four of them would sit down to the meal that had been arranged, with Rosie beside them in a high chair. Once they'd eaten, the bride and her new husband would set off for the honeymoon they'd planned, leaving Zoey to look after Rosie until they came back.

It would all seem a bit of an anticlimax once they'd gone, especially for Zoey, and he knew he wasn't going to be able to ignore her over the two days of Christmas. Every time he saw her he felt as if his very bones would melt with longing and knew that if he was fasting it was his own choice.

CHAPTER EIGHT

THE vows had been made, the knot tied. The wedding was over.

All the time the ceremony had been taking place Zoey had been remembering how Alex had found out about Mandy's light-hearted suggestion for a double wedding.

Was he recalling it, too, she wondered, and thinking he'd had a lucky escape from the local flibbertigibbet? That he'd made one mistake and wasn't going to make another in a hurry? It was because he wasn't in a hurry that everything kept going wrong, Zoe thought wryly.

They all went back to the house so that Mandy could change her clothes before she and Harry left for a short break in Spain. Now, just Zoey, Alex and the baby were left and, as if she sensed that her mother had left her, Rosie was becoming fretful.

Zoey was eyeing her in perplexity. She was usually such a good little soul that an unhappy Rosie was unheard of. But fretful she was, and Alex asked, 'Do you think she's sickening for something?'

She was trying to soothe her into sleep but Rosie wasn't to be coaxed and she said, 'It will be incredible if she is. It's the first time that Mandy has left her for anything other than a few hours.'

Alex was standing beside them, and as he looked down at her bent head tenderness washed over him. They were a beautiful sight, Zoey and the baby.

Rosie, blue-eyed like her big sister and with a golden

142

down on her small head, and Zoey, young and beautiful, watching over her like an anxious madonna.

'I have to go,' he said reluctantly. 'There are a couple of things I have to see to at the station before Christmas Day dawns, but I'll be back as soon as I can.'

'Thanks, Alex,' she said gratefully. 'I'm sure she'll be fine. I'll see you later.'

But as time passed, Rosie's temperature began to rise and she was far from well. Mandy always had infant paracetamol on hand and Zoey tried to coax the baby to take it, but it seemed difficult for Rosie to swallow and she tried to push the spoon away with a hot little hand.

Fearful of meningitis, Zoey lifted Rosie's vest, looking for the tell-tale rash that would be the forerunner to a nightmare. Thankfully the baby's skin was clear, and when Zoey shone a light in her eyes there was no increase in the discomfort.

Mandy and Harry would be somewhere in the sky at this moment, she thought, so she couldn't reach them if she wanted to, and she would have to be desperate to break into their brief time together.

The obvious thing to do was ring the GP, but she'd forgotten that it was the late afternoon of Christmas Eve and the only help available was a voice message giving details of the emergency service.

Rosie was coughing now, harsh, rasping noises that were quite frightening. It was going to have to be A and E at the nearest hospital, she decided, and hoped that the place wouldn't be full of those who'd drunk too much. Or people who'd slipped on icy pavements that hadn't thawed out from a drastic drop in temperature the night before.

Wrapping the baby up snugly, she ventured forth. As she pulled out of the drive she glanced quickly at the house across the way. It looked warm and welcoming, with an illuminated tree in the garden and coloured lights framing the porch. The curtains hadn't been drawn and she caught a glimpse of Gloria looking out, an unruffled figure with glass in hand, which made her gloom deepen.

There was no sign of Alex, but there wouldn't be. He'd said he had some work to do at the fire station before the day was out. Maybe the wedding had interfered with headquarters business and he'd gone to catch up. The place would be closed during the festivities but the men would all be on call if any major emergencies arose.

As Rosie's coughing broke into the silence, Zoey thought anxiously that she had an emergency of her own to cope with and hoped that he would find her somewhere along the way.

The casualty department of the hospital was as she'd expected it to be on Christmas Eve—full. But after the triage nurse had noted that Rosie was now having difficulty in breathing, they were seen almost immediately.

'It's a bad case of croup,' the doctor said. 'It's common in children under four and in most cases clears up when moist warmth is introduced into the atmosphere. Croup comes from a viral infection that affects the voice-box, the epiglottis that covers the larynx, and the trachea or windpipe. It seems to occur at this time of year for some reason and in the case of your little one we're going to have to hospitalise her so that she can be put inside a tent and given humidified oxygen.'

'I'm not her mother,' Zoey explained. 'Rosie is my half-sister. I'm looking after her while her mother is away.'

He nodded. 'I'll send for a nurse from the children's

ward to come and collect you,' he said, 'and one of the paediatricians will start the baby's treatment as soon as you're settled in there.'

Zoey had kept calm all through the crisis, but now that the treatment seemed to be working and Rosie was sleeping peacefully she was beginning to feel the after-effects.

It was just gone midnight. Seated in the dimly lit ward with the only sounds the restless stirrings of the small patients and the soft padding of the night nurse's rubber-soled shoes as she went to and fro, she felt isolated and exhausted.

For the first couple of hours she'd debated whether to get in touch with Mandy, but she didn't want to intrude into Mandy's honeymoon unless it was absolutely necessary.

Yet there'd been the dread of Rosie becoming worse and her mother not having been informed. Now, thankfully, that crisis was past. She might even be able to take the baby home in the morning. But it didn't take away the feeling of terrible aloneness.

Zoey could feel her eyelids drooping and knew that wouldn't do. She was there to watch over Rosie. It happened again and this time when she blinked them open she looked up, startled. She wasn't alone in the shadows. Alex was there, only inches away, his expression full of grave concern.

'Alex!' she breathed. 'How did you know where we were?'

'Simple deduction,' he said in a low voice. 'I was very late leaving the station because I discovered a burst pipe in the kitchen and had to rustle up a plumber, which is no mean feat on Christmas Eve, I can tell you. And when

I did eventually get away I saw that your place was in darkness.

'I naturally concluded that Rosie had improved and you'd gone to bed. Until Gloria said she'd seen you "gallivanting" off in the car earlier. I knew that couldn't be right. That you wouldn't leave the baby, even if she was well, and she was far from that the last time I'd seen her, so I decided to try the hospital...and here I am.'

He bent over the sleeping child.

'What was it?'

'A bad case of croup. Rosie is being given humidified oxygen as it's affected her larynx and trachea. She started to cough and it was dreadful. I've never heard anything like it. By the time we arrived here her breathing was affected and they saw to us immediately.'

'And?'

'It seems to be working. The doctor said if it didn't they might have to do a tracheostomy and I was frantic, trying to decide whether I should get in touch with Mandy or not.'

'But you didn't?'

'No.' There was a wobble in her voice. 'Do you think I did the right thing?'

'Yes. Now that she's improving. But I can see that it was no easy decision to make.'

'It was awful. The responsibility was immense. I felt so alone.'

She bent her head so that he wouldn't see tears on her lashes but she was forgetting that she was with a man who missed nothing.

'Come here,' he said gently, holding out his arms. 'You've had one heck of a night.' As she went into them like a homing pigeon, he went on, 'It's been some

Christmas Eve! You being worried sick over Rosie and ending up here and me chasing the plumber so that the station wouldn't be flooded.'

As she snuggled against him she could tell that he was smiling when he said, 'You're still in your bridesmaid's dress, I see. Couldn't you bear to take it off?'

She looked down blankly at the long folds of blue velvet.

'I haven't had a chance. Rosie was still in hers when I brought her here, but the nurse found her a little cotton baby suit.'

'So what happens next?' he asked.

'I don't know. It will depend on what the doctor says in the morning whether she's allowed home. If he's not happy to discharge her, I shall be here until he does. I can't believe that this has happened the moment her mother was out of sight.' Zoey sighed. 'What a nightmare.'

'You coped brilliantly, Zoey.'

She lifted her head to see his expression and as their eyes met she asked, 'So you don't think I'm the village nitwit after all?'

'I never did. I might have thought other things of you, but never that. You're strong and brave...and sometimes er...unpredictable and impatient. Shall we say that getting to know you is quite an experience.'

The night nurse was hovering and they stood back while she checked on Rosie.

'Her breathing is much better,' she told them, 'but I think the paediatric consultant might want to keep her in for another day, even though we are trying to keep the ward as empty as possible with it being Christmas.'

She smiled. 'So prepare yourselves for having Christmas lunch on the children's ward.'

'No problem,' Alex told her smoothly, and when Zoey eyed him in surprise he said, 'Well? Is there?'

'Not for me,' she agreed, 'but surely you'll want to be getting back.'

'What for? To watch Gloria spend the day beside a box of chocolates and a bottle of wine? I'll be where I want to be, so does that answer your question?'

It certainly did, Zoey thought as the night ticked away. Not so long ago she'd thought this was going to be the worst Christmas ever, but that wasn't how it was turning out. Rosie was getting better and incredibly Alex was here beside her and content to be so. If he thought that she was unpredictable, what was he?

The nurse had found them a couple of comfortable chairs and Zoey was dozing when Alex said suddenly, 'Were you disappointed that it wasn't a double wedding?'

Her eyes flew open. It was the last thing she'd expected him to say. She shook her head.

'No. The man I marry will have to be really sure that he wants to marry me. Not feel as if he's been rushed into something he might regret.'

'I take it that you are referring to me?'

'Mmm. Maybe.'

'And do you think the fact that I've been feeling rather disillusioned with you of late could have added to any doubts I might have? Especially as I've recently gone through a divorce?'

'It might have, I suppose,' she conceded. 'But you know how I feel about you.'

He raised a quizzical eyebrow.

'Do I? Should I be asking forgiveness for losing my cool when I saw you wrestling with Osbourne?'

'Exactly!' she exclaimed. 'Wrestling! Not romancing!

I was at a loose end when you cancelled our arrangements and he was there. But I didn't ask him to walk me home, or to start taking it for granted that I was going to be falling into his arms like a piece of putty.'

'That is a substance I would never liken you to,' he said laughingly. But he was serious again as he said, 'It will be daylight soon. The ward will be a hive of activity then. So while peace still reigns, merry Christmas, Zoey.'

As she observed him with her mouth a round 'O' of surprise, he put a small gift-wrapped box in her hand and told her, 'I wasn't sure if I would get the opportunity to give it to you, but the Fates had other ideas, didn't they?'

'Er…yes,' she said awkwardly, for once almost lost for words. 'Is it all right if I open it?'

'Of course. It is Christmas morning.'

She slowly unwrapped the gift to discover a bracelet of diamonds and sapphires. As she gasped with delight he said, 'Sapphires to match your eyes, and diamonds because they sparkle almost as brightly as you do.'

She held out a slender wrist for him to fasten it on and once it was in position she looked down at the glowing gems.

'It's beautiful,' she breathed, and getting to her feet she bent over and kissed him on the cheek.

He'd been right about her sparkle. It might have been missing of late, but now it was brighter than the diamonds as she told him, 'If we weren't here I would do better than that. But the children's ward is hardly the place to be kindling our desires, is it?'

Alex was smiling.

'You're assuming that the kindling would be mutual, then?'

'Wouldn't it?'

'It would depend,' he said with the smile still in place.

'On what?'

'Just how much will-power I was able to dredge up.'

At that moment there was an interruption. A porter, with anxious parents one on either side of him, was wheeling in a trolley with a sick child on it, and the moment was broken into.

'What about Gloria?' Zoey asked as a winter dawn streaked the sky.

'What about her?' Alex said smoothly.

'Won't she wonder where you are?'

'She knows that I went to find you.'

'And she didn't mind?'

'No, of course not. She's busy winding up her aunt's estate and then she'll be off.'

Gloria and her concerns seemed a long way off on this Christmas morning. Zoey said sleepily, 'We're like Mary and Joseph, watching over the child.'

Alex smiled. 'You've certainly got the blue dress on,' he quipped, 'and if I stay here much longer I'll have the beard that goes with the part.'

It was ten o'clock when the consultant came on his rounds, and when Zoey asked if Rosie could go home he shook his head.

'She's recovering satisfactorily,' he told her, 'but I'd like to keep her here under observation for another day at least. It was a bad attack. We nearly had to perform a tracheostomy, but fortunately the oxygen seems to be doing the trick instead.'

He turned to Alex.

'It's your wife that should go home. She looks exhausted.'

'I'm just a friend,' he said, 'but I agree with what you say.' He turned to Zoey. 'The doctor's right. You need some sleep. Rosie is in good hands. We can come back later.'

As she opened her mouth to protest he said, 'Shush. I'm taking you home. We'll come back after lunch.'

'What lunch?' she said wearily. 'All the food that Mandy bought is still in the freezer.'

He led her gently but purposefully out onto the hospital's main corridor.

'We'll call it breakfast, then. You don't keep your eggs and bacon or your cereal in the freezer, do you?'

'That's hardly what you would call festive fare. It's Christmas Day,' she protested weakly.

'So what? It will still have twenty-four hours in it. Become light, then go dark in the late afternoon, like any other day at this time of the year. At the risk of sounding trite, Christmas is where the heart is, not where the turkey's thawing out.'

Zoey had to smile even though she was drooping with tiredness.

'Very profound, I'm sure. But one can't eat pearls of wisdom, or thread them for that matter.'

'So what do you have in cereals?' he countered, ignoring the comment. 'Something other than cornflakes, I hope.'

This is fantastic, she thought as Alex tucked her into the car. We're friends again. Proper friends! We can laugh and joke together, and if we get back to doing other things together life will be great.

The promised breakfast didn't materialise. Zoey fell asleep in the car and when Alex awoke her at the other end the need for rest outweighed the need to eat.

She didn't undress, just flung herself onto the bed. The

last thing she remembered was Alex planting a kiss on her brow before he covered her with the duvet.

If she'd gone to sleep feeling cherished, she didn't waken up to the same feeling of contentment.

There was panic in her. Rosie! She'd left her at the hospital. What if she'd had a relapse or, confused by all the strange faces, was crying for her mother? She should never have let herself be persuaded to come home.

As the thoughts came crowding in, she found herself on her feet. Hair tousled, black smudges beneath her eyes, already back on the children's ward in her mind's eye. The turkey could stay in the freezer for ever.

'It's all right,' Alex's voice said from the open doorway. 'I've just phoned the hospital. Rosie has eaten all her lunch and after a quite lively time has gone back to sleep again, so there's no need to rush.'

She sank down onto the bed and looked at herself blearily. She was still wearing the blue dress, for goodness' sake! Alex had said that they needn't hurry back, so she was going to have a shower and then change into something else. If she never saw the dress again it wouldn't matter. It would always remind her of Rosie coughing and gasping for breath.

'You have to eat before you do anything else,' he said as if he were reading her mind. 'We have a nice line in muesli, porridge or fresh fruit. What would you like?'

Suddenly she felt light-hearted. She could relax. Rosie wasn't fretting and Alex was here, offering her a mundane menu that sounded mouth-watering when she thought about how hungry she was.

What had he said? Christmas was where the heart was. She'd given her heart to him, but what about his? He still wasn't committing himself to anything more than friendship.

When she went to eat the breakfast that he'd prepared, the turkey was glistening on the kitchen unit, looking as if it had just arrived from outer Siberia.

'If you like, I'll come over this evening and cook the meal while you're at the hospital,' he said. 'The bird should be thawed out by late afternoon, and if it isn't I'll use the microwave. You can decide then whether you just come back to eat and then return to the hospital for the night, or come back to stay if you think Rosie will be all right without you.'

'I don't deserve you,' Zoey said with a catch in her voice.

He smiled as he put a generous helping of bacon and eggs in front of her.

'You haven't got me yet.'

Her face sobered.

'Sorry. I keep forgetting that you don't want to be rushed.'

Alex's smile was still in place but his thoughts didn't match it. What was the matter with him, letting her think that? She was wearing the jewellery he'd bought her. Was thrilled with it. But he knew deep down that it should have been a ring. That was what he'd gone to buy. So why hadn't he? He knew that he wanted Zoey Lawrence in his arms, in his bed, in his life. So what was he waiting for?

When Zoey had finished eating she went up to shower and to rid herself of the blue dress, leaving Alex to clear away. After the lows of yesterday she was on a high. Thankful that Rosie was going to be all right and delighted that she had Alex all to herself for Christmas.

He hadn't been across to his own place since they'd

got back from the hospital, but she reckoned he would have to check up on Gloria sooner or later, and as far as she was concerned later would be fine.

She paused in the middle of towelling herself dry, viewing her nakedness in the bathroom mirror. At that moment she longed to feel his touch, his strength against her as they gave in to their need for each other.

But as far as she knew, Alex was still downstairs in the kitchen, clearing up after their impromptu Christmas breakfast. Making love to her would be the last thought in his head. With sudden recklessness she threw on a robe and ran downstairs, her bare feet making no sound.

He wasn't in the kitchen. All was neat and tidy, and as she hesitated in the doorway he asked from behind her, 'Are you looking for me?'

As she turned quickly the robe swung open, and with a bravado that was far from how she was really feeling she made no attempt to pull it together again.

'What are you trying to tell me?' he asked in a low voice. 'That you're beautiful, desirable...and available? I know all those things, Zoey. And I also know that if and when I make love to you, it won't be because you've made the first move. We're not Adam and Eve in the garden of Eden. It will be because we both want it more than anything else on earth.'

If the robe had been loose before, it wasn't now. She was pulling it so tightly around her it was cutting into her middle.

'Well, thanks for making that clear,' she said stonily. 'I hope that whenever you reach that state of bliss I'll be around to share it.' And on that note she marched back upstairs and got dressed.

When she went back downstairs Alex was reading a book, but he put it down when she came into the room.

'Could you drop me off at the hospital, please, Alex.' she asked. 'My car's still there.'

'All right. If you'll ring me when you know what time you'll be back to eat.'

'So you're still going to cook for us?'

'Why not? I said I would, didn't I?'

'I thought that you might have had enough of me and my crazy assumptions.'

He shook his head.

'I'm the one who's crazy.'

'You're just saying that to make me feel less rejected,' she said dolefully, 'and to make yourself seem not so cold and unfeeling.'

He was on his feet and moving towards her. 'So that's how you see me, is it?' he said with a purpose in him that was unmistakable.

Swinging her up into his arms, he began to climb the stairs.

'Put me down,' she gasped, her face scarlet with humiliation. 'You think I'm begging for it, don't you? Well, I'm not!'

He didn't answer. Just continued on his way up the staircase. When he laid her on the bed she gazed up at him in outrage for the briefest of moments and then she was rolling over to get out of his reach. He made no move to detain her and once she was on her feet allowed her to push past him as if she thought that the devil himself was about to ravish her.

She hadn't said a word all the way to the hospital, Alex thought with a wry smile on his face as he defrosted the turkey.

Zoey must be out of her mind if she believed he didn't want to make love to her, he told himself. When she'd shown him her nakedness it would have been so easy to have taken her there and then. To accept what she'd offered and worry about the implications afterwards. But he hadn't kept a hold on his desires for this long to have it end in swift lust. He was his own man. Not to be knowingly manipulated.

Just the same, there was no way he would have made love to her during those moments in the bedroom. Taking her up there had been merely a gesture brought about by her description of him.

When eventually they did make love it would be a joyous thing, combining passion, tenderness and respect, and he was prepared to wait until then.

He was still regretting not having bought the ring. But there was the New Year ahead of them with its hopes and aspirations. What better time for new beginnings?

And in the meantime he'd promised her a Christmas meal. Whether she would want to have anything to do with him after their little episode in the bedroom he didn't know. But if that did prove to be the case all she had to do was throw him out.

While the food was cooking he went across to his own house. Gloria wanted to know where he'd been.

'I was in the children's ward at the hospital for most of the night,' he informed her, 'and am now cooking a meal.'

'I see,' she said. 'So I'll be eating alone?'

He couldn't let her do that. Not on Christmas Day.

CHAPTER NINE

FOR the rest of the day Zoey put her own needs to one side and devoted herself to Rosie. The baby was no longer on the oxygen treatment and was sitting up and taking notice of all that was going on around her.

Some of the children in the ward were noisy and fretful and others, those who were really sick, were very quiet. There was sadness in Zoey as she watched them. Rosie's problem had been serious enough, but it was minor compared to what some of these young ones were coping with.

'When you take her home, keep the atmosphere warm and moist,' a staff nurse told her. 'It might sound odd, recommending a damp atmosphere, but that's what she needs for a day or two.'

She cast a sympathetic eye over the youthful figure by the cot.

'Not much of a Christmas you're having, is it? Being a parent isn't all sweetness and light.'

'I'm Rosie's half-sister,' Zoey explained. 'Her mother got married again yesterday and had only just left on her honeymoon when the baby became ill.'

'Have you told her?'

Zoey shook her head.

'No. I was very undecided, worried sick, in fact, but when Rosie began to improve I left it.'

'Where's your friend?' the nurse asked curiously, adding when Zoey eyed her questioningly, 'The guy you were with this morning.'

'I told him that he didn't need to come,' Zoey told her, thinking that 'friend' rather than 'lover' was an apt description of Alex's place in her life.

Yet she should be grateful for that, she supposed, as she had a feeling that those who had Alex Carradine for a friend were fortunate people. There was a strength and integrity about him that made other men seem insignificant.

Stop fretting over what's not on offer, she told herself, and make the most of what you've got. If he doesn't want to go to bed with you, at least he's making Christmas dinner. Just don't start thinking about which you would prefer.

She had Rosie on her knee and as the little one reached up and pressed a chubby fist against her face, Zoey said, 'You know what I want, don't you, little sister? So do I. It's just Alex who can't see the wood for the trees.'

It was six o'clock in the evening. The baby had been bathed and fed and was now sleeping soundly.

'Does she usually sleep through the night?' one of the nurses asked.

Zoey nodded.

'Then go home and enjoy what's left of Christmas Day. She'll be fine, and tomorrow it's almost certain that the doctor will discharge her.

'Go on,' she insisted as Zoey hesitated. 'We know where you are if we need you and, with the progress the baby is making, it's not likely that we will.'

Zoey's smile beamed out.

'All right. I will. I'll be back first thing in the morning.' And with a lighter heart than she'd had at the same time the day before, she went.

She was smiling as she drove home. Whatever dos and don'ts Alex had in mind, at least they were going to spend the evening together, shutting out the winter dark and relaxing in the cosy warmth of the house that her father had bought for his young wife.

Alex was at the stove when she went in and he immediately asked about Rosie.

'She's fine,' Zoey told him breezily.

'Good,' he said crisply, then said in a more subdued tone, 'Mandy rang to wish you a merry Christmas.'

She paused in the act of taking off her long winter coat.

'What did you say?'

'I'm afraid that I told her a whopper. I said you'd taken Rosie out in the pram for some fresh air and would ring her when you got back.'

'And what did she say to that?'

'To leave it until later as they were going out for a meal.'

'Phew! So we have a reprieve. Was she surprised that you answered the phone?'

'Not in the least. I explained that I was doing the cooking.' He paused and she was conscious of unease in him. 'And...er...with regard to that, I hope you don't mind, I've invited Gloria across. I can't leave her stuck there on her own on Christmas Day. She hasn't an awful lot going for her at the moment. It seemed the charitable thing to do.'

Zoey felt her brief lifting of spirits dwindle as she took in what he'd said. Once again his was the sweet voice of reason.

But it was the same old thing again, wasn't it? Keeping her at a distance. Safety in numbers. She was being unkind and knew it, but she couldn't help herself.

What on earth was she doing, pining for a man whose interest in her was so restrained?

'By all means,' she said coolly. 'Why not go out onto the highways and byways and see who else you can find?'

Alex was eyeing her sombrely.

'I knew that was how you would see it.'

'Yet you still did it.'

'If I think something is right, yes, I go ahead and do it. So, do I ring across and tell her to forget it?'

Zoey was already contrite, but wasn't going to let him see it.

'No, of course not,' she said blandly. 'She'll be able to chaperone us. Stop us from giving in to our animal desires…as if that were likely. I notice that you didn't try to stop me when I fought my way out of the bedroom.'

'Disappointed, were you?' he asked drily.

'No. I wasn't. I was more the nervous virgin,' she said with a toss of her head. 'But seriously, getting back to Gloria…'

'Yes?'

'It's been a strange Christmas all round. Sharing it with your ex-wife can't make it any more strange. It's fine by me for her to join us.'

'Good. My invitation to her stemmed from nothing more than a guilty conscience.'

'Why would that be, then?'

'Because I have so much. I have a job I enjoy immensely. I live in beautiful countryside and—' with a quizzical smile '—I've got you, babe.'

'Oh, no, you haven't…"babe",' she hooted. 'You've passed up too many chances for that…and—' looking over his shoulder at the stove '——there's a pan about to boil over.'

As he went to adjust the flame she walked towards the door.

'I'm going upstairs to change and when I come down you can tell me what there is left to do.'

He waved his hand over the worktops.

'It's done…babe…and Gloria will be across shortly.'

Zoey smiled.

'Great! I can't wait.'

'Are you going to wear your bracelet?' he asked as she paused in the doorway.

Her mouth softened as she held out her arm.

'I haven't taken it off.'

'So I did manage to do something right?'

'Mmm. You did.'

It was on the tip of his tongue to tell her it should have been a ring, but that would have put to waste all the will-power he'd been hanging onto. So he just smiled and told her to get a move on as the meal was almost ready.

When she came downstairs a little later Zoey realised that the spectre at the feast had arrived. She could hear Gloria's flat tones coming from the sitting room and braced herself before entering.

'Hello, there,' Gloria said when she went in. 'Hope you don't mind me gatecrashing, but Alexander was so insistent.'

Zoey hid a smile. 'Alexander' was looking rather uncomfortable.

'No,' she said easily. 'Not at all.' And was surprised to find that she meant it. 'Christmas is not the time to be alone. Especially after a recent bereavement.'

For a moment the other woman looked disconcerted, but she rallied quickly enough and said, 'Yes, that is so.'

Alex looked away and Zoey thought, He's thinking I've done a quick about-turn. But, then, he already thinks I'm unpredictable.

Gloria was dressed in black from head to toe. She looked understated and elegant, and Zoey wondered if Alex would think she'd overdone it in her favourite dress of sapphire-coloured silk. One of her most treasured possessions, it matched her eyes and turned her silky bob into white gold.

Her glance met his and she knew she'd made the impact she'd desired. His gaze was telling her that she was beautiful and that would have been fine if they'd been alone and could have hopefully gone on from there.

She was beginning to feel deflated again. What she'd said to Gloria had been genuine enough, but the disappointment was still there. Would she and Alex ever be alone at the right moment...in the right surroundings?

As she ate the food that he'd cooked and drank the wine that he'd chilled, Zoey put on a show of good humour that had him glancing at her thoughtfully when he thought she wasn't looking.

For his own part, Alex was silent most of the time, leaving the two women to keep the conversation going. Zoey wondered if he was comparing them...the past and the present.

At last Gloria yawned and got to her feet. Zoey felt relief sweep over her. The ordeal was over. Maybe now she and Alex could... But his ex-wife was saying, 'I'm not too keen on going into the house on my own at this hour, Alex.'

It took Zoey all her time not to groan out loud as he responded, 'I'll come with you.'

When they'd gone she locked up and went wearily to bed. If Alex had said he was coming back she would have waited, but she wasn't a mind-reader. Certainly not where his was concerned.

It was proving to be a see-saw sort of Christmas, she thought, frustratedly punching the pillows on her bed. Up, down, up, down.

One of the ups had been getting through to Mandy during the evening and hearing that she and Harry were having a wonderful time. When she'd asked about Rosie, Zoey had felt able to tell her what had been happening now that the crisis was past and there was no more cause for alarm. But it hadn't stopped Mandy from saying anxiously that she would come home.

'There's no need, dearest,' Zoey soothed. 'Rosie is fine. I would have been on to you straight away if she'd got any worse, but she didn't. So enjoy your honeymoon.'

'I'm glad that you've got Alex around for moral support,' the anxious mother said.

Zoey found herself laughing.

'Oh, it's that all right.'

'What?'

'Moral.'

It was Mandy's turn to chuckle.

'So you're not making much progress with that gorgeous man.'

''Fraid not. I'm spending the evening with Alex and his ex.'

'Sounds delightful,' Mandy said, still amused.

'Tell me about it,' Zoey groaned, and after promising each other to speak again soon they said an affectionate farewell.

It was lovely to talk and Zoey felt better now that

Mandy knew about her small daughter's illness. It had been no problem telling her now, but Zoey shuddered at the thought of what it would have been like if she'd had to ask Mandy to come home because Rosie was in a critical condition. It had been on the cards, but thankfully the treatment had worked.

Sleep claimed her eventually and her last thought before it did was that she hoped that Alex's solicitations on Gloria's behalf weren't going to include anything further than the invitation to eat with them.

Alex had intended to go back. If only to make sure that Zoey wasn't too upset at having Gloria foisted upon her. He'd spent most of the evening in a state of longing for which he had only himself to blame. Yet he couldn't have left Gloria on her own on Christmas Day.

Every time he'd looked at Zoey he'd told himself that he was a fool to keep her in suspense. She was divine. Even at her most subdued she was like a bright beacon in his life, and what was he doing? Playing hard to get. As if he were the catch of the season. Once Gloria was safely inside he would go back and tell her all that was in his heart.

But he'd no sooner crossed the road than he turned to see that the house opposite was in darkness, and he thought ruefully that the message was clear enough. She wasn't expecting him to return.

Zoey brought Rosie home the following morning and might have been feeling more perky if it hadn't been for two things. They'd warned her at the hospital that the croup might recur, and she'd seen nothing of Alex since the night before.

Obviously he wasn't yearning for her company. The

whole affair was too one-sided, she decided glumly. Maybe she would ask for that transfer in the hope that out of sight would be out of mind.

Mandy was due back in two days' time and she still hadn't found anywhere to live. Obviously she and Harry wouldn't be rushing her, but it was only right and proper that she find somewhere.

She knew where she'd like to take up residence. In the slot that a certain brunette was occupying. But she was about to give up on that one.

And so Boxing Day dragged on, with Rosie's return being the only bright thing about it.

Alex phoned in the early evening and when Zoey heard his voice she sighed. She was about to bathe Rosie and took the call on a phone on the upstairs landing, holding the baby in one arm.

He'd had all day to phone. Why leave it until now? she wondered.

'What's the matter?' he asked when she answered. 'You sound rather distant.'

'I'm about to commence bathtime.'

'So? What's wrong? Do you want your back scrubbed?'

'You're living dangerously, aren't you?' She couldn't help but laugh. 'It's Rosie's bathtime that we're talking about.'

'Which answers my next question. I was about to ask if she was home.'

'Yes, she is, and she's fine, but they told me at the hospital that the croup may come back.'

'Just hope it doesn't,' he advised, and added, as if anxious to say his piece and be gone, 'I just wanted to check that you weren't too put out by having Gloria with us last night.'

'I can think of things I would have enjoyed more, but taking everything into account I suppose she served her purpose.'

'Meaning?'

'She kept us apart.'

'You think that's what I wanted?'

'Possibly.'

It was his turn to sigh.

'I'm not going to argue with you, Zoey, and in view of what you said about little miss about to have her bath, I'm going. But first let me ask, when are you back on duty?'

'Next Monday. I can't have any more time off. I've used up all my leave.'

'Right. So I'll see you when I get back. I'm going away for a few days.'

'Who with?' she asked before she could stop herself.

'No one. It's a course that headquarters have suddenly dreamed up out of the blue, and if I'm going to get the station officer's position it's sensible that I go on it.'

'Why didn't you tell me before?' she said listlessly.

'Because I've only just found out myself. There was a notification in the post that came on Christmas Eve and I've only just had a chance to open it.'

'I'll see you when you get back, then,' she told him, and in the silence that followed she replaced the receiver.

Her responsibility for Rosie was at an end. Mandy and Harry were back and looking extremely happy.

'I'm going to apply for a transfer back to the main station,' she told them on their first night home. 'I spoke to the station officer there before Christmas when the thought first came to me, and he said there should be no problem. As soon as it comes through I'll look for a flat in the city centre.'

Mandy was observing her anxiously.

'What about you and Alex?' she asked.

'It turned out to be just one of those things,' Zoey said lightly. 'It never got off the ground.'

'Are you sure?' Mandy persisted. 'He was here with you at Christmas.'

'Hmm. Briefly. But I haven't seen him since. In fact, he's away.'

'Not with that ex-wife of his, I hope.'

'No. He's gone alone.'

Mandy was like a dog with a bone.

'Where to?'

'On a course.'

On Sunday night she went to the pub. It was the first time she'd been out over the festive season. There'd been no signs of Alex so she'd concluded that he was still away and, that being so, she'd felt no urge to sally forth. But by the time Sunday had come she'd been getting restive.

She'd missed the men at the station while she'd been off. Their friendship and that of their wives and partners meant a lot to her and she would miss them even more when she transferred back to the city centre. The local station might be small in the vast organisation that was the fire service, but the staff's efficiency and camaraderie were second to none.

Zoey told them that she was thinking of moving back now that her stepmother had remarried. It wasn't the real reason but it would have to do. She wasn't going to tell them she was in love with Alex Carradine and that he wasn't doing anything about it.

There were cries of disappointment.

'You haven't been here five minutes,' Geoff said. 'Won't you change your mind?'

'Yes,' someone else cried. 'Don't leave, Zoey. You're one of us.' But she'd just smiled.

It was almost time to go when Alex came in and she wondered why she was considering torturing herself by leaving this place. How would she cope away from him?

He looked tired but perked up when he saw them and answered their questions about the course willingly enough. But his glance was on Zoey, standing on the edge of the group, struggling with her doubts and uncertainties.

She was getting ready to go when she found him beside her.

'How's the little rosebud?' he asked.

'She's fine, thank you,' she told him gravely, as her mind went back to the night they'd spent in the darkened ward, fraught with anxiety on the baby's behalf. 'And how are you? Did you enjoy the course?'

'Not particularly.'

'Why was that?'

'I just didn't want to be away at this time.'

'Why?'

'I thought you would know,' he said softly.

His eyes had darkened and she found that she was holding her breath, but before he could say anything else one of the men called across, 'Has Zoey told you she's leaving us?'

If he'd looked tired before, his jawline was as tight as a bowstring now.

'Is that correct?' he asked in a low voice.

'Yes,' she muttered. 'I'm thinking of moving back to where I came from.'

'And I'm the last to know?'

'You weren't around to tell.'

'And you couldn't wait?'

'You would have known tomorrow when I made a formal application to transfer.'

He took her to one side.

'Is it because of me, Zoey? Am I driving you away?'

'I don't want to talk about it.'

'Fair enough,' he said levelly. 'Let me have your transfer application and I'll send it to the appropriate department.'

He hadn't exactly tried to persuade her to change her mind, Zoey thought as she climbed the stairs to bed. Far from it. If she had been dithering at all, that had settled it. If Alex had told her he didn't want her to go, she would have stayed. It was as simple as that. But he hadn't, and that fact had a message of its own. He wasn't bothered.

It serves you right, she told herself. You rush into everything without giving it enough thought. You took it for granted that because you fell in love with Alex he would respond likewise, and he hasn't. You might have had your moments with him, but that's what they were, and moments don't make a lifetime's commitment.

He probably sees you as young and foolish, which is his mistake. But are you going to point that out to him? No! You've done enough of the running. Time to stop. Get on with your life.

It all sounded so sensible and definite when presented like that, but as she turned her face into the pillow it was misery rather than determination that was the uppermost feeling.

* * *

If Alex had been feeling low in spirits before, he was devastated now. If Zoey was leaving the crew so soon she couldn't have felt much empathy with the men and, with regard to her feelings for himself, she was soon giving up on them.

He'd come back aching to see her again and when she'd been in the pub his spirits had lifted immediately. It was always great to meet the rest of the crew outside working hours and when she was with them it was the icing on the cake.

But she'd had a knockout blow waiting for him. She'd asked for a transfer and that could mean only one thing. The romance that never had been was over. She'd given up on him, and who was to blame for that?

As he'd marched home with frustration churning inside him he'd known that no matter how much he hated the idea of her going, Zoey had to make up her own mind whether she was giving up on the rapport between them.

He smiled a grim smile. He'd like to bet it wasn't the word she would have used to describe their relationship. Phrases like 'one-sided affair' or 'playing hard to get' sprang to mind.

He supposed he should be grateful that she wouldn't be all that far away. They were only a few miles from the city centre. It wasn't as if the fire service had a station on the moon and she'd asked to be transferred there.

But the worrying thing was that there was a finality about what she was doing. As if she was shutting the door on an episode in her life that had turned out to be less than her expectations.

Gloria was in the lounge, watching television, but she took her eyes off the screen long enough to say, 'So you're back.'

He nodded. 'Yes, I'm back.'

'You don't look very happy.'

'I'm not,' he told her bluntly. 'Zoey has asked for a transfer.'

She got to her feet.

'I'm sorry about that. Maybe I can cheer you up.'

'Meaning?'

'Aunt Mary's affairs are settled. Sometimes it comes in handy, being a solicitor, and it's been a great help being on the spot instead of having to rely on correspondence. So I'm ready for off, Alex. I'm packed and will be out of your hair tomorrow.'

Her smile was wry.

'When I first came back I did wonder if we'd made a mistake and might get together again. But since then I've seen you with Zoey Lawrence and I know where your heart lies. Put what happened between us behind you, Alex, and go forward with my blessing.'

Gloria left early next morning and as Alex watched her car pull away from the front of the house, his feelings were a mixture of relief and sadness.

It was a great burden off his shoulders that she'd gone in the same frame of mind as before, with no rancour between them. He hoped that one day she might find the right person, as he had.

And that was where the sadness was coming from. He'd found Zoey and had let her slip through his fingers. Admittedly from the best of motives. But it was what he'd done nevertheless. If he started to plead with her to change her mind at this late stage, would he be influencing her against what was best for her in the long run? He wished he knew.

Sleeping in the house across the way was a woman

who was loving and totally unselfish, and he'd been keeping her at a distance for what were turning out to be ridiculous reasons.

Well, one problem was solved. Gloria had gone. Zoey would have no worries about her presence any more. But that didn't matter so much now. She was asking for a transfer because of him, not his ex-wife.

It was the day of New Year's Eve and the crew had already been out on two minor calls when a big 'shout' came through. A store in the city centre was on fire and all available fire crews were being asked to attend.

As they raced to climb aboard the engine Zoey was glad to be back. There was less time to think when she was working. When they weren't on a 'shout' there was the equipment to check, talks about fire safety to charity functions, and general station duties that they all took turns to do.

And now here was a big one. Made even bigger because it was a furniture store that was on fire in the midst of the crowds jostling each other in the after-Christmas sales.

Three fire-engines were already there when they arrived. Firemen from other stations were manning the hoses while others were helping people who were trapped in the upper storeys onto aerial ladder platforms.

Grim-faced policemen were keeping back the gaping public and asking them to disperse, but with no obvious effect, and as they pulled up alongside, a nearby church bell began to toll sonorously as if a harbinger of doom.

Zoey felt a shiver run down her spine and Alex's face was tense. This was a bad one. They could all see that.

'What's the score?' he asked of a fellow sub-officer.

'Suspected incendiary device,' he said tersely. 'We

think there could be others. The fellow who owns the store says there have been bad feelings between him and his ex-partner. That he's been threatened by him.'

Zoey took a deep breath. On one of the busiest shopping days of the year somebody wanted to blow up a furniture store.

'There are people trapped inside,' the man told them. 'The place was full when it went off. So your lot will be needed in there.'

'If danger has a taste to it, it's in my mouth,' Geoff said sombrely as they donned their breathing apparatus. 'Let's see if we can get some of these poor devils out.'

'The upper floors are cleared!' somebody shouted as they approached. 'Concentrate on the basement!'

As she groped her way down the stairs with Geoff and Alex in front, Alex turned and said, 'Think on Zoey. No heroics. Just do what you can, then get out.'

'Yes, boss,' she said levelly.

There were other things she wanted to say but it was neither the time nor the place. She wanted to tell him that tragedies like this made their own ups and downs seem as nothing, and that she wasn't going to give up on him.

'Over here!' came the call, and as they groped towards a smoking jumble of three-piece suites Zoey saw a mother and child lying unconscious on the floor. Close by was an elderly couple in a similar state.

'Take the child,' Alex commanded. 'We'll see to the others.'

Geoff had already hoisted the younger of the two women over his shoulder, and as Zoey picked up the child he pushed her in front of him.

'Get moving, Zoey, girl,' he grunted. 'Before there are any more explosions.'

And she did. Aware with a tight knot of anxiety around her heart as she staggered up the stairs that they'd left Alex in the basement with the old couple, and strong as he was he wouldn't be able to carry them both.

The moment she handed the child over to waiting paramedics she was back in there, dreading the sound of further explosions, but for the moment there was only the crackling of burning wood and rumblings…and smoke and flames more dense than before.

CHAPTER TEN

ALEX was coming up the stairs, carrying the old man, and when Zoey would have gone past him to get to the woman he shook his head and pointed over his shoulder.

As she peered through the smoke Zoey saw Greg bringing up the rear with the woman in his arms.

There seemed to be no sign of anyone else in that area. Other firefighters were at the other end of the basement and they were shouting the all-clear when there was another explosion that rocked the building.

It was either a fractured gas main or another incendiary, she thought frantically, and as Alex pushed on with his burden she saw that Greg and the old lady were buried beneath a pile of rubble that a few moments earlier had been a brick pillar.

There was silence where the shouts had been coming from and her heart sank. At that moment it looked as if she was the only one in there. So it was up to her to act fast before anything worse occurred.

But the flames were coming nearer. It was as if the air released by the second explosion had fanned them and Zoey could see that in a matter of minutes the whole area would be engulfed.

As she heaved the rubble off them she could see a hand with knotted veins sticking out. Then a scrawny leg appeared and she began to work even faster.

A moaning sound from under the bricks at the other side of the elderly victim told her Greg was alive, though for how long she didn't know. But she had grave doubts about the inert figure that was still half-buried beneath the debris.

There was no pulse in the frail wrist, or heartbeat when she managed to find her chest, and the flames were like dancing dervishes coming ever nearer.

Zoey was flinging bricks and pieces of concrete off them with a strength she wouldn't have believed she possessed, and now Greg was visible. Mercifully he was conscious and she sent up a silent prayer.

'How badly hurt are you?' she gasped.

'My legs,' he groaned. 'I think they're broken.'

She was picking up the woman, desperate to try resuscitation but knowing there was no time.

'It's clear that we haven't been missed,' she told the injured firefighter. 'Try to drag yourself away from the flames, Greg, and I'll send help.'

Then she was off, staggering under the weight of her burden and dodging the flames as she went.

When Alex had deposited the elderly man into the care of ambulance personnel, he leant against the wall and took a deep breath. Thank goodness they'd got out of that lot before yet another explosion occurred.

Zoey and Greg had been right behind him so they must be somewhere around, and both of them feeling just as relieved as he that they'd made it out in time.

But when he'd got his breath back he saw that they weren't around…anywhere. He froze. Surely they weren't still in there? Zoey, his bright morning star, trapped in that inferno!

He'd known fear in his time. It went with the job, but never like this…the sick churning of terror.

'Two of my crew are missing,' he cried. 'I'm going back in.'

'Hold on!' somebody cried. 'There's one of 'em here now!'

As Zoey staggered into the light of day, carrying the body of the old lady, a cheer went up.

But there was no time for rejoicing.

'No pulse or heartbeat,' she croaked as the paramedics took over. Addressing Alex, who was as white as a sheet beneath the grime, she said, 'Greg's still in there, Alex. He's got leg fractures and goodness knows what else. He was trying to drag himself away from the flames when I left him.'

If she hadn't known him better she would have said Alex was traumatised, but it seemed that as usual his brain was working at top speed.

'Stay where you are,' he told her. To the others he cried, 'One of my men is still in there!' Then he disappeared into the smoke and flames. There was a surge forward amongst the firefighters. He didn't need to ask for volunteers. It was their job.

The old lady was dead. She'd been unconscious before being trapped in the rubble and hadn't stood a chance. Her husband, as yet unaware of her death, had fared better.

By the time Alex had passed him over to the paramedics, who were working with a team of doctors and nurses from the hospital, he was showing signs of recovery and had been taken to hospital. But he was still too much in shock to be told the sad tidings.

'His wife is the only casualty so far,' one of the policemen told her. 'Let's hope it stays that way.'

Zoey couldn't agree more. Her eyes were riveted on the burning building. Alex was inside there, along with other men who were prepared to risk their lives as part of the job.

They were strong, physically fit and kitted out for it, but there was always the dread that circumstances might prove too much for them.

The fire on the outside was under control now, but she knew that the basement, which was less accessible, was a different matter. Suppose there was yet another explosion?

Policemen were talking to the store's owner who was standing nearby with a look of such sick horror on his face that she thought grimly it would be a long time before he could forget what had stemmed from a disagreement, if that was what it had been.

Someone had passed her a mug of tea and as she sipped it slowly it felt as if her throat had seized up. Where were they amongst the rumblings and cracklings of the damaged building? she thought frantically. Had there been another fall of masonry?

When they came out, with Alex leading them and Greg on a stretcher, it was as if a huge weight had been lifted off her heart.

She wanted to hold him and never let him go again. Her love for him was in her eyes as she ran towards him. If she was transferred to the ends of the earth, nothing would ever change the way she felt.

But Alex was bending over Greg, his concern with the injured firefighter as they carried him to safety and the waiting hospital team.

When she appeared at Alex's side he said tersely, 'That was touch and go. Another few seconds and we would have lost him. It's a good job he was wearing the right gear and had the oxygen or he wouldn't have survived.'

Greg was conscious and he weakly caught at Zoey's arm.

'Zoey, I'm sorry for the way I behaved that night after the pub. I was so drunk—I really am sorry.'

Zoey regarded the contrite face of the injured man for a moment and then took his hand. 'Yes, you were drunk, but nothing really happened. You're forgiven, Greg. Just make sure you don't drink so much next time we're all out.'

Greg looked relieved and even managed a smile for her.

'Trust me to have to be rescued by action man,' he mumbled. 'I'd rather it had been you, blondie.'

'Next time I'll make sure it is,' she said with an answering smile.

'Promise?'

'Absolutely.'

She could sense Alex's relief in finding Greg able to talk coherently, but it didn't stop him from tutting impatiently and commenting, 'When you two have finished passing the time of day, this guy needs a different kind of attention from what he's getting now.'

Zoey managed a smile. If Greg was still able to flirt a little it showed that he was facing up to what had happened in his own way. Of course she knew he needed medical attention. She was the crew's trauma technician, for heaven's sake. But what had Alex expected her to do? Ignore the man's brave flippancy? Well, Greg wasn't the only one who could be flippant.

'Point taken,' she told him, 'but you'll have to excuse me. I always chat to men on stretchers.'

As the doctors took over he gave her a long level look. 'I'll leave you to it, then.' And went back to where the fire was trying to take hold again.

What exactly was he leaving her to? she wondered.

*   *   *

'That was a job well done,' Alex announced as they drove back to the station, minus Greg who was now hospitalised with two fractured femurs, a broken clavicle and minor burns.

They'd stayed to assist with the inspection of the premises once the fire had been brought under control, and it had looked as if they were dealing with arson.

'What sort of a person would blow up a building out of spite?' Geoff said incredulously.

'There are a few around, I'm afraid,' Alex told him. 'The police have been to his address but, needless to say, he wasn't there.'

He was still shaken from the horror of finding that Zoey had still been in the burning building, having believed that she'd followed him out. If anything had happened to her he would have had nothing to live for. To lose her would be like losing his life blood.

Gloria had told him to move forward, put the past behind him, and she'd been right. That was what he was going to do and not before time...if he hadn't left it too late.

Zoey had yet to discover that Gloria had gone. But if he told her, would she think it was a ploy to keep her with him, after all these weeks of trotting out excuses to hold her at arm's length?

Then, running true to form, he'd been snappy with her when she'd been talking to Greg. Letting the nightmare they'd just gone through make him less than understanding, when all she'd been doing was being her usual caring self. Not to mention the fact that Greg had confirmed Zoey's innocence that night he'd found them together. What was he like?

Those moments when he'd realised she hadn't followed him out of the building had been the worst of his

life, and before he'd been able to tell her about his agony
of mind there'd been the need to bring Greg to safety.

He could have told her then, when they'd been beside
the stretcher. Yet what had he done? Pulled rank instead
of joining in the brave banter of a badly injured member
of his crew.

The day had gone by the time they docked the engine
on the forecourt of the station and when Alex had made
his report and checked that all was safe and sound before
he and the others left, he found that Zoey had gone.

In a painful sort of way he was glad. At least while
they were apart he wasn't likely to disenchant her further. It was New Year's Eve. The end of one year. The
beginning of another. Whatever it held for them was in
his hands.

Her transfer application was on his desk, waiting to
go through. The coming days and months stretched
ahead like a black abyss. Why didn't he tear it up?

When Zoey got home Mandy was setting the table for
the evening meal and Rosie was in her high chair, playing with a plastic duck.

They both looked up and smiled when she walked in,
and that did it. The scene was achingly tranquil. She was
with those who loved her and suddenly it was all too
much.

'That is it!' she exclaimed, flinging her bag down onto
the nearest chair. 'I have had it with that man!'

Mandy looked up.

'I take it that we are talking about Alex Carradine?'

'Yes, we are,' she said wearily. 'Nothing I do is right
for him. He is insensitive, snappy and—'

'You love him,' Mandy finished off for her.

'Yes, I do,' Zoey wailed, as the annoyance subsided.

'I can't believe what the two of you are like,' the other woman said. 'It's like missing the bus every time you run for it.'

'Yes, because the driver won't pick up any passengers that he thinks might cause him grief. He's not a chancer!'

'Can you blame him?' Mandy persisted gently. 'He has had Gloria for the last few years and is still being charitable towards her. If you want the man, do something about it. It's New Year's Eve, for goodness' sake. What better time to think of fresh beginnings?'

'I've done all I'm prepared to do,' Zoey told her. 'In fact, I've already accepted that it's over…not that it ever really began.'

'I never thought of you as someone who would give up so easily,' Mandy said chidingly, 'but if you aren't going to spend the last night of the old year with the man of your dreams, would you mind if I went to give Harry a lift to the pizzeria? We didn't want anything to stop you from spending it with Alex, but if you're not bothered I know he'd be glad of the help, as he's given time off to the people who staffed the place while we were on honeymoon over Christmas.'

'Of course go and help Harry,' Zoey said immediately. 'I'm going nowhere. I might stay up to watch the New Year in and that will be it.'

'You're too young and beautiful to be alone on New Year's Eve,' Mandy protested.

Zoey shook her head.

'Even if I wanted to go across the road, Alex has probably arranged to spend the evening with Gloria. He didn't want to leave her on her own on Christmas Day, and it will be the same tonight. So go and get ready.'

*   *   *

She had never known the house so quiet. Once Rosie had gone to sleep in cherubic innocence, a silence had settled over the rooms as if the whole place were waiting for something.

Zoey had switched the television on and off a few times, prowled around the lounge looking for something to read, and had finally ended up staring into space.

She had no yearning to be out there with the merry-making crowds if she couldn't be with the one person who mattered.

You ought to be making resolutions for the coming year, she told herself as she stared into the glowing coals of the fire. But with the shambles that was her present state of mind, she felt it would take her all her time to decide whether to get up in the mornings, let alone start mapping out the year ahead.

She'd been to the window a few times and gazed bleakly at the house across the way. All the lights were on so someone was still in there. Maybe it was Gloria, and Alex was out partying somewhere. That thought brought no cheer with it.

As the night wore on she weakened. If he was over there, the least she could do was wish him a happy new year. Surely he wouldn't read anything provocative into that.

At five minutes to twelve she checked on Rosie and went to find a coat. If Alex wasn't there, her absence would be only seconds. If he was, it still wouldn't be much longer than that if what had happened earlier in the day was anything to go by.

Alex had seen Mandy's car drive off, which meant that Zoey and the baby were alone in the house, as it stood to reason that the new husband would be at his restaurant. Why was she in there, though? Surely she wasn't going to stay in on New Year's Eve, even if it only meant going to the pub.

But the evening wore on and Mandy didn't come back. Finally it dawned on him that she must be helping her husband at the pizza parlour.

So Zoey had been left with the baby again. It seemed a bit unfair. But he knew how she loved the child. If she was like that with Rosie, what would she be like with a baby of her own…theirs?

His smile was wry. He'd handled it so that the chances of that were remote. He could count the number of times he'd kissed her on one hand, let alone made love to her. He'd let ridiculous concerns detract him from what really mattered and had been so determined that he wasn't going to make the same mistake twice that he'd fallen over backwards to keep his blonde enchantress in her place.

He looked at the clock. Ten minutes to twelve. He couldn't let the old year go out without telling her how much he loved her.

As Zoey lifted her hand to open her front door, the bell rang. When she opened it Alex was there in the porch. She felt her heart jolt in her breast, but her greeting gave no sign of it.

'Yes?'

He smiled.

'Can I come in?'

She stepped back without speaking.

'Where were you off to?' he asked, observing that she had her coat on.

Swallowing hard, she said the first thing that came into her head.

'I was going to feed the birds.'

'Seems a funny time to think of doing that.'

'Er...yes...maybe it is. There was some bread left over from the meal and I thought...' Her voice trailed away when she saw the amusement in his eyes. Determined not to be undermined, she said stiffly, 'So what can I do for you, Alex?'

'You can tell me that you'll marry me.'

'Wha-at?'

'I love you, Zoey. I always have from the moment I saw you, but I kept trying to convince myself that the timing wasn't right. As if that mattered.'

She was gripping the back of a chair for support, her wide blue gaze full of amazement.

'Why the change of mind?' she breathed. 'It's taken you so long!'

'It's not a change of mind. More an acceptance of what's been in it ever since we met. Please, tell me that I haven't messed things up completely. That your feelings for me haven't changed.'

'They won't ever do that, Alex,' she told him with a sweet gravity that made his bones melt. 'What I feel for you is deep and true, not just a girlish crush. I want to give you babies, spend every second I can with you, if you'll let me.'

'Oh!' he groaned. 'I'll let you! If you only knew the number of times I've wanted to put every other thought to one side and accept that I love you.'

She was still clutching the chairback and he smiled.

'Wouldn't you rather hold onto me?'

'Every day and always.' She beamed.

'So come on then, Zoey, darling. Let me show you

how much I really care.' And this time as she went into his arms there were no doubts, no uncertainties, just joyful amazement that what she'd longed for was going to be hers.

Later, Zoey asked, 'What do you think Gloria is going to say about this?'

'Gloria has gone,' he said drily. 'She finally sorted out her aunt's affairs and had no further reason to stay. She accepted that I was head over heels in love with you and actually told me to do something about it. So it would seem that we have her blessing.'

'Oh, Alex!' Zoey breathed. 'And I thought that she wanted you back.'

'It might have been like that when she first appeared, but after she'd seen what you mean to me she was happy to bow out gracefully.'

'We'll invite her to the wedding,' she vowed.

He laughed.

'If that's what you want. The way ahead for us is crystal clear now, my darling. I'm the one who's been muddying it up, but not any more. It's going to be you and I putting out fires, until the time comes for you to produce those babies that you've promised me. And as to the flame that we have kindled between us, it will burn more brightly with every moment we're together.'

Rosie was a bridesmaid again, but this time she was making her progress down the aisle in her mother's arms and it was a different bride, a different groom.

When the ceremony was over there was something else that was different. The sight of it made her wriggle excitedly in her mother's arms.

The traditional wedding car had been replaced with a big red fire-engine, and as the beautiful bride and her new husband climbed aboard they were cheered on their way by men in funny coats and big yellow hats.

Rosie didn't know what it was all about, but maybe one day her big sister would tell her.

0906/05a

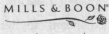

MILLS & BOON®

Live the emotion

In October 2006 Mills & Boon bring back two
of their classic collections, each featuring three
favourite romances by three of our bestselling
authors…

Red-Hot
Revenge

Featuring
The Greek Tycoon's Revenge by Jacqueline Baird
The Millionaire's Revenge by Cathy Williams
Ryan's Revenge by Lee Wilkinson

Make sure you buy these
irresistible stories!

On sale 6th October 2006

*Available at WHSmith, Tesco, ASDA, Borders, Eason,
Sainsbury's and most bookshops*

www.millsandboon.co.uk

MILLS & BOON®

Live the emotion

0906/05b

More Than a Mistress

Featuring
His Virgin Mistress by Anne Mather
Claiming His Mistress by Emma Darcy
Mistress on His Terms by Catherine Spencer

**Make sure you buy these
irresistible stories!**

On sale 6th October 2006

*Available at WHSmith, Tesco, ASDA, Borders, Eason,
Sainsbury's and most bookshops*

www.millsandboon.co.uk

0906/01a

MILLS & BOON
Live the emotion

Modern
romance™

PURCHASED BY THE BILLIONAIRE
by Helen Bianchin

Three years ago, under pressure from her father, Kayla removed bad-boy billionaire Duardo Alvarez's wedding ring. Now circumstance has forced Kayla to ask her ex-husband for help. But Duardo's price is high: marry him again, or he'll walk away...

MASTER OF PLEASURE *by Penny Jordan*

Sasha ran out on millionaire Gabriel Cabrini ten years ago – and he has never forgiven her. Now Sasha is shocked to discover that Gabriel has been named heir to her late husband's wealth. She is completely in his power, and he wants revenge...

THE SULTAN'S VIRGIN BRIDE *by Sarah Morgan*

Sultan Tariq bin Omar-Sharma gets everything he wants – except Farrah Tyndall. Farrah was crushed when she discovered that he wanted her, but only in his bed. Now Tariq needs to marry Farrah to secure a business deal. But having broken her heart, can she love again...?

WANTED: MISTRESS AND MOTHER
by Carol Marinelli

Ruthless barrister Dante Costello hires Matilda Hamilton to help his troubled little girl. Then Dante decides he will offer Matilda the position of mistress – and nothing more... But what Dante thought was lust turns out to be something far greater...

On sale 6th October 2006

Available at WHSmith, Tesco, ASDA, Borders, Eason, Sainsbury's and most bookshops

www.millsandboon.co.uk

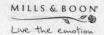

MILLS & BOON®

Live the emotion

0906/01b

Modern
romance™

THE RICH MAN'S ROYAL MISTRESS
by Robyn Donald

Princess Melissa Considine is captivated by womanising
billionaire Hawke Kennedy. His seduction leads the
virginal princess to decide she will let Hawke teach her
how to love…and be loved. But Melissa knows that she
must put duty before their affair…

AT THE SHEIKH'S COMMAND *by Kate Walker*

Abbie Cavanaugh can obtain her brother's freedom – but
only if she marries the Sheikh of Barakhara. The passion
between Sheikh Malik and Abbie could mean a marriage
of delight… But neither of them knows the other's real
identity, and the truth creates a desert storm…

THE SPANIARD'S PREGNANCY PROPOSAL
by Kim Lawrence

Having been burned badly before, Fleur Stewart reckons
staying away from Spanish billionaire Antonio Rochas
should be no problem. But Antonio is sexy, smouldering,
and attracts women like moths to a flame. And he doesn't
intend to let Fleur go easily…

AN ITALIAN ENGAGEMENT *by Catherine George*

Max Wingate is broodingly handsome. But his romantic
charm won't persuade Abigail Green to fall into his arms.
There's something vulnerable about Abby, but Max is
driven by desire. He's determined to have her surrender
to him, and he'll use any means at his disposal…

On sale 6th October 2006

*Available at WHSmith, Tesco, ASDA, Borders, Eason,
Sainsbury's and most bookshops*

www.millsandboon.co.uk

0906/03a

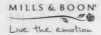

MILLS & BOON®

Live the emotion

_MedicaL
romance™

RESCUE AT CRADLE LAKE by *Marion Lennox*

Top surgeon Fergus hopes to soothe his broken heart with life at Cradle Lake – something which just might be possible with the help of local emergency doctor Ginny Viental. Is Fergus ready to make a life with Ginny, and her little niece? Especially when it means taking on a role he thought he would never face again – that of a father.

A NIGHT TO REMEMBER by *Jennifer Taylor*

A&E DRAMA

A tanker loaded with toxic chemicals is headed straight for an oil rig. A team, led by Dr Seb Bridges, is ready and waiting. Meanwhile, Dr Libby Bridges is on her way to ask Seb for a divorce... For Seb only two things matter: saving lives and saving his marriage. This will be the most important night of his life. And the clock is ticking...

A SURGEON, A MIDWIFE: A FAMILY
by *Gill Sanderson*

Dell Owen Maternity

Neonatal surgeon Jack Sinclair has learned to keep his professional and personal life separate. Until Dell Owen Hospital's new midwife, Miranda Gale, joins the team and breaks through his cool, detached façade. While Miranda is just as attracted to Jack, she has a secret...

On sale 6th October 2006

Available at WHSmith, Tesco, ASDA, Borders, Eason, Sainsbury's and most bookshops

www.millsandboon.co.uk

MILLS & BOON®
Live the emotion

0906/03b

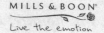

_MedicaL
romance™

THE DOCTOR'S NEW-FOUND FAMILY
by Laura MacDonald

Renowned surgeon Nathan Carrington has put his
marriage behind him, and devoted his attention to
his young son. Paediatrician Olivia Gilbert's world
has been turned upside down – now she lives for her
children. But Nathan and Olivia discover that single
parenthood just isn't enough...

HER VERY SPECIAL CONSULTANT
by Joanna Neil

Dr Amelie Clarke's first day at work doesn't go
as expected when she is rushed into A & E – as a
patient. She is mortified that her gorgeous new boss,
Gage Bracken, has seen her in her underwear! But
caring for her four-year-old nephew combined with
her job leaves Amelie no time for romance. Having
healed her body, it is up to Gage to heal her heart
as well.

THE ITALIAN DOCTOR'S BRIDE
by Margaret McDonagh

Mediterranean Doctors

Dr Nic di Angelis's arrival has stirred considerable
interest in the rural Scottish village of Lochanrig!
The GP has won the hearts of the whole community
– apart from that of his boss, Dr Hannah Frost.
It will take all of Nic's powers to break through
Hannah's defences. Only then can Hannah fully
embrace all that the fiery Italian has to offer...

On sale 6th October 2006

*Available at WHSmith, Tesco, ASDA, Borders, Eason,
Sainsbury's and most bookshops*

www.millsandboon.co.uk

0906/108/MB051

Seductive, Passionate, Romantic
There's nothing as sexy as a Sheikh!

THE SHEIKH'S BRIDE

Featuring *The Sheikh's Virgin Bride* and *One Night with the Sheikh* by Penny Jordan

Available 1st September 2006

THE SHEIKH'S WOMAN

Featuring *The Arabian Mistress* by Lynne Graham and *The Sheikh's Wife* by Jane Porter

Available 15th September 2006

Collect both exotic books!

www.millsandboon.co.uk

First comes love, then comes marriage...

That was Gracie's plan, anyway, at the ripe old age of fourteen. She loved eighteen-year-old heart throb Riley with a legendary desperation. Even now that she's all grown up, the locals in her sleepy town won't let her forget her youthful crush.

...but it's not as easy as it looks.

And now she's face-to-face with Riley at every turn. The one-time bad boy has come back seeking respectability – but the sparks that fly between them are anything but respectable! Gracie's determined to keep her distance, but when someone sets out to ruin both their reputations, the two discover that first love sometimes is better the second time around.

On sale 1st September 2006

0806/121/MB043

From No. 1 *New York Times* bestselling author Nora Roberts

Atop the rocky coast of Maine sits the Towers, a magnificent family mansion that is home to a legend of long-lost love, hidden emeralds— and four determined sisters.

Catherine, Amanda & Lilah
available 4th August 2006

Suzanna & Megan
available 6th October 2006

Available at WHSmith, Tesco, ASDA, Borders, Eason, Sainsbury's and all good paperback bookshops

www.silhouette.co.uk

"People look at me and they see this happy face, but inside I'm screaming. It's just that no-one hears me."

While breaking the news of Princess Diana's death to millions, reporter Isabel Murphy unravels on live television. *But Inside I'm Screaming* is the heart-rending tale of her struggle to regain the life that everyone thought she had.

21st July 2006

Can you tell from first impressions whether someone could become your closest friend?

Lydia, Jacqueline, Carol and Alix are four very different women, each facing their own problems in life. When they are thrown together by the hands of fate, none of them could ever guess how close they would become or where their friendship would lead them.

A heartfelt, emotional tale of friendship and problems shared from a multi-million copy bestselling author.

On sale 18th August 2006